47 RONIN

www.purplerosebooks.com

Copyright © 2013 Purple Rose Publishing

This Purple Rose edition first published 18 October, 2013

Cover design by Purple Rose Publishing

ISBN: 9781907960086

CONTENTS

INTRODUCTION

The legend of the 47 ronin is one of the most popular and best known stories about the samurai in Japan. It is often referred to as the country's "national legend" and is the most revered example of the samurai code of honor, bushido, put to the ultimate test.

The story tells of a group of samurai who, in 1701, were left leaderless (becoming ronin) after their daimyo (feudal lord) Asano Naganori, whose title was Takumi no Kami, was compelled to commit seppuku (ritual suicide) for assaulting a court official named Kira Yoshinaka, whose title was Kozuke no suke. The ronin avenged their master's honor by killing Kira, after waiting and planning for almost two years. In turn, the ronin were themselves forced to commit seppuku for committing the crime of murder. The revenge plot was led by Asano's chief councilor, Oishi Yoshio, who is best known by his title, Oishi Kuranosuke.

With much embellishment, this true story was popularized in Japanese culture as emblematic of the loyalty, sacrifice, persistence, and honor that people should preserve in their daily lives. The popularity of the almost mythical tale was enhanced by rapid modernization following the fall of the shogun during the Meiji era of Japanese history, when it is suggested many people in Japan longed for a return to their cultural roots.

Although it was a real event, so much has been written about the revenge of the 47 ronin that doubt has been cast over many of the details. The story was popularized in numerous plays, but because of the censorship laws of the shogunate, which forbade portrayal of current events, the names were changed. Fictionalized accounts of these events are known as Chushingura, the first being written some 50 years after the event. The story has also been one of the most popular themes in Japanese art.

The earliest known account of the incident to appear in English was in Isaac Titsingh's *Illustrations of Japan*, published in 1822. An official of the Dutch East India Company, Titsingh held audiences with the shogun and other high officials. His writings were widely read throughout Europe, describing the land of the rising sun to a public fascinated with the 'exotic East'. He was the first to record the story of the 47 ronin as one of the significant events of the era and his descriptions of life in Japan became the standard references for many years.

In 1863, Rutherford Alcock published in two volumes *The Capital of the Tycoon: A Narrative of a Three Years' Residence in Japan* which included a section on the 47 ronin tale. Alcock was the first British diplomatic representative to live in Japan, and the first non-Japanese person to climb Mount Fuji. Alcock was the author of several works, and was one of the first to awaken in Britain an interest in Japanese art. In *The Capital of the Tycoon* he paints a very comprehensive picture of nineteenth-century Japan, all stamped with the authenticity of his own personal observations and experiences.

The Meiji Restoration in 1868 brought Japan into the modern age. A chain of events, it restored imperial rule to Japan under Emperor Meiji and Japan underwent a massive reform and restructure. The Restoration led to enormous changes in Japan's political and social structure, and was responsible for the emergence of Japan as a modernized nation in the early twentieth-century. The Meiji period marked the re-opening of Japan to the West, and a period of rapid industrialization.

After the Restoration several new versions of the story of the 47 ronin emerged. Algernon Bertram Freeman-Mitford was the first to retell the story in English in any great depth. Mitford, Lord Redesdale, was in the British Foreign Service as a young man. He was assigned to Japan for several years and was one of the first foreign diplomats there. He acquired a life-long fascination with Japanese culture. His most well known work, *Tales of Old Japan* (1871), is credited with making the story of the 47 ronin known to a wider Western public. The book forms an introduction to Japanese literature and culture, both through the stories, all adapted from Japanese sources, and Mitford's supplementary notes. These stories focus on various aspects of Japanese life. Also included are Mitford's eyewitness accounts of a selection of Japanese rituals, ranging from hara-kiri (seppuku) and marriage to a selection of sermons. The book was a standard source of information about Japanese folklore and customs for many years.

Mitford's telling of the story of the 47 ronin varies greatly from that of Titsingh and Alcock. It may be that he translated it from a Japanese version he found, but it may also be that he embellished the story somewhat, since his focus was on the storytelling rather than the historical facts. It was the most well known version of the events for some time and continues to be popular today.

Published in 1880, just nine years later, *The Loyal Ronins: An Historical Romance* is a loose translation of the Japanese book *Iroha Bunko* by Shunsui Tamenaga, a Japanese novelist. Translated by a

Japanese man, Shiuichiro Saito, and a British diplomat, Edward Greey, it has since been seen as a fanciful take on the story of the ronins, with Saito and Greey influenced in their translation by the hope of improving Japan's status in the West. Adding a very British feel to the work, Saito and Greey translated the names of the characters in the story into English, so Lord Asano was translated into Lord Morning (asa) Field (no) and Oishi was translated as Sir Big (oo) Rock (ishi) etc. This was done, as Greey explains, to avoid "those stumbling-blocks to readers, Japanese names for persons and places." Their focus in translating the story was most certainly in attracting Western readers to a Japan newly restored under the Meiji Restoration. Both Mitford's *Tales of Old Japan* and Tamenaga's *The Loyal Ronins* had a significant impact on how Japan was viewed by the West at the end of the nineteenth-century.

James Murdoch's *The Forty-Seven Ronin* is the last of our retellings of the story. Murdoch was a scholar and journalist who worked as a teacher in Japan. From 1903–1917, he wrote the three-volume *A History of Japan*, the first comprehensive history of Japan in the English language. A single chapter in *A History of Japan* is dedicated to the 47 ronin. It is a short yet well researched piece and mentions all of the previous English versions. Of Alcock's he says that it is still "one of the most interesting books that has been written on Japan" and of Mitford's he says: "His volume has become a classic, and it is well worthy of the distinction, for no other single book has succeeded in conveying a sense of the real social and moral atmosphere of Tokugawa Japan so thoroughly and effectually as Mr. Mitford's perennially interesting volume has done." *A History of Japan* remained the standard work on Japanese history for many years.

Many versions of the events surrounding the revenge of the 47 ronin exist today. Many claim to be more historically accurate than the last, many are fictionalized, dramatized and romanticized for effect. The story of the 47 ronin continues to be popular both in Japan and throughout the world. The story holds considerable power, and its popularity grows with every new retelling. A beloved legend and among the best known tales in Japanese history, the story of the 47 ronin continues to attract interest and fascination to this day.

FROM: ILLUSTRATIONS OF JAPAN

BY ISAAC TITSINGH

PART I: PRIVATE MEMOIRS AND ANECDOTES OF THE REIGNING DYNASTY OF THE SOVEREIGNS OF JAPAN

On the 14th of the 3d month of the 14th year *Gen-rok* (1701), Assan-no-takoumi-no-kami-Naganori, prince of Ako, who had been several times treated contemptuously by Kira-kotsouki-no-ski, having received a fresh affront from him in the palace of the Djogoun, drew his sabre with the intention of revenging the insult. Some persons, on hearing the noise, ran up and separated them, and Kotsouki was but slightly wounded. It is an unpardonable crime to draw a sabre in the palace; the prince was therefore ordered to rip himself up, and his descendants were banished for ever. His adversary who, out of respect for the palace, had abstained from drawing his sabre, was pardoned.

This injustice exasperated the servants of the prince so much the more, since it was Kotsouki, who, by his repeated insults had caused the destruction of their master. Forty-seven of them, having agreed to revenge his death, forced their way, in the night of the 14th of the 12th month of the following year, into the palace of Kotsouki; and, after a combat which lasted till day-light, they penetrated to his apartment and dispatched him. The Djogoun, on the first intelligence of this desperate attack, sent troops to the assistance of the unfortunate Kotsouki, but they arrived too late to save him. The assailants, not one of whom lost his life in the scuffle, were all taken and condemned to rip up their bellies, which they did with the greatest firmness, satisfied with having revenged their master. They were all interred in the temple of Singakousi, near the prince. The soldiers, in token of respect for their fidelity, still visit their graves, and pray before them. Kotsouki's son, who had been withheld by cowardice from hastening to the assistance of his father, though he was then in the palace, was deprived of his post and banished, with all his kindred, to the island of Awasi.

FROM: THE CAPITAL OF THE TYCOON, VOLUME I

BY SIR RUTHERFORD ALCOCK

HER MAJESTY'S ENVOY EXTRAORDINARY AND MINISTER
PLENIPOTENTIARY IN JAPAN

CHAPTER XVII

A strange history—strange if true, and scarcely less so if invented. Not less, but more illustrative, perhaps, in the latter case, of the popular idea of heroism and poetic justice, as these are, moreover, exemplified in a hundred legends and traditions, which form the staple of their theatrical pieces, their picture-books, and their popular tales. One of the most celebrated of these is a story of a small daimio, who, having a feud in past times with one of the Tycoon's Council of State, determined to avenge himself by slaying his enemy when he met him in the palace. He made the attempt and failed, inflicting only a slight wound, some of the attendants having seized him from behind as he was aiming his blow. Foiled in his object, he returned to his house; and having collected his officers and retainers about him, and made his preparations for disemboweling himself, he deliberately performed the operation in their presence, and then, handing the short sword covered with his blood to his secretary, he laid his dying injunctions upon him, as his liege lord, with that very weapon to take the life of his enemy. The latter, being freed from his antagonist, seized upon the house and property of the deceased daimio, and turned out all his faithful servitors. These, to the number of forty-seven, became Lonins, under the command of the secretary, all bound together by an oath to accomplish the destruction of their master's enemy! Accordingly, choosing their time, they stormed his castle during the night when they knew he was inside, and entered into a terrible conflict with all his retainers, to the number of some three hundred; and such was their valor and heroism that they finally vanquished them, and immediately proceeded to search for their chief victim. He was concealed in a secret recess between two rooms, with one of his friends; but they had obtained information of the existence of such a hiding-place, and one of them thrust a spear through the partition. The blade wounded the daimio, but not in a vital part; and as it was drawn out he took care to wipe it with his sleeve, so that on examining it and seeing no mark of blood, they came to the conclusion that no one was there, and that he had escaped their vengeance. Nothing then remained but an act of self-immolation; and, stripping off their armor and dress, they were just in the act of performing the Hara-kiru, when a stifled cough reached their ears from the very hiding-place they had pierced in a vain search. Satisfied now that their enemy was still in their grasp, they sprung to their feet, tore down the walls, and dragged him and his friend out, when the secretary, with the very sword received from his dying chief, struck off both their heads. Their vengeance thus satisfied, and not a living being remaining to be slain, they then performed the disemboweling with the greatest heroism and complacency. They were all buried in one cemetery in Yeddo, which was pointed out to me, and they live to this day in the hearts of all brave and loyal men in Japan as types of true heroism! As this story was recited to me, I could not help reflecting on what must be the influence of such a popular literature and history upon the character, as well as the habits of thought and action of a nation. When children listen to such fragments of their history or popular tales, and, as they grow up, hear their elders praise the valor and heroism of such servitors, and see them go at stated periods to pay honor to their graves centuries after the deed—and such is the fact—it is quite obvious this general talk and unhesitating approval of what with us, perhaps, would be considered great crimes, may have very subtle and curious bearings on the general character and moral training of the people. What its exact influence may be we can not determine, perhaps; but that it is deep and all-pervading, affecting their general estimate of all deeds of like character, whether it be the slaying of a Regent or the massacre of a Foreign Legation, is very certain, and presents a state of things well worthy of serious consideration.

FROM: TALES OF OLD JAPAN

BY LORD REDESDALE, G.C.V.O., K.C.B. (A. B. MITFORD)

FORMERLY SECOND SECRETARY TO THE BRITISH LEGATION IN JAPAN

WITH ILLUSTRATIONS
DRAWN AND CUT ON WOOD BY JAPANESE ARTISTS

PREFACE

In the Introduction to the story of the Forty-seven Rônins, I have said almost as much as is needful by way of preface to my stories.

Those of my readers who are most capable of pointing out the many shortcomings and faults of my work, will also be the most indulgent towards me; for any one who has been in Japan, and studied Japanese, knows the great difficulties by which the learner is beset.

For the illustrations, at least, I feel that I need make no apology. Drawn, in the first instance, by one Ôdaké, an artist in my employ, they were cut on wood by a famous wood-engraver at Yedo, and are therefore genuine specimens of Japanese art. Messrs. Dalziel, on examining the wood blocks, pointed out to me, as an interesting fact, that the lines are cut with the grain of the wood, after the manner of Albert Dürer and some of the old German masters,—a process which has been abandoned by modern European wood-engravers.

It will be noticed that very little allusion is made in these Tales to the Emperor and his Court. Although I searched diligently, I was able to find no story in which they played a conspicuous part.

Another class to which no allusion is made is that of the Gôshi. The Gôshi are a kind of yeomen, or bonnet-lairds, as they would be called over the border, living on their own land, and owning no allegiance to any feudal lord. Their rank is inferior to that of the Samurai, or men of the military class, between whom and the peasantry they hold a middle place. Like the Samurai, they wear two swords, and are in many cases prosperous and wealthy men claiming a descent more ancient than that of many of the feudal Princes. A large number of them are enrolled among the Emperor's body-guard; and these have played a conspicuous part in the recent political changes in Japan, as the most conservative and anti-foreign element in the nation.

With these exceptions, I think that all classes are fairly represented in my stories.

The feudal system has passed away like a dissolving view before the eyes of those who have lived in Japan during the last few years. But when they arrived there it was in full force, and there is not an incident narrated in the following pages, however strange it may appear to Europeans, for the possibility and probability of which those most competent to judge will not vouch. Nor, as many a recent event can prove, have heroism, chivalry, and devotion gone out of the land altogether. We may deplore and inveigh against the Yamato Damashi, or Spirit of Old Japan, which still breathes in the soul of the Samurai, but we cannot withhold our admiration from the self-sacrifices which men will still make for the love of their country.

The first two of the Tales have already appeared in the *Fortnightly Review*, and two of the Sermons, with a portion of the Appendix on the subject of the Hara-Kiri, in the pages of the *Cornhill Magazine*. I have to thank the editors of those periodicals for permission to reprint them here.

LONDON, *January 7, 1871.*

CHAPTER I

THE FORTY-SEVEN RÔNINS

The books which have been written of late years about Japan, have either been compiled from official records, or have contained the sketchy impressions of passing travelers. Of the inner life of the Japanese, the world at large knows but little: their religion, their superstitions, their ways of thought, the hidden springs by which they move—all these are as yet mysteries. Nor is this to be wondered at. The first Western men who came in contact with Japan—I am speaking not of the old Dutch and Portuguese traders and priests, but of the diplomatists and merchants of eleven years ago—met with a cold reception. Above all things, the native Government threw obstacles in the way of any inquiry into their language, literature, and history. The fact was that the Tycoon's Government—with whom alone, so long as the Mikado remained in seclusion in his sacred capital at Kiôto, any relations were maintained—knew that the Imperial purple with which they sought to invest their chief must quickly fade before the strong sunlight which would be brought upon it so soon as there should be European linguists capable of examining their books and records. No opportunity was lost of throwing dust in the eyes of the new-comers, whom, even in the most trifling details, it was the official policy to lead astray. Now, however, there is no cause for concealment; the *Roi Fainéant* has shaken off his sloth, and his *Maire du Palais*, together, and an intelligible Government, which need not fear scrutiny from abroad, is the result: the records of the country being but so many proofs of the Mikado's title to power, there is no reason for keeping up any show of mystery. The path of inquiry is open to all; and although there is yet much to be learnt, some knowledge has been attained, in which it may interest those who stay at home to share.

The recent revolution in Japan has wrought changes social as well as political; and it may be that when, in addition to the advance which has already been made, railways and telegraphs shall have connected the principal points of the Land of Sunrise, the old Japanese, such as he was and had been for centuries when we found him eleven short years ago, will have become extinct. It has appeared to me that no better means could be chosen of preserving a record of a curious and fast disappearing civilization than the translation of some of the most interesting national legends and histories, together with other specimens of literature bearing upon the same subject. Thus the Japanese may tell their own tale, their translator only adding here and there a few words of heading or tag to a chapter, where an explanation or amplification may seem necessary. I fear that the long and hard names will often make my tales tedious reading, but I believe that those who will bear with the difficulty will learn more of the character of the Japanese people than by skimming over descriptions of travel and adventure, however brilliant. The lord and his retainer, the warrior and the priest, the humble artisan and the despised Eta or pariah, each in his turn will become a leading character in my budget of stories; and it is out of the mouths of these personages that I hope to show forth a tolerably complete picture of Japanese society.

Having said so much by way of preface, I beg my readers to fancy themselves wafted away to the shores of the Bay of Yedo—a fair, smiling landscape: gentle slopes, crested by a dark fringe of pines and firs, lead down to the sea; the quaint eaves of many a temple and holy shrine peep out here and there from the groves; the bay itself is studded with picturesque fisher-craft, the torches of which shine by night like glow-worms among the outlying forts; far away to the west loom the goblin-haunted heights of Oyama, and beyond the twin hills of the Hakoné Pass—Fuji-Yama, the Peerless Mountain, solitary and grand, stands in the centre of the plain, from which it sprang vomiting flames twenty-one centuries ago.[1] For a hundred and sixty years the huge mountain has been at peace, but the frequent earthquakes still tell of hidden fires, and none can say when the red-hot stones and ashes may once more fall like rain over five provinces.

In the midst of a nest of venerable trees in Takanawa, a suburb of Yedo, is hidden Sengakuji, or the Spring-hill Temple, renowned throughout the length and breadth of the land for its cemetery, which contains the graves of the Forty-seven Rônins,[2] famous in Japanese history, heroes of Japanese drama, the tale of whose deeds I am about to transcribe.

On the left-hand side of the main court of the temple is a chapel, in which, surmounted by a gilt figure of Kwanyin, the goddess of mercy, are enshrined the images of the forty-seven men, and of the master whom they loved so well. The statues are carved in wood, the faces colored, and the dresses richly lacquered; as works of art they have great merit—the action of the heroes, each armed with his favorite weapon, being wonderfully life-like and spirited. Some are venerable men, with thin, grey hair (one is seventy-seven years old); others are mere boys of sixteen. Close by the chapel, at the side of a path leading up the hill, is a little well of pure water, fenced in and adorned with a tiny fernery, over which is an inscription, setting forth that "This is the well in which the head was washed; you must not wash your hands or your feet here." A little further on is a stall, at which a poor old man earns a pittance by selling books, pictures, and medals, commemorating the loyalty of the Forty-seven; and higher up yet, shaded by a grove of stately trees, is a neat inclosure, kept up, as a signboard announces, by voluntary contributions, round which are ranged forty-eight little tombstones, each decked with evergreens, each with its tribute of water and incense for the comfort of the departed spirit. There were forty-seven Rônins; there are forty-eight tombstones, and the story of the forty-eighth is truly characteristic of Japanese ideas of honor. Almost touching the rail of the graveyard is a more imposing monument under which lies buried the lord, whose death his followers piously avenged.

And now for the story.

At the beginning of the eighteenth century there lived a daimio, called Asano Takumi no Kami, the Lord of the castle of Akô, in the province of Harima. Now it happened that an Imperial ambassador from the Court of the Mikado having been sent to the Shogun[3] at Yedo, Takumi no Kami and another noble called Kamei Sama were appointed to receive and feast the envoy; and a high official, named Kira Kôtsuké no Suké, was named to teach them the proper ceremonies to be observed upon the occasion. The two nobles were accordingly forced to go daily to the castle to listen to the instructions of Kôtsuké no Suké. But this Kôtsuké no Suké was a man greedy of money; and as he deemed that the presents which the two daimios, according to time-honored custom, had brought him in return for his instruction, were mean and unworthy, he conceived a great hatred against them, and took no pains in teaching them, but on the contrary rather sought to make laughing-stocks of them. Takumi no Kami, restrained by a stern sense of duty, bore his insults with patience; but Kamei Sama, who had less control over his temper, was violently incensed, and determined to kill Kôtsuké no Suké.

One night when his duties at the castle were ended, Kamei Sama returned to his own palace, and having summoned his councilors[4] to a secret conference, said to them: "Kôtsuké no Suké has insulted Takumi no Kami and myself during our service in attendance on the Imperial envoy. This is against all decency, and I was minded to kill him on the spot; but I bethought me that if I did such a deed within the precincts of the castle, not only would my own life be forfeit, but my family and vassals would be ruined: so I stayed my hand. Still the life of such a wretch is a sorrow to the people, and to-morrow when I go to Court I will slay him: my mind is made up, and I will listen to no remonstrance." And as he spoke his face became livid with rage.

Now one of Kamei Sama's councilors was a man of great judgment, and when he saw from his lord's manner that remonstrance would be useless, he said: "Your lordship's words are law; your servant will make all preparations accordingly; and to-morrow, when your lordship goes to Court, if this Kôtsuké no Suké should again be insolent, let him die the death." And his lord was pleased at this speech, and waited with impatience for the day to break, that he might return to Court and kill his enemy.

But the councilor went home, and was sorely troubled, and thought anxiously about what his prince had said. And as he reflected, it occurred to him that since Kôtsuké no Suké had the reputation of being a miser he would certainly be open to a bribe, and that it was better to pay any sum, no matter how great, than that his lord and his house should be ruined. So he collected all the money he could, and, giving it to his servants to carry, rode off in the night to Kôtsuké no Suké's palace, and said to his retainers: "My master, who is now in attendance upon the Imperial envoy, owes much thanks to my Lord Kôtsuké no Suké, who has been at so great pains to teach him the proper ceremonies to be observed during the reception of the Imperial envoy. This is but a shabby present which he has sent by me, but he hopes that his lordship will condescend to accept it, and commends himself to his lordship's favor." And, with these words, he produced a thousand ounces of silver for Kôtsuké no Suké, and a hundred ounces to be distributed among his retainers.

When the latter saw the money, their eyes sparkled with pleasure, and they were profuse in their thanks; and begging the councilor to wait a little, they went and told their master of the lordly present which had arrived with a polite message from Kamei Sama. Kôtsuké no Suké in eager delight sent for the councilor into an inner chamber, and, after thanking him, promised on the morrow to instruct his master carefully in all the different points of etiquette. So the councilor, seeing the miser's glee, rejoiced at the success of his plan; and having taken his leave returned home in high spirits. But Kamei Sama, little thinking how his vassal had propitiated his enemy, lay brooding over his vengeance, and on the following morning at daybreak went to Court in solemn procession.

When Kôtsuké no Suké met him, his manner had completely changed, and nothing could exceed his courtesy. "You have come early to Court this morning, my Lord Kamei," said he. "I cannot sufficiently admire your zeal. I shall have the honor to call your attention to several points of etiquette to-day. I must beg your lordship to excuse my previous conduct, which must have seemed very rude; but I am naturally of a cross-grained disposition, so I pray you to forgive me." And as he kept on humbling himself and making fair speeches, the heart of Kamei Sama was gradually softened, and he renounced his intention of killing him. Thus by the cleverness of his councilor was Kamei Sama, with all his house, saved from ruin.

Shortly after this, Takumi no Kami, who had sent no present, arrived at the castle, and Kôtsuké no Suké turned him into ridicule even more than before, provoking him with sneers and covert insults; but Takumi no Kami affected to ignore all this, and submitted himself patiently to Kôtsuké no Suké's orders.

This conduct, so far from producing a good effect, only made Kôtsuké no Suké despise him the more, until at last he said haughtily: "Here, my Lord of Takumi, the ribbon of my sock has come untied; be so good as to tie it up for me."

Takumi no Kami, although burning with rage at the affront, still thought that as he was on duty he was bound to obey, and tied up the ribbon of the sock. Then Kôtsuké no Suké, turning from him, petulantly exclaimed: "Why, how clumsy you are! You cannot so much as tie up the ribbon of a sock properly! Any one can see that you are a boor from the country, and know nothing of the manners of Yedo." And with a scornful laugh he moved towards an inner room.

But the patience of Takumi no Kami was exhausted; this last insult was more than he could bear.

"Stop a moment, my lord," cried he.

"Well, what is it?" replied the other. And, as he turned round, Takumi no Kami drew his dirk, and aimed a blow at his head; but Kôtsuké no Suké, being protected by the Court cap which he wore, the wound was but a scratch, so he ran away; and Takumi no Kami, pursuing him, tried a second time to cut him down, but, missing his aim, struck his dirk into a pillar. At this moment an officer, named Kajikawa Yosobei, seeing the affray, rushed up, and holding back the infuriated noble, gave Kôtsuké no Suké time to make good his escape.

Then there arose a great uproar and confusion, and Takumi no Kami was arrested and disarmed, and confined in one of the apartments of the palace under the care of the censors. A council was held, and the prisoner was given over to the safeguard of a daimio, called Tamura Ukiyô no Daibu, who kept him in close custody in his own house, to the great grief of his wife and of his retainers; and when the deliberations of the council were completed, it was decided that, as he had committed an outrage and attacked another man within the precincts of the palace, he must perform *hara-kiri*,—that is, commit suicide by disemboweling; his goods must be confiscated, and his family ruined. Such was the law. So Takumi no Kami performed *hara-kiri*, his castle of Akô was confiscated, and his retainers having become Rônins, some of them took service with other daimios, and others became merchants.

Now amongst these retainers was his principal councilor, a man called Oishi Kuranosuké, who, with forty-six other faithful dependants, formed a league to avenge their master's death by killing Kôtsuké no Suké. This Oishi Kuranosuké was absent at the castle of Akô at the time of the affray, which, had he been with his prince, would never have occurred; for, being a wise man, he would not have failed to propitiate Kôtsuké no Suké by sending him suitable presents; while the councilor who was in attendance on the prince at Yedo was a dullard, who neglected this precaution, and so caused the death of his master and the ruin of his house.

So Oishi Kuranosuké and his forty-six companions began to lay their plans of vengeance against Kôtsuké no Suké; but the latter was so well guarded by a body of men lent to him by a daimio called Uyésugi Sama, whose daughter he had married, that they saw that the only way of attaining their end would be to throw their enemy off his guard. With this object they separated and disguised themselves, some as carpenters or craftsmen, others as merchants; and their chief, Kuranosuké, went to Kiôto, and built a house in the quarter called Yamashina, where he took to frequenting houses of the worst repute, and gave himself up to drunkenness and debauchery, as if nothing were further from his mind than revenge. Kôtsuké no Suké, in the meanwhile, suspecting that Takumi no Kami's former retainers would be scheming against his life, secretly sent spies to Kiôto, and caused a faithful account to be kept of all that Kuranosuké did. The latter, however, determined thoroughly to delude the enemy into a false security, went on leading a dissolute life with harlots and winebibbers. One day, as he was returning home drunk from some low haunt, he fell down in the street and went to sleep, and all the passers-by laughed him to scorn. It happened that a Satsuma man saw this, and said: "Is not this Oishi Kuranosuké, who was a councilor of Asano

Takumi no Kami, and who, not having the heart to avenge his lord, gives himself up to women and wine? See how he lies drunk in the public street! Faithless beast! Fool and craven! Unworthy the name of a Samurai!"[5]

And he trod on Kuranosuké's face as he slept, and spat upon him; but when Kôtsuké no Suké's spies reported all this at Yedo, he was greatly relieved at the news, and felt secure from danger.

THE SATSUMA MAN INSULTS OISHI KURANOSUKÉ.

One day Kuranosuké's wife, who was bitterly grieved to see her husband lead this abandoned life, went to him and said: "My lord, you told me at first that your debauchery was but a trick to make your enemy relax in watchfulness. But indeed, indeed, this has gone too far. I pray and beseech you to put some restraint upon yourself."

"Trouble me not," replied Kuranosuké, "for I will not listen to your whining. Since my way of life is displeasing to you, I will divorce you, and you may go about your business; and I will buy some pretty young girl from one of the public-houses, and marry her for my pleasure. I am sick of the sight of an old woman like you about the house, so get you gone—the sooner the better."

So saying, he flew into a violent rage, and his wife, terror-stricken, pleaded piteously for mercy.

"Oh, my lord! Unsay those terrible words! I have been your faithful wife for twenty years, and have borne you three children; in sickness and in sorrow I have been with you; you cannot be so cruel as to turn me out of doors now. Have pity! Have pity!"

"Cease this useless wailing. My mind is made up, and you must go; and as the children are in my way also, you are welcome to take them with you."

When she heard her husband speak thus, in her grief she sought her eldest son, Oishi Chikara, and begged him to plead for her, and pray that she might be pardoned. But nothing would turn Kuranosuké from his purpose, so his wife was sent away, with the two younger children, and went back to her native place. But Oishi Chikara remained with his father.

The spies communicated all this without fail to Kôtsuké no Suké, and he, when he heard how Kuranosuké, having turned his wife and children out of doors and bought a concubine, was groveling in a life of drunkenness and lust, began to think that he had no longer anything to fear from the retainers of Takumi no Kami, who must be cowards, without the courage to avenge their lord. So by degrees he began to keep a less strict watch, and sent back half of the guard which had been lent to him by his father-in-law, Uyésugi Sama. Little did he think how he was falling into the trap laid for him by Kuranosuké, who, in his zeal to slay his lord's enemy, thought nothing of divorcing his wife and sending away his children! Admirable and faithful man!

In this way Kuranosuké continued to throw dust in the eyes of his foe, by persisting in his apparently shameless conduct; but his associates all went to Yedo, and, having in their several capacities as workmen and pedlars contrived to gain access to Kôtsuké no Suké's house, made themselves familiar with the plan of the building and the arrangement of the different rooms, and ascertained the character of the inmates, who were brave and loyal men, and who were cowards; upon all of which matters they sent regular reports to Kuranosuké. And when at last it became evident from the letters which arrived from Yedo that Kôtsuké no Suké was thoroughly off his guard, Kuranosuké rejoiced that the day of vengeance was at hand; and, having appointed a trysting-place at Yedo, he fled secretly from Kiôto, eluding the vigilance of his enemy's spies. Then the forty-seven men, having laid all their plans, bided their time patiently.

It was now midwinter, the twelfth month of the year, and the cold was bitter. One night, during a heavy fall of snow, when the whole world was hushed, and peaceful men were stretched in sleep upon the mats, the Rônins determined that no more favorable opportunity could occur for carrying out their purpose. So they took counsel together, and, having divided their band into two parties, assigned to each man his post. One band, led by Oishi Kuranosuké, was to attack the front gate, and the other, under his son Oishi Chikara, was to attack the postern of Kôtsuké no Suké's house; but as Chikara was only sixteen years of age, Yoshida Chiuzayémon was appointed to act as his guardian. Further it was arranged that a drum, beaten at the order of Kuranosuké, should be the signal for the simultaneous attack; and that if any one slew Kôtsuké no Suké and cut off his head he should blow a shrill whistle, as a signal to his comrades, who would hurry to the spot, and, having identified the head, carry it off to the temple called Sengakuji, and lay it as an offering before the tomb of their dead lord. Then they must report their deed to the Government, and await the sentence of death which would surely be passed upon them. To this the Rônins one and all pledged themselves. Midnight was fixed upon as the hour, and the forty-seven comrades, having made all ready for the attack, partook of a last farewell feast together, for on the morrow they must die. Then Oishi Kuranosuké addressed the band, and said—

"To-night we shall attack our enemy in his palace; his retainers will certainly resist us, and we shall be obliged to kill them. But to slay old men and women and children is a pitiful thing; therefore, I pray you each one to take great heed lest you kill a single helpless person." His comrades all applauded this speech, and so they remained, waiting for the hour of midnight to arrive.

When the appointed hour came, the Rônins set forth. The wind howled furiously, and the driving snow beat in their faces; but little cared they for wind or snow as they hurried on their road, eager for revenge. At last they reached Kôtsuké no Suké's house, and divided themselves into two bands; and Chikara, with twenty-three men, went round to the back gate. Then four men, by means of a ladder of ropes which they hung on to the roof of the porch, effected an entry into the courtyard; and, as they saw signs that all the inmates of the house were asleep, they went into the porter's lodge where the guard slept, and, before the latter had time to recover from their astonishment, bound them. The terrified guard prayed hard for mercy, that their lives might be spared; and to this the Rônins agreed on condition that the keys of the gate should be given up; but the others tremblingly said that the keys were kept in the house of one of their officers, and that they had no means of obtaining them. Then the Rônins lost patience, and with a hammer dashed in pieces the big wooden bolt which secured the gate, and the doors flew open to the right and to the left. At the same time Chikara and his party broke in by the back gate.

Then Oishi Kuranosuké sent a messenger to the neighboring houses, bearing the following message:—"We, the Rônins who were formerly in the service of Asano Takumi no Kami, are this night about to break into the palace of Kôtsuké no Suké, to avenge our lord. As we are neither night robbers nor ruffians, no hurt will be done to the neighboring houses. We pray you to set your minds at rest." And as Kôtsuké no Suké was hated by his neighbors for his covetousness, they did not unite their forces to assist him. Another precaution was yet taken. Lest any of the people inside should run out to call the relations of the family to the rescue, and these coming in force should interfere with the plans of the Rônins, Kuranosuké stationed ten of his men armed with bows on the roof of the four sides of the courtyard, with orders to shoot any retainers who might attempt to leave the place. Having thus laid all his plans and posted his men, Kuranosuké with his own hand beat the drum and gave the signal for attack.

Ten of Kôtsuké no Suké's retainers, hearing the noise, woke up; and, drawing their swords, rushed into the front room to defend their master. At this moment the Rônins, who had burst open the door of the front hall, entered the same room. Then arose a furious fight between the two parties, in the midst of which Chikara, leading his men through the garden, broke into the back of the house; and Kôtsuké no Suké, in terror of his life, took refuge, with his wife and female servants, in a closet in the verandah; while the rest of his retainers, who slept in the barrack outside the house, made ready to go to the rescue. But the Rônins who had come in by the front door, and were fighting with the ten retainers, ended by overpowering and slaying the latter without losing one of their own number; after which, forcing their way bravely towards the back rooms, they were joined by Chikara and his men, and the two bands were united in one.

By this time the remainder of Kôtsuké no Suké's men had come in, and the fight became general; and Kuranosuké, sitting on a camp-stool, gave his orders and directed the Rônins. Soon the inmates of the house perceived that they were no match for their enemy, so they tried to send out intelligence of their plight to Uyésugi Sama, their lord's father-in-law, begging him to come to the rescue with all the force at his command. But the messengers were shot down by the archers whom Kuranosuké had posted on the roof. So no help coming, they fought on in despair. Then Kuranosuké cried out with a loud voice: "Kôtsuké no Suké alone is our enemy; let some one go inside and bring him forth, dead or alive!"

Now in front of Kôtsuké no Suké's private room stood three brave retainers with drawn swords. The first was Kobayashi Héhachi, the second was Waku Handaiyu, and the third was Shimidzu Ikkaku, all good men and true, and expert swordsmen. So stoutly did these men lay about them that for a while they kept the whole of the Rônins at bay, and at one moment even forced them back. When Oishi Kuranosuké saw this, he ground his teeth with rage, and shouted to his men: "What! Did not every man of you swear to lay down his life in avenging his lord, and now are you driven back by three men? Cowards, not fit to be spoken to! To die fighting in a master's cause should be the noblest ambition of a retainer!" Then turning to his own son Chikara, he said, "Here, boy! Engage those men, and if they are too strong for you, die!"

Spurred by these words, Chikara seized a spear and gave battle to Waku Handaiyu, but could not hold his ground, and backing by degrees, was driven out into the garden, where he missed his footing and slipped into a pond, but as Handaiyu, thinking to kill him, looked down into the pond, Chikara cut his enemy in the leg and caused him to fall, and then, crawling out of the water dispatched him. In the meanwhile Kobayashi Héhachi and Shimidzu Ikkaku had been killed by the other Rônins, and of all Kôtsuké no Suké's retainers not one fighting man remained. Chikara, seeing this, went with his bloody sword in his hand into a back room to search for Kôtsuké no Suké, but he only found the son of the latter, a young lord named Kira Sahioyé, who, carrying a halberd, attacked him, but was soon wounded and fled. Thus the whole of Kôtsuké no Suké's men having been killed, there was an end of the fighting; but as yet there was no trace of Kôtsuké no Suké to be found.

Then Kuranosuké divided his men into several parties and searched the whole house, but all in vain; women and children weeping were alone to be seen. At this the forty-seven men began to lose heart in regret, that after all their toil they had allowed their enemy to escape them, and there was a moment when in their despair they agreed to commit suicide together upon the spot; but they determined to make one more effort. So Kuranosuké went into Kôtsuké no Suké's sleeping-room, and touching the quilt with his hands, exclaimed, "I have just felt the bed-clothes and they are yet warm, and so methinks that our enemy is not far off. He must certainly be hidden somewhere in the house." Greatly excited by this, the Rônins renewed their search. Now in the raised part of the room, near the place of honor, there was a picture hanging; taking down this picture, they saw that there was a large hole in the plastered wall, and on thrusting a spear in they could feel nothing beyond it. So one of the Rônins, called Yazama Jiutarô, got into the hole, and found that on the other side there was a little courtyard, in which there stood an outhouse for holding charcoal and firewood. Looking into the outhouse, he spied something white at the further end, at which he struck with his spear, when two armed men sprang out upon him and tried to cut him down, but he kept them back until one of his comrades came up and killed one of the two men and engaged the other, while Jiutarô entered the outhouse and felt about with his spear. Again seeing something white, he struck it with his lance, when a cry of pain betrayed that it was a man; so he rushed up, and the man in white clothes, who had been wounded in the thigh, drew a dirk and aimed a blow at him. But Jiutarô wrested the dirk from him, and clutching him by the collar, dragged him out of the outhouse. Then the other Rônin came up, and they examined the prisoner attentively, and saw that he was a noble-looking man, some sixty years of age, dressed in a white satin sleeping-robe, which was stained by the blood from the thigh-wound which Jiutarô had inflicted. The two men felt convinced that this was no other than Kôtsuké no Suké, and they asked him his name, but he gave no answer, so they gave the signal whistle, and all their comrades collected together at the call; then Oishi Kuranosuké, bringing a lantern, scanned the old man's features, and it was indeed Kôtsuké no Suké; and if further proof were wanting, he still bore a scar on his forehead where their master, Asano Takumi no Kami, had wounded him during the affray in the castle. There being no possibility of mistake, therefore, Oishi Kuranosuké went down on his knees, and addressing the old man very respectfully, said—

"My lord, we are the retainers of Asano Takumi no Kami. Last year your lordship and our master quarreled in the palace, and our master was sentenced to *hara-kiri*, and his family was ruined. We have come to-night to avenge him, as is the duty of faithful and loyal men. I pray your lordship to acknowledge the justice of our purpose. And now, my lord, we beseech you to perform *hara-kiri*. I myself shall have the honor to act as your second, and when, with all humility, I shall have received your lordship's head, it is my intention to lay it as an offering upon the grave of Asano Takumi no Kami."

Thus, in consideration of the high rank of Kôtsuké no Suké, the Rônins treated him with the greatest courtesy, and over and over again entreated him to perform *hara-kiri*. But he crouched speechless and trembling. At last Kuranosuké, seeing that it was vain to urge him to die the death of a nobleman, forced him down, and cut off his head with the same dirk with which Asano Takumi no Kami had killed himself. Then the forty-seven comrades, elated at having accomplished their design, placed the head in a bucket, and prepared to depart; but before leaving the house they carefully extinguished all the lights and fires in the place, lest by any accident a fire should break out and the neighbors suffer.

THE RÔNINS INVITE KÔTSUKÉ NO SUKÉ TO PERFORM HARA-KIRI.

As they were on their way to Takanawa, the suburb in which the temple called Sengakuji stands, the day broke; and the people flocked out to see the forty-seven men, who, with their clothes and arms all blood-stained, presented a terrible appearance; and every one praised them, wondering at their valor and faithfulness. But they expected every moment that Kôtsuké no Suké's father-in-law would attack them and carry off the head, and made ready to die bravely sword in hand. However, they reached Takanawa in safety, for Matsudaira Aki no Kami, one of the eighteen chief daimios of Japan, of whose house Asano Takumi no Kami had been a cadet, had been highly pleased when he heard of the last night's work, and he had made ready to assist the Rônins in case they were attacked. So Kôtsuké no Suké's father-in-law dared not pursue them.

At about seven in the morning they came opposite to the palace of Matsudaira Mutsu no Kami, the Prince of Sendai, and the Prince, hearing of it, sent for one of his councilors and said: "The retainers of Takumi no Kami have slain their lord's enemy, and are passing this way; I cannot sufficiently admire their devotion, so, as they must be tired and hungry after their night's work, do you go and invite them to come in here, and set some gruel and a cup of wine before them."

So the councilor went out and said to Oishi Kuranosuké: "Sir, I am a councilor of the Prince of Sendai, and my master bids me beg you, as you must be worn out after all you have undergone, to come in and partake of such poor refreshment as we can offer you. This is my message to you from my lord."

"I thank you, sir," replied Kuranosuké. "It is very good of his lordship to trouble himself to think of us. We shall accept his kindness gratefully."

So the forty-seven Rônins went into the palace, and were feasted with gruel and wine, and all the retainers of the Prince of Sendai came and praised them.

Then Kuranosuké turned to the councilor and said, "Sir, we are truly indebted to you for this kind hospitality; but as we have still to hurry to Sengakuji, we must needs humbly take our leave." And, after returning many thanks to their hosts, they left the palace of the Prince of Sendai and hastened to Sengakuji, where they were met by the abbot of the monastery, who went to the front gate to receive them, and led them to the tomb of Takumi no Kami.

And when they came to their lord's grave, they took the head of Kôtsuké no Suké, and having washed it clean in a well hard by, laid it as an offering before the tomb. When they had done this, they engaged the priests of the temple to come and read prayers while they burnt incense: first Oishi Kuranosuké burnt incense, and then his son Oishi Chikara, and after them the other forty-five men performed the same ceremony. Then Kuranosuké, having given all the money that he had by him to the abbot, said:—

"When we forty-seven men shall have performed *hara-kiri*, I beg you to bury us decently. I rely upon your kindness. This is but a trifle that I have to offer; such as it is, let it be spent in masses for our souls!"

And the abbot, marveling at the faithful courage of the men, with tears in his eyes pledged himself to fulfil their wishes. So the forty-seven Rônins, with their minds at rest, waited patiently until they should receive the orders of the Government.

At last they were summoned to the Supreme Court, where the governors of Yedo and the public censors had assembled; and the sentence passed upon them was as follows: "Whereas, neither respecting the dignity of the city nor fearing the Government, having leagued yourselves together to slay your enemy, you violently broke into the house of Kira Kôtsuké no Suké by night and murdered him, the sentence of the Court is, that, for this audacious conduct, you perform *hara-kiri*." When the sentence had been read, the forty-seven Rônins were divided into four parties, and handed over to the safe keeping of four different daimios; and sheriffs were sent to the palaces of those daimios in whose presence the Rônins were made to perform *hara-kiri*. But, as from the very beginning they had all made up their minds that to this end they must come, they met their death nobly; and their corpses were carried to Sengakuji, and buried in front of the tomb of their master, Asano Takumi no Kami. And when the fame of this became noised abroad, the people flocked to pray at the graves of these faithful men.

THE WELL IN WHICH THE HEAD WAS WASHED.

Among those who came to pray was a Satsuma man, who, prostrating himself before the grave of Oishi Kuranosuké, said: "When I saw you lying drunk by the roadside at Yamashina, in Kiôto, I knew not that you were plotting to avenge your lord; and, thinking you to be a faithless man, I trampled on you and spat in your face as I passed. And now I have come to ask pardon and offer atonement for the insult of last year." With those words he prostrated himself again before the grave, and, drawing a dirk from his girdle, stabbed himself in the belly and died. And the chief priest of the temple, taking pity upon him, buried him by the side of the Rônins; and his tomb still remains to be seen with those of the forty-seven comrades.

This is the end of the story of the forty-seven Rônins.

A terrible picture of fierce heroism which it is impossible not to admire. In the Japanese mind this feeling of admiration is unmixed, and hence it is that the forty-seven Rônins receive almost divine honors. Pious hands still deck their graves with green boughs and burn incense upon them; the clothes and arms which they wore are preserved carefully in a fire-proof store-house attached to the temple, and exhibited yearly to admiring crowds, who behold them probably with little less veneration than is accorded to the relics of Aix-la-Chapelle or Trèves; and once in sixty years the monks of Sengakuji reap quite a harvest for the good of their temple by holding a commemorative fair or festival, to which the people flock during nearly two months.

THE TOMBS OF THE RÔNINS.

A silver key once admitted me to a private inspection of the relics. We were ushered, my friend and myself, into a back apartment of the spacious temple, overlooking one of those marvelous miniature gardens, cunningly adorned with rockeries and dwarf trees, in which the Japanese delight. One by one, carefully labeled and indexed boxes containing the precious articles were brought out and opened by the chief priest. Such a curious medley of old rags and scraps of metal and wood! Home-made chain armor, composed of wads of leather secured together by pieces of iron, bear witness to the secrecy with which the Rônins made ready for the fight. To have bought armor would have attracted attention, so they made it with their own hands. Old moth-eaten surcoats, bits of helmets, three flutes, a writing-box that must have been any age at the time of the tragedy, and is now tumbling to pieces; tattered trousers of what once was rich silk brocade, now all unraveled and befringed; scraps of leather, part of an old gauntlet, crests and badges, bits of sword handles, spear-heads and dirks, the latter all red with rust, but with certain patches more deeply stained as if the fatal clots of blood were never to be blotted out: all these were reverently shown to us. Among the confusion and litter were a number of documents, yellow with age and much worn at the folds. One was a plan of Kôtsuké no Suké's house, which one of the Rônins obtained by marrying the daughter of the builder who designed it. Three of the manuscripts appeared to me so curious that I obtained leave to have copies taken of them.

The first is the receipt given by the retainers of Kôtsuké no Suké's son in return for the head of their lord's father, which the priests restored to the family, and runs as follows:—

"MEMORANDUM:—
ITEM. ONE HEAD.
ITEM. ONE PAPER PARCEL.
The above articles are acknowledged to have been received.

Signed, { SAYADA MAGOBEI. (*Loc. sigill.*)
{ SAITÔ KUNAI. (*Loc. sigill.*)

To the priests deputed from the Temple Sengakuji,
His Reverence SEKISHI,
His Reverence ICHIDON."

The second paper is a document explanatory of their conduct, a copy of which was found on the person of each of the forty-seven men:—

"Last year, in the third month, Asano Takumi no Kami, upon the occasion of the entertainment of the Imperial ambassador, was driven, by the force of circumstances, to attack and wound my Lord Kôtsuké no Suké in the castle, in order to avenge an insult offered to him. Having done this without considering the dignity of the place, and having thus disregarded all rules of propriety, he was condemned to *hara-kiri,* and his property and castle of Akô were forfeited to the State, and were delivered up by his retainers to the officers deputed by the Shogun to receive them. After this his followers were all dispersed. At the time of the quarrel the high officials present prevented Asano Takumi no Kami from carrying out his intention of killing his enemy, my Lord Kôtsuké no Suké. So Asano Takumi no Kami died without having avenged himself, and this was more than his retainers could endure. It is impossible to remain under the same heaven with the enemy of lord or father; for this reason we have dared to declare enmity against a personage of so exalted rank. This day we shall attack Kira Kôtsuké no Suké, in order to finish the deed of vengeance which was begun by our dead lord. If any honorable person should find our bodies after death, he is respectfully requested to open and read this document.

"15th year of Genroku. 12th month.

"Signed, OISHI KURANOSUKÉ, Retainer of Asano Takumi no Kami, and forty-six others."[6]

The third manuscript is a paper which the Forty-seven Rônins laid upon the tomb of their master, together with the head of Kira Kôtsuké no Suké:—

"The 15th year of Genroku, the 12th month, and 15th day. We have come this day to do homage here, forty-seven men in all, from Oishi Kuranosuké down to the foot-soldier, Terasaka Kichiyémon, all cheerfully about to lay down our lives on your behalf. We reverently announce this to the honored spirit of our dead master. On the 14th day of the third month of last year our honored master was pleased to attack Kira Kôtsuké no Suké, for what reason we know not. Our honored master put an end to his own life, but Kira Kôtsuké no Suké lived. Although we fear that after the decree issued by the Government this plot of ours will be displeasing to our honored master, still we, who have eaten of your food, could not without blushing repeat the verse, 'Thou shalt not live under the same heaven nor tread the same earth with the enemy of thy father or lord,' nor could we have dared to leave hell and present ourselves before you in paradise, unless we had carried out the vengeance which you began. Every day that we waited seemed as three autumns to us. Verily, we have trodden the snow for one day, nay, for two days, and have tasted food but once. The old and decrepit, the sick and ailing, have come forth gladly to lay down their lives. Men might laugh at us, as at grasshoppers trusting in the strength of their arms, and thus shame our honored lord; but we could not halt in our deed of vengeance. Having taken counsel together last night, we have escorted my Lord Kôtsuké no Suké hither to your tomb. This dirk,[7] by which our honored lord set great store last year, and entrusted to our care, we now bring back. If your noble spirit be now present before this tomb, we pray you, as a sign, to take the dirk, and, striking the head of your enemy with it a second time, to dispel your hatred for ever. This is the respectful statement of forty-seven men."

The text, "Thou shalt not live under the same heaven with the enemy of thy father," is based upon the Confucian books. Dr. Legge, in his "Life and Teachings of Confucius," p. 113, has an interesting paragraph summing up the doctrine of the sage upon the subject of revenge.

"In the second book of the 'Le Ke' there is the following passage:— 'With the slayer of his father a man may not live under the same heaven; against the slayer of his brother a man must never have to go home to fetch a weapon; with the slayer of his friend a man may not live in the same State.' The *lex talionis* is here laid down in its fullest extent. The 'Chow Le' tells us of a provision made against the evil consequences of the principle by the appointment of a minister called 'The Reconciler.' The provision is very inferior to the cities of refuge which were set apart by Moses for the manslayer to flee to from the fury of the avenger. Such as it was, however, it existed, and it is remarkable that Confucius, when consulted on the subject, took no notice of it, but affirmed the duty of blood-revenge in the strongest and most unrestricted terms. His disciple, Tsze Hea, asked him, 'What course is to be pursued in the murder of a father or mother?' He replied, 'The son must sleep upon a matting of grass with his shield for his pillow; he must decline to take office; he must not live under the same heaven with the slayer. When he meets him in the market-place or the court, he must have his weapon ready to strike him.' 'And what is the course in the murder of a brother?' 'The surviving brother must not take office in the same State with the slayer; yet, if he go on his prince's service to the State where the slayer is, though he meet him, he must not fight with him.' 'And what is the course in the murder of an uncle or cousin?' 'In this case the nephew or cousin is not the principal. If the principal, on whom the revenge devolves, can take it, he has only to stand behind with his weapon in his hand, and support him.'"

I will add one anecdote to show the sanctity which is attached to the graves of the Forty-seven. In the month of September 1868, a certain man came to pray before the grave of Oishi Chikara. Having finished his prayers, he deliberately performed *hara-kiri*,[8] and, the belly wound not being mortal, dispatched himself by cutting his throat. Upon his person were found papers setting forth that, being a Rônin and without means of earning a living, he had petitioned to be allowed to enter the clan of the Prince of Chôshiu, which he looked upon as the noblest clan in the realm; his petition having been refused, nothing remained for him but to die, for to be a Rônin was hateful to him, and he would serve no other master than the Prince of Chôshiu: what more fitting place could he find in which to put an end to his life than the graveyard of these Braves? This happened at about two hundred yards' distance from my house, and when I saw the spot an hour or two later, the ground was all bespattered with blood, and disturbed by the death-struggles of the man.

THE LOYAL RONINS

AN HISTORICAL ROMANCE,
TRANSLATED FROM THE JAPANESE
OF
SHUNSUI TAMENAGA
BY
SHIUICHIRO SAITO AND EDWARD GREEY

ILLUSTRATED BY
KEI-SAI YEI-SEN, OF YEDO

"This is the Legacy of the Loyal Samurai. The friction of Time, which
obliterates most things, adds lustre to their fame."
SHUNSUI TAMENAGA.

INTRODUCTION

The brilliant display made by Japan at the International Exhibition
at Philadelphia gave an impetus to the interest already excited among
Western nations concerning Japanese art, and from that time the
subject has commanded the wonder and admiration of the world.
Indeed, at no distant period, the names of Hokusai and of the Kano
Brothers are destined, like those of Raphael and Hogarth, to become
household words in every American and European family.

The literature of a people and their works of art are signs by which
the student is enabled to learn the degree of civilization and
refinement attained by a nation, and it cannot be denied that the
Japanese, who have achieved so much in art, possess a literature of no
mean order.

Foremost in the ranks of her celebrated writers are Bakin and
Tamenaga, and the Western world, which has already acknowledged
the genius of Hokusai and of the Kano Brothers, will not fail to
appreciate the wit and pathos to be found in the writings of the
authors whose names I have quoted.

For many reasons, which I need not here mention, the works of our
writers have been sealed to American and English readers. It is true, in
"Mitford's Tales of Old Japan," something has been related of the
social condition of the people; but as an example of Japanese literature,

the book possesses little value. Within the last ten years the pages of the "Japan Mail" have contained many articles of great interest; however, few persons are aware of the existence of such a periodical.

Three years ago I determined to translate a standard Japanese novel, and thus supply a want I knew was greatly felt by those interested in my country.

After some thought I decided to take the "I-ro-ha Bunko" of Tamenaga; first, because he is one of the most popular of our writers; secondly, on account of the romance containing a wonderful description of Japanese life under the feudal system, and of an institution, which, for more than seven hundred years, has exerted a most powerful influence over the nation.

Notwithstanding many misrepresentations and expressions of disgust heaped upon Roninism, I feel sure those who have written upon the subject have only seen "one side of the picture." While I am the last person to defend lawless acts, I cannot avoid feeling a certain admiration for the much-despised institution, believing that it contained the germ of patriotism.

The author and book having been decided upon, I, in the summer of 1879, began my task; but finding myself unequal to the work, sought and obtained the assistance of an estimable lady residing in Boston. Although I had her hearty and sympathetic cooperation, I failed to make satisfactory progress and we abandoned the attempt.

In October, my attention was called to the Japanese stories of Mr. Edward Greey, of Manchester, Mass., which greatly delighted me, they giving most graphic, amusing, and instructive descriptions of the manners and customs of my countrymen, and showing the author's thorough familiarity with our literature. I wrote to him at once, and our acquaintance, so interestingly begun, soon ripened into friendship. I discovered Mr. Greey had not only lived many years in the East, and knew Japan from Yezo to Kiusiu, but that he is also an accomplished Japanese artist. During the following January, I mentioned to him my attempt with "I-ro-ha Bunko," when he recognized the work and agreed to join me in its translation. The result is before the reader.

To those who have assisted Mr. Greey and myself, I tender my most hearty thanks, especially to Mr. Gilbert Attwood, of Jamaica Plain, Mass., who has for many years been a sincere friend to Japan and the Japanese, and without whose kind and generous surrender of his copy of "I-roha Bunko," we would not have been able to complete this translation. To Mrs. Edward Greey, who so kindly copied the MSS. for the printers, I return my best thanks; also to Mr. Makoto

Fukui, of New York, and Mr. A. Van Name, Librarian of Yale College, for the loan of copies of Tamenaga's works; and to Mr. John A. Lowell, of Boston, who has done so much to bring Japanese art before the public, and who so freely gave us the use of his library of Japanese books.

I feel especially happy in being able to offer this trifling tribute of my gratitude to the American people, with whom I have lived for the last five years, and in one of whose institutions of learning I have received the education of which, I hope, with the help and guidance of the spirits of my ancestors, I shall make good use in the service of my sovereign and country. Wherever I have been I have received a most kind welcome, and the memory of the generous hospitality extended to me will always be retained in my heart.

By the time this work reaches you I shall be crossing the broad Pacific on my way home, yet I trust the day is not far distant when I shall again be among you to study more thoroughly your noble institutions, which are founded upon the principles of freedom I so greatly love and admire.

Till then I say *Sayonara* (farewell).

SHIUICHIRO SAITO.
Manchester-by-the-Sea, Mass.,
July 19, 1880.

NOTES

"The Loyal Ronins" is one of seven stories written by Shunsui Tamenaga (For-the-sake-of-perpetual Spring-water), and published under the title of "I-ro-ha Bunko" ("The ABC Writing-desk"). The edition used by Mr. Saito and myself bears the imprint of Nakamura-ya Kozo (Middle-village-store Happy-store-house) of Yedo, and was issued in parts, at irregular periods, between the seventh year of Tempo (Heaven-secure) and the first year of Kayei (Fortutunate-perpetual)—A.D. 1836–1848. It is in eighteen volumes, containing over a hundred and eighty illustrations by Kei-sai Yei-sen (Valley-cottage Superior-spring).

Tamenaga founded the modern school of Nihonese fiction, and was the Charles Dickens of Japan.

The author's arrangement of the romance, while perfectly intelligible to a Japanese, would, if literally followed, have utterly bewildered our readers—Tamenaga taking for granted that his patrons were thoroughly acquainted with the story of the forty-seven ronins. We were therefore compelled not only to rearrange the sequence of the chapters, but to supply the links in the story omitted by the author.

These were obtained by referring to "Ako Shijiu hichi-shi Den" (The Biography of the Forty-seven *Samurai* of Ako), "Sei-chu gi-shi mei-mei ga-den" (The Pictorial Biography of the Truly Loyal *Samurai*), and other works.

We have endeavored to reproduce Tamenaga's romance without making use of foot-notes or those stumbling-blocks to readers, Japanese names for persons and places. These are, in nearly all instances, translated literally. In the cases of individuals either the surname, the given name, or the military title is used. Our reason for retaining Japanese words, such as *samurai, ronin, sambo, saké*, etc., was the impossibility of translating them concisely.

The original illustrations are in two pieces, an arrangement peculiar to Japanese works, and one that, to the Western eye, totally destroys the effect of the pictures. Before reproducing the engravings I was compelled to unite them and retouch the lines of junction.

Some of the half-cuts were engraved independently of the others, and no amount of ingenuity would make them join correctly.

Many very interesting pictures had to be rejected on account of their not having any connection with the letterpress.

Those who are acquainted with the Japanese language will fully understand the difficulties we had to overcome in preparing this work for the press, and none better than ourselves know its imperfections. We have not attempted to translate the quaint sentences into elegant English, but have done our utmost to retain the unique, naive style of the author, believing it were "best to leave well alone."

If this specimen of Nihonese literature pleases our readers, we are prepared to give them other works by Tamenaga, and the romances of Bakin, the Sir Walter Scott of the Japanese literary world.

EDWARD GREEY.

Manchester-by-the-Sea, Mass.,

July 19, 1880.

AUTHOR'S PREFACE

During the long winter evenings of my childhood, when the lamp burned dimly in the paper lantern and but partly revealed the pictures on the screens, I often sat by the fire-bowl and listened with awed face to my honored mother, who, to compensate me for the gloom of the apartment, would relate stories of the Forty-seven Ronins; and thus illuminate my soul with the light of loyalty. It was from her honored lips I received the histories embodied in this work; therefore, if the book pleases, I beg the reader not to think of the old man of Yedo whose brush traces these characters, but to pay grateful respect to the spirit of my honored parent, whose eloquent descriptions I have so imperfectly reproduced, and whose body is now resting beneath the tall grass.

CONTENTS

CHAPTER I.
UNSHEATHING THE SWORD.

In the month of November, A.D. 1698, during the reign of the Shogun Iyetsuna, the president of the Council of Elders in Yedo, was officially informed that three commissioners were on their way from the Imperial Court at Kioto, and was directed to appoint two officials to receive them; in consequence of which he nominated Lord Morning-field of Ako, and Lord Tortoise-well, *daimio* (great lords) of equal rank, who were instructed to place themselves under the orders of Kira, Master of Ceremonies to the Shogun.

This man, not being a *daimio*, lacked the true principles of nobility: was greedy, corrupt, and insolent in the discharge of his duties, treating the customary presents brought by the lords with scorn and addressing them in terms of undisguised contempt. At first they bore his behavior with quiet dignity, however, when it became insufferable, they determined to resent it and even went the length of resolving to kill him.

Sir Reedy-plain, the chief councilor of Lord Tortoise-well, learning of his Lord's annoyance secretly visited Kira, and bribed him with offerings which he diplomatically represented came from his master, and thus averted evil from their house.

Sir Big-rock, chief councilor of Lord Morning-field, was less fortunate. When he heard his chief had been appointed one of the officials to receive the commissioners he felt troubled, knowing, as he did, the reputation of the upstart Kira, besides which, being in charge of the castle of Ako, in the province of Harima, distant nearly three hundred miles from Yedo, he could not leave his post and personally propitiate the Master of Ceremonies.

After pondering over the matter, he summoned a *samurai* (knight or military gentleman) of the clan, named New-well, to whom he said:

"I wish you at once to start for Yedo, on most important business. Are you ready to go?"

"Yes, sir, yes," was the response. "I am always at your service, at any moment, day and night? "

"Very good," said Sir Big-rock, adding, in a lower tone, "I have here a letter and some money that I desire swiftly conveyed to our lord's councilors, Sir Arrow-stand and Sir Wisteria-lake. The communication instructs them to wait privately on Kira, and hand him the gold, two hundred *rio* (dollars), as though it came from our chief. I have written urging them, on no account to neglect this duty, as by so doing they might expose our lord to serious annoyance"; then, giving him a smaller package containing fifteen *rio*, continued, "This sum will be sufficient to defray your travelling expenses. I am sure you will not fail speedily to discharge this important commission."

Sir New-well bowed respectfully and after receiving the letter and money, said:

"I am honored by your selecting me for this responsible duty; please accept my thanks. I will do my utmost in return for your great favor."

Before the sun had set the faithful *samurai* was on his way, and he traveled day and night until he arrived at his destination.

Unfortunately for Lord Morning-field his councilors, Sir Arrow-stand and Sir Wisteria-lake, were men of little intelligence, parsimonious in their ideas and stupid in the execution of their duties. Upon receiving Sir Big-rock's letter they hesitated to carry out his commands, deeming the money would be as good as thrown into the bay. Therefore, when their chief next presented himself to Kira he was treated with neglect and covert disdain, while Lord Tortoise-well was welcomed with obsequious flattery and carefully initiated in his duties.

On the morning the commissioners were expected from Kioto the two lords proceeded to the castle of Oshiro for the purpose of receiving their final instructions. Kira, after complimenting Lord Tortoise-well, turned to the latter's companion and said:

"Here, my Lord Morning-field, the string of my sock has become loosened. Tie it for me."

Although the noble's patience was almost exhausted, he complied with the insolent command, deeming it an imperative duty to obey the representative of the Shogun, at the same time resolving, later on, to seek Kira and demand satisfaction at his hands.

After awhile the Master of Ceremonies excused Lord Tortoise-well, who was permitted to retire to the reception hall. Then, addressing the other noble more contemptuously than before, he said:

"How exceedingly clumsy you are to-day. One would think you were a countryman, ignorant of the manners of Yedo."

At this provocation Lord Morning-field rose, and, clutching the hilt of his sword, cried:

"Defend yourself, Sir Kira, I will no longer submit to your unjust treatment."

"DEFEND YOURSELF, SIR KIRA, I WILL NO LONGER SUBMIT TO
YOUR UNJUST TREATMENT."

Instead of bravely drawing his weapon and facing his challenger,
Kira trembled and endeavored to escape, whereupon the noble dealt
him a blow that, had it not been for the cap worn by the official, would
have cleft his head in twain. Kira, finding himself wounded, uttered
loud cries, and, pressing his hand to his forehead, rushed away, hotly
pursued by Lord Morning-field who, as his victim fled, once more
attacked him, but missing his aim, buried his weapon in a pillar
behind which the fugitive had retreated. The incensed noble was
following him up when an officer arrived on the scene, and advancing
behind the *daimio*, threw his arms around his waist, thus giving Kira
ample time to escape.

An hour afterward Lord Morning-field was commanded to retire to
his residence and consider himself under arrest.

CHAPTER II.
HOW A DAIMIO MET HIS DEATH.

"The *man-rio* is developed and beautified by the snows of winter.
Injustice to the lord reveals and intensifies the devotion of the
samurai."

Thus wrote the Lord of Ako one lovely morning in December, two
weeks after his encounter with Kira. The noble, costumed in his official
garb, was kneeling before a writing table in his study engaged in
verse-making, his manner betraying no anxiety concerning the
impending decision of the Council of Elders. Upon the desk were some
volumes of poetry, an inkstone bearing his crest, falcon's feathers
crossed and enclosed in a circle, some brushes resting on a lacquered
holder and a small kettle of inlaid metal containing water with which
to moisten his ink.

He grasped the slender bamboo-stemmed writing-brush firmly and
formed the characters with a swift motion. Then, when he had
completed the poem, turned his head and glanced into the veranda,
where stood a porcelain flower-pot containing the object of his
inspiration, a *man-rio* plant, upon the bright green leaves of which was
piled the snow of the previous night, contrasting charmingly with the
clusters of ruddy berries hanging beneath. As he gazed upon this
the rising sun sent its rays across the scene and made the crystals
sparkle like a cluster of stars.

While the master of the house was thus calmly employed, his
retainers were moving silently about their duties. No song came
from the kitchen, no voice was heard speaking above a whisper.
The main gate was closed, a temporary fence of green bamboo
had been built before it—a sign the lord was a prisoner—and a
friend of the family, surety for the chief, gave orders and decided
who should enter or quit the

THE *MAN-RIO* (TEN-THOUSAND-
GOLDEN-BERRY PLANT).

mansion. A great sorrow was upon the household and all, save its head, trembled with apprehension.

In the midst of his reverie, a screen behind him was moved noiselessly aside and Lady Fair-face, his wife, entered the apartment; her features too plainly betraying the disturbed state of her soul. Advancing toward him she sank upon the floor and bowing until her forehead touched the mat, said in an agitated voice:

"I trust my lord is in the enjoyment of good health."

The noble regarded her tenderly and replied:

"I am well, Fair-face; why are you so sad?"

The lady conquered her grief and said:

"My lord, when you are in danger, how can I appear happy?"

Although her words moved him he did not betray any emotion, but inviting her to approach nearer, pointed to the poem.

Lady Fair-face read it slowly, and glancing at him, remarked:

"Ah, my lord, you are prepared for the worst! Kira is all powerful with the Shogun, and his friends will do their utmost to crush the house of Ako."

"Have no fear, Fair-face! My greatest anxiety is on your account. I know what is passing in your mind. Your actions have betrayed you."

"My actions, my lord?"

"Yes," indicating the *man-rio*. "You cannot deceive me. Last evening, when you tended that plant, you used one of your hair-pins to remove a dead berry and left the trinket on the rim of the vessel, also your paper handkerchiefs near it—they are there this morning."

"How forgetful of me," she murmured, gazing sadly at him. "I can deceive all the world but you."

Uttering these words she leaned forward, and placing her hands on his knees, rested her face upon them. The noble glanced sorrowfully at her and laying his hand on her shoulder, said:

"Fair-face, the bird driven from its nest always finds some shelter from the storm. Whatever may occur, I desire you will place implicit confidence in my chief-councilor and regard his words as though they were mine. When I succeeded to the rank and estates of my honorable father, I imagined myself wiser than Big-rock, however, I quickly discovered my error and learned to value him at his true worth. He is a man of a hundred thousand, brave, honorable, fertile in resource, patient under difficulties and a thorough statesman."

"Statesman!" she cried. "Ah, then why has he not averted this danger from us? Kira was most polite to Lord Tortoise-well."

Lord Morning-field did not reproach her for this wifely outburst, merely replying:

"I am certain Big-rock has done his duty. If harm overtakes our house it will not be through any fault or neglect of his. He is a mirror of loyalty. I pray you not to forget my estimation of him."

The lady bowed her head and clung to her husband, knowing full well that she was soon to part from him for ever. Lord Morning-field endeavored to comfort her and when she became somewhat composed, led her toward the entrance to her apartments, saying:

"Fair-face, I will send for you later on. I understand, you have passed a sleepless night—lie down and endeavor to seek refreshment in slumber."

She tottered into the passage-way and sinking upon the floor saluted him, sobbing as though her heart would break. Lady Pine-island, her chief attendant, advanced quickly and drawing the screens between the rooms, shut the pitiful sight from her lord's view.

The noble slowly returned to his desk, and kneeling before it, remained in profound thought until the hour of the Dragon (8 A.M.), when he was disturbed by the entrance of Sir Common, who, prostrating himself near the doorway, announced the arrival of the Commissioners from the Shogun.

Lord Morning-field arose and quitted the study, passing Sir Common who was still respectfully upon his hands and knees and who presently followed him. Upon reaching the main entrance the noble received and gravely saluted his visitors, whom he conducted to the reception hall where they seated themselves in the place of honor; he kneeling on the mats, lower down, the apartment, facing them.

Neither of the officials spoke nor returned his salute, they being there as the representatives of the Shogun. After a moments pause, the elder drew a folded document from his bosom, and extending it toward the noble, said:

"My Lord Morning-field, we are ordered by the Shogun to announce the decision of the Council of Elders in the matter of your unsheathing your sword within the precincts of the castle of O-shiro. We request you will at once read and carry out this decree."

The noble gravely received the paper and having reverently lifted it to his forehead, calmly perused its contents, then addressing the commissioners, said:

"This commands me to commit self-despatch and announces the confiscation of my estates and extinction of my family name, to all of which I most respectfully submit."

The chief commissioner listened with unmoved countenance and replied:

"In that case we are ready to act as your witnesses."

Lord Morning-field, who had not anticipated any other judgment, summoned Sir Common and bade him remove some screens concealing a recess in the hall, when the visitors beheld the preparations necessary for the solemn ceremony. He advanced to the place and removing his outer garments revealed the *shiromuku* (white suit used during mourning and sacrificial ceremonies) after which he seated himself on the thick mats and signaled Sir Common to summon Sir Pure. When the latter had entered, bowed and taken his place behind his chief, Lord Morning-field, addressing the commissioners, remarked:

"With your permission I will give my final instructions to my councilors."

No objection being offered to this he bade Sir Common approach close to him, then pointing to a white pine-wood box resting on a *sambo* (stand) of like material, whispered in his ear; presently drawing a letter from his bosom and handing it to the *samurai*, who listened with the deepest attention and, after his lord had ceased to speak, saluted him reverently and retired to his left hand.

The scene was most impressive. In the centre of the group knelt the noble, calm and resolute, before him were seated the commissioners, cold and stern, and behind him crouched the faithful *samurai*, ready to render the last services to their chief.

Outside the mansion all was still, there being a light covering of snow upon the ground. Inside reigned a dead silence for, though the retainers set their teeth and clenched their fingers in agony, no sound escaped their lips.

Lord Morning-field gazed through the open screens upon the beautiful view beyond and, mutely bidding it farewell, calmly reached for the dirk placed near his right hand.

That afternoon a mournful procession wended its way toward the cemetery of the Spring-hill Temple in the southern suburb of Yedo. In the midst of the cortege was borne a *norimono* (enclosed litter) containing the dead body of the Lord of Ako, which was conveyed to its final resting place amid the tears, lamentations and prayers of thousands of people.

CHAPTER III.
THE MOTHER OF SIR STRAIGHT-GROVE.

"The hungry, persistent fly quickly discovers a dead body.
The great man's misfortune fattens the news-seller."

This was said, many years ago, by a learned man of Kioto who had thoroughly studied human nature, and these words equally apply to our own time.

Early on the morning of the day after the tragedy, the city of Yedo swarmed with men shouting themselves hoarse in their endeavors to dispose of news-sheets containing full particulars of the death of the Lord of Ako. In one hand they carried their paper lanterns and in the other the broad-sides which had been printed during the night. After awhile their cries aroused the inhabitants, who quitting their beds hastened into the streets and, as they made their purchases, eagerly inquired if the latter contained an account of the self-despatch of Sir Kira.

"What are you asking?" laughingly exclaimed one of the venders, a merry-looking boy who had folded his pocket-towel and secured it on the top of his head, as a protection against the dew, and whose muddy clogs indicated he had traveled from the suburbs. "Do not expect too much! My honorable masters, you will find your fifteen cash worth of horrors in this sheet. One seldom discovers two nuts in a single shell."

"When will Sir Kira die?" demanded an old man, who wore horn-spectacles and was nervously fumbling in his bag for coins. "I am anxious to know, as I have relations in the clan of Ako."

The news-seller comically rolled his eyes and stuck out his tongue, then replied:

"Don't worry yourself—Sir Kira will die a natural death."

This announcement amazed the listeners who were fully aware of the law, which required that equal punishment should be meted out to all parties engaged in a quarrel.

At the hour of the Horse (noon), the people learned Kira was to escape with the loss of his office and a few days nominal imprisonment, on hearing which they became very indignant and secretly condemned the partiality of the Shogun.

Among the minor instructions, contained in the decree sentencing the Lord of Ako to self-despatch, was one directing that the three residences of the *daimio* in Yedo were to be given up to commissioners accredited by the Shogun, who would take possession of them within two days of the noble's death. This news spread consternation in the hearts of the clansmen residing in the city; they, in the absence of Sir Big-rock, being at a loss how to act in such a sudden emergency. By the mandate a thousand families were rendered homeless, and as they entirely depended upon the annual allowances received from their lord, their situations were pitiful in the extreme. Some, who lacked the true spirit of loyalty, disposed of their effects and took service under new masters; however, the greater number, after attending to the immediate wants of their families, packed their armor and set out for the castle of Ako.

Everything was in confusion and loud were the lamentations of the women who, unlike their husbands, did not hesitate openly to denounce the severity of the sentence, which not only ended the life of their chief, but broke up their homes and deprived them of subsistence.

"MY HONORABLE MASTERS, YOU WILL FIND YOUR FIFTEEN
CASH WORTH OF HORRORS IN THIS SHEET."

One of the unfortunates was a *samurai* named Straight-grove, whose aged parent had been the foster-mother of the dead lord. On the day of his death she visited his residence in order to bid farewell to his body, and upon seeing the sad sight became frantic with grief. Lady Fair-face, fearing the old woman would do herself some injury, commanded Sir Straight-grove to conduct her home, which he did with many expressions of tenderness and affection. After awhile his words appeared to comfort her and she recovered her usual calmness of manner, whereupon her delighted son softly retired to the kitchen and poured out a cup of *saké* (rice wine), which, having placed on the family altar, he drained to soothe his agitated nerves.

When the members of his household returned from the funeral, he assembled them and announced that they were to depart on the morrow for his brother's residence in the province of Izu, at the same time stating he would proceed to join Sir Big-rock at the castle of Ako.

As that was to be their last night in the old home, he directed his wife to prepare a little feast, and about the hour of the Rooster (6 P.M.), they gathered in the dining-room and partook of various delicacies which the careful house-wife had made with her own hands. His mother appeared heartily to enjoy the viands and when the children went to bed, cheerfully remarked to her son:

"Our time here grows short so I will seek my room and do some writing."

All present bowed respectfully, and Sir Straight-grove said:

"Honorable mother, I trust you will sleep well."

When, later on, he retired for the night he saw the lamp was still burning in her apartment and knew she had not sought her bed.

The next morning the family rose earlier than usual and began to pack their effects, even the little ones assisting, but no sound came from the chamber of the grandmother. Sir Straight-grove, imagining she was tired through sitting up late, refrained from disturbing her; however, as the hours passed and she did not make her appearance, he grew uneasy and approaching the door of the room, knocked gently, saying:

"Honorable mother, I pray you will make haste to arise. It is very late and the bearers are waiting outside to convey your baggage to Izu. Excuse my thus rudely summoning you.

He paused and listened for a reply. Receiving none he became thoroughly alarmed and drawing back the sliding door entered the apartment, then moving toward the bed, pushed aside the screen, saying:

"Honorable mother—!"

To his horror he saw her face was unnaturally white and the bed-clothes were crimson with blood.

"What!" he exclaimed, as he tremblingly surveyed the shocking sight. "Was my mother crazy that she should do this? Alas for me!"

Advancing and weeping bitterly, he knelt, raised her in his arms and gazed upon the placid face, calm in the majesty of death. As he held her left hand in his and supported her with his right, he beheld the weapon with which she had ended her life; its appearance plainly denoting the will and courage that had sustained her last moments—a courage worthy of the mother of a brave *samurai*.

His lamentations quickly attracted the members of his family who crowded into the room, and falling upon their knees, saluted the dead.

By the side of the mat, which had proved an altar for her loyal sacrifice, was a writing-case, and near it a folded paper inscribed:

"LAST WORDS."

When the body had been removed from the room, Sir Straight-grove noticed the letter and proceeded to read it, stopping every now and then to wipe the tears from his blinded eyes.

"SIR STRAIGHT-GROVE GAZED UPON THE PLACID FACE, CALM
IN THE MAJESTY OF DEATH."

This was the communication, written in a firm hand by the heroic matron:

"I leave you a few words. To-day a dreadful calamity overtook our lord and I have almost lost myself. When he entered the world my hands received him. My tongue taught his to say *uba* (nurse—literally milk-mother). It was I who watched his infant steps and my heart that swelled with pride when he first walked the length of a mat. I saw him bloom into childhood and develop into a glorious youth. I was present, behind the screens, when he first received the clansmen in public audience, when his consummate tact, dignity and manhood, brought tears to my aged eyes. He was my foster-son, my chief, my lord. Therefore, to-day, when I saw his murdered body, I determined he should not, unattended, travel the Lonely Road. I am about to end my life in order that my spirit may accompany his on its journey. When our lord hears the sound of my clogs behind him he will be comforted, knowing in death as in life, his old nurse is in attendance upon him.

My son, my heart dwells upon you, although I can but feebly express my thoughts. As you read this, grasp the hilt of your sword and swear swift vengeance upon the enemy of our master—vengeance which will cause you to follow me so quickly that I shall hear behind me the echoing of your clogs and ere long welcome you to the land of shadows.

"In my closet, wrapped in a purple cloth, are three volumes of a novel I borrowed from Mrs. Moat, Jr. You will return them with my thanks. I also desire you will give two of my robes and one of my girdles to my maid, Miss Angel.

"Take good care of your health until the day arrives for you to avenge our master, when you will not consider yourself.

To my dear son,

From your mother."

Sir Straight-grove dropped the document, and grinding his teeth with rage, presently exclaimed:

"Who is the cause of all this? Is it not solely due to the insult Kira offered my honored master? I call the gods to witness he shall not escape punishment."

When the day of retribution arrived Sir Straight-grove was the first to cross swords with the retainers of Sir Kira.

CHAPTER IV.
SIR UNCONQUERABLE MEETS THE MESSENGERS FROM YEDO.

"To-o ke moya
Ikura to-o kumo nani kamaya senu
Yeube no furi de mizu ga mashi
Masu nomi dekiru kio no kawa bito"

"May the distance between the banks of the river be great. What is troubling you? The water is high through the storm of last night, and our fares being high in proportion, we can afford to indulge in big cups of *saké.*"

Such was the song chanted by a number of lightly-clad coolies, whose occupation consisted in carrying passengers and vehicles across the Kagosa river, which formed the eastern boundary of Harima. They were a turbulent, lawless party, the terror of solitary travelers from whom, notwithstanding the instructions of the village elders, they generally contrived to extort more than the legal amount of fare. Some of them were squatting on the banks smoking and gambling, others stretched upon their backs dozing or watching the rays of the setting sun that gilded the swift waters of the stream, while the rest stood waist-deep in the flood and amused themselves by splashing their comrades.

As they were thus employed one of the party, shading his eyes with his hands, espied two travelers signaling them from the opposite bank, on seeing which he exclaimed:

"A great beauty is making signs to me from the other side of the river. I will hasten over and attend to her."

"What is that? What is that?" cried the others, springing to their feet. "A beauty—who is she?"

Instead of replying, the fellow rushed into the water and began to breast the stream, laughing and shouting:

"I am coming, great lady, I am coming."

The other coolies followed him like a flock of ducks anxious to secure a choice morsel.

The object of their attention was a charming girl of eighteen with a complexion like a *momo* (peach-flower), whose costume and manner denoted her to be the daughter of a *samurai*, and who was accompanied by a young man-servant, armed with one sword. The attendant remained a few paces behind his mistress and anxiously watched the coolies. Night was coming on, the banks of the river were almost deserted, the place had a bad reputation and the *yakago* (cylindrical net of split bamboo filled with stones, used as an embankment) cast a deep shadow on the spot where they stood and hid them from the view of approaching travelers.

On came the men and presently the foremost, emerging from the water, staggered up the slippery incline, shouting:

"Come, young lady, mount on my shoulders, the stream is deep and no one can carry you as easily as myself."

The frightened maiden shrank from him and would have fled, when he rudely seized her and endeavored to raise her from the ground. As he did so another coolie quitted the water, exclaiming:

"Look here, man. I am already engaged by that lady! You shall not rub your unshaven chin against her pearly face."

"Here, boys," cried the third, a tall, muscular wretch. "It is useless for you to make love to her. Cannot you see she prefers me? Among the gallants of the Kagosa river who is better looking than I?" and tearing her from the embrace of his companion, he continued "Don't flutter so, my little crow, I will carry you safely over the rough water."

On hearing this outrageous speech, her servant, no longer able to restrain his indignation, threw down her baggage and rushing into their midst, rescued his mistress, then drawing his sword, exclaimed:

"Dogs, what do you intend to do? My lady is not alone, I am here to defend her. Dare again to lay a finger upon her and you will experience the consequences."

The coolies stared as though amazed at his audacity and seizing their cudgels fell upon the brave lad, whom they beat and kicked cruelly, after which their leader seized the young lady and made off with her, followed by his triumphant companions. Ere they had gone many paces a *ronin-samurai* was seen approaching along the road, noticing which they halted and clustered around their victim. The face of the newcomer was concealed by a straw hat that effectually masked his features, and at the same time permitted him to see; like a person who peeps behind the grating of a prison.

This stranger was Sir Unconquerable, a man whose name fitted him like his *tabi* (socks) and who, some years before, had belonged to the clan of Ako. One day having purchased a sword, he had thoughtlessly tried its temper upon an impertinent peddler whose friends brought the matter to the notice of his chief. Although the latter admired the bravery of his follower and greatly valued his services, he could not condone his offence, so giving Sir Unconquerable a sum of money, he dismissed him and the knight became a *ronin* (wave-man, one who, though still a *samurai*, owes allegiance to no master).

Such was Sir Unconquerable who, on seeing the young lady in the hands of her captors, advanced, seized them one after the other by their hands, twisted them like broken bamboos and hurled them to the ground, having done which he turned to the affrighted maiden and said:

"The atrocious conduct of these scoundrels must have sorely troubled you."

The young lady was too much agitated to reply, however, her servant who, spite of his wounds, had risen to his knees, said:

"Honorable Sir, you have indeed arrived at an opportune moment."

Sir Unconquerable placed his hand upon the hilt of his sword, and advancing upon the prostrate coolies, exclaimed:

"Much to be hated dogs, prepare for death."

The fellows made off like birds alarmed by a hunter or ants whose nest is disturbed by a husbandman.

"SIR UNCONQUERABLE SEIZED THEM ONE AFTER THE OTHER
AND HURLED THEM TO THE GROUND."

The young lady and her servant, overjoyed at their escape, knelt before their deliverer, folded their palms and expressed their gratitude, the lady saying:

"Sir stranger, accept my profound thanks."

"And mine," murmured the servant. "Though my spirit sprung like an arrow, I was alone and could do but little to defend the daughter of my master. Through your bravery we have escaped a great danger. The gratitude of your humble servant knows no bounds. We expect to meet my master in the next village when we will, without fail, present ourselves at your residence and thank you for your kindness. Be pleased to let me know your honorable name?"

Sir Unconquerable listened grimly and replied:

"I do not require such thanks for so trifling a matter. Do not trouble yourself further about this, but conduct your mistress back to the nearest inn, the sun will soon be set."

"You are very kind," said the young lady. "Still I would much like to know to whom I am indebted for my deliverance."

While she and her servant were urging him to divulge his name, they heard loud voices proceeding from the other side of the river and presently beheld a host of travel-stained coolies, carrying a light litter and running with all their might. As this party plunged into the stream a second one was seen in the distance.

Sir Unconquerable watched the approach of the procession, and as the first litter was borne up the bank, glanced at its occupant and said:

"Pardon me, but is not the honorable *samurai* who travels post-haste, Sir Common of the clan of Ako?"

The person addressed ordered his bearers to halt a moment, then said:

"Strangely met, Sir Unconquerable."

"Sir Common," said the former, approaching the litter, "your manner of traveling alarms me. Has any harm befallen my lord?"

Sir Common pointed to a little frame fixed in the front of the litter, on which was secured the *sambo* and white pine box, referred to in a former chapter, and said:

"Your fears are well founded. We have, in five days, traveled nearly three hundred miles to convey this," bowing respectfully, "to Sir Big-rock and announce to him the great calamity that has overtaken our lord. You must excuse my relating the particulars; you will learn them from Sir Pure who is following me."

Ere he had uttered the last word, the bearers once more lifted the litter and starting at a run, vanished in the direction of Ako.

The *ronin*, too impatient to wait for the arrival of the second litter upon the bank, waded into the river, approached the vehicle and shouted:

"Sir Pure, Sir Pure, it is I, Unconquerable! I pray you tell me what misfortune has occurred to our lord?

"Sir Pure waited until his bearers had carried him alongside the speaker, when, placing his mouth close to Sir Unconquerable's ear, he whispered the sad news, adding:

"We have made up our minds what to do. If you still remember the gracious favors of your late lord, you will not hesitate to join us."

Sir Unconquerable, who, as he spoke, waded by the side of the litter, answered:

"Sir Pure, it is not necessary you should remind me of such a thing. Although my spear is somewhat rusty and my armor dilapidated, I can make good use of them."

Sir Pure hastily saluted him and they ascended the bank, on reaching the summit of which the bearers broke into a run and rapidly followed the other litter; leaving Sir Unconquerable with the young lady and her attendant.

For some moments he remained as though lost in thought, the sad fate of his lord, profoundly affecting his loyal soul. He felt that, beginning with Sir Big-rock, all the *samurai* of the clan should die defending the castle against the army of forfeiture, and, as he turned to conduct the strangers to a place of safety, did not notice the dim outlines of the trees and rocks, but only beheld the *sambo* and white pine box carried in the litter of Sir Common.

When they arrived at the office of the road-commissioners, in the little village near the ferry, he made a formal complaint against the coolies, then, requesting the officers to take care of the travelers and see them to an inn, returned to his humble lodging, where he took his armor from its rest and busied himself in mending and polishing it.

The next morning he disposed of his few effects and started on foot for Ako.

CHAPTER V.
SIR BIG ROCK RECEIVES THE LAST FAVOR FROM HIS LORD.

"Better have a dishonest servant than a stingy one," was the golden maxim of the ancients, by which they meant, he who is too careful with his master's money, often becomes the means of ruining him. Meanness is not economy. The unpardonable failure of Sir Arrow-stand and Sir Wisteria-lake to pay over the gold sent by Sir Big-rock as a bribe for Kira, was treason against their lord and indirectly the cause of his death.

After the chief councilor had despatched Sir New-well, he felt somewhat easy in his mind and looked with little apprehension for the return of his messenger. Therefore, imagine, if you can, his grief and indignation when he heard the awful news brought by Sir Common and Sir Pure, who reached Ako upon the night of their meeting Sir Unconquerable on the bank of the Kagosa river.

When Sir Common handed the letter, entrusted to him by his dead chief, to Sir Big-rock, the latter raised it reverently to his forehead, then with trembling fingers essayed to break the seal. As he did so he beheld the *sambo* and pine box from which Sir Pure had removed the white covering; whereupon the chief councilor, unable to restrain his grief, bowed his head to the mat and wept, his emotion being shared by the messengers.

After awhile he conquered his sorrow, and addressing Sir Common, said:

"I trust the spirit of our lord will forgive my exhibition of weakness. These are the only tears I will allow myself."

Thus speaking he opened the letter and slowly perused its contents, and having thanked the exhausted messengers for their loyal devotion in hastening to carry out the instructions of their chief and given directions that their wants should be attended to, dressed himself in his robes of ceremony, and taking the *sambo* and its sacred burden in his hands, proceeded to the castle where he deposited his charge on the *tokonoma* (raised recess corresponding to our mantlepiece), and that accomplished, sent out couriers to summon the clansmen to an extraordinary council.

While awaiting their arrival he knelt, motionless as a statue, with his eyes fixed upon the white pine box, thinking how he should best carry out the wishes of his lord. Presently his hand sought the bosom of his robe and he drew from it the letter, which he again read; the communication being as follows:

"THOU KNOWEST."

This was signed with the military name of the late noble.

In a short time the clansmen began to assemble, each, as he arrived, silently taking his place on the matted floor according to his rank and respectfully saluting the chief councilor, their blanched faces and grave looks plainly denoting the anxiety that possessed their souls. The hours passed slowly as they knelt, mute and mournful, with their right hands grasping the hilts of their long swords, which they held vertically and used to support their bent bodies.

The first gray streaks of dawn were illuminating the horizon when an aged soldier ascended the castle-tower, and approaching the big bell sorrowfully drew back the suspended beam used as a clapper and swung it against the metal; repeating his action seven times and thus proclaiming the hour of the Tiger (4 A.M.). After he had completed his task he leaned over the parapet, and placing his withered hand to his wrinkled ear listened, presently muttering to himself:

"The last of the clansmen has come in. I hear the warden closing the great gate. Now the council will begin."

His surmise was correct. At that moment Sir Big-rock raised his head and announced the reason for so suddenly assembling the members of the clan.

The news fell upon the *samurai* like a thunderbolt upon an egg. A dead silence reigned in the apartment, and the dumbfounded clansmen glanced at one another as though utterly unable to comprehend the full meaning of the communication. After awhile one of the juniors uttered a cry of indignation. Then a loud clamor arose all over the hall and, notwithstanding their respect for the chief councilor, everybody spoke at once.

"Now is the moment to remember the golden words of the ancients," excitedly exclaimed a young *samurai*, "When the master is insulted it is for the servant to die. Our lord is no more, therefore let us follow him, dying gallantly defending his castle, the ramparts of which shall be our pillow. Sir Chief-councilor, this is our determination, frankly spoken. How and when it is to be accomplished, we leave to your decision."

Sir Big-rock understanding their excitement permitted them freely to express themselves. Then once more calling the meeting to order, said:

"Fellow clansmen, your exhibition of loyalty, while admirable in its intent, savors too much of haste. You desire to die like true *samurai*. Where is your enemy to be found? It will be easy enough to throw away your lives but the height of folly to sacrifice yourselves without obtaining some return. Our duty is to petition the authorities to appoint Lord Great-learning, the honored brother of our late master, chief of our clan and thus restore the house of Ako. As yet we only partially know the decision of the council of elders. I expect, as our lord was directed to commit self-despatch, Sir Kira, unless he has already died of his wound, will have received a similar sentence. This matter was not known on the afternoon of our lord's death when Sir Common and Sir Pure left Yedo. I propose we despatch two competent persons to the capital for the double object of presenting the petition and ascertaining the fate of Sir Kira. How say you, fellow clansmen?"

The assembly almost unanimously signified its assent, then Sir Moat, Sr., addressing the president, said:

"Sir Chief-councilor, there is one matter to which I desire to call your attention. I understand when you heard of the danger likely to overtake our late lord, you gave certain instructions to his councilors in Yedo, which, if carried out, would have averted this calamity. They, without doubt, failed in their duty and their treasonable neglect should be punished with death at our hands."

"Yes, with death at our hands," echoed the clansmen.

Sir Moat, Sr., paused until the sound of their voices had died away, when he continued:

"Sir Chief-councilor, I trust you will assent to this."

Sir Big-rock bowed gravely, after which he turned to Sir Shell and Sir Pigeon-field, and said:

"I shall have to trouble you with the mission to Yedo. You will travel post-haste and return in the same manner. Fellow clansmen," once more addressing the assembly, "from to-day until further orders, you will remain in the castle, every one at his post, and the clan will be ready under arms. We will now close the council."

The members saluted and retired, and before night the castle was in a state of complete defense, every one anxiously waiting for information from Yedo.

Two days afterward Sir New-well arrived post-haste from the capital, bringing news of the sentence passed upon Sir Kira.

This announcement caused the whole clan to grind their teeth and say:

"There is now no hope for us, however we will not be cowards and bring upon ourselves the ridicule and contempt of the world. We will fight and die, and our bodies, hanging over the ramparts, will show that we deserve the name of loyal *samurai*. Although the clan of Ako may no longer exist, people will say 'the master who observes his duties, shall have servants who do the same.' This is the only return we can render for the well-remembered favors of our dead lord."

Filled with these lofty sentiments, the whole clan swarmed to the castle, each carrying his armor, swords and spear, eager to be the first to enter the portal and report himself for duty.

CHAPTER VI.
THE CLANSMEN PREPARE TO DEFEND THE CASTLE.

"The beautiful lotus springs from the mud.
Loyalty knows no distinction of rank."

This ancient maxim admirably describes the feeling that animated the clan of Ako. It is true, on hearing of their lord's misfortune, some of the *samurai* had sought safety in the service of other masters; however, these were exceptions, the majority of the clansmen, including the foot soldiers, forgetting all else but their duty, loyally rallying round the standard hoisted by the chief-councilor.

Sir Big-rock, ever wise and watchful, placed certain officers at the castle gate with instructions to take down the names of all who presented themselves and assign them duty according to their rank and merit.

"THE CASTLE OF AKO, PROVINCE OF HARIMA,
ON THE SHORE OF THE INLAND SEA."

Among those who approached the portal, were three *ronin-samurai* whose appearance plainly betrayed their spirit and determination. These men had some time before lost the good will of the lord of Ako. Instead of obtaining service elsewhere they had wandered about the country, waiting for the day when he would forgive them and restore them to their former positions. Upon hearing of his fate they had vowed to die in his cause, and although their armor was rusty and their clothes ragged, hastened to present themselves before the registering officers.

"Wait a moment, if you please," remarked the latter."While admiring your spirit I cannot permit you to enter the castle, the orders of the chief councilor excluding all but clansmen from enrollment."

Sir Cliff-field, speaking for the others, replied:

"Honorable Sir, you are quite right, yet, though only *ronin*, we are determined to die for our lord; therefore, be good enough to report our presence to Sir Big-rock. If you do not grant us this favor we will end our lives where we stand."

The official did as he was requested. In a few moments a messenger came out, and after thanking the three *ronin*, in the name of Sir Big-rock, presented them with money and clothing, then, taking down their addresses, said:

"You may, at some future day, hear from the chief-councilor. At present he is unable to avail himself of your services."

Upon hearing this decision Sir Cliff-field, unable to restrain his tears, replied in a husky voice:

"The kindness of Sir Big-rock is well known to us. Taking pity upon our wave-like fortune he, even in the hour of his trial, forgets not to remember our needs.

Under these circumstances we dare not refuse his bounty or disobey his order to withdraw. We most sincerely trust, when his plans are decided upon, he will communicate with us."

The others added their entreaties to his, and after the messenger had promised to inform the chief-councilor of the same, they departed, commenting upon the goodness of Sir Big-rock.

During the succeeding days the registering officers were kept busily employed by the arrival of the loyal clansmen from Yedo, in addition to whom came merchants from the city and farmers from the provincial villages, who, catching the loyal spirit of the clansmen, were anxious to offer their services.

In the midst of the bustle there appeared a very poorly clad man, carrying on his back a set of dilapidated, purple armor and bearing in his hand a formidable spear. He advanced without any demonstration and attempted to enter the portal, noticing which the registering officer contemptuously motioned him to retire, remarking with a sneer:

"We have no occasion for your services."

His words were caught up by the bystanders who began to mock the new-comer; one of them saying:

"Look at the fellow's clothes! I wonder at his impudence in desiring to be registered; it would be good for him to take a glance in a mirror."

"O, don't you understand!" said another. "He fears to die of hunger, so wishes to enter the castle where he knows there is plenty of rice. He is willing to meet a soldier's death, if he can first of all satisfy the craving of his appetite."

"I do not even give him that much credit," whispered a third. "My opinion is he has heard of those three men whom the chief-councilor supplied with money and clothing and wants to share their good fortune."

"That is it! That is it!" cried the others.

"IN THE MIDST OF THE BUSTLE THERE APPEARED A VERY POORLY CLAD MAN, CARRYING ON HIS BACK A SET OF DILAPIDATED, PURPLE ARMOR AND BEARING IN HIS HAND A FORMIDABLE SPEAR."

"Yes," said a weazened-faced tailor. "A tramping dog often happens upon a good dinner."

The grim-looking *samurai* did not trouble himself to listen, but, taking his seat upon the stump of a tree near the gate, waited patiently as though expecting a summons from within.

In a few moments an aristocratic, martial-looking *samurai*, named Hatchet, came to the portal and enquired of the registering officers:

"Among those who are waiting for admittance, is there not one— Sir Unconquerable."

The official scanned his list, and bowing respectfully, replied:

"The honorable *samurai* you mention has not yet arrived."

Upon receiving this answer, Sir Hatchet raised his voice and shouted:

"Sir Unconquerable! Are you among the crowd? Sir Big-rock is impatient to see you."

"Sir Unconquerable! Sir Unconquerable!" echoed the officials at the gate; the cry being taken up by the loungers outside.

On hearing his name called, the saturnine stranger slowly rose and advanced toward the gate, the people falling back as he approached.

Sir Hatchet saluted him with profound respect and said:

"Well met, Sir Unconquerable! The chief-councilor has been expecting you. Now, Sir, please accompany me to his presence."

Sir Unconquerable turned slowly round and, after glancing contemptuously upon the crowd, followed Sir Hatchet to the council-chamber, leaving the people in amazement; the tailor presently remarking:

"Great Buddha, we can no longer tell a gentleman by his clothes."

That afternoon when a number of the clansmen were assembled in the council-chamber, talking over their plans and prospects, one of them exclaimed:

"What has become of Sir Island-in-the-front? He has always been noted for his bravery and loyalty. Surely he has not sought safety in flight. It is now five days since the enrollment began, yet his name does not appear on the lists."

This remark aroused the ire of some young *samurai*, who, clapping their hands to their swords, rose, saying:

"We will attend to the matter and pay a visit to Sir Island-in-the-front. If we find him preparing to retire like a crab, we will send him upon a different journey."

Away they went rattling their swords and clattering their clogs, fully determined to carry out their words.

Upon reaching the house they entered without ceremony, and rushing into the reception-room found everything in confusion.

"Ah!" exclaimed their leader. "I knew it; it is as we expected; he is in his private apartment. I will be the one to despatch him."

He motioned his companions to remain quiet and advanced to the entrance of the room, when instead of drawing his sword he halted a moment and, pointing forward, said:

"I cannot make this out. There is his armor hanging from the beam ready to be put on at a moment's notice. We have been too hasty."

As he spoke the wife of Sir Island-in-the-front entered from the yard, and falling upon her knees enquired in an agitated voice:

"Honorable sirs, what is your pleasure?"

To which their leader answered:

"We desire to know whether your husband is preparing to assist in the good work?"

"Honorable sirs, he is down upon the shore attending to his business."

"Ah!" said the *samurai*. "On the shore is he? Come, gentlemen, we will seek him. After all this looks suspicious."

They swaggered off, three abreast, like stage *daimio*, and presently reached the custom-house on the wharf, where they discovered Sir Island-in-the-front busily engaged loading coolies with packages of provisions, on seeing which they rudely demanded what he was about, and why he had not enrolled his name.

The *samurai* listened gravely and replied:

"Those packages are destined for the castle. While you have been doubting my loyalty I have been providing the means for your support. That is the reason why I have not had time to enroll my name."

The faces of the young men crimsoned with shame, and, bowing respectfully, their leader said:

"Ten thousand pardons for the ignorance of youth. 'The sparrow cannot comprehend the mind of the eagle.'"

CHAPTER VII.
SEALING THE COMPACT.

"A million evils are not so heavy as a command of the master;
Balanced against the latter my life is as light as a feather."

These words were uttered by Sir Big-rock upon the occasion of his receiving an official notification from the Shogun, commanding him, within thirty days, quietly and respectfully, to surrender the castle of Ako to the commissioners who would be despatched for the purpose of taking possession of the same. This document reached him about the time Sir Shell and Sir Pigeon-field arrived in Yedo. However, he did not communicate its contents to the clansmen, deeming it wisest to await the return of their envoys from the capital. Meanwhile preparations for the defense were continued and the fortress was victualled to sustain a long siege.

On the morning of the fourteenth day Sir Shell and Sir Pigeon-field presented themselves at the gate, and were immediately conducted to the presence of Sir Big-rock. Their travel-stained costumes and fatigued appearance betokened the severity of their journey.

Sir Pigeon-field being too much exhausted to speak, Sir Shell made the report, which was as follows:

"Sir Chief-councilor, we duly delivered the petition to the proper authorities then made searching enquiry regarding Sir Kira. Alas! Alas! he still lives and though deprived of his office, basks in the sunshine of the Shogun's favor. We hear his manner is as insolent as ever and that he triumphs in the disgrace of our house. He has trebled the guards at the gates of his residence and his spies dogged our steps wherever we went. He boasts of the wisdom of Sir Small-grove, his chief councilor, and of the fidelity of his retainers, and laughs at the idea of our avenging the death of our lord. While the latter lies under the shadows of the tall pines of the Spring-hill cemetery, his enemy gazes at the rising sun, the stately Fuji, and the moon illuminating the Sumida river and mocks the noble spirit. How can the gods permit such injustice?"

Sir Big-rock listened with deep attention, then replied:

"I thank you for your zeal in the discharge of your mission. Please retire and take the refreshment and repose you so greatly need. I desire you will not make known this intelligence to any one, as I wish to think the matter over before I communicate it to the clan."

The messengers bowed and retired, leaving Sir Big-rock to his meditations.

Two days afterward he assembled a second council, and thus addressed its members:

"Fellow clansmen, it is my duty to inform you that the Shogun has commanded me to deliver up the castle to an army of occupation, which, bowing to his authority, I shall do. I have not lightly come to this conclusion. To oppose the lawful authorities would be to dishonor the memory of our late lord, who upon receiving the decree of the Shogun, immediately proceeded to carry out its purport."

The *samurai* listened with grave attention, and when he ceased to speak, looked inquiringly at one another, as though expecting he would say something more; however he remained with his head bowed, whereupon Sir Common said:

"Sir Chief-councilor, while we do not doubt the wisdom of your decision, we hesitate to abide by it without first knowing what is to become of us. Are we to forget our loyalty? Perish the thought!"

The chief-councilor respectfully saluted the speaker, and taking a document from his bosom, said:

"This is my reply!" unfolding the paper and reading, "We, the undersigned, retainers of the Lord of Ako, remembering the countless favors we have received at his hands and those of his ancestors, and the words of the sage 'When the master is insulted, it is for the servant to die,' hereby vow to commit self-despatch and follow his spirit on the Lonely Road, thus demonstrating to the world our respect for lawful authority and devotion to our chief. If we fail to carry out this vow, may the vengeance of the hundred million gods of heaven and earth be visited upon us. January, 1699."

The chief-councilor paused in order to note the effect of his words upon the assembly, then continued:

"To-morrow at the hour of the Horse (noon), we will re-assemble for the purpose of signing this. The council is now dismissed."

At the appointed time sixty-three of the clansmen were kneeling upon the matted floor of the council-chamber. These men represented the rice separated from the husks.

After a brief delay Sir Big-rock entered and, saluting them gravely, produced the paper which he unfolded and reverently deposited on the *tokonoma* in front of the *sambo*. Turning to the assembly he drew a little knife from the scabbard of his sword, cut the back of the third finger of his left hand and placed the bleeding member upon the document, beneath his own name. He then invited Sir Moat, Sr. to follow him, but the old *samurai* declined the honor and requested that the son of the chief-councilor, Sir Big-rock, Jr., a lad of thirteen, should sign next to his father. The boy advanced and performed the ceremony, after which the others, one by one, did the same; the last to sign being a foot soldier named Temple-cliff, addressing whom Sir Big-rock said:

"Your presence here gratifies the spirit of our chief and adds lustre to the reputation of his loyal retainers." Then speaking to the entire assembly, added: "Immediately after the surrender of the castle, we will meet at the family temple of our late lord for the purpose of fulfilling our vow."

The next day Sir Big-rock paid off the paper currency of the clan, and, having set aside a large sum of money for a special purpose, divided the balance left in the treasury among the sixty-three *samurai*, each of whom received twenty-five *rio*.

On the morning of the thirtieth day, the army of occupation arrived before the gate and demanded possession of the fortress, whereupon the chief-councilor ordered Sir Common to marshal the clansmen and march them out of the castle. The occasion afforded an opportunity for the official to display his military knowledge, the manner in which he manoeuvred his forces exciting the envy and admiration of the beholders.

The clansmen emerged two abreast from the portal, their arms and accoutrements glistening in the cold sunlight. Crossing the stone causeway they deployed to the right and left and formed into two bodies, one under the command of Sir Common and the other under Sir Unconquerable. They stood motionless, spear in hand, as though ready to obey any order, whether to attack or retire.

While they were thus waiting, Sir Island-in-the-front quitted the castle, bearing the standard of the late chief. Following him came Sir Big-rock, Jr., clad in ceremonial costume, who carried in his hands the *sambo* covered with the white cloth, the intention being to screen the sacred relic from the profane gaze of the vulgar. Behind him, at a short distance, marched the chief-councilor, guarded by *samurai*, holding in his right hand the key of the main gate.

He waited until his son had joined the body of clansmen under Sir Common, when he despatched a messenger to the commanders of the army of occupation, who advanced with their retinues and received the key, during which ceremony Sir Big-rock and his attendants prostrated themselves upon the ground, while the representatives of the Shogun were seated upon camp-chairs.

When all was over Sir Big-rock rejoined the clansmen whom he thus addressed:

"The house of Ako no longer exists. I bid you a sorrowful farewell. I trust those among you who may seek new masters will serve them as faithfully as you have served your late lord."

All present bowed low and the clan dispersed.

At the hour of the Horse Sir Big-rock entered the temple of the Snow-clad Pine, bearing reverently in his hand a tablet inscribed with the posthumous name of his lord, behind him being his son carrying the *sambo*. Upon reaching the main hall they were met by the chief priest who received their burdens and deposited them on the altar. The sixty-two were all assembled with their swords placed upon the mats ready for use.

Sir Big-rock advanced to the post of honor and kneeling, prostrated himself; then, without drawing his sword, said:

"The time has not arrived for us to use our weapons upon ourselves, and the reason is to be found in the words of Confucius, 'Thou shalt not live under the same heaven or tread the same earth with the enemy of thy master or thy parent.' The death of our lord must first be avenged. His enemy, knowing full well the spirit that animates us, will render our task a most difficult one, nevertheless we must accomplish it. The king-fisher always finds its prey even though the latter hide at the bottom of the river."

The conspirators listened attentively, and Sir Moat, Sr., replied:

"Sir Big-rock, we will, in all things, be guided by your example and counsel."

The chief priest provided them with paper and other writing materials, upon receiving which their leader wrote a new compact. This the sixty-four sealed with their bloody hands.

From that hour they became in the eyes of men, as they were already in the eyes of the law, *ronin*, owing allegiance to no one but their dead lord.

The clansmen not concerned in the league did what they considered wisest for the welfare of themselves and families, the greater number taking service under a favorite of the Shogun, who had lately been created Lord of Sabaye.

Within a week of the surrender of the castle, Sir Big-rock despatched Sir Shell, Sir Cliff-side, Sir Unconquerable and Sir Thousand-cliffs with other conspirators to Yedo, instructing them minutely to watch Sir Kira and report his movements, having done which he gave up his residence in Ako and purchased a house in Yamashina, a little town near the city of Kioto.

Upon the death of the Lord of Ako, his wife, Lady Fair-face, assumed the religious name of Pure-gem, and took up her abode in her only possession, a mansion situated in the Blue Hill district in the western part of Yedo, where, attended by Lady Pine-island and a few faithful maidens, she dwelt secluded from the world, waiting for the time to arrive when the *ronin* would avenge the death of her husband.

CHAPTER VIII.
THE STORY OF A YOUNG WIFE'S SORROW.

In the fashionable, northern suburb of Yedo, called Root-bank, stood a cottage surrounded by beautiful grounds containing many lovely trees, plants and flowers, which were kept green and fresh by a little stream that flowed through the domain. The result of an artistic taste could be seen on every side but, alas, she who had created the paradise had passed away and her late home was inhabited by a young bride, who, only a few months before, had been a famous singing-girl. At the expiration of her contract she had married a young merchant named Mr. Bright-stone, and he, proud of his lovely wife, had installed her in that charming spot. This lady, whose name was Little-tiger, was left much alone, her husband being absent at his place of business in the city, and as solitude naturally induces feelings of gloom, she often thought of her former gay life and contrasted it with the quietness and stagnation of her new state.

One evening, when the shadows were deepening, she took up her guitar, which rested against a pillar, and after tuning it, commenced to sing a well-known song.

"As I wandered the Niphon road, alone and sad, my heart beat fast and became as round as the Imon Hill that lay before me.

"Neither the nightingale nor the umbrella man noted the approach of rain, yet my sleeves were wet with showers of tears.

"As the wood vines render the foot of Uyeno Hill difficult to ascend, so is the path of love crossed with thorny obstacles.

"The waters of the Sumida river tranquilly pursue their course, but when my thoughts flow toward my love, I am full of uncertainties."

Instead of completing the song she suddenly laid aside the instrument, and resting her chin upon her hands, said in a musing tone:

"Although my husband will not own it, I am sure, since we have been married, his business has decreased. I believe it is a mistake for any one in his position to disregard public opinion and sacrifice his comfort. Why has he brought me to dwell in such a secluded place? Surely this cannot be the summer-house of which I have heard so much, but one he has hurriedly hired for my reception. He goes off very early to the city and does not return until late at night. The empty state of his money-bag and his worried looks tell the story of his trouble. Though shame and consideration for my feelings, may keep him from imparting the disastrous news to me, I would prefer to learn the worst and share his sorrow, knowing the pangs of unspoken grief are doubly hard to bear."

The chirping of the birds, calling their mates to their resting-places among the trees, and the dusk of the evening added to her sadness, and tears began to course down her cheeks.

Presently she heard some one opening the gate, upon which she dried her eyes, rose, hurried to the entrance and welcomed her husband, saying:

"Dear Bright-stone, you are very late; I began to have fears about you."

"Do not be alarmed, Little-tiger; I have been very busy to-day running all over the city and must make another visit before retiring to rest."

He followed her into the house, when his wife, after closing the outer door, knelt close to him and said:

"Dear Bright-stone, please do not go out again this evening; I know not why but something tells me to ask you this; my heart is full of sadness."

He drew her toward him, rested her head upon his knees, and patting her on the back, replied:

"I understand all, Little-tiger. I suppose the contrast between your gay home and this place is too great. In a few days we will remove to our city residence when I am sure you will feel more cheerful."

"Oh, Bright-stone!" she sobbed. "You do not understand me. It is not my loneliness but your secret sorrow that renders me so unhappy."

"Little-tiger! Little-tiger!" he exclaimed, "who has been speaking to you about my business affairs?"

"No one," she said. "I have learned all by watching your face. Please do not conceal the nature of your misfortune from me. If I am not worthy to share your trouble, I am unworthy to be your wife."

Her speech greatly affected him and it was some moments ere he could reply, when he said:

"Dear Little-tiger, your love magnifies your fears. The fact is my business compels me to take a journey, and, truth to tell, I must set out to-night. Now you know all."

"To-night?" she cried, in a despairing voice. "No, not to-night. Wait until morning."

"I cannot, little one, I must set out at once. Here," withdrawing a package containing five *rio* and a sealed letter from his bosom, "is what I came to bring you. Now I must return to the city. You will here find necessary instructions, and the money will be sufficient to last you until my return."

"Oh, please wait awhile," she cried, clinging to him. "If you must depart this evening, let me accompany you."

"How can I take you where I myself dislike to go. Come, be brave, my Little-tiger."

Her womanly perception penetrated his loving stratagem, and regarding him with overflowing eyes, she pleaded:

"Oh, my dear husband, sit down again. I understand all. A sudden calamity has overtaken you and you are about to end your life. That letter contains your farewell. Friendless as I am, if I must part from you, I have no need of money. I shall follow the path you take."

She clung to him with one hand and with the other broke the seal of the letter, noticing which he cried:

"My dear, that is not intended for you to read now. I must hurry away."

The agonized wife only grasped him more firmly, as she did so quickly glancing over the epistle, which she presently dropped, exclaiming:

"Ah! I find it is as I thought. What can I say? You are blameless. It is I, a woman of low birth, once a singing girl, who has brought this ruin upon you. Still, as you have chosen me for your wife, do you imagine I could survive your death?"

"No, dear and admirable one," he sobbed, "I have never thought you would be thus unfaithful. Had I done so, I would not have taken pains to provide for you after my death. I know full well the world will brand me as a coward for shirking my responsibilities instead of bravely facing them; but, alas, I have of late been so unfortunate that I am disgusted with my life and am determined to end it. You quitted your gay circle to please me, and have been only a prisoner in this wild place, so I thought if I were out of the way, you would be better off. This small sum of five *rio* will not go far, still it was obtained honestly, therefore I pray you to accept it."

So saying he sunk down at her feet, prostrated with grief.

By and by, when she had somewhat comforted him, she said:

"The gods decree all things for our good. We will go to the 'Well-of-the-woods' near by, and there end our lives, dying in the beautiful spot rendered sacred by the devotion of the singing-girl, White-oak, who is buried near her lover beneath the spreading branches of the weeping willow, planted in her memory."

Bright-stone rose, and regarding her tenderly, said:

"The willow tree you mention is said to possess miraculous power. Come, we will seek its shelter."

They quitted the house, hand in hand, and proceeded toward the Three-points in the direction of the 'Well-of-the-woods,' pausing to pray at the willow tree, to one of the branches of which the wife tied her silken girdle-string, a sign she had renounced all hope of life.

As they approached the well they saw the pale moon reflected upon the placid water, noticing which they knelt and said their last prayers. All was lonely and sorrow-inviting.

After a few moments they rose, joined hands and prepared for the fatal leap when a *samurai* advanced along the path and, divining their intention, rushed forward and seized them.

The new comer was Sir Small-grove, chief councilor of Sir Kira, a man whose loyalty would at any time cause him to cross swords with the enemy of his master, and who, though that master erred, always counseled him rightly, even at the risk of incurring his displeasure.

When Sir Small-grove had drawn them from the edge of the well he enquired the cause of their sorrow, and, upon learning the truth, became greatly interested and did his best to console them, saying:

"My good friends, you are both very young, therefore, doubtless, feel unable to bear such great shame and sorrow. Probably, in your despair, the course you had decided to take appeared the best under the circumstances. It was in truth a very foolish one. There are changes in the career of every man, and though he may fall very low yet who can say he will not rise again. I came here to-night to pray under yonder venerable tree for my honored lord, that the dangers now besetting him may be averted. In being able to save your lives, I recognize a good omen for him. As you have, by my interposition, been delivered from death, so will he be saved from his enemies. I pray you dry your tears and come with me."

Bright-stone and his wife were touched by the kindness of Sir Small-grove, and after gratefully saluting him and returning their thanks, accompanied him to his house where they remained a few days.

It fortunately happened that one Mr. Young-island, an old friend of Sir Small-grove and a mirror-maker by trade, desired to adopt a son, so, at the *samurai*'s suggestion Mr. Bright-stone and his wife were received into the merchant's family.

In a future chapter I will tell how these young people were enabled to return the great kindness rendered them by Sir Small-grove, who, though he served a bad master, was, like Sir Big-rock, a man of a hundred thousand.

"BRIGHT-STONE AND HIS WIFE WERE TOUCHED BY THE KINDNESS OF SIR SMALL-GROVE."

CHAPTER IX.
THE CONTEMPTIBLE BEHAVIOR OF THE TWO COUNCILORS.

"At the first signs of a storm the timid hare seeks safety in the
earth.
When trouble overtakes the master, the disloyal servant fills his
pouch and departs."

I came across this maxim the other day while reading a history of
the forty-seven *ronin*; and as birds collect various substances with
which to form their nests, so authors search out and use the thoughts
of others, which they weave into their stories. I quote the foregoing
saying in order to illustrate the cases of those cowardly wretches, Sir
Arrow-stand and Sir Wisteria-lake.

On the night of their lord's death they met in the apartment of Mrs.
White-stocking, wife of Sir Arrow-stand, and began to talk over their
prospects.

"What shall we do?" nervously enquired Sir Wisteria-lake, who
was the younger of the two men.

"We are blamed for everything that has occurred and our position
has become a very hot one."

"Yes," mournfully answered Sir Arrow-stand, pouring out a big
cup of *saké* which he raised to his lips with a shaking hand. "The fact
is, Sir Wisteria-lake, we are in a well. Everyone else can go to Ako, but
we must seek other and more pleasant quarters. Sir Big-rock will never
overlook our blunder. I think the wisest thing for us to do, will be to
commit self-despatch and thus secure a good name for the future."

The lady uttered a peculiar sound, indicative of dissent, and resting
the palms of her hands upon her knees, gave her husband a significant
look, wagging her head as she did so, after the manner of young
women mated to old husbands whom they have tamed to wear
petticoats.

Sir Arrow-stand, who, though used to that sort of demonstration,
was anxious to keep his friend in ignorance of it, gazed at her over his
horn-spectacles and mildly remarked:

"Your cough is again troubling you?"

"I did not cough," she tartly replied. "I said pewgh!"

Sir Wisteria-lake, who was respectfully waiting for the termination
of this domestic encounter, looked enquiringly at Sir Arrow-stand,

who he expected would reproach the lady; however the husband merely replied:

"The noise outside renders conversation somewhat difficult. Honorable wife, what are you condemning?"

"Your determination," she said. "You always forget me. If you commit self-despatch, what am I to do?"

Sir Wisteria-lake bent forward and murmured, as though thinking aloud:

"Follow his honorable example."

Mrs. White-stocking pretended not to hear this remark which, in no manner, agreed with her inclination; so, after filling and lighting her pipe, she glanced at her husband and said:

"Honorable Sir, listen to me. You and Sir Wisteria-lake have the keys of the treasury, why not accept the benevolent provision of the gods? To-morrow the commissioners will arrive and pocket all that is left."

Sir Arrow-stand turned to his comrade and remarked in an under-tone:

"The strongest is not always the wisest."

"This is no time to quote poetry," she cried. "If you mean business, go to the treasury at once. I will accompany you and, while you are filling your bags, select some of the soul-stirring robes from my lady's presses; there are eye-hitters stored there. Now that my mistress is a widow she will no longer have use for such things and, I am sure, would rather know they decorated my back than see them in the possession of the commissioners' favorites."

At first her husband affected to be shocked by her proposition, and Sir Wisteria-lake waved his hand as though signifying he could never consent to such a thing; however, when they had exhausted their stock of moral maxims, they took their lanterns and proceeded to the fire-proof building, where the robes and other treasures of their dead master and living mistress were stored.

The men, who now forgot all scruples, set to work to fill their bags with *koban* (oval, gold coins of various values), for which purpose they kicked open the treasure-boxes and otherwise conducted themselves like burglars. Sir Wisteria-lake secured the plunder while Sir Arrow-stand made entries in a note-book, he being determined, when the time came for them to divide their prize, his companion should not have more than his share.

This matter kept him very busy, as Sir Wisteria-lake instead of depositing the *koban* in the common purse, betrayed a tendency to slip them into his sleeve; therefore Sir Arrow-stand failed to notice the actions of his wife.

When they were filling the last bag he observed Mrs. White-stocking on her knees before an immense bale, which she was securing with a silken cord, while between her teeth she held a pocket-book, containing paper-currency, wrapped in a white cloth. Seeing her thus employed he said:

"What are you doing?"

"That is my affair," she mumbled, the pocket-book preventing her from speaking very plainly. "Go on with your business, I will attend to mine."

Hearing this remark Sir Wisteria-lake paused in the act of placing a *koban* in the bag and said:

"We shall be unable to carry anything so weighty."

"Don't you trouble yourself," she retorted. "I will be my own coolie."

"My dear," whispered her husband, "do not burden yourself with those bulky things; take money. That will purchase you all the dresses you require."

"THAT IS MY AFFAIR," SHE MUMBLED. "GO ON WITH YOUR BUSINESS, I WILL ATTEND TO MINE."

"Pewgh!" she contemptuously returned. "There are robes in this bale that cannot be duplicated. When a man meddles with a lady's wardrobe, he attempts something he does not understand."

"As you will, as you will, my dear," he hurriedly replied.

"Yes," she said, leaning back and tightening the cord of the package. "It has been and shall always be as I will."

Sir Arrow-stand uttered a deep sigh and returned to his work. When they had collected as much as they could carry he secured the door of the building and they proceeded toward their house.

Mrs. White-stocking soon dropped her burden and exclaimed:

"It is too heavy!"

"I told you so," said her husband in a low tone. "Let us hurry! I do not wish to be discovered in the vicinity of the treasury."

"Not one step will I advance without my bundle," she resolutely answered. "Come, pick it up and carry it between you."

The over-burdened men did as they were required, both being in her power.

They soon reached the house, when she made them pack the money among her movables. An hour before the dawn the party quitted the *yashiki* (mansion), going forth like burglars anxious to avoid the gaze of honest people.

Later on I will describe the punishment that overtook this disloyal trio. Meanwhile we will leave the wretched men to be tormented by the bitter tongue of the shrew.

CHAPTER X.
WHAT OCCURRED AT THE RESTAURANT OF THE ROYAL CHRYSANTHEMUM.

"The perfect state is only to be obtained by prayer. We will not kill the birds and will even feed the wild eagles, and by such deeds shall our lives be rendered pure."

This was the prayer of a pious priest, who many years ago dwelt in a hermitage on the spot now occupied by the Temple of Asakusa. From that little germ grew a mighty fabric, which during the prosperous reign of a wise sovereign, flourished and attracted great crowds of people, who daily visited it and made their supplications to the goddess Kuwannon, the mother of mercy.

The approaches to this beautiful place were lined with restaurants, among them being a celebrated one bearing the sign of the Royal Chrysanthemum.

One day, in April, when the cherry-blossoms were just budding in the Temple gardens, an old, gray-haired man, accompanied by a beautiful girl of seventeen years, entered the inn and took their places on the matted floor of the public room. An attendant quickly placed a screen before them and having obtained their order retired.

The patriarch, whose cheeks were moistened with tears, said to his companion:

"My dear Home, it is not fear that drives me away from Yedo. I am becoming too old to properly take care of you and am afraid that your beauty will prove a source of misery to you. I have therefore made up my mind to quit the city and live in the country. Although you may at first feel lonely and dislike to reside among strangers, you will soon become accustomed to the life. Keep a good heart and bear my decision with patience."

To this explanation and entreaty the maiden affectionately replied:

"Grandfather, as long as you are with me I shall not be friendless, and once in the country no one will annoy us. Still I cannot help feeling regret at having to part with my dear friends and my kind music-teacher."

The old man watched her closely and endeavored to lessen her distress, saying:

"I described our new home as being in the country while in reality Golden-shore is not far from Yedo; it is also a famous watering-place and neither dull nor lonesome. When you desire to see your old friends you can join a party of pilgrims coming hither to pray to the goddess Kuwannon and thus reach the city quite safely."

His words were cheerful, but his heart was sorely troubled at being compelled to take his grand-child from her companions and install her in a strange home, and for awhile he remained silent, absorbed in sad thoughts.

In a short time the quick-footed attendant spread a humble repast before them, and Miss Home was in the act of pouring out *saké* when two strangers swaggered into the room. One of the new comers appeared to be a merchant and the other, a person of rough demeanor, was a middle-man.

Upon seeing the grandfather they advanced to where he was seated, and pushing aside the screen, squatted before him, the middle-man exclaiming:

"Mr. Left-gate-keeper, we have met in a very good place."

The person addressed trembled with apprehension, noticing which his granddaughter glanced uneasily at the intruders whose behavior greatly distressed her.

"Oh, you need not look so very innocent, Mr. Left-gate-keeper," rudely continued the fellow. "To judge from your face, no one would think you knew that your son had borrowed money of this gentleman. You act as though you had a perfect right to take your granddaughter where you please. But, kind Sir, I say you no."

The bewildered grandfather did not reply, simply clasping his hands and regarding the speaker, seeing which the merchant said in a conciliatory tone:

"Mr. Prosperity, have a little patience with him. I will take this young girl by way of payment, and thus wipe out the obligation."

"That is a bright thought of yours," said the middle-man, and addressing Mr. Left-gate-keeper, he added: "Do you hear that, Mr. Grandfather, surely it will satisfy you? See here, Miss Home, you are to be the pay for your parent's debt, therefore cannot accompany your relative. The obligation having been incurred by your father, you will not say no, so come along with me, at once."

While the men were making ready to start, the terrified girl turned to her troubled companion and said:

"My dear grandfather, what am I to do? Is it true I must accompany these persons? Can you not help me?" Thus speaking she grasped the sleeve of his robe and began to weep.

Mr. Prosperity laughed heartily and sneeringly exclaimed:

"Come now, don't give us any more trouble."

He seized the girl's hands and endeavored to drag her away, whereupon the old man arose and thrusting him back, cried:

"What, shall I part with my dear granddaughter for the paltry sum of five *rio*? No, no! You shall not take advantage of my age and the death of my son! You say he borrowed money of you; where is your proof? Have you his writing to show? Whether you have or not I will, upon reaching Golden-shore, borrow the amount you demand and forward it to you by a swift messenger. Under no circumstances will I give up the charge of my granddaughter."

"By the sacred mountain!" ejaculated the merchant. "We are not such fools as to depend upon a mere promise, even though it proceed from the mouth of the old and honorable Mr. Left-gate-keeper."

"Our patience is exhausted," cried the middle-man. "We must and will have this girl."

He once more seized her and dragged her toward the entrance, shouting: "Stop your whimpering and come along."

"Here, man, you go too far," passionately exclaimed the grandparent. "Although I am aged I can still use my sword and will not see my son's daughter kidnapped."

He endeavored to draw his weapon but his palsied hand refused its office, seeing which the merchant retorted:

"Look here, Mr. Left-gate-keeper, I shall not excuse such words."

"Nor I," said the middle-man. "What is the good of your wasting your feeble breath. You know full well you were compelled to leave your house on Buddha-river Street on account of being in arrear with your rent and were not even allowed to remove your furniture. Your promise to pay is a mere trick. We have caught you in the act of running away. You cannot deceive me. Everyone knows what sort of man I am. My name is Mr. Prosperity and I am termed the backbone of the middle-men of Yedo."

As he uttered these bombastic words he glanced menacingly around at the guests, in order to intimidate them and prevent their interference, then renewed his attempt to drag Miss Home from the apartment.

The poor girl, who was almost terrified out of her senses, broke from him and darted toward a screen behind which a *ronin-samurai* was seated, partaking of refreshments. The middle-man pursued her, and in his struggle kicked over the screen which fell upon the gentleman, who, enraged at the double outrage, sprang to his feet and dealt Mr. Prosperity a blow that sent him upon the floor, then, drawing his sword, stood over him, exclaiming:

"Dog, what do you mean?"

The *samurai* was Sir Shell, who had been refreshing himself after a tour of inspection, the object of which was to learn something of the movements of Sir Kira. He certainly was a handsome young man, and as he stood there his white complexion, aquiline nose, clear eyes, rosy lips and brave demeanor, captivated the heart of Miss Home, who, kneeling by the side of her grandfather, timidly glanced up at her deliverer.

"You impudent wretch," continued the *samurai*, "although social distinctions lose their sharpness in a restaurant, your kicking over my table in the midst of my dinner is more than I ought to permit. I shall therefore punish you."

Both the merchant and the middle-man were greatly frightened and, prostrating themselves with their foreheads to the floor, besought his forgiveness, explaining that they were there to arrest some runaways, in doing which they had not intended to offend the guests, least of all a noble *samurai* like himself.

Sir Shell glanced disdainfully at them and returned:

"I am not about to punish you for your lack of courtesy toward myself, but for your disrespect for age. You men of low degree, taking advantage of this old gentleman's years and helplessness, have sought to kidnap this young lady, in doing which you have violated the laws of your country. Your foot kicked over the screen upon me, I will have that foot."

He drew his sword and flourished it, seeing which the middle-man humbly pleaded:

"Honorable sir, I deserve the punishment, but the noble *samurai* will surely stay his hand when he hears I have a mother and a little son who are entirely dependent upon me for their support."

"Yes, yes," murmured the merchant. "I can vouch for all he says."

Sir Shell deliberated a moment, then observed:

"I should only stain my good sword with the blood of such a reptile. In case I spare you, will you assent to my proposal?"

"We will agree to anything," they answered. "Name your own conditions."

"Good," he cried. "In the first place you will renounce all claim upon this old gentleman. As for the sum you demand I will pay that. Under no circumstances will I permit you to interfere with this young lady;" then turning to Miss Home, he continued, "perhaps I am taking too great a liberty—will you permit me to interfere in this matter?"

The maiden, who felt very bashful in the presence of the handsome stranger, could only faintly utter:

"I thank you, honorable sir."

Her grandfather came to her aid, saying:

"We are deeply indebted to you. I am really ashamed to figure in such a disgraceful affair. I shall regard the money as a loan which I will endeavor speedily to repay."

Sir Shell bowed and said:

"Honored sir, I beg you not to refer to that, I will settle this matter."

After which, addressing the prostrate pair, he sternly said:

"Let me have your decision. Will you take my money or a thrust of my sword? Ah! I see you prefer the former. Be quick, make out the receipt and be off."

The exchange was soon made, and in a few moments the kidnappers were out of the house.

"YOUR FOOT KICKED OVER THE SCREEN UPON ME,
I WILL HAVE THAT FOOT."

The guests, who had been much alarmed by the blustering of the intruders, loudly expressed their admiration for the courage and charity of the *samurai*, while the latter, turning to Mr. Left-gate-keeper, said:

"Honorable sir, you must have felt very anxious, however, thanks to my good sword, the danger has passed from you. Still, even now, you will have to use caution, and it is not safe for you to tarry here. I would advise you to quit the place at once."

The old man bowed profoundly and gratefully replied:

"By some mysterious providence we have received a great charity at your hands." Then, whispering to Miss Home, said: "My dear granddaughter, why do you not thank the honorable gentleman?"

"Indeed I—I feel under a great obligation to you," she stammered.

"I beg you will not mention it," said Sir Shell. "I know it was discourteous to draw my sword in the presence of so fair a lady, yet the exigency of the case demanded it. I cannot leave you without asking your pardon for my rudeness. I have an urgent duty to perform, therefore must now say farewell. I hope at some future day to be again illuminated by the light of your countenance."

These words caused her heart to beat violently. Poor girl! She was already deeply in love with her gallant rescuer, not because he was young and handsome but on account of his goodness of heart, which had induced him to bestow the large sum of five *rio* upon a passing stranger. His manly generosity touched her soul, and she felt that to trust her life to such a one would be like confiding in the gods themselves. However, being in a public restaurant and unaccustomed to such places, she was diffident and instead of replying, whispered something to her grandfather, who, nodding to her, thus addressed the *samurai*:

"Honorable sir, I desire to make a little explanation. I have long been annoyed by those men, who had made up their minds to deprive me of my granddaughter, so I determined to retire to Golden -shore out of their way. Now, thanks to your kindness in getting rid of them, all my plans are in confusion. May I ask where you reside?"

The ronin's face flushed slightly, as he evasively replied:

"Honorable sir, I am bound for Original-place (the district in which Sir-Kira resided). Why do you enquire?"

"Because I desire to return your kindness," whispered Mr. Left-gate-keeper. "This is no place for conversation and I—I—I was about to say—"

Instead of completing his speech he paused and glanced downward with a puzzled air, on which the young lady sighed and said:

"Would it were possible always to remain in the place of one's birth."

Sir Shell, comprehending her meaning, urged her relative to return to the city, to which the old man agreed.

This decision so delighted Miss Home that, forgetting her bashfulness, she exclaimed:

"Oh! Great happiness, then we shall travel the same road as this gentleman. Our home is in the district of Original-place."

Such incidents as these teach us the mysterious ways and workings of the gods who preside over the tying of the thread of love.

CHAPTER XI.
THE OLD, OLD STORY.

"Who can oppose the will of the god of Izumo (fate).
Even the great warrior is conquered by love."

Sir Shell, Mr. Left-gate-keeper and Miss Home quitted the restaurant together and the young people were so delighted with each other's society, that the distance between the Temple-grounds and Original-place appeared but a few paces.

By the time they reached Buddha-river Street the sun had sunk below the horizon and the shadows of the evening were gathering over the city.

Mr. Left-gate-keeper called upon his landlord, who dwelt near by, and after paying the arrears of rent, received a new lease of his old home, whereupon he invited Sir Shell to enter it and partake of a cup of *saké*. How simple are the ways of the poor!

It was too late for Sir Shell to call upon his friend, Sir Unconquerable, who wished to consult him with regard to a despatch received from Sir Big-rock, so accepting the pressing invitations of Miss Home and her grandparent, he remained as their guest, fully intending to leave early the next morning.

At daybreak he drew aside the paper-screen and glanced out, when he saw the rain descending in a perfect deluge from the leaden sky. The down-pour continued, finding which he made it an excuse and spent the whole day listening to the charming voice of Miss Home, who delighted him with songs and her spirited performance upon the guitar.

While the young lady was preparing the evening meal he looked round the house and noticed the poverty-stricken appearance of the apartments, it being plain enough to him that the inmates would be at a loss to procure even the next day's rice. He entered the kitchen, took two *rio* from his purse, presented them to Miss Home and said:

"This is a very small amount but I pray you to accept it and expend the money in purchasing some delicacies for your venerable grandfather. He has few years to live and it is every one's duty to make him happy."

As he was speaking Mr. Left-gate-keeper came from an adjoining room and, bowing low, said:

"Those who remember the aged will themselves attain the honorable years."

This remark pleased Sir Shell, and after they had chatted for awhile, he said:

"Pardon the question I am about to ask. Have you any occupation? If one lives without earning, even a mountain-high fortune will soon be spent."

The old man and young maiden felt sorely ashamed; however, she, innocent of hypocrisy, frankly informed him her relative had peddled candies in the streets and she had earned something by assisting her music teacher.

"What you received could hardly pay for your necessaries," said Sir Shell, and leading the old man aside he whispered to him: "It seems to me the young lady is of an age to be married; when that takes place you will have some one to support you comfortably."

"That is very true," answered Mr. Left-gate-keeper. "But we are exceedingly poor; in addition to this we were once *samurai* in the service of the Lord of Ako who recently met such an untimely fate. With his death ended the life-long hope of my late son that, at some future day, one of his descendants might be permitted to return to the service in which he had himself been employed. My only wish now is, my granddaughter may be married to a *samurai*."

His strange speech quite startled Sir Shell, who was so deeply impressed by it that he spent the next day in talking over the misfortunes of their late lord, the recital greatly agitating the old man and making him very unhappy.

Before day-break on the following morning, Miss Home knocked at the door of Sir Shell's apartment and said in a troubled voice:

"I pray you come to my grandfather. He has been seized with a fit. I heard him moaning and upon going to his aid discovered he was speechless."

The *ronin* arose and accompanied her to the miserable apartment, on the floor of which lay Mr. Left-gate-keeper, whose features were ashy with the pallor of death.

He glanced up at the young man, then, closing his eyes, gave a gentle sigh, and the thread of his existence was snapped in twain.

Sir Shell and the young lady knelt by the body until the morning light illuminated the placid face of the dead, when Miss Home summoned the neighbors, to whom she sorrowfully communicated her bereavement.

In a short time the corpse was prepared for burial, and as the smoke of the burning incense circled about the apartment, the poor girl knelt and wept—the women present uniting their lamentations with hers and exclaiming:

"Alas! Alas! The venerable man is no more."

Sir Shell, who looked on sorrowfully, could not find it in his heart to abandon Miss Home in her hour of trouble, and the landlord, who took a fatherly interest in the orphan, patted her on the shoulder and whispered words of consolation.

Now her relative was dead all seemed to look upon Sir Shell as her guardian or brother.

The young man gave full scope to his generosity and not only saw the dead properly buried, but provided the neighbors with funeral gifts, in fact, treated them with so much respect and attention that they would not permit him to depart for three or four days.

On the fifth morning he informed Miss Home he must start early on the following day, after which, he busied himself with certain transactions, which through the helplessness of the young girl, devolved upon him.

"THE LANDLORD, WHO TOOK A FATHERLY INTEREST IN THE ORPHAN, PATTED HER ON THE SHOULDER AND WHISPERED WORDS OF CONSOLATION."

As the shades of evening deepened and the hum of the city grew faint, Miss Home sat in the veranda and watched the fire-flies flitting through the tall grass. These, as they came and went, seemed to her like the spirits of her departed friends. Her thoughts were full of sadness and her tears flowed freely. A few months before she had lost her father; now her grandparent and only relative was gone, her future was full of uncertainty; how could she support herself? The man to whom she had in secret given her heart, was indeed kind, but his was the devotion of a brother. During their five days of almost constant companionship no word had fallen from his lips which she could interpret otherwise than as the utterance of pure friendship. If she allowed that opportunity to pass without letting him know the state of her heart, he might never learn the truth. She had heard the neighbors whisper:

"In the midst of her affliction Miss Home has found happiness. She is really to be envied. She and Sir Shell will make a handsome couple."

These reflections inspired her with both joy and sorrow. Joy that any one should think she had found favor in the eyes of him whom she so loved, and sorrow for fear he merely pitied her and that congratulations might be turned to sneers.

She made up her mind if he went away without expressing affection for her, to follow her grandfather.

Thus thinking, she hid her face in the sleeves of her garment and sobbed bitterly. Her grief quickly attracted the attention of Sir Shell, who, coming to her assistance, tenderly conducted her indoors, placed her by the fire-bowl and, seating himself near by, said:

"My dear Miss Home, what is troubling you? You must not grieve so much for the loss of your relative. The gods are good and, though they do not restore our friends, give us new ones."

The agitated girl sobbed on and, glancing downward, replied:

"When you are gone, who will be left to care for me?"

She paused and not a sound was heard but the beating of their hearts.

Presently some crows, roosting in the trees surrounding the dwelling, began to cry to the moon, hearing which Sir Shell said:

"The bird of love makes me feel bold. Dear and beautiful Miss Home, I would wish ever to be near you. Can you look with favor upon an unfortunate *ronin*?"

Her reply was drowned by the voices of the birds, while the moon, peeping through the open window, revealed the beautiful scene. She knelt with her head bent, hiding her blushing face and exhibiting only her snow-white neck, with her tapered fingers interlaced on her lap, looking more charming than the half-opened bud of a chrysanthemum.

"Sir Shell—Sir Shell—will your loyalty prove greater than your love for your dainty bride?"

CHAPTER XII.
SIR KIRA.

"He who has committed a great wrong hears in the scampering of a
   mouse the footsteps of the avenger.
No sound alarms the placid soul of the well-doer."

This accurately describes the feelings of Sir Kira, who, dreading the
vengeance of the loyal *ronin*, hid himself in his private apartments and,
like a bat, only went out at night.

A more miserable existence could scarcely be imagined—his
enormous wealth yielded him no happiness, his suspicious soul feared
a traitoress in each of his beautiful attendants, he trusted no one but
his chief-councilor, Sir Small-grove, and while waiting for the just
retribution he knew must sooner or later follow his crime, died a
thousand deaths. His residence was guarded not only by his own
retainers, but by a body of men belonging to his son, Lord Uyesugi,
spite of which he would start at the slightest noise and worry his
people by complaining of their negligence and disregard for his safety.

Instead of feeling regret he took comfort in the fact that Lord
Morning-field was dead. He spent his days in sending out spies to
watch the man whom he most feared, Sir Big-rock, and in consulting
with his friends how to bring his political influence to bear against the
scattered members of the clan of Ako. His bitter hatred extended even
to the innocent widow, Lady Pure-gem, whom he surrounded with
detectives and watched as a tiger does his prey.

When the autumnal flowers were blooming in the gardens of his
residence, a messenger arrived post-haste from Kioto, on hearing
which Sir Kira directed his attendants to conduct the man to his
presence and thus addressed him:

"I hope you have brought me good news?"

The kneeling retainer raised his head and murmured:

"My lord, the information I have is for your ear alone."

Sir Kira motioned his servants to retire and bidding the messenger
approach close to him, said:

"Now speak."

"My lord, your instructions have been fully carried out. My wife,
Convolvulus, is installed in the house of Big-rock as an attendant upon
his children, my brother is in his employ as gate-keeper, and five of
your loyal retainers are living within bow-shot of his dwelling."

"Yes, yes!" impatiently remarked Sir Kira. "What is the news?"

"My lord, I have learned this much. A week before I left Kioto, Big-rock received a communication from the Council of Elders. Their letter evidently caused him great annoyance. I, therefore, instructed my wife to ascertain its contents. This proved a very difficult matter; however, by dint of using caution, she succeeded in getting a sight of the document."

"Well, well!" testily exclaimed Sir Kira. "What was in it?"

"The council neither granted nor denied the prayer of the petitioners for the restoration of the clan, and at the same time gave Big-rock plainly to understand if he made any attempt to avenge the death of his lord, both he and whoever joined him would experience the full power of the law. That night he went to the house of Hatchet, where he met a number of other *ronin*. The notification from the council was evidently a death-blow to their hopes. They emptied many bottles of *saké* and sent to a neighboring restaurant for refreshments. I was hanging round the spot, and bribed one of the waiters to let me take his place, and thus obtained admission to the house. Said Big-rock 'This news is a skull-cracker. I have made up my mind what to do. The honorable Sir Kira has the best of the game. It is useless for us to worry about re-establishing the clan. Each must look out for himself. As for me, for many years I have worked hard, so, in future, intend to enjoy my life. What say you, Hatchet?'

"The poet replied very indignantly, and the other *ronin* joined him, whereupon Big-rock took the bottle, and filling a cup, remarked '*Saké* is the medicine for all diseases.'

"The next day Big-rock was drunk, and he has not since been sober. Now, my lord, have no apprehension. Without their leader the clansmen can do nothing; they will be like a flock of geese that has lost its pilot."

Sir Kira thought for a while, then summoning Sir Small-grove, bade the man repeat the story, after which he said:

"What think you, Sir Councilor?"

"My lord, this news astounds me. We must continue to watch our enemy."

"Yes, we will not relax our vigilance. Let the messenger return and take with him some young men in my service, whom you will instruct to follow Big-rock closely, and, if possible, engage him in a quarrel that will result in his no longer being able to trouble us."

The next day a number of Sir Kira's retainers started for Kioto, and, from that time, Sir Big-rock was surrounded by an army of spies, who reported everything he did to their anxious employer.

CHAPTER XIII.
SIR BIG-ROCK DIVORCES HIMSELF.

"The hunted badger shams death."
"With an unscrupulous enemy, even a nobleman has to resort to
    trickery."

Sir Big-rock, having always been famous for his virtues, astonished
the world when he gave himself up to drunkenness and dissipation,
yet, though his neighbors shook their heads and secretly condemned
his conduct, his good wife uttered no word of reproach, and neither by
look nor action showed her sorrow and amazement.

One morning in December, after he had been absent from home all
night, she saw him staggering up the pathway, noticing which she
hurriedly sent her two little children into her private apartment, being
anxious they should not see their father in such a disgraceful state.

Sir Big-rock entered the house with his clogs on, and sinking upon
the floor, said to her:

"I want some *saké*."

She replied as though he had treated her with the greatest
politeness, and bringing him a cup of the best, knelt by his side and
presented the liquor, saying:

"My honorable husband, you are fatigued. Shall I prepare a bed for
you?"

He took a sip of the liquid, and throwing the rest upon the matted
floor, drowsily answered:

"Is that the sort of stuff you give me?"

"My dear husband, it is the finest *saké* in Kioto. You are tired with
your journey and everything tastes badly!"

"Journey, journey? I have only been to the tea-house on Gi-on
Street."

Just then some of the servants entered, seeing whom the lady said
in a low tone:

"Do not disturb your master, he is not well. Fetch a pillow for his
head."

Sir Big-rock, who appeared to fall into a deep sleep, permitted
them to arrange a bed for him, after which his wife knelt by his side,
fearing his head would slip from its support and that he would lie
uncomfortably. As she watched him, she unconsciously gave vent to
her thoughts, little imagining he heard what she said.

"I am an unhappy woman. Evidently I have been remiss in my duty, else why does my husband turn from me and seek the society of others. Alas! Alas! I fear the death of our lord has disturbed the beautiful balance of Sir Big-rock's mind. He, who used to be so just, so kind and thoughtful, has of late strangely found fault and blamed me for what I have not done. Still I think I must have been negligent in some way, though I cannot remember in what. When he sobers I will respectfully ask him how I have offended, as I can no longer bear this terrible agony. Better die than incur the displeasure of my husband. I will leave him and see that his bath is ready. Ah me! The happy days of the past when he thought his wife was without fault."

The poor lady conquered her sobs, and drying her eyes, softly retired, as she did so, regarding the sleeping man with the utmost tenderness.

When she was well out of hearing, Sir Big-rock arose with no trace of intoxication in his manner, but with features expressive of the deepest agitation.

"Ye gods!" he moaned. "How faithful she is! I cannot bear this!"

As he spoke the tears trickled down his cheeks.

"She is a model of a wife. Instead of blaming me for what would appear to be a crime on my part, she invents thousands of excuses for my conduct and takes upon herself all the odium. I will end this at once. She shall not witness the scenes I must enact in order to carry out my plan of deceiving Sir Kira. Then again my little children shall not remember me as a drunken sot. I will put her away; yet how can I do it?"

This brave, strong man paced the floor, grasped his arms and clenched his teeth in his agony. Wise as he was, he had, in undertaking to play the role of a dissolute man, forgotten how impossible it would be to overcome the devotion of his wife. The only thing left to him was to give her a letter of divorce and send her, with their younger offspring, to his father-in-law, who he knew would understand the true reason for his act and afford her comfort and advice.

Presently he heard the sound of his children's voices, and his wife saying in a low tone:

"Do not make a noise, my little ones. Papa is not well, you will disturb him."

"Has he got that funny sickness again?" demanded the elder boy.

"Hush! Hush!" said the mother. "Papa has many troubles and you must not speak thus."

The unhappy man thought of his duty to his dead lord, and, steeling himself against all else, returned to his bed and once more pretended to slumber.

About noon his wife entered and kneeling beside him, waited until he opened his eyes, when she said:

"Honorable husband, your bath is ready."

"Bath?" he exclaimed, rising and taking a flageolet from its rest. "I am going out."

He moved in the direction of the door, seeing which she picked up his *ronin* hat and kneeling presented it to him, saying:

"Honorable husband, I pray you to put this on. You have enemies about."

Sir Big-rock turned toward her and said:

"Enough. You talk too much. I shall give you a letter of divorce and you must go back to your father. I will, however, if you wish, grant you permission to take charge of our two younger children. My servant Happy-seven will accompany you."

"HONORABLE HUSBAND, I PRAY YOU TO PUT THIS ON.
YOU HAVE ENEMIES ABOUT."

Ere she could reply he had put on the hat and was staggering down the pathway, leaving her gazing after him like one just awakened from a dream.

When the neighbors heard the news and saw her and the little ones depart, they whispered to one another:

"Sir Big-rock must be crazy. In addition to wasting his substance in tea-houses, he now puts away his model of a wife, and gives up the guardianship of his children. How strange are the ways of some men! He has soon forgotten the goodness of his lord."

CHAPTER XIV.
THE STORY OF DOCTOR BUTTERFLY-COTTAGE.

"Some soldiers accomplish great military deeds while running
away from the enemy.
The ignorant attempts of quacks occasionally result in good
consequences."

No one is more to be pitied than he who places his life in the hands
of a quack. Unfortunately many such foolish persons exist, because,
throughout all ages, people have been more inclined to listen to rogues
than to follow the advice of honest men. Must we not be cautious?

There are many mock-doctors to be found everywhere. These
fellows, utterly ignorant of the science of medicine, which the ancients
so closely studied and reduced to a system, pretend to cure diseases of
which they do not even know the names, and entrapping their victims
by a great show of books and scientific instruments, by threats and
deceit, compel them to swallow the most nauseating compounds.

If, once in a while, they make a hit, the whole country rings with
their praise, and they walk the earth with their heads in the clouds.

The ancient professors of medicine established certain rules which
are followed to this day. They first ascertained the comparative value
of drugs, then mixed them in specified proportions, taking care that
the effects of one ingredient should counterbalance the others, and
thus produce a harmonious result. A patient suffering from fever
requires medicines containing *in* (cold) properties, and one shivering
with a chill should be dosed with *yo* (hot) drugs, to equalize the
temperature of the system. However, a person afflicted with fever
must not take only cold-producing physic, or the one who has a chill
be treated with drugs that merely create heat. A skilful physician gives
certain quantities of each remedy, in addition to which he uses
acupuncture and the moxa. In the foregoing consists the science of
medicine, which is only acquired by long study and serving a number
of years as assistant to a regular practitioner. Some drugs ought to be
administered in their natural state, others require careful preparation,
or their effects prove very injurious to the patient. Now a quack, not
having studied these principles, blindly administers his nostrums,
trusting to the god of luck to carry him through. If his patient dies, he
solemnly shakes his shaven head and says to the weeping relatives:

"I was sure of this from the beginning."

Beware of quacks! They live upon the weakness of human nature and may be known by the long pole of their *norimono* (enclosed litter), their assumption of profound gravity, and the audacious manner in which they promise to cure most incurable diseases. At the same time they take care never to approach a person suffering from a contagious malady without having their sleeves stuffed with disinfectants, while their meanness is such they will keep their bearers walking all day, never so much as thinking to give the tired men a lunch or a cup of *saké*. There is another kind of quack who is too parsimonious to have a *norimono* or even a man to carry his medicine-case. These scarecrows trot round the streets, from morning till night, with their pockets puffed out with packages of nostrums, and slip through the crowds, like eels between the rushes, as though in great haste to visit innumerable patients. Such creatures are well described by the proverb:

"A quack looks like a man who has stolen a cat and hidden it in his pocket."

My friends, if you wish to live, keep away from the doctors, though, in giving this advice, I do not mean to assert there are no able physicians. These, like all good people, follow their profession quietly, and after performing a cure, do not go clucking about like hens.

On Gold-mountain Street in the city of Yedo, lived a physician named Butterfly-cottage, whose establishment presented an imposing appearance. In front, was a magnificent lodge, occupied by a porter in livery who answered all inquiries, and, by his important air, added greatly to the respectability of his master. Once inside the yard the visitor noticed a tablet, inscribed as follows:

"Those who require to be examined are requested to come before the hour of the Snake (10 A.M.), not later.

"We refuse to visit patients living any great distance from our residence."

This was intended to impress his clients with an idea that he had more business than he could attend to.

Thus lived Dr. Butterfly-cottage, physician to Sir Kira, who was, in his day, the greatest quack in the metropolis.

One morning in February, 1700, this worthy approached the rear gate of his house, carrying in his hand a horse-mackerel, wrapped about with rushes. The snow was falling lightly and he protected his shaven head with a paper umbrella, while his feet were kept from the wet by high clogs. Under ordinary circumstances the doctor would not have been seen bearing his own dinner; however, his old bohemian taste sometimes returned and led him to do things incompatible with his new dignity. He was the brother of the cowardly renegade, Sir Arrow-stand, and, like him, crafty, treacherous and over-reaching. When quite a young man he had behaved so badly that he incurred the disfavor of the Lord of Ako, who, notwithstanding Sir Arrow-stand's pleading, banished him from the Province of Harima. Being but imperfectly educated, he was at his wits' end how to obtain a living, and for some years wandered aimlessly about the country, finally drifting to Yedo where he established himself as a go-between in marriages, and real-estate agent. By-and-by, he contrived to creep into the good graces of Sir Kira, whom he cured of a trifling, though painful ailment. After accomplishing this feat he set up as a physician, and by dint of making great display, and through the influence of his patron, soon became well known. His library was the talk of the neighborhood, his collection of medical appliances was mysterious and appalling, and his furniture and ornaments were unique and elegant, notwithstanding which he could neither read nor write. His only stock in trade was his ready wit and a thorough knowledge of human nature.

As he entered the house he handed his burden to his kneeling servant, saying:

"Tell the cook to prepare that for my mid-day meal. I wish it stewed with leeks. Bring me a cup of hot *saké*, I feel the cold principle predominating in my body."

The man hastened to obey, and the doctor, after casting aside his heavy outer garment and unwinding the white silk wrap from about his throat, crouched over the *hibachi* (fire box), and warmed his chilled fingers.

The attendant soon returned with the tray on which were a kettle of hot *saké* and a cup. Kneeling by his master he served him, saying:

"There is a man from the Blue-hill district waiting to see you."

"He is early," said the doctor, holding out his cup for more *saké*. "Tell him I am very busy studying a case and will see him presently. I must smoke a few pipes before I can receive patients. People should not expect a doctor to wait on them at once like a store-keeper."

After he had refreshed himself and taken a bath, the visitor was ushered into his presence. The new-comer was dressed in the costume of a merchant in easy circumstances, and had a simple, polite manner which favorably impressed the doctor, who, responding to his salutation, blandly observed:

"You are the gentleman from the Blue-hill district, are you not?"

"THE SNOW WAS FALLING LIGHTLY AND HE PROTECTED
HIS SHAVEN HEAD WITH A PAPER UMBRELLA."

"I have the pleasure of seeing you for the first time," said the man. "I am from the place you name, and have come to consult you concerning a relative of mine, who is employed in an apothecary store on Main Street. Of late, he has been much disturbed in his mind, and talks the wildest nonsense. I would like you to prescribe for him. Your fame has been noised all over the city."

Dr. Butterfly-cottage simpered like a vain woman who is complimented, and replied:

"Under ordinary circumstances I could not take a new patient, still as you have come from such a distance, I will see your relative; besides, the treatment of crazy people is my specialty. But there is something I have to tell every new-comer. Doctors resemble dried fishes; you cannot know their quality by looking at them. Then again, you remember the saying, 'the pay of a physician is like the cherry-blossoms on the high mountain, it cannot be reached' (literally demanded). That is why definite prices have been fixed for certain kinds of medicine. We, of our honorable profession, being prevented from demanding recompense for our advice, have to compensate ourselves by charging for drugs. I will not be strict with you and exact payment in advance, though I must have an understanding concerning my fees. This is my invariable practice, yet I find it does not decrease the number of my patients. I commence mixing early in the morning and begin my rounds after mid-day, often not returning until late at night. My great reputation and large practice excite the envy and hatred of all my brother practitioners, who maliciously term me the 'scavenger doctor.' Is it not ridiculous? Now you understand my way of doing business. If you wish to engage me I am at your service."

His visitor bowed low and replied:

"Honorable doctor, if you will undertake my relative's case, I care not how much I have to pay you. I am even ready to give a sum in advance, only I must first be assured you can cure him."

"Cure him, cure him!" ejaculated the quack, clapping his hands together. "Honorable sir, I always cure my patients. The illustrious nobleman, Sir Kira, who is in such favor with the Shogun, calls me Doctor Never-fail. When I have clients who appreciate me, I do my best, which means cure. Tell me the symptoms of your friend's disease."

"Honorable doctor, he is crazy. Imagines all manner of things."

"Yes, yes," patronizingly interposed the other. "Those are the symptoms described in the ancient books on lunacy. Of course he thinks himself somebody else and believes he is pursued by enemies?"

"Not exactly," quietly answered the man. "My relative's illusion is a very peculiar one. He is continually saying: 'I would like to have the money for the pearls.'"

"Ah I will soon cure him of that. Suppose we say five *rio* for my attendance and medicine during the period of ten days. Will that be satisfactory to you?"

The simple one bowed and murmured:

"I would not care if it were a little more."

"Well, then, give me six *rio*."

The man produced his purse, and handing the sum to the doctor, remarked:

"Honorable sir, I will bring the patient early tomorrow. Please do not be harsh with him. Remember he will say, 'I would like to have the money for the pearls.'"

When the visitor had departed, the doctor gleefully polished his shaven pate with his right hand, and after chuckling awhile, cried:

"Gracious me! That customer does not appear to know what avariciousness is. Unless I add some new patients to my list I shall be compelled to give up my *norimono*. I must fill the gaps caused by my little mishaps. I have earned six *rio* of his money and will keep him paying as long as he has a coin in his pouch."

While he was rejoicing, the clock on the *tokonoma* struck the hour of the Horse (mid-day).

The next morning the merchant presented himself at a celebrated drug store on Main Street, and handing a letter to the proprietor, boldly remarked:

"Will you please attend to this matter at once?"

The druggist opened the communication, and after reading it, said:

"This is from Dr. Butterfly-cottage. I see he requires a number of pearls of the very best quality. One of my people shall pick them out and take them round to Gold-mountain Street."

"I will wait and accompany him," said the messenger.

He walked around the place as though it belonged to him, and after the clerk had the pearls ready, observed:

"You must go quickly. The doctor is anxiously awaiting my return."

Upon arriving at the house, the merchant stepped into the reception room, and addressing the clerk, who stood respectfully in the entrance, said:

"Give me the package and remain here until you are summoned. The doctor wishes to send some things back to your master."

The man bowed, but when the merchant turned to enter the inner apartment, derisively stuck out his tongue, then laughingly exclaimed:

"That fellow, although he looks simple, talks very big! I suppose he thinks because he is in the service of this quack he has a right to put on airs."

He waited in the ante-room for some time, the proprietor of the house being unusually busy with patients. At last an attendant came out and said:

"Are you the young man from the apothecary on Main Street?"

"Yes, sir, I am."

"Then follow me."

When Dr. Butterfly-cottage saw him, he enquired:

"THE MAN BOWED, BUT WHEN THE MERCHANT TURNED TO ENTER
THE INNER APARTMENT, DERISIVELY STUCK OUT HIS TONGUE."

"Well, sir, how do you find yourself to-day?"

"Quite well, doctor."

"Quite well, eh? Come into my private office and let me examine
you."

The clerk, though not comprehending his meaning, did as he was
requested. To his amazement, the doctor felt his pulse, saying:

"Ah! I knew it, the hot principle predominates. Now your tongue?"

"What do you mean, doctor? I am not sick. If the pearls are
satisfactory, I would like to have the money."

"All right, all right," was the soothing response. "I understand
your case. Now loosen your girdle and let me look at your chest."

"I shall do no such thing, doctor. I would like the money for the
pearls."

"Don't be so stubborn, but do as I bid you. How can I prescribe
before I make an examination. Where is the man who came with you?"

The clerk regarded him with surprise, noticing which the servant
said:

"Honorable master, if you mean the merchant who called
yesterday, I saw him pass out of the rear gate an hour ago."

"How very annoying," muttered the doctor. "Come, young man, be reasonable and let me examine you. I suppose your relative has returned to his home in the Blue-hill district."

"Will you give me the money for the pearls?" angrily demanded the clerk. "I have no relative living in the Blue-hill district. The man who accompanied me was your own messenger. I would like to have the money for the pearls."

"I understand your saying that. It is one of your symptoms. Now loosen your girdle. It is the hardest thing in the world to manage you crazy people."

The clerk, provoked at being termed a lunatic, placed his hands upon his knees, and, making a mock obeisance, cried:

"Will you pay me for those pearls? I don't care what you call me, as long as you hand me over the money. It is not I who am out of my senses."

"Young man," sternly returned the doctor, "there is no end to your tongue. I am not accustomed to be addressed in such a disrespectful manner. Cease your clamor. Your demanding payment for pearls I have never received is calculated to throw a blemish upon my honorable face. Being a person of the highest respectability, I can afford to treat such a charge with the contempt it deserves, still I do not intend you shall rush about the city with your mouth full of such accusations. I will have you secured until I can communicate with your relative."

Upon hearing this the clerk produced the order from his bosom, remarking in a satirical voice:

"Will you deny your own writing? Here is a note signed by yourself, ordering a number of pearls of the best quality. Perhaps this is a symptom of my sickness?"

Doctor Butterfly-cottage took the letter, which he held upside down and regarded with blank amazement.

"Is not that your signature?" cried the man. "Turn it the right way and look at it."

The doctor reversed the paper, and being unwilling to acknowledge his ignorance of reading and writing, said, in a bewildered manner:

"Yes, I always sign my orders thus—though I do not remember issuing this one."

"At last we are beginning to arrive at an understanding," said the clerk. "Of course, as that document is correct, you will pay me for the pearls?"

A few moments calm talk convinced both parties they had been swindled by an adventurer. When the clerk returned to his master, the latter insisted upon receiving his due saying, as the doctor had written the order, he must be held responsible. Finally, the quack paid the large sum demanded, (six hundred *rio*) preferring to lose his gold rather than acknowledge his profound ignorance. Although he did his utmost to keep the affair quiet, it gradually leaked out, and soon the song sellers on the streets were heard chanting a poem that made flushes of shame glow through the thick skin of the doctor's face.

CHAPTER XV.
SIR CLIFF-SIDE'S STRANGE ADVENTURE.

The reader will remember that soon after the surrender of the castle of Ako, Sir Big-rock despatched certain of the conspirators to Yedo, with instructions to watch Sir Kira and report his movements. Among these loyal men was Sir Cliff-side, who had a most extraordinary adventure, which I will now relate.

This *samurai*, like his companions, had been very diligent, never heeding what fatigue he underwent. For twenty months he traveled all over the city and suffered the extremes of heat and cold, finally contracting a disease that rendered him partially blind and confined him to his home, a small house far from any other dwelling, in the part of Yedo called Preaching-court, in the district of Made-land. Here he resided with his servant, Original-help, who, in the month of February, 1700, had unexpectedly presented himself, saying:

"Honorable master, the news of your sickness has reached Ako. I have come to nurse and attend upon you."

Sir Cliff-side was over-joyed and placed himself entirely in the faithful man's hands. During eight months Original-help tended him day and night, and watched him with the greatest solicitude.

Toward the end of autumn when the leaves were red, the sick man began to show signs of improvement and would sit for hours in the little veranda, watching the ships going and coming on the blue waters of the bay. One afternoon as he was thus employed, the cackling of a flock of geese passing overhead brought to his memory thoughts of the home where he had left his wife and children.

"Ah!" he sighed. "Who would not feel sad to hear that sound. There go the winged messengers, yet they have brought no news to me. I have, since spring, been sick, helpless and unable to do my duty, like Sir Shell and the rest. I fear I shall leak out of the conspiracy. Although I have constantly and fervently prayed to the god of medicine, he has been slow to hear me, added to which this prolonged suspense with regard to Sir Big-rock's plans and my lack of funds, have rendered me doubly miserable."

He sat for some time in a deep reverie, watching the receding line of geese until it vanished upon the horizon, when he was aroused by Original-help saying:

"My honorable master, at last your medicine is ready, please take it while it is hot. The days are getting so short I could not have it prepared earlier. I had no idea it was such a great distance to Yeast Street. Doctor Original-course was absent attending our lady. When he returned he told me she had inquired most kindly after you."

"That was very good of her," said Sir Cliff-side. "Though my trouble has been hard to bear, it is, when compared with hers, as light as down. The gods give her comfort and hasten the day when we can look at the sun without blushing."

Original-help knelt by his side and poured some of the hot medicine from a pot into the cup, saying:

"Honorable master, I think your eyes look better."

"Yes, I can see yonder mountains of Kazusa, and Awa, and the sails far away down on the bay."

"Indeed, indeed! The gods be praised, you will soon be quite well again. Can you discern that boat next to the fishing craft, the one in which a man is tending a net?"

Sir Cliff-side, pointing in the indicated direction, replied:

"Yes, he is pulling the line from the water. See he grasps the buoy of the net. He is taking out a fish. What a large one, how it struggles!"

"SIR CLIFF-SIDE, POINTING IN THE INDICATED DIRECTION, REPLIED:
"YES, HE IS PULLING THE LINE FROM THE WATER.""

"My honorable master, you are all right. You must thank Dr. Original-course. He seems to understand your constitution."

"That he does. He is a most skilful physician. He treated me when I was a boy at Ako, and our late lord highly esteemed him. He is a very different man from Doctor Butterfly-cottage. Have you ever heard of that knave?"

"Yes, my honorable master, I once had occasion to consult him."

"How foolish of you. He is an unscrupulous pretender. Of how much did he rob you?"

Original-help cast down his eyes and respectfully answered:

"Honorable master, there are some things to which we do not like to refer. I promise you I will never go near him again. Dear me, it is growing dusk and you will not be able to see, I must get the light ready."

He rose and quitting the veranda, went in-doors, leaving his master to watch the setting sun, which presently sank below the horizon. Then the color of the water changed from blue to black, the angry wind began to whistle and the scene, lately so enjoyable, became sad and gloomy. Sir Cliff-side followed his servant and seating himself by the *tokonoma*, on which stood his sword-rack, covered with a cloth, lighted his pipe and resumed his meditation.

When the shadows had deepened into night he was aroused by voices outside, and some one demanding:

"I beg your pardon. Does Sir Cliff-side live here?"

Original-help being engaged in the attic, Sir Cliff-side answered the summons, saying:

"Yes, I am here. Who might you be?"

"What, my honored master, is that yourself? I am so glad. It is I, Original-help, who have traveled all the way from Ako as escort to your honorable wife."

The speaker then turned to some one who was with him and said:

"Come, the honorable wife, this is the temporary residence of my master. Young master-babies, you will now see your father."

Sir Cliff-side was both puzzled and surprised; puzzled at the strange speech of Original-help and surprised at the sudden arrival of his wife and children.

"Mamma, mamma, please untie my sandals. I want to go in quickly," cried the elder boy. "Papa, papa, it is I, your little son, New-six. Brother Help-of-six is with us."

"Come in, come in," joyfully answered Sir Cliff-side. "I cannot rise to welcome you, as I am suffering from a sickness called bird's-eye, and am unable to see anything in the twilight. Welcome, Bamboo, my wife! So you have arrived from home. Lave your feet and enter at once. Original-help will furnish you with water and towels. If I try to move I shall fall over something. How pleased I am! Be quick, send the children to me and come yourself."

"I wonder where the buckets are kept," said Original-help, stumbling about in the entry. "Wait a moment. I will use my flint and steel."

When the servant had lighted a candle, Bamboo surveyed the place and noted its miserable appointments. The mats covering the floor were old and full of holes, there were great rents in the paper-screens through which came strong draughts, the plastering on the walls was cracked in all directions, and the only handsome article of furniture was the *katanakake* (sword-rack) which stood on the *tokonoma* and held Sir Cliff-side's weapons.

"My honorable husband, are your eyes still bad?" she remarked, as she hastily made her toilet. "I was most anxious to know how you were, so as we came through the city, called upon Dr. Original-course. He told me you would soon be quite well."

"Yes, that is correct. I don't mind my sickness now you and the little ones have arrived."

She entered the room, knelt before Sir Cliff-side, placed her hands on the floor, and bending her forehead to the mat, respectfully saluted him, saying:

"My honorable husband, I have not seen you for many, many months, during which time I have been longing to look once more upon your face. You must have lived very uncomfortably in this wretched habitation. Who has attended upon you?"

"Original-help," said Sir Cliff-side. "He is as industrious and kind as ever."

"I understand, my honorable husband, you have a servant whom you call Original-help, after the faithful man who has escorted me from home."

"Escorted you from home, Bamboo? Why he has been with me since February." Then he called, in a loud voice, "Original-help, come and see your honorable mistress!"

"I am coming, honorable master."

Thus speaking Original-help No. 1 descended from the attic with a lantern in his hand, at the same time Original-help No. 2 entered from the veranda, leading the elder child and carrying the younger in his arms. In the excitement of beholding his children, Sir Cliff-side forgot the extraordinary phenomenon of the duplicate Original-help, and affectionately rubbing his elder boy on the head, said:

"My son, New-six, you have grown quite a big fellow. I am so glad to set eyes upon you again, I hope you have been good and obeyed your mother. I see Help-of-six is afraid of me and hides his head in Original-help's short coat."

New-six looked up anxiously at his father's face and enquired in a gentle voice:

"Dear papa, do your eyes pain you? I am glad I have come, now you will have some one to rub your back, you know that is a good thing to do to sick people?"

Little Help-of-six, encouraged by Original-help No. 2 glanced timidly around and said, "Is my papa sick?" Then, descending from the servant's arms, he toddled toward his parent and fondled him, saying, "I, too, will rub your back, papa. You will soon get quite well."

Sir Cliff-side was moved to tears by the tender speeches and affectionate manner of his children, and for some moments was unable to speak. At last he held them close to him and said:

"O, both of you have become most gentle. My dear Bamboo, you must feel very tired, lie down without any ceremony and rest."

Bamboo stretched herself upon the mat and the little ones reclined upon their father's knees, while he caressed them and talked with his wife about their dead lord.

Original-help No. 2 softly rose and retired to the kitchen where he found Original-help No. 1 busily engaged preparing supper. Although he had heard the man addressed by the same name as himself, he was unaware how exactly they resembled each other.

"Mr. Original-help," he whispered, "I do not wish to disturb our master and mistress who have much to talk about. I have brought from Ako many letters and messages for the attendants on Lady Pure-gem. As it is some distance from here to Blue-hill I wish to start soon. Will you require any aid from me?"

"No, Mr. Original-help," laughingly answered the other. "You start at once. I will attend to our master and mistress. You need not hurry back to-night. The road between here and Blue-hill is none of the safest I will explain the reason of your absence to our master."

"Thank you," said Original-help No. 2. "I will return early in the morning."

Sir Cliff-side and his wife had ceased their conversation in order to listen to the foregoing talk, and, when the man departed, the lady said:

"I am very much perplexed by the resemblance between those men. Did you not tell me that your servant was our Original-help?"

"So he is, Bamboo. He came from Ako in February."

"But, my honorable husband, Original-help has never left me. Your man must be my servant's twin-brother."

"That is impossible," replied Sir Cliff-side. "They are evidently strangers to one another. I am as much puzzled as yourself."

The lady thought for a while, then said in a low, terrified tone:

"My honorable husband, now I understand the mystery. It is a case of the soul-dividing disease."

"THE TWO ORIGINAL-HELPS."

CHAPTER XVI.
THE GOD FOX.

The ancient book called *Kishitzuho* (prescriptions for strange sicknesses) thus describes the *ri-kon-bio* (soul-dividing disease):

"If any person suddenly becomes two beings, exactly resembling each other, it is a case of soul-dividing disease. You may know this by the fact of the duplicate person being unable to speak. The remedy for such an affliction is as follows:

"Take equal parts of gentian, asafoetida and ginger, pound them in a mortar and make a strong infusion. Give the person who can speak, one *saké* cupful every half hour. The medicine will make the patient bright and cheerful, and cause the duplicate, wandering spirit to return to its proper body.

"This disease is a very rare one."

Sir Cliff-side quoted the fore-going extracts to his wife adding:

"Bamboo, I do not believe any such sickness exists out of books. Doctors are very fond of explaining things that no human being can fathom. Even, according to their statement, this cannot be a case of the soul-dividing disease, for both men speak. Do not permit the affair to worry you. Leave a mystery alone and it will explain itself. Tell me about Sir Big-rock and what has brought you hither. See, our dear children are both fast asleep on my knees. Leave them so until supper is ready."

Bamboo moved closer to her husband, and, fearing Original-help No. 1 might be a spy of Kira, whispered:

"I have very important news for you. I suppose you have heard how strangely the chief-councilor has behaved; how he divorced his wife, gave up the care of his children and spends his time with the butterflies of the tea-houses. Such things would not have been surprising in an ordinary man, but coming from the chief-councilor have amazed every one. The conspirators in Kioto have been terribly exercised, spite of which he carries himself in a most reckless manner. Is this not incomprehensible? Can he have forgotten the kindnesses of our late lord?"

"Bamboo, I have every faith in Sir Big-rock. We know of his proceedings, and have many times met to consult about the matter, finally agreeing to continue our work of watching Kira, and to wait patiently. Sir Big-rock is not a man to indulge in such pleasures for the sake of gratifying himself. Our enemy, although skulking in the retirement of his residence, has immense influence, and is guarded vigilantly. I, and many of the conspirators, believe Sir Big-rock acts as he does to throw Kira off his guard. If our conjecture is correct all will yet go well, and when the proper moment arrives, Sir Big-rock will give us the signal. Our present anxiety is to learn what are his real sentiments; Sir Hatchet and Sir Common have this matter in hand, and, being on the spot, know what is best to do. In a few days they will be joined by Sir Thousand-cliffs who will represent the conspirators residing in this city. Now tell me what you have to communicate."

"My honorable master," said Original-help No. 1, speaking from the kitchen, "at last the supper is ready. The honorable wife and master-boys must be very hungry. I am ashamed to say there is nothing good to give them."

The father awoke his children and the servant brought in the repast, which was really a most excellent one and was heartily enjoyed. During the meal Original-help No. 1 laughed with the boys, who in their innocence, took the man to be Original-help No. 2, though the wife was secretly troubled and regarded him askance.

The supper being over, the mother made up beds for her little ones, and, when the attendant had retired for the night, reclined close to her husband and observed in a low tone:

"At last I can speak freely. About a week before I left Ako, the chief-councilor called upon me and said: 'I am informed Sir Cliff-side has been very sick and that he has not yet fully recovered. Of course, under the circumstances, you have desired to be with him, still, knowing his position, have submitted patiently, fearing lest your presence might interfere with our plans. That is as it should be and your loyal conduct merits my thanks. I, however, now desire you will join your husband and take your children with you. When a man is sick it is not good for him to be left to the mercy of strangers.' He then gave me thirty *rio* for you and ten for my traveling expenses," producing the money. "Honorable husband, although I have practiced the utmost economy, I have only been able to save four *rio*. The boys were both of them sick and I had to pay for many extras."

"My dear Bamboo, you have done well to save anything. This present from the chief-councilor," raising the package to his forehead, "gives me double hope. It shows he has neither forgotten his vow nor myself."

"Honorable husband, that is not all. The chief-councilor said: 'Later on I will despatch Sir Hatchet or Sir Island-in-the-front with money for those who are in Yedo.' Here," producing another package, "are thirty-eight *rio* I received for the sale of our house and furniture, and five *rio* paid me by the District-overseer. He said: 'I know you must be sorely pinched by being so suddenly cut off from the income allowed by your lord, and thinking you needed the money, have brought five of the ten *rio* I owe your husband.' He expressed the deepest regret at his inability at once to pay the entire sum borrowed of you, and promised to do all in his power soon to liquidate the debt. Though I did not like to act without consulting you, I was so much touched by his goodness, that I gave him a receipt for ten *rio*. Instead of trying to cheat us, like some people I could mention, he did his best."

"I thank you, Bamboo. You acted just as I would have done. The overseer was one of our lord's retainers, yet he lives a great distance from the city, and could safely have assumed a know-nothing face with regard to his debt. I thank the gods there are some honest men in the world."

"Yes, he is honest through and through. At first he refused to take the receipt and, finally, said: 'Tell your honorable husband, after the harvest is over I intend to visit Yedo, when I will call on him and clear my conscience.' Now you have learned what brought me hither, I would like to know about your sickness. How came your eyes in such a state?"

"Mine is a case of drying up of the water of the pupil. At first, Dr. Original-course felt very anxious about me, saying the only thing to cure my disease would be to use the very best pearls; yet how could I obtain things of such great value. I believe our lady must have given him some for me as, since February, I have been regularly supplied with them."

"Ah, honorable husband, our lady is very good!"

"Yes, indeed she is. Only to-day she spoke to the doctor about me. So the children were sick during the journey?"

"Yes, at one time I feared little Help-of-six would die. You must know they have both had the smallpox. I was compelled to stay a month in the city of Mulberry and was at my wit's end. Poor Help-of-six, not being as old and sensible as his brother, cried all day, was very irritable, and would never sleep except on my lap. As many as three physicians gave him up, and twice his breathing ceased altogether. But for our good Original-help, I should not be here today. He attended upon us with the greatest devotion, going without sleep, treating the boys as his own, and encouraging us by word and deed. I prayed to the gods constantly, and vowed if my children were spared not to eat sugar or oranges for three years, so please don't tempt me with those things. My prayers were heard and the dear boys got well. I have the happiness of presenting them to you without their showing any signs of the trouble. You don't know how much I have endured."

"The gods be praised, they have safely passed through one calamity of their lives. You say Help-of-six suffered the most? That is a thing I cannot understand. New-six, being the elder, should have had most disease in his body, at least so say the doctors, though I believe many of their assertions are mere guesses. When I think of the great calamity that has overtaken our lord, I am perfectly willing to die. My duty to him is before all other; still, remembering the uncertain future of our poor babes, I cannot help feeling anxious."

Bamboo wiped her eyes with her sleeves, and gazing earnestly at him, replied:

"My honorable husband, though you cannot leave your children a fortune, you will bequeath them something better—a reputation that will keep them straight through life. All the world is waiting for you and your honorable companions to strike at the cowardly wretch who deprived us of our benevolent and beloved lord. Remember, in the sad days when my eyes will no longer behold you, our two brave boys will constantly visit your tomb, deck it with flowers, and burn incense to your spirit. Let that comfort you."

"My loyal wife, I am ready, at any moment, to do my duty. Your words, indeed, cheer me, for I know after I have gone the Lonely Road, you will bring up our children like true *samurai*."

"Yes, my honorable husband, I will endeavor to do so. You are tired, let me give you your medicine."

She procured the pot, and, while pouring out the liquid, whispered to him:

"I shall not sleep a wink to-night. You are brave and above superstition; I am only a woman full of the fancies of my sex. I really believe my good Original-help must have had an attack of the soul-dividing disease."

The next morning Original-help No. 2 arrived at the house and found everything ready for breakfast, but Original-help No. 1 was nowhere to be seen.

As Sir Cliff-side, his wife and children, entered the room, the man saluted them and said:

"My honorable master, did your Original-help deliver my respectful message?"

"No," said Sir Cliff-side, then raising his voice, he shouted:

"Original-help, where are you?" The echo outside repeated: "Where are you?"

"Come," said Bamboo to her attendant, "I see you are now all right."

The man hesitated, as though ashamed, and said:

"My honorable mistress, I thought I had walked off all traces of last night's indulgence. The servants of our lady plied me with *saké*. You see they were very glad to get news from Ako and it was first 'drink with me,' then 'drink with me,' until your miserable Original-help was as red as *Shut-ten-do-shi* (the demon of drink). I beg you will forgive me this time."

The lady waited until her husband had gone into the veranda, then whispered to the penitent servant:

"Original-help, I am going to tell you something. Do not be alarmed; you have lately suffered from a dreadful malady."

"Yes, my honorable mistress, *saké* always has been my weakness. I have a chronic trouble termed dry-throat."

"No, not that, good Original-help. You have been afflicted with a most wonderful complaint, called the soul-dividing disease. One half of you has been here, in Yedo, with my honorable husband, and the other in attendance upon me. Your double has returned to your body. Do not tremble so, you are perfectly cured."

The bewildered man gaped at her, as though fearing she was not in her right senses, but remembering a *samurai* lady must know more than a common fellow like himself, proceeded to dish the breakfast, murmuring as he did so:

"That fellow, who called himself Original-help, like me? If I thought I looked as homely as he does, I would go and drown myself."

In a little while he announced the meal was ready, and the family seated themselves. They had scarcely begun to eat when a paper fluttered in through the porch and fell at Sir Cliff-side's feet.

"What is this?" he cried, picking it up, then read its contents, which were as follows:

"Since last February I have assumed the form and manner of your servant, Original-help, and nursed you during your sickness. Now your family and attendant have arrived from Ako, you no longer require my aid. Your eyes are fast getting well, yet be advised by me and continue taking the pearls. I have left a good number of them for you in the hands of your doctor, who believes they came from Lady Pure-gem. Using my supernatural power I assumed the shape of a merchant, and—while punishing that avaricious quack, Dr. Butterfly-cottage, who, forgetting the benefits conferred upon him by his former lord, is consorting with your enemies—obtained what you so sadly needed. You may expect still further assistance from me.

"To Sir Cliff-side

"From an inhabitant of the residence of Lady Pure-gem."

After reading this the *samurai* remarked to his amazed wife and servant:

"Then the one whom I deemed to be a man was the god Fox of the residence of our lady. He has taken pity upon me and saved me much suffering. How can I forget his great mercy!"

Overcome by this discovery the three shed tears of gratitude; while the children, witnessing their emotion, uttered piercing cries and wept as profusely as their elders.

When Sir Cliff-side recovered the full use of his sight, he paid a visit to Lady Pure-gem, to whom he related the wonderful story here recorded. She was greatly moved by the miraculous interposition of the god, and, assembling her attendants, reverently made offerings at his shrine.

From that time he was referred to as the "Omnipotent god Fox Original-help," which name he continues to bear to the present day.

If the reader desires to satisfy himself of this fact, he has only to visit the Blue-hill district where he will find the shrine, which is kept in beautiful order by the neighboring inhabitants; yet there are some sceptics who sneer at the supernatural powers of the god Fox.

CHAPTER XVII.
CONVOLVULUS OVERHEARS A CONVERSATION.

"The cherry blossoms were blushing in the temple gardens; the air was mild and full of vernal incense sent up by the flowers to the gods; the swiftly-flowing water of the Kamo River glittered like the spears of a vast army; pic-nic parties swarmed out to the hills surrounding the city; and all creation reveled in the warm sunshine."

On such a day as this, Sir Big-rock was seen staggering along Temple Street, Kioto. He was dressed in a black costume, marked with his crest, and carried himself with the exaggerated dignity of a man who has taken an extra cup; seeing which the beggars and tradesmen nimbly got out of his way, knowing, from experience, that the sword of a drunken *samurai* rests uneasily in its scabbard. As he turned the corner of Temple Avenue he was stopped by a *ronin* wearing a pilgrim's hat, who saluted him, and said in a low tone:

"Well met, Sir Big-rock, I have been looking for you everywhere."

The councilor steadied himself against the trunk of a cherry-tree, and, peering at the speaker through his half-closed eye-lids, replied:

"Well met, Sir Common. I was just hoping to see some thirsty friend who would assist me in emptying a bottle of the best. There is an excellent shop not far from here, where the *Bozu* (Buddhist priests) obtain their nourishment. Come along, come along."

Thus speaking, he grasped Sir Common by the arm and led him down a side-street to an inn called the "Eight Supreme Delights." When they were seated in a private room, Sir Common began to question his friend with regard to his intentions concerning Sir Kira. Sir Big-rock listened indifferently, and presently remarked:

"We came to drink, not talk about impossible things. It is useless for a sickle-insect to attack a team of horses. Is that all you have to tell me?"

Sir Common lowered his voice to a whisper and said:

"Honorable comrade, I have something important to communicate. Do you remember the woman who was lately attendant upon your children? She called herself Peach-blossom."

"Yes, I recollect the creature; her true name was Convolvulus. She was a spy of Sir Kira and is the wife of Black-field, his trusted retainer. I, at one time, thought of using her as a means of deceiving her master, but now have given up the idea. She lives not far from here, next door to a very worthy man who is a money-changer. I spent last evening at his house, and he was so hospitable that on my way home I dropped one of my swords. When you met me I was endeavoring to find it."

"I understand, honorable comrade, Convolvulus listens to everything that passes between you and your friend. Her husband and a band of Kira's people are secreted in her house, waiting for a chance to kill you. They have been following you for several months. Be warned by me, and do not go near the place to-night."

As he ceased speaking he looked at Sir Big-rock, whom, to his annoyance, he found fast asleep; noticing which he arose and summoning the landlord, said:

"This noble *samurai* is suffering from over-fatigue. Here is a *rio*, I pray you let him remain as long as he desires. When he awakens, give him some of your best *saké*", and do everything in your power to detain him here all night. I will call again to-morrow."

He quitted the room, and the landlord, closing the door after him, significantly replied:

"Judging by your honorable friend's symptoms, he will not awaken until sunset. Your instructions shall be strictly followed."

No sooner had Sir Common departed than Sir Big-rock arose, and reassuming an intoxicated expression, staggered out of the apartment and, spite of the landlord's persuasion, sallied into the street. His zig-zag walk highly amused a number of children, who, falling into line, mimicked his gestures and followed him as far as the house of the money-changer.

Sir Big-rock seated himself upon the edge of the platform at the entrance to the store, which was shaded by an over-hanging pine tree, and glanced drowsily at the proprietor, who, after saluting him respectfully, ordered his boy to bring some tea, then observed:

"Honorable sir, I presume you have come for your sword?" producing the weapon and handing it to his visitor. "My boy found it lying on the *tokonoma* in the back room."

At that moment the lad came forward with the cup of tea on a small lacquered tray and kneeling near the guest, presented it, thinking as he did so:

"The honorable *samurai* is very much confused this morning, what comical grimaces he makes."

Sir Big-rock did not take the cup, being busily engaged in attempting to draw the sword from its sheath. While he was thus employed Mrs. Convolvulus emerged from a neighboring house, and noiselessly approaching the money-changer's residence, listened at a side window.

"This sword," said Sir Big-rock, "was presented to me by my late lord. There are people who reproach me for not having avenged his death. I laugh at all such idiots. What can one person do against a powerful noble like Sir Kira. Moreover, remembering the saying, 'man's life is but fifty years,' who would care to shorten it. Turning to the boy he murmured: "*Saké*? Yes, I can always take a cup."

"This is Uzi tea," responded the lad, stifling an inclination to snicker.

"The honorable *samurai* knows that," said the money-changer, frowning at his servant. "Why did you not bring *saké* as I directed?"

The boy retired and on reaching the rear apartment, performed a pantomimic dance, and sang to him self:

"*Saké* and tea are all the same to a man who has been to see the flowers."

"Mr. Gold-help," hiccoughed the visitor, as though replying to an invitation, "certainly, certainly, I will visit you again this evening."

"You honor me, Sir Big-rock. At what time may I expect you?"

"SIR BIG-ROCK DID NOT TAKE THE CUP, BEING BUSILY ENGAGED IN ATTEMPTING TO DRAW THE SWORD FROM ITS SHEATH."

"About the hour of the Hog (8 P.M.)," drowsily answered his guest. "We will indulge in a royal carouse."

"You shall have some more of that old *saké*," said the delighted merchant.

"Good, good!" muttered the other "I cannot wait now. Permit me to leave this sword here until tonight. It will never do for me to go through the streets at mid-day with three weapons in my girdle. People might imagine me to be intoxicated."

As he rose to depart he saw the shadow of Convolvulus vanish from the window.

About the hour of the Rat (midnight), when most honest men were slumbering, Sir Big-rock quitted the house of the money-changer. The latter had long been oblivious of anything his guest said, and was lying on his back, with his right arm in a dish of stewed lampreys. His visitor had done the talking and he the drinking; though the tradesman imagined the reverse.

The *samurai* assumed an intoxicated air and walked very eccentrically, pausing frequently to gaze at the moon. He did not appear to observe three men who had emerged from a neighboring tenement and, sword in hand, were creeping after him, their bare feet making no sound upon the pavement. After going some distance he turned down a lane and entered a lonely spot at the rear of the shrine of Hachiman (the god of war). In the midst of the ground was a gnarled, feathery pine, the trunk of which was completely shaded by the drooping branches. Sir Big-rock staggered toward the tree and placed his back against the stem, when, all of a sudden, the men rushed forward and attempted to cut him down.

This proved a very difficult task, he being in the shadow and his assailants in the full light of the moon; added to which he fought with the greatest coolness and skill. The bravos finding they were getting the worst of it, took to their heels, never stopping until they reached the house of Convolvulus, who expended a large package of paper in patching their mutilated bodies.

They forgot to report the result of their encounter to Kira, and as their intended victim kept his own counsel, the loyal *ronins* remained in ignorance of the affair.

From that time the spies contented themselves with watching Sir Big-rock and reporting his vagaries to their master, who, as the days passed, gradually began to regard his enemy with profound contempt.

CHAPTER XVIII.
SIR UNCONQUERABLE PERFORMS AN ACT OF JUSTICE.

"An arrow aimed at a private soldier sometimes slays a general.
A chance word is often more effective than a premeditated speech."

In the vicinity of Kamakura, within bowshot of the great bronze image of Buddha, was a fashionable inn, that, in the spring of 1701, was conducted by two men and a woman, whose dialect betrayed them to be natives of Ako, though they assured every one they had come from the South.

Their establishment was managed in a very peculiar way, none of the servants being permitted to remain in the house at night, and strange rumors were circulated regarding the proprietors, who were said to be bandits. One of them was an old man called Quick-sand, and the other, who was supposed to be his relative, was addressed as Long-radish; though few imagined those were their true names. Both stood in the greatest fear of the hostess, who, while she sat in her private room and enjoyed every luxury, ordered them about like beggars, and compelled them to do the work of four servants. This woman had a very hot tongue, and ruled the house, even the guests sometimes experiencing the effect of her temper.

One evening Sir Unconquerable, dressed as of old and wearing his *ronin* hat, presented himself at the inn, and marching into the best apartment, ordered refreshments, at the same time curtly announcing that he intended to remain all night.

A few days before, he had been told of the bad reputation borne by the establishment, on hearing which he felt a burning desire to visit it; his old spirit of adventure prompting him to go where hard knocks were likely to be given and taken. He was also informed Sir Kira's chief-councilor was in the habit of frequenting the inn.

When the attendant had delivered the new-comer's order to her mistress, she said:

"I do not keep a house for the entertainment of poor *samurai*."

"Mrs. Rose-bud, he is not poor. I believe he is Sir Plain-field who made a large sum of money by the misfortunes of his lord. He carries a big purse."

"Big purse, does he? That settles the case. You are not beautiful enough to wait on such a valuable guest; send Tiger-lily here. She is the one to make him order expensive food and drink."

While the grim-visaged *ronin* was being served, her husband and his partner entered her room, when she said:

"Quick-sand and Long-radish, go and look through the spy-hole at our new guest. He is laden with money. You will have to attend to him to-night."

The elder of the men put on his horn-spectacles, and advancing to a place where some holes had been made in the wall, peeped, then began to tremble.

"Are you going to have a stroke?" she snapped. "What has overtaken you?"

He turned his ashen features toward her and hoarsely whispered:

"Ye gods! It is Sir Unconquerable! Now the end has arrived and we shall have to give up what we have stolen."

"Phewgh!" she returned. "We will do no such thing. You were always a coward, Arrow-stand. Who cares for Sir Unconquerable?"

"But, honorable madame," faltered the other man, "Unconquerable is a perfect demon. Our lives are not worth a cash each."

"Listen," she said. "He does not know my face, I will go and entertain him. To-night, when he is happily sleeping, you can rid us of his troublesome presence."

"Steal his swords, my dear," suggested her husband, in a tremulous voice. "We dare not attack him while he is armed."

"Leave it all to me," she said. "You become more timorous every day. Cease quaking and look like a man. That old *saké* will conquer him!"

At the hour of the rat (mid-night) Sir Unconquerable saw the door of his room pushed back, and by the dim light from the corridor, beheld two men enter the apartment. In an instant he was upon his feet, and as the intruders attacked him with their long swords, seized one by the neck and the other by the sleeve and hurled them to the floor, then picking up a weapon, dropped by the elder of the two, proceeded to demonstrate the strength of his arm. The intruders uttered loud cries, on hearing which the landlady, spear in hand, rushed upon the scene and assisted in entertaining their guest.

Alas for their calculations! In a short time the thread of her existence was severed, and her husband and his partner were extended on the mats in the agonies of death.

The tumult had aroused the other guests, who crowded into the chamber and demanded the cause of the disturbance. Sir Unconquerable explained what had occurred, and calling for a light, observed:

"Let us take a look at these rascally inn-keepers."

A lamp being brought he discovered who they were, whereupon he sternly exclaimed:

"So, it is you, unfaithful, disloyal wretches. While striking in the dark I have accomplished an act of justice. The vengeance of heaven may be slow but it is sure. Now I shall sleep comfortably."

Thus perished those contemptible creatures, Sir Arrow-stand and Sir Wisteria-lake, whose lives, like their deaths, were miserable.

CHAPTER XIX.
MISS QUIET'S DOWER.

In chapter the sixth I described how three *ronin-samurai* presented themselves at the castle of Ako and offered their services to avenge the death of Lord Morning-field. Although Sir Big-rock could not then avail himself of their aid, he determined to communicate with them later on, as he knew they were men whose loyalty was beyond question. A few days after the surrender of the castle, one of the three, Sir Cliff-field was seized with a fatal sickness which confined him to his bed. On finding his end near he sent for his son, a youth of sixteen, to whom he was tenderly attached. When the boy had saluted him, he grasped his short sword in his right hand and said:

"My son, I am about to climb the Hill of Death and shall soon arrive at the place where the three roads meet. I do not desire to take the one leading to the infernal regions, or the path from this world, preferring, as I am a good Buddhist, to go to *Gokuraku* (Paradise). When *Sanzu-no-baba* (the old woman who is the toll-keeper of the Sanzu-river) comes forward to receive my clothes, she will ask me why I bring this sword with me. I have therefore determined to give it to you."

He paused, through weakness, and his daughter said:

"My honorable father, let me give you a cup of tea, it will cheer your spirits."

The dying man waited until she had served him, then bade her retire and said to his son:

"This morning I was reading the book you see before me. It is the history of *Kusunoki Masashige*, which you, of course, know by heart. I desire to follow the example of that mirror of loyalty and bequeath a legacy to you. Soon after the surrender of the castle of Ako, Sir Big-rock privately sent for me, and to my delight admitted me into the noble band of men who have vowed to avenge the death of our never-to-be-forgotten chief. The gods have decreed that the thread of my life shall soon be snapped. I charge you to take this sword, the gift of our dead chief, and to assume the responsibility of my vow, so that my spirit may pass happily to a future state."

He slowly recited the oath he had taken, his boy repeating the words after him and receiving the sword, which he solemnly swore to use as his father directed.

"Farewell, my son," exclaimed the old *ronin*. "When I meet our lord in Paradise, I shall not be ashamed to look upon his face."

The young Sir Cliff-field buried his father, and after mourning sixty days, went to Sir Big-rock, who was much moved by the loyal devotion of the *samurai*, and accepted him as a member of the conspiracy. He was directed to assume the name of Three-help, and ordered to Yedo, where he joined Sir Cyprus-village, who had opened a grocery called the Three Springs, on a street not far from the residence of Sir Kira.

Sir Cliff-field entered into business with the greatest ardor, and being very handsome, attracted many customers to the shop. Among these were the servants of Sir Kira, whom he treated with special civility, hoping thereby to gain admittance to the noble's mansion. In this he was doomed to disappointment, for, though he gave many bribes, he was never so much as invited into the porter's lodge.

One day a young girl named Miss Quiet, a nurse-maid in the service of Sir Small-grove, entered the Three Springs, and asked for a cake of *tofu* (bean-curd). Sir Cliff-field, who received her order, said in an insinuating tone:

"It is a shame you should be obliged to carry this home. Will you permit me to take it for you?"

"You are too kind," she replied, modestly closing her eyes. "I am only a poor little servant girl."

"You are very beautiful," he whispered. "Do you not reside in the honorable house of Sir Kira?"

She answered in the affirmative, and finally accepted his offer. From that day Miss Quiet became a constant visitor at the store.

Some of the shop-men, who were not in the conspiracy, wondered how a good-looking fellow like Three-help could fall in love with such a homely girl as Miss Quiet, and passed many witty remarks upon the matter, to all of which he would reply:

"The sensible man looks to the heart. The morning-glory soon withers."

In the course of a few months Miss Quiet accepted the young grocer as her betrothed and introduced him to her uncle, Mr. Plain, a retired architect, who lived snugly upon the earnings of his younger days, in a comfortable house on Divinity Street.

The girl loved her affianced very tenderly, yet never invited him to visit her at her master's residence, which, being within the enclosure containing Sir Kira's mansion, was guarded closely. The meetings of the lovers always took place at her uncle's home, and the young people did not appear together upon the street.

After awhile Sir Cliff-field became really enamored with her; notwithstanding which he eagerly kept his eyes and ears open, and was as anxious as ever to gain admission to Sir Kira's mansion.

Who can predict what sort of chicken will be hatched from an egg.

This *samurai* who had, in the beginning, made certain plans, found them defeated by his attachment to this humble but virtuous girl; still, in the end, it was through her he obtained what he so greatly desired.

At first the old architect treated him very coolly, but when he found the young people really loved each other, he gradually took a liking to the grocer and called him nephew, while Sir Cliff-field, who highly esteemed the old man, addressed him by the familiar title of uncle.

One day, in July, 1701, when the lovers were paying the architect a visit, he produced a number of plans, which he proudly exhibited, saying:

"Let me show you some of my handiwork."

"Excuse me, honorable uncle, I must go," said his niece, rising and stepping into the "mouth of the house" where she slipped on her clogs. "*Sayonara* (farewell). Three-help, you will have great pleasure in looking at those beautiful drawings. You must not accompany me, for, if I were seen walking with any one, my mistress would dismiss me from her service. In our house we have to be doubly particular. That fidgety old Sir Kira suspects everybody."

As soon as she had departed, the architect said:

"What do you think of these specimens?"

"You have wonderful talent, uncle. This must be a plan of a *daimio's* mansion. Have you designed many such?"

"Yes, a great number. I drew the plan of Sir Kira's *yashiki* (mansion). He was very crotchety and gave me lots of trouble. This," unrolling a large paper, "is what I did for him. It contains more passages and secret rooms than a fashionable tea-house."

"What a beautiful piece of work. How I envy you the ability to do such a thing."

"That is nothing, nephew. I really ought not to keep this, yet on account of its exquisite finish, hesitate to destroy it. When I die you must be very careful with my papers; I am like a doctor, I know the mysteries of many houses."

He rolled up the drawings and showed the young man a recess beneath the *tokonoma* where he kept his treasures, as he did so, remarking:

"THREE-HELP, YOU WILL HAVE GREAT PLEASURE IN LOOKING AT THOSE BEAUTIFUL DRAWINGS."

"You, without doubt, remember how the Lord of Ako was treated by Sir Kira, do you not, nephew?"

"Yes, uncle, I know something about the matter; will you kindly give me the full particulars?"

The old man related the story of the tragedy and concluded his narration by saying:

"Although I once had Sir Kira for a client I heartily detest him. The Lord of Ako was a noble man, just and humane. I am amazed that his retainers have not avenged his death. I know it is wrong to talk in this manner, still, were I a *samurai*, I would never rest until I had done my duty."

"Uncle, you forget the law forbids men taking justice into their own hands. No doubt the members of the clan have loyal hearts—they do not desire to oppose the authorities."

This reply made the architect very angry.

"Go to," he cried. "Were you a *samurai*, you would not utter such words."

"I am a *samurai*," was the proud response. "My true name is Cliff-field."

The architect leaned back upon his elbows, and regarding his visitor with amazement, joyfully exclaimed:

"Well met, Sir Cliff-field, I am Green-mountain, who was once a councilor of the Lord of Tamba, the bosom friend of Lord Morning-field. Through the intrigues of a fellow-official, I lost the favor of my honored chief and was forced to become a *ronin*. Though I wear the garb of a tradesman I have the heart of a *samurai*. I believe I understand what you are doing in Yedo." Taking the plans from their hiding place, he continued: "Future nephew, here are some important papers, accept them as the dower of my niece."

Sir Cliff-field received the documents with trembling hands, and, raising them to his forehead, murmured:

"Sir Green-mountain, future uncle, I cannot find words with which to express my thanks. You give your niece a priceless dower. Up to this time the hearts of my loyal comrades have been sorely troubled, and we have hoped against hope. Our enemy, strong in his political power, guarded like the Shogun himself, has defied our attempts and mocked at our misery. Your kindness will enable us to clear the stain of disloyalty from the name of the clan of Ako."

Within ten days the plan was delivered into the hands of Sir Big-rock, who, after examining it, exclaimed:

"I see one star shining through the darkness of the night."

CHAPTER XX.
SIR BIG-ROCK WINNOWS THE RICE.

"Even a high mountain may in time become a hillock.
How a few vows stand the test of years."

Upon a hot day in August, 1701, Sir Big-rock was seated in his library, thinking of the news he had received from Yedo.

"Only one thing is now required," he said, thinking aloud. "Kira has sent away the guard furnished by his son, and evidently no longer fears me. I will now try the loyalty of the conspirators, and when I have winnowed the rice, proceed to Yedo and carry out the plan I have so long had in my mind. It is most certain Kira will never give us an opportunity to attack him upon the street, so we will storm his residence and kill the badger in his hole. Had I not obtained the plan from Sir Cliff-field we should have been compelled to grope our way in the dark; I now know every nook and corner of our enemy's house better than he does."

"Honorable master," said the servant, Left-six, from the passage, "Sir Hatchet and Sir Common desire to see you."

"Admit them."

When the visitors entered the room, Sir Big-rock exclaimed:

"Welcome, my friends! Sir Common, I presume you are feeling annoyed because I defeated you at our last game of *go*, and have come to wipe out the stain. I suppose Sir Hatchet is here to help you with his suggestions."

The guests knelt quite close to him, and Sir Common answered:

"No, Sir Big-rock, our business is to talk about something more important. We are fortunate in finding you at home."

"After this," said their host, "I shall always be here. I have of late spent much foolish money, and am now beginning to feel stingy. Had I invested all I have thrown away, I should to-day be a rich man. Luckily I have some few *rio* left, which I intend to loan upon collateral security. Do you notice the large storehouse I have built in the back-yard? It is to hold the pledges. I had a very nice fish sent me this morning; will you not eat some of it and drink a cup of *saké* with me?"

He was about to strike his hands together, in order to summon a servant, when Sir Common prevented him and said:

"You must excuse us to-day. Pardon me, Sir Big-rock, why are we thus mistrusted? What are we to understand by your words? Surely you do not intend that Sir Kira shall die in his bed. Are the sacrifices and sufferings of the loyal clansmen, of our wives, children and dependants to go for nothing, like bubbles that rise on the surface of water. This long delay has sorely tried many of our number, and we fear some of them may lose heart, and when the time comes, refuse to perform their vow. You must surely comprehend all these things. We have come to ask you, once and for all, what is your determination with regard to our enemy?"

"Yes, Chief-councilor," said Sir Hatchet, "Sir Common has exactly expressed my sentiments. Many of the conspirators, discouraged by this long delay, are losing their grip."

"I understand," calmly answered Sir Big-rock. "In the beginning, carried away by anger and a desire for revenge, I made up my mind, come what might, to attack Sir Kira. I now think better of it. All the reports show any attempt on our part would result in ignominious defeat. I do not desire to become the laughing-stock of the world, and thus bring additional disgrace upon the memory of our honored lord. Our best plan will be again to petition the Council of Elders to reestablish the house of Ako. That is my idea; what do you think?"

""YES, CHIEF-COUNCILOR," SAID SIR HATCHET, "SIR COMMON
HAS EXACTLY EXPRESSED MY SENTIMENTS."

Sir Common, who had listened most impatiently, angrily replied:

"I do not agree with you! I never expected to hear such words from the mouth of Sir Big-rock. You know full well the council has not the slightest intention to grant what you propose. We have waited nearly three years for them to move in the matter, and might wait three hundred, could we live so long. There is only one course open to us, namely, to take the head of Sir Kira, and thus wipe out our too prolonged disgrace."

"You jump at conclusions," said Sir Big-rock. "The fact of our having conspired has reached the ears of the authorities at Yedo, who naturally agree that, as long as we entertain such feelings, we are unworthy to be restored to our old positions. I have thought the matter over and have resolved to return the written oaths intrusted to my charge. It would be making the affair too important were I specially to summon the late conspirators for that purpose. I will therefore give the papers into your charge. When you come across our friends, communicate my ideas to them, and return their pledges."

He then took a roll of documents from his writing-desk and held the package toward them.

For some moments the visitors remained speechless with indignation.

"Sir Big-rock," cried Sir Common, "are you endeavoring to fathom our hearts? I did not take that oath in jest. If you mean what you say, Chief-councilor as you are, I will not spare you."

Having thus spoken he grasped the hilt of his sword and impatiently waited for a reply.

"Sir Common, you provoke yourself about a trifle. If my decision does not suit you and others, follow your own judgment, only exclude me from your arrangements, as I have a plan of my own. All I ask you is to take charge of these papers."

"I will not accept them," thundered Sir Common. "Have you forgotten the sacred charge I brought from Yedo? Go to the temple of the Snow-clad Pine and refresh your loyalty by gazing at the last gift from your lord. If, after that, you refuse to keep your vow, I will cut off your head and offer it to the god of war, which act will show our fellow conspirators that, at least, they have one man who is not afraid to lead them! These are strong words to use to a Chief-councilor, but this is no time for compliments. My heart is full of sorrow for my dead lord, therefore my tongue brooks not the restraint of ceremony. I will call upon you to-morrow, in order to receive your reply."

Sir Hatchet waited a few moments, then interposed, saying:

"Calm yourself, Sir Common. I begin to understand the meaning of Sir Big-rock's words. We will do as he desires and receive the documents."

"What?" cried Sir Common, trembling with rage. "Are you, too, a coward?"

"Come," said Sir Hatchet, grasping his companion by the arm and hurriedly saluting their leader. "I will take charge of the papers. The Chief-councilor has determined wisely. We will retire."

The next day, while Sir Hatchet was perusing a volume of ancient poems, his daughter came to him and said:

"Honorable father, there is a fan-dealer outside."

"Thank you, Plum. I do not require any of his wares this morning."

The girl retired, but presently returned with a folded paper which she handed to her parent, who, upon opening it, said:

"My dear Plum, will you please send the gentleman in?"

When the stranger entered, Sir Hatchet saluted him, and exclaimed:

"Welcome, Sir Thousand-cliffs, you have arrived at a most opportune time."

"Dear me," cried the young lady, who was lingering at the door. "Honorable sir, can it be possible you are my cousin, Thousand-cliffs? I did not know you. How completely you are disguised."

The *samurai*, who was dressed in the humble garb of a merchant, deposited his sample box upon the floor, and wiping his perspiring brow, turned to the lady and replied:

"So you did not recognize me, cousin Plum? Don't you think I make a good-looking fan merchant?"

"You could not spoil your handsome features," she merrily answered. "I will go and prepare some refreshments. My mother and grandmother have gone to the temple."

Sir Hatchet waited until she was out of hearing, then related what had passed at the house of Sir Big-rock. On hearing which, Sir Thousand-cliffs said:

"I perfectly understand his intention. This news is indeed delightful. I have come from Yedo in order to consult with you about his eccentric behavior. Now I comprehend it, and believe the day of attack is close at hand."

"That is also my opinion. Last night I argued the matter for several hours with worthy Sir Common, and at length brought him to reason. How would you advise me to return these documents?"

"Nothing could be easier," said Sir Thousand-cliffs. "You visit the conspirators who are in this city, and I'll attend to those in Yedo. You will hear from me as soon as possible. When Kira learns the oaths have been returned he will deem the league broken. What a wonderful man the Chief-councilor is! I, for one, though often feeling despondent, have never doubted his wisdom and loyalty."

Within a month a package arrived from Yedo, on receipt of which Sir Common and Sir Hatchet once more visited Sir Big-rock, who, seeing the papers were greatly diminished in number, said:

"These men can be trusted. When the time comes we shall act as one person. They, like refined gold, have been thrice tried. Never mind what may be the odds we will accomplish our purpose. Do not doubt me, I am for the attack. Now you know what is in my heart. I would, however, caution you about one thing; be more vigilant than ever. You remember the saying of Iyeyasu, 'After a victory knot the cords of your helmet.'"

He then showed his visitors the plan of Sir Kira's residence, and consulted with them.

Sir Hatchet and Sir Common were so encouraged and pleased, that they felt as though they were climbing up to heaven.

"SO YOU DID NOT RECOGNIZE ME, COUSIN PLUM? DON'T YOU THINK I MAKE A GOOD-LOOKING FAN MERCHANT?"

CHAPTER XXI.
THE MOTHER OF SIR COMMON.

"The *samurai* lady has the soul of a warrior.
When the son hesitates, the mother leads."

Sir Big-rock having returned the written oaths and ascertained the intentions of his followers, felt in a position to execute his plans. Knowing the clansmen in Yedo were beginning to exhibit impatience, and fearing they might precipitate matters by ill-timed action, he determined to send a representative to pacify and watch over them, for which purpose he summoned Sir Common, whom he thus addressed:

"I have been considering the intelligence brought from Yedo by Sir Thousand-cliffs, and would much like to visit our comrades, however, at present that is impossible; besides my appearance among them would re-awaken Sir Kira's suspicions and defeat our project. I, therefore, desire you will take my place. When can you be ready to depart?"

Sir Common bowed and replied:

"I offer you my heartfelt thanks for selecting me, a man of inferior judgment and little wisdom, to represent you on this important mission. Nothing would give me greater pleasure than to start at once, but I have one favor to ask. My aged mother, my wife and child are at my home in Middle Village, near Ako. If I go to Yedo now, I cannot expect to return. For this reason I am most anxious to once more see my dear mother and family, and to bid them a last farewell. Although I cannot openly speak the words, I can, at least, do so mentally. Will it be possible for you to grant me this great indulgence? I shall only be absent one or two days."

Sir Big-rock nodded and answered:

"Everybody thinks of his mother, especially you who have always been such a dutiful and affectionate son. I will grant your request with the greatest pleasure. By all means visit your home and do not be stingy with your farewells. A few days' delay will be of trifling consequence, as Sir Thousand-cliffs will have somewhat quieted the apprehensions of our brothers in Yedo. Present my regards to your honorable mother and family. The perfume of the plum-blossom soon passes away. Make the most of the delightful moments."

The tears stood in the eyes of Sir Common as he respectfully took his leave. He felt that Sir Big-rock was allowing him a happiness he denied himself.

Sir Common purchased a few presents, which he made into a bundle to be carried over his shoulders, then dressed himself in his best, and putting on his striped cloth overcoat, proceeded upon his way, the journey occupying one day and a half. On nearing home his thoughts reverted to the time of his prosperity, when he was a great *samurai* with an allowance of three hundred *koku* of rice.

"Ah!" he exclaimed, "then I was enabled to lodge my mother in a beautiful residence, now all I can afford is yonder mean cottage. My breast is well nigh closed." (An expression of suppressed grief.)

He paused, and regarding the humble abode, the white roof of which could be seen peeping from among the branches of the pine-trees, dashed the tears from his eyes, and restraining his emotion, assumed an unconcerned air, murmuring to himself:

"It will not do for my mother to see me looking miserable."

As he approached the dwelling he heard his wife, Mrs. Cloth, singing, and knew by the sound of splashing water that she was washing linen. He noiselessly advanced from behind the reed-fence, and halting, watched her, she being unaware of his presence.

Mrs. Cloth, who had her babe upon her back and her sleeves bound with her *tasuke* (a cord carried by ladies to loop up their dresses), was seated upon a clog behind a shallow tub. As she vigorously rubbed the garment and plunged it into the water, she talked to her child, never for a moment imagining he was fast asleep and that his father was listening to what she said.

"Yes, my brave son," she exclaimed, "have a little patience; eat heartily and enjoy yourself, so that when your papa returns he will not recognize his big, strong Fusa Bo" (literally Apartment baby).

Mrs. Cloth then sang a nursery song, and not hearing his voice in reply, turned to look at him, when she beheld Sir Common, whereupon she ceased her occupation and said:

"Oh, honorable husband, I am so glad to see you! Mother has been feeling very anxious on your account. Honorable mother, where are you? My husband has come home!"

Hearing this, Sir Common's mother, who was over eighty years old, advanced to the window in the side of the entry, and gazing lovingly at her son, said:

"Common, I am delighted once more to behold your face. You must have suffered greatly during this season of returning heat (Indian summer). I pray you not to trouble yourself about saluting me. Lave your feet and enter without ceremony."

""OH, HONORABLE HUSBAND, I AM SO GLAD TO SEE YOU! MOTHER HAS BEEN FEELING VERY ANXIOUS ON YOUR ACCOUNT."

"As you please, honorable mother," was his respectful answer. "Your happiness at seeing me is not greater than mine at beholding you."

He slipped, off his straw sandals, and laying aside his sun-hat, entered the house, his wife following with the child.

Having prostrated himself and performed the respectful salutation, Sir Common said:

"Honorable mother, I have for a long time expected to come back, in order to ascertain the good or bad that has occurred to you, but the pressure of business has detained me."

The aged lady smiled kindly upon him and replied:

"I understand, my son. Although you were unable to visit me you have written very frequently from Kioto. This has afforded me great comfort. I have not seen you for six months, yet cannot observe any change in your appearance. Your presence fills my heart with happiness. During your absence our good Cloth has been most affectionate, and has proved an admirable daughter. Look at our darling Fusa Bo. Has he not grown? He is very healthy, and can almost balance himself upon his feet. He also says a few words, and is most lovable. See the pretty fellow; he is still asleep, little thinking his papa has come home."

When she ceased speaking, Sir Common's wife took up the current of the old lady's thought, and said:

"We knew you would feel proud of our boy. A moment before you came he was talking to me, not in words that every one could understand, but in his own baby language. In an instant, he was off to the dream-country and I felt his soft cheek rest upon my neck. Since our honorable mother loves and pets him so much, he is always about her, and, during the day, she is his nurse and guardian."

"He is truly a fortunate fellow," said the delighted father. "I pray you not to disturb him. When he awakens we will make each other's acquaintance. Tell me where my brother, Total-three, is?"

"He has only gone to a neighbor's," said Mrs. Cloth, then, listening for a moment, added: "Here he comes."

As she spoke his brother entered, and saluted Sir Common with respectful delight.

While the *samurai* were conversing, Mrs. Cloth, assisted by the old lady, who disliked to be unoccupied, cooked fish and rice and warmed *saké*. When the baby awoke, the family sat down to a feast and celebrated the safe return of its head, their happiness being unmixed and unrestrained.

Sir Common waited until the smiling face of his parent indicated a good opportunity for him to communicate what he desired to say, then observed:

"My honorable mother, since I have been away from you in Kioto, I have done my best to find some place where I could settle and repair my fortune. Luckily I have met a certain prince of the Kuwan To provinces, who desires me to enter his service, so I am about to go to Yedo. I have come hither to announce this happy news and bid you farewell; I must start to-morrow morning, but will return next spring and take you to my new home. Until that time I beg you will regard my brother, Total-three, as the head of the family, and remain well and happy. Brother and wife, you now know my errand. Take every care of our honored mother. This," producing a sum of money, "will serve for your present needs. Remember our honorable mother must not suffer for anything."

Total-three received the package and, like Cloth, felt sad at the thought of losing Sir Common almost as soon as they had recovered him.

"My honorable brother," said the young man, "rest assured nothing shall be lacking on my part."

"Nor on mine," murmured Mrs. Cloth.

While they were speaking, the venerable lady watched the face of her eldest born, and, correcting her attitude (assuming a serious pose), observed:

"My son, I am very happy to hear you are going to Yedo, though I would, if possible, like to know the real reason of your journey."

"What does my honored mother mean?" he cried, affecting amazement. "Have I not fully stated my business?"

"My son," she gravely replied, "there is no one here but our family and you can speak without restraint. I presume your telling us a certain prince is to take you into his service is a fiction, and am sure the real reason for your trip to Yedo is to avenge the death of our lord. Do you fear to tell me the truth, believing that I, one in ten thousand, might prevent you from going, or that my tears would weaken the vow you have made? I comprehend your motive for concealment, but you misunderstand me. Woman as I am, the proud mother of *samurai*, I will not give way to undisciplined feeling. I conjure you to speak out, so that there will be no after regret concerning the matter."

Sir Common, surprised and delighted that his mother's loyalty was as true as the needle to the pole, was about to reveal all, when he checked himself, imagining, though she spoke so bravely, when the time came for her to say farewell she would become distracted with grief. This determined him to continue his loving deception. Placing both hands upon the floor, he respectfully said:

"Honorable mother, I grieve to hear your suspicions, as I deemed my explanation would be satisfactory. With regard to avenging the death of our honored lord, the matter is still undecided. While we held the castle we had many consultations, and were resolved to kill Sir Kira. Since that time a great number of our comrades have changed their minds, and even Sir Big-rock is trying to mend his fortune by entering into business. Why should I deceive my honored mother? I pray you to banish your suspicions and wait until spring, when I will return from Yedo."

While his tongue uttered these words, his heart rebelled against the deceit he was practicing upon his parent, and he bowed his head close to the mat, in order to hide his shame.

His mother understood his feelings, but pretending not to do so, answered:

"Since you say so, I am re-assured, and will anxiously wait for the spring to come. My dear son, I pray you be careful of yourself upon your journey. Start at sunrise, do not travel during the heated hours of noon, and avoid the evening dews. You must be tired. Have a good rest to-night. I will awaken you early."

He thanked her for her minute and careful concern, and after saying good night, retired to rest.

The next morning the old lady arose before daybreak and busied herself in preparing luncheon for him, making rice-cakes and other delicacies of which she knew he was very fond.

When Sir Common came from his apartment and beheld her thus employed, he endeavored to appear cheerful, while she thought to herself:

"Whatever others may do, it shall not be said that his mother, by word or deed, caused him to be untrue to his lord."

After the morning meal had been eaten, he took his little child upon his knee, and, gazing lovingly at him, said in a low, tender voice:

"My son, your father is going upon a long journey. You must be a very good boy. I shall often think of you and of the comfort you will be to your grandmother and mother. Grow strong, my second self, grow strong. Farewell—my boy!"

Thus speaking, he handed the babe to his sobbing wife, who, with averted face, received the child, and after listening to her husband's farewell, hurriedly quitted the apartment. When she was gone and Sir Common had said good-bye to his brother, he prostrated himself before his mother, and, in broken accents, bade her adieu.

The aged lady listened with unmoved countenance, and, counseling him to remember her advice, accompanied him to the porch and watched his departure.

He last saw her standing in the door-way regarding him affectionately.

Sir Common hastened from the place, being desirous of quickly returning to his duty, and thus banishing the sad thoughts that filled his soul.

About noon, when he had travelled nearly eighteen miles, he seated himself in the shade of a tree and opened his luncheon-box, in which he found the rice-cakes and food prepared by his mother. Taking a cake in his hand, he reverently lifted it to his forehead, then proceeded to partake of the repast, at the conclusion of which one rice-cake remained in the receptacle.

"What can I do with this?" he mused. "If I keep it until night it will be spoiled and I cannot throw away her gift."

He glanced about him and noticed a pigeon's nest in the fork of a tree above his head, seeing which he placed the cake in a suitable spot and presently had the pleasure of beholding the pigeons feed their brood with his offering.

Sir Common watched their actions with a dreamy curiosity, his mind being preoccupied with thoughts of those who were far away. He was awakened from his reverie by the noise of the young birds clamoring for the food, which they devoured as fast as the old ones could procure it, the parents never once swallowing a morsel. Seeing this, Sir Common thought:

"Although the pigeon is a small bird, its parental instinct causes it to deny itself everything for its off-spring. Do human beings think as much of their children? If I go to Yedo I shall either die fighting or by *hara-kiri*, and my life will be lost to my family. I have, in bidding farewell to my mother, been guilty of a grave falsehood. When all is over and she becomes acquainted with my deceit, she will most surely say: 'Though I have thought so much of my son, his affection for me was so slight that he did not hesitate to deceive me,' and will feel displeased and lament. I have made a great mistake."

These reflections caused him to feel very unhappy, and prevented him from resuming his journey.

"I must return to her," he said. "I will reveal the true motive of my visit to Yedo and bid her farewell in a proper manner."

He then rose and retraced his steps, reaching home about sun-set.

Having allayed the apprehensions of his wife and brother by stating he had forgotten an important matter, he went to his mother's chamber and narrated the circumstances that had influenced him to revisit her, then said in a husky voice:

"I thoroughly feel my wickedness in confessing the truth at this late hour. It is as you have suspected; I am going to Yedo for the purpose of avenging the death of our honored lord. Sir Big-rock and others of the clan have vowed to accomplish this act of duty; therefore it will be impossible for me to visit you again. You are my only parent and I am conscious I ought to live with you and do my utmost to make your life happy, yet I cannot forget the grace of our late lord. How am I to fulfil both my loyal and filial duties? I pray you will put your ungrateful and unworthy son out of your heart."

The lady listened with a delighted expression and gently replied:

"You lovingly tried to conceal the truth from me, yet I was not for a moment deceived. Now that you have spoken frankly, my heart is rejoiced. My son, do your duty to our lord. That is the first thing a *samurai* should consider. Remember, your brother will be with me to comfort my last years. I am perfectly satisfied. Even had I no other son, you would have to keep your word and leave an untarnished name to your child. You could not, in any way, more perfectly fulfil your obligation to me than by acting thus. Dismiss me from your thoughts and concentrate your whole mind upon your duty. We will now drink a farewell cup."

She procured *saké* and entertained him, never by word or look showing the least indication of her grief.

Sir Common, overjoyed with her loyalty of spirit, talked with her until nearly midnight, when they retired to their respective apartments.

At day-break he rose and waited outside his mother's room, knowing it was her custom to be up before the rest of the household. The hours passed and the sun mounted high into the heavens, yet there was no sign of her being awake. His wife came and went, and glanced at him uneasily, still he did not notice her or appear to observe the affectionate demonstrations of their child, who alternately peeped round the door-way at his papa and clamored for his grandmother.

At the hour of the dragon (8 A.M.), Sir Common, unable any longer to bear the suspense, entered his parent's chamber, and, to his horror and grief, discovered she was dead. By her pillow was a letter, stained with the life-blood of the noble and courageous lady.

"Brother! Wife!" he cried, "come hither and see what mother has done for my sake!"

Total-three and Cloth hurried into the room, and when Sir Common had somewhat mastered his grief, he reverently opened the letter and read:

"I leave you a few words. My dear son, your kindness and affection toward me are beyond my poor expression. That you should come back the distance of eighteen miles, thinking of your mother, is only a slight evidence of your love for me. How happy is the woman who possesses such a son! After I parted from you I thought over your position, and saw that my duty is as clear as yours. You must go to the attack unfettered by any concern about me. Were a thought of that kind to enter your mind, your fortitude might forsake you, and you might afford the enemy a chance to behold the inside of your helmet. I am old and my life can well be spared. I joyfully end it in order to free you from anxiety, that you may die the death of a *samurai*. My son, I precede you to the land of shadows. Look upon Sir Kira not only as the enemy of our honored lord, but also as the executioner of your mother, and set an example of heroism to your comrades. Knowing you will surely do this, I die contented, and, smiling upon the knife, hasten to sever the thread of my existence. My last farewell to Total-three, to dear little Fusa Bo, to Cloth and to you, my dear son.

"MOTHER."

When Sir Common had read this he cried like a child at the top of his voice, after awhile observing:

"There are many sons who do not fulfil their filial duties, but none so wicked as I. Had I foreseen this I would not have returned. Indeed, I have done the most foolish thing imaginable. How can I ever forget the noble example set me by my mother! A thousand times be accursed the wretch who caused all this misery!"

His brother and wife united with him in lamenting the death of their parent, and by turns embraced the inanimate form.

"WHEN SIR COMMON HAD SOMEWHAT MASTERED HIS GRIEF,
HE REVERENTLY OPENED THE LETTER AND READ."

Grief, though natural, will not restore the dead to life; so Sir Common, after having buried his mother with all honors and spent fourteen days in mourning at her tomb, bade farewell to his wife, child and brother, and, returning to Kioto, presented himself to Sir Big-rock, who, saluting him, said:

"Well, Sir Common, you have been absent longer than you promised, moreover, you do not look as usual. Have you been sick?"

"No, Sir Big-rock, there is nothing the matter with me. Unhappily, I have lost my honored mother. I disregarded the usual limit of mourning and returned as soon as possible."

"I regret to hear of your bereavement. Did your honorable mother die suddenly?"

Sir Common related all that had occurred, even reading the letter, which so moved Sir Big-rock that the tears trickled down his cheeks, and he exclaimed:

"Ah! The loyal heart of the *samurai* woman! Your honored mother is like the noble parent of Sir Straight-grove. Their united names will be reverently remembered by posterity. Those courageous ladies make us men blush with shame. I can well imagine your grief and that of your family. All this misery is the result of the meanness and wickedness of Sir Kira—the death of our lord, the sufferings of our clan—how can I express myself! The time of retribution is at hand. When you arrive in Yedo you may freely communicate my plans to our comrades, then wait for the day when we shall be able to return the sacred charge entrusted to me by our honored chief."

Sir Common, encouraged by Sir Big-rock's words, banished his sorrow, and, having stayed one day in Kioto, started for Yedo.

CHAPTER XXII.
MR. NOBLE-PLAIN.

"A glittering grain of gold is seen amid a hundred million particles
   of sand.
The humble garb of the peasant often covers a noble heart."

At the sign of the Heaven Stream (milky way) in the town of Sakai,
near the seaport of Osaka, dwelt a man named Noble-plain, who,
during the lifetime of Lord Morning-field, lived by supplying the clan
of Ako with arms and other equipments. Upon hearing of the
misfortune that had overtaken his employer, he hastened to the castle
and sought an interview with Sir Big-rock, whom he thus addressed:

"Sir Chief-councilor, though only a *chonin* (literally street-people, a
class including citizens, artizans and peasants), my heart is heavy with
the calamity that has befallen my gracious patron, and I desire to do
something to prove my gratitude for the many kindnesses I have
received at his hands. Oh, that I were a *samurai*! Even were my rations
no more than a handful of rice, I could then join in your noble
enterprise and die an honorable death. As it is, I know not what to do."

Sir Big-rock listened with pleasure, and replied:

"Your generous devotion will gratify our dead chief. Be patient and
await the time when you will receive a communication from me. I
have long been aware of your honesty and fidelity, and will some day
call upon you to render us an important service."

"Sir Chief-councilor, I am henceforth at your command. My
fortune, my life, all I possess is at your disposal. Be it to-morrow or ten
years hence, you will find me in the same mind. Your words have
comforted my heart. I shall look forward for the moment to arrive
when you will avail yourself of my humble aid."

He then took his leave and returned to Sakai.

The years passed, and, like the rest of the world, Noble-plain heard
strange stories concerning the behavior of Sir Big-rock,
notwithstanding which he was always expecting a summons from the
Chief-councilor.

In October, 1701, a few days after the departure of Sir Common for
Yedo, a messenger entered the merchant's store and said:

"Are you Mr. Noble-plain?"

"That is my name. What can I do for you?"

The new-comer approached him and whispered:

"Would you like to earn a large sum of money? I perceive your shop is not so well stocked as formerly and that you have only one assistant. Surely business must be very bad with you?"

The proprietor sighed and answered:

"Since the death of my noble patron my affairs have become all of a heap. I shall be most happy to better my condition."

"That is good. The service I require is a very easy one. You have heard of Sir Kira, late master of ceremonies to the Shogun. He wishes you to supply him with some arms."

Noble-plain's eyes flashed and he ground his teeth with rage, then exclaimed:

"You dog! How dare you propose such a thing to me. Quit this place or I will kick you out."

The stranger, instead of complying with this command, drew a letter from his bosom and handed it to the merchant, saying:

"Before I go, I desire you will read this."

Noble-plain glanced at the superscription and saw that the communication was from Yamashina, and the bearer was designated as Temple-cliff. He opened the note and read as follows:

"An old employer desires to see you at your earliest convenience. He is about to engage in business, and wishes to give you a little commission.

"PEACEFUL-VALLEY,

"of Yamashina."

The overjoyed merchant prostrated himself before the messenger, and, after returning thanks, invited him to enter his private apartment, where he regaled him with *saké* and fish."

That night the two men started for Yamashina, and on the following morning Noble-plain presented himself to Sir Big-rock, who said:

"You must excuse the trick played by Temple-cliff. I am compelled to test even those whom I deem most faithful. I hear you are very poor, therefore am rejoiced to know, though you have lost your fortune, you still remember the goodness of your late patron."

"Sir Chief-councilor," replied the merchant, "it is true I have but little left, still what there is, is at your service."

Sir Big-rock produced a paper which he handed him, saying:

"Enclosed you will find a list of certain articles I require delivered to the care of the chief-priest of the Spring-hill Temple in the High-rope district of Yedo. I wish you to attend to this matter at once, and will leave the details to your judgment; merely remarking that absolute secrecy must be observed in the matter."

Noble-plain opened the document, and after scanning it, said:

"I understand what you want and will have everything at the place you mention before the snow begins to fly. The uniforms I will procure in Yedo, also the bamboo pins and pocket writing materials. I will start at once and you may rely upon your secret being well kept. Sir Chief-councilor, I am overjoyed at receiving this commission; I feel as though I were walking upon the air."

"With regard to funds—" said Sir Big-rock.

"I shall sell my stock and business," replied the merchant. "Have no apprehension on the score of money, I will attend to that."

Sir Big-rock sent for a package which he gave to the man; remarking as he did so:

"Here are two hundred *rio*; if this sum be insufficient, call upon Sir Common, who is living at the Three-springs grocery store, near the residence of Sir Kira, in Yedo. He will hand you any further funds you may require."

Noble-plain took his leave, and returning to his home, informed his wife that he was going to the province of Bingo, then secretly set out post-haste for Yedo.

A few days after the merchant's departure, Sir Big-rock received the following communication from the capital:

"The late beautiful weather has been very favorable for eeling and the Associated Anglers have been out early and late. Yesterday we tried our fortune in the old stream, containing the big eel. Although we searched every nook and corner we failed to get sight of him. At last, toward the evening, we learned that he had quitted his usual retreat and taken refuge beneath the shade of a tall cedar. You remember the saying of Confucius: 'It is foolish to go to a tree in order to catch fish.' This case will prove an exception to the rule. Your experience as an angler will enable you to suggest some means by which we can secure the monster.

"ASSOCIATED ANGLERS."

After Sir Big-rock had read this, he laughed to himself and exclaimed:

"So, Sir Kira has left his house and sought refuge with his son Lord Upper-cedar. When I join the Associated Anglers we will capture that slippery eel."

CHAPTER XXIII.
SIR BIG-ROCK DEPARTS FOR YEDO.

Among the celebrated ladies of the clan of Ako was Mrs. Brilliant, wife of Sir Hatchet, who, like him, was a poet, and wrote many verses that have been preserved to this day. She was famous for her virtues, wisdom and talents, and possessed a noble and loyal soul. Gentle in manner, obedient to her husband, and kind to her mother-in-law, she not only managed her household affairs with consummate ability, but found time to continue her studies in Japanese and Chinese literature, in addition to which her whole heart was in the conspiracy, and she made her house the rendezvous of the loyal leaguers.

During the lifetime of Lord Morning-field, Sir Hatchet was the governor of his chief's residence in Kioto, and after the noble's death, the poet continued to reside in that city, where he earned his living by instructing pupils in the art of composing elegant stanzas.

Toward the end of October, when the tempests had stripped the autumnal garb from the trees, an epidemic appeared in Kioto, and among its first victims were the mother of Sir Hatchet, and his daughter, Miss Plum. While the sleeves of the mourners were yet wet with tears, Sir Hatchet was instructed to depart for Yedo. Mrs. Brilliant received the news with heroic fortitude, and bade adieu to her husband as though he was going to a festival, congratulating him that he would soon accomplish what they both so greatly desired.

Brave and wise woman, where can we find her equal?

Sir Hatchet was accompanied by Sir Big-rock, Jr., and, in order to deceive their enemies, they left Kioto under the pretence of making a pilgrimage to the shrine of the goddess Amaterasu Omi-kami, in the province of Ise (the Mecca of believers in the Shinto faith).

On their way the poet delighted his companion by describing the objects and places of historic interest, which he made the subjects of impromptu verses.

After crossing a river, that in the morning sun sent up a heavy mist, he observed:

"As I emerge from the Kamo, I take with me the vapor of the stream."

At Shiga, he said:

"Lonely and cold stands the solitary pine-tree on the shore of Shiga.

"So lives a person (meaning his wife) at home."

These poems showed the young man, that while Sir Hatchet was apparently unconcerned, he was thinking of the beloved one whom he had left in Kioto.

When the travelers reached the town of Kanagawa, they halted for a day to celebrate the majority of Sir Big-rock, Jr., who, that morning, had his forelock shaven, and received the military name of Good-gold.

Upon the following day, as they were proceeding on their journey, the fog that had for the previous twenty-four hours enveloped Fuji-yama, suddenly lifted, noticing which, Sir Hatchet looked across the glittering water upon his right, and said:

"I see, reflected upon the bosom of the bay, the snow-clad peak of Fuji-san."

His companion, hearing this, turned, and glancing at the mountain, joyfully exclaimed:

"Oh, happy omen! Fuji-yama salutes me on attaining my majority! May it thus greet me upon the morning of my accomplishing the desire of my heart!"

"SIR HATCHET LOOKED ACROSS THE GLITTERING WATER UPON HIS RIGHT, AND SAID: "I SEE, REFLECTED UPON THE BOSOM OF THE BAY, THE SNOW-CLAD PEAK OF FUJI-SAN.""

Toward evening they arrived at their destination, and were warmly welcomed by their fellow conspirators. From that time Sir Big-rock, Jr. assumed a position of responsibility, and assisted in the task of watching the enemy.

Soon after Sir Hatchet and his companion departed for Yedo, Sir Big-rock began to examine his papers and arrange them in order, like one who prepares for death. When he had completed this task, his maid-servant, Carnation, entered the room, bringing a cup of tea, which she presented to him, remarking:

"Honorable master, you have not taken any refreshment to-day. I beseech you to drink this."

He drained the vessel and gave it back; then, as she turned to depart, called to her, saying:

"Carnation, I am growing tired of this lonely life, and am about to go upon a journey which will occupy me until the end of the year. Here are your wages, and money to cover the house expenses while I am absent. Have everything in readiness, so that if I return suddenly I may not be annoyed by finding the place in disorder. It is possible my son may come back before me and bring some friends with him."

The girl listened attentively to his instructions, and bowing, said:

"Honorable master, everything shall be done as you command. Will you, before leaving, kindly speak to Mr. Left-six and Mr. Happy-seven, who annoy me with their attentions?"

Her employer smiled, and regarding her, replied:

"Have no fear, Carnation, I intend to take those men with me. The only person who will remain with you will be old Grandson-left-gate-keeper."

The overjoyed girl retired, and Sir Big-rock presently heard her informing the aged servant of his determination. In a few moments Grandson-left-gate-keeper appeared in the doorway, and prostrating himself, said in a troubled voice:

"Honorable master, is it true you have decided that I shall not accompany you?"

"Yes," was the reply. "I require a responsible person here to receive any of my friends who may call. You will, in my absence, take charge of the house."

This delighted the old man, who saluted his master, and retired with an important air.

That evening Sir Big-rock proceeded to the temple of the Snow-clad Pine, and received the *sambo* and white-wood box.

Early the next morning, the neighbors saw the Chief-councilor and his two servants quit the house, behind them being a hired coolie laden with their baggage.

"HER EMPLOYER SMILED, AND REGARDING HER, REPLIED:
"HAVE NO FEAR, CARNATION, I INTEND TO TAKE THOSE MEN
WITH ME.""

CHAPTER XXIV.
SIR HATCHET'S LETTER TO HIS WIFE.

"I met my love and talked with her until the moment of parting.
No sooner had I quitted her presence than I remembered a
thousand things I had left unsaid."

One night toward the end of December, 1701, the wife of Sir
Hatchet received a package from her husband, and upon opening it,
discovered a box, some poems, and a letter. Proceeding to her room,
she lighted the lamp in a tall lantern, and kneeling upon the matted
floor, spread the epistle before her, then clasping her hands, regarded
the characters and exclaimed:

"When I see the writing of my husband, my tears fall like a shower.
Even in the midst of his anxiety he remembers me."

After she became somewhat composed she read the
communication, which was as follows:

"I send you a few lines. I have not heard from you since I left home,
and in consequence feel very unhappy. Rest assured I am quite well.

"I said you might begin to write about five days after my
departure, and thinking there might be a letter from you at the address
I named, yesterday made inquiry, but found none had arrived. Are
you still at our home? If you are lonely, why not take some one to live
with you or go to reside with a friend? Oh how I pity you, knowing
you must miss the beautiful objects of art and the furniture to which
you have been so long accustomed and which you sold to defray my
expenses hither! You must feel in the absence of those things as though
the house had grown larger. I dare say you also miss the many callers
who visited us when we were together. I fancy I can see you sitting
lonely and comfortless. I pray you will endeavor to conquer your grief,
as I am trying to do mine.

"Has Wisteria-three returned the money I loaned him? You had
better urge him to do this. I hope Wisteria-help has paid the principal
and interest due me. Be careful not to be cheated or robbed.

"Yesterday, the first monthly anniversary of our mother's death, I
felt very sad, not being able to visit her tomb, so, in order to disperse
my melancholy, called upon our adopted son, who gave me some
good *saké*, and comforted me by saying you would do everything
necessary and pay the priests for praying for the repose of our dear
parent's soul.

"WHEN I SEE THE WRITING OF MY HUSBAND, MY TEARS FALL
LIKE A SHOWER."

"I resume my pen to-day, the 29th November, having written the foregoing whenever I had a few moments to spare.

"Last night I received your letters of the 15th and 16th inst., which gave me great happiness. I seemed, while perusing them, to be talking with you, and read them slowly, so as to get the full sense of every word.

"You say you still have the pain in your left ribs; that you cannot sleep on that side; also that your pulse is weak. You have done well to consult Dr. Village-cottage. Remembering what you have suffered, I am not surprised you are sick. Sorrow always produces diseases of the body. You must not allow yourself to grieve so much; you are friendless enough, and it is important you should take care of your health. Your answer to Wisteria-help, the district registrar, was perfectly correct. If he troubles you with further enquiry, tell him to wait until the end of the year, when he will hear from me. I am not astonished there are many rumors with regard to Sir Big-rock, and it pleases me to hear none of the people suspect the truth.

"I am glad you visited the tomb of our mother and distributed the alms; also that the tomb-stone was finished and placed in position, and the stone-cutter's bill was so reasonable.

"Although our separation is the result of a determination made long ago, yet we both sorely feel the sadness it has brought about. You say, during the day your occupation prevents you from dwelling too much upon your misery, yet when night comes you cannot sleep from thinking of me. My poor, dear wife, I feel the same as you do. The saying, 'Not seeing is forgetting,' does not apply either to you or me. As the days pass, the greater grows our sorrow; still, if we reason correctly, we will find each misfortune is a step toward the attainment of wisdom. You already know these things, yet, by reflecting upon them, will gradually learn the philosophy of human life, and thus soothe your sorrow. Our duty is not to lament over what is irreparable, but to bear the misfortunes inflicted upon us by the gods; yet, my dear wife, I pity you.

"You tell me you are pleased with my poems, especially that upon the Osaka Pass. I greatly admire those enclosed in your letters. By the way, I hope you will not give up composing verses, but will write one whenever you have a spare moment and send it to me. During my journey hither, I had little to disturb my mind and could think about verse-making; however, since my arrival here, I have been surrounded by visitors and have had little time for correspondence.

"I am sorry to tell you bad news. The fact is, Sir Kira is hiding somewhere, and, like a badger, does not give any sign of his whereabouts. I hope, now that every arrangement has been made, our enemy will not slip through our fingers.

The younger members of our party are full of courage. Sir Lucky-field, Sir Common, Sir Unconquerable, Sir Early-crop and myself being the seniors, are in hourly consultation and arrange everything for the others. Yesterday the theatres opened for the winter season, and the boys, including our son, took a holiday and went to witness the performances. We live in bachelor style, the juniors doing the house-work and waiting upon us at meals. They treat us very kindly. We all have nicknames. They call me 'doctor,' saying I have a forelock growing like a physician's. The sleeves and linings of my clothes are beginning to wear, but, remembering I shall only be here for a little while longer, I have let them go. To-day our son, noticing a large rent in my coat, insisted upon sewing it up, and I allowed him to have his way. During the night I put on all my garments, as it is very cold here. You said I had better take another suit with me, I am exceedingly sorry I did not follow your advice.

"Yesterday I went to a store to buy some geese, and seeing they were very nice and reasonable in price, bought an extra one, which I have had boned and salted. You will receive it in a box with this letter. There is no necessity for you to soak it, as it is only slightly corned. Make it into soup, and when Dr. Valley-cottage calls, give him some of it with *saké*.

"Since writing the above I have removed to the house of Big-rock, Jr., which is some distance from where our son is staying.

"Remember, my beloved wife, I am well in health, so try to comfort yourself. You may at any moment receive the welcome news.

"I have written this letter under circumstances of great difficulty. You will hear from me up to the last moment.

"November the 30th,

"To my dear Brilliant,

"HATCHET."

CHAPTER XXV.
THE MEETING IN THE SPRING-HILL TEMPLE.

"Our most fervent vows of vengeance are made in the peaceful abodes of the gods."

The leaguers knew Sir Big-rock was in Yedo, but few of them saw him, though all felt the power of his presence. From the first to the tenth of December, everyone was actively employed in endeavoring to discover the whereabouts of Sir Kira, spite of which they were unsuccessful, their enemy having vanished like a cloud. They haunted the vicinity of his son's residence and even penetrated into the mansion, yet all they could learn was that he had quitted the place for parts unknown. The younger of the conspirators became greatly excited, finding which Sir Big-rock summoned them to meet him in the Spring-hill Temple.

At the hour of the Fox (10 P.M.) on the 11th of December, a number of men stealthily approached the sacred building, and by midnight the leaguers were all assembled in a large apartment behind the main altar. The priests guarded every entrance and took care that no one should surprise their visitors. A dead silence reigned in the dimly-lighted hall, and the conspirators, who knelt in two rows, eagerly awaited the arrival of their chief. As the midnight hour was struck upon the great bell, Sir Big-rock slowly entered the hall. In his hands he bore the *sambo* and white pine box, which, having placed upon the *tokonoma*, he respectfully saluted. After returning the bows of his comrades, he directed Sir Common to call the roll.

Forty-seven *ronins* answered "Here."

The flickering, red light of the candles feebly illuminated the apartment, and little could be seen save the pale faces of the clansmen, who, advancing close to their leader, crouched in a semicircle about the *sambo*, the contents of which were unknown to most of them.

Sir Big-rock remained for a moment with his head bowed, as though in deep thought, then, gazing upon them, said:

"Brothers, three years ago our beloved lord committed this legacy to my charge. Since that time some of his followers have proved faithless to their plighted words; those we leave to the vengeance of the gods and the contempt of their fellow-men. We, who are here assembled, have been thrice tried and I have waited patiently, bearing everything that we might some day be in a position to perform our too-long deferred duty. Our enemy, powerful and vigilant, had to be deceived into believing that we were disloyal and many things had to be done ere we were prepared to strike the blow. I yesterday received information that Sir Kira, disbelieving in our devotion to our honored chief, is about to return to his home, and that on the anniversary of the death of our beloved lord he will give a feast to his friends. On that night he shall cease to live. We care not how closely he may be guarded. Be there ten thousand men at his command, we will cut our way through them and accomplish our aim."

This speech was received with murmurs of approval, the conspirators grasping the hilts of their swords, as though eager to attack their enemy.

Sir Big-rock removed the lid of the box, and took from it a package wrapped in a purple cloth. After raising this to his forehead, he opened the folds and revealed a blood-stained dirk, exclaiming as he exhibited it to the assembly:

"This is the weapon that shall end Sir Kira's life. I swear by the hundred million gods never to leave his residence until our duty is performed."

The conspirators, aroused to frenzy by his words, pressed forward, and reverently touching the dirk, joined in his vow; then, after receiving instructions as to their places of rendezvous on the night of the 14th, silently departed to their lodgings, leaving him kneeling, and regarding the legacy of his chief, in which attitude he remained till daybreak.

Before quitting the temple he gave audience to Noble-plain, the contractor, and inspected the uniforms and accoutrements provided by the latter, and that done, retired to his lodging in a house opposite the residence of Sir Kira.

CHAPTER XXVI.
SIR SHELL AND HIS FAMILY.

"At the call of duty, the *samurai* bids farewell to those who are dear
   to him.
"Though the face be calm and resolute, the heart may be
   surcharged with sorrow."

"My dear husband, are you going to Original-village to-day?"

"Yes, my love, it will never do for me to remain idle. If I were to die
suddenly and we had nothing laid by, how you would suffer."

The speakers were Sir Shell and his wife, Mrs. Home, who had
been married nearly three years. In the ardor of his wooing he had not
reflected upon the consequences of tying the thread of love; however,
after their union, when he had time for reflection, he thought:

"I know I have acted indiscreetly, still what could I do? I tenderly
love my wife, yet cannot prove faithless to my lord, and when the time
comes, must tear myself away. The past cannot be recalled. Home is
young and attractive, and will, I hope, find some one to console her for
my loss."

This comforted him until their son was born, when he discovered
the grievousness of his mistake and found he had two helpless beings
dependent on him. Thus, while the advent of the babe was a source of
great happiness to the mother, the sight of the little one filled the
father's heart with pity and sorrow, and he secretly reproached himself
with being the cause of the misery he knew must soon overtake them.

On the morning of the 12th of December, when Sir Shell was
proceeding home from the Spring-hill Temple, he determined to
inform his wife of their approaching separation. Upon beholding her,
his courage failed, so, after eating his breakfast, he went out for the
day to watch the residence of Sir Kira.

As he quitted the house, his wife thought to herself:

"What is the trouble that has come upon my husband? He goes out
late in the evening and returns at all hours, and is often moody and
thoughtful. I wonder whether I have done anything to make him so
unhappy? Even the smiles of our little one have ceased to attract his
attention."

That evening after sunset, Mrs. Home lighted the charcoal in the
fire-bowl, and seating herself near her work-box, began to sew upon a
garment for her husband. Her babe, Also-five-boy, was sleeping

peacefully on a rug by her side, with his arms extended and his head resting on a cushion, near him being his toys—a mottled dog, a rattle, and a rag doll. While she was thus employed, Sir Shell entered, and after depositing his sword in the *katana-kake* (sword-rack), seated himself by the fire-bowl, and having lighted his pipe, said:

"Dear Home, there is something I have long desired to tell you."

"What is it?" she enquired, glancing anxiously at him.

He thought for awhile and replied:

"It is necessary I should go upon a long journey. I may have to start very soon."

"My dear husband, I am ready to accompany you at any moment. Also-five-boy is now old enough to travel and will not be any trouble. Really, the news delights me. I hope we are going to Ako, as I would like to visit your native place."

Sir Shell laid down his pipe, and folding his arms, said in a gentle voice:

"My dear Home, I am not going to Ako. The journey I am about to make is not a matter of one or two hundred miles, but a long and tiresome one, and there are many perils to be encountered on the road. Indeed, I may never return alive."

"Still I would prefer to accompany you," she pleaded.

"That will be impossible," he said. "I have thought it all over and decided it is best for you and our son to remain here. Surely you do not desire to risk his life? It will be bad enough for you to part with me. No, no, my dear wife, you remain here and take care of our boy while I go to better our fortune."

He then produced a package of money which Sir Big-rock had given him that afternoon, and handing it to her, continued:

"This sum will last you for a long time."

The agitated woman burst into tears and covering her face with her sleeves sobbed convulsively.

Sir Shell, who felt as though his heart were torn to pieces, regarded her pityingly without being able to reply. He realized, for the first time, the full force of the sacrifice he was about to make, and as he watched her and their sleeping babe, scalding tears trickled down his cheeks and dropped upon his hands.

After awhile the agonized woman made a great effort and said, as she pointed to the child:

"My honorable husband, I understand all. You wish to cast me off. I, who have brought you nothing but anxiety and misery. I feared this was coming and have no reproaches to make; but, even though you do not love me, I beg you will think of our child, and put off your intention until he is old enough to remember your face. Oh, bear with me for his sake and do not let him suffer for my faults! You tell me you have to go upon a long journey, that is your kind pretext for putting me away. Alas, alas, that we ever met in the restaurant at Asakusa! Would I had died before that day, then I should never have known this great sorrow! Were you a cruel husband I might find comfort in your decision, but you have always been most kind and affectionate. When this child was born I felt doubly happy in believing he would be the means of strengthening our love."

She threw herself at his feet, and after uttering a despairing cry, exclaimed:

"O honorable husband! I pray you to put an end to our lives! I cannot exist without you!"

The distracted man bowed his head and was utterly unable to reply. He suffered untold agony in the conflict between his love and duty, and in the prospect of leaving his dear ones for the journey to the unknown; and, biting his lips, felt as though he would have to break his loyal vow.

"AS HE WATCHED HER AND THEIR SLEEPING BABE, SCALDING TEARS TRICKLED DOWN HIS CHEEKS AND DROPPED UPON HIS HANDS."

The babe awoke and crawling toward his mother peered up at her face; then, hearing her sobs, began to cry piteously, thus adding to their sorrow.

Sir Shell, no longer able to bear the sight, hastily arose, and quitting the house, paced the street, leaving his wife to comfort the babe.

The hours passed until the distant sound of the temple bell announced the arrival of midnight, when Sir Shell crept back to his home and, halting in the porch heard Mrs. Home singing:

"Nen neko okorori nen neko yo.
Obo san yoiko da nen neko yo;
Obo san ga nen neko shita ato dé,
Yama saka koyete ikimashite,
Aka no omamma ni toto soyete
Oriko na obo san, no mezameni agema sho."

TRANSLATION.

Sleep, sleep, my good baby, sleep.
While my gentle baby slumbers,
I will go over the mountains and through the valleys
and fetch some red-bean rice and fish.
When my clever baby awakens,
I will feed him with the red-bean rice and fish.
I will go over the mountains and through the valleys.
Sleep, sleep, my good baby, sleep.

The husband listened with heaving breast and troubled face; then, as the sad air died away, quietly entered his dwelling and stretched himself upon his bed.

At last the angel of sleep threw his shadow over the abode of sorrow, and, for a brief space, caused the inmates to forget their unhappiness.

CHAPTER XXVII.
SIR BIG-ROCK MAKES REPARATION TO HIS WIFE.

"Judge no one until the grass has grown upon his grave.
Only the gods know the secrets of our souls."

On the morning of the 13th of December, Sir Big-rock rose early, and after devoting several hours to writing, summoned his servants, Happy-seven and Left-six, whom he thus addressed:

"The time has arrived when I no longer require your services. I desire you will both proceed to Rich-cliff and take with you these letters and this package, which you will personally deliver into the hands of my father-in-law."

The men, having been in constant attendance upon him, were aware of the conspiracy and had hoped to die with their employer. Happy-seven bowed humbly and said:

"Honorable master, we pray you will allow us to remain with you to the end. We desire to attend you upon your last journey. This is the determination we made long ago."

Sir Big-rock listened attentively and replied:

"I will be frank with you. The hour is at hand when the clansmen will carry out their long-cherished plan. It is impossible for me to grant your prayer, as none but the members of the league will be permitted to join in the attack. If you wish to serve me, do as I request, and devote the remainder of your lives to attending upon my family."

When the men heard this they wept and begged he would reconsider his decision, and it was with difficulty he restrained them from ending their lives there and then. At last, Left-six dried his tears and said in a choking voice:

"Honorable master, we will obey. I see it is not fit for such common fellows as we are to take part in your glorious enterprise."

"Yes," said Happy-seven, "as long as we live we will remember your goodness, and serve your honorable family as faithfully as we have done you."

They then received their wages and the letters and package, and set out for their destination, feeling sure that the time of attack was close at hand.

Sir Big-rock's communications were addressed respectively to his father-in-law, his wife and his children. The first was a long epistle in which the *samurai* narrated the history of the conspiracy, and commended his family to the guardianship of his father-in-law. The third was to his sons, giving, among other things, a list of books he desired they should read, also minute instructions for their guidance. The second letter was to his wife, Mrs. Stone, and read as follows:

"By Happy-seven and Left-six, whom I now dismiss from my service and commend to your care, I send you a few lines.

"In the first place I ask you, my dear and honored wife, to forgive me for the apparently brutal conduct with which I treated you. Oh! How I suffered that cold December morning, when my sense of duty compelled me to tear myself away from you and put upon you the stigma of divorce. It was my only means of deceiving our enemy, and nothing I have done has been so effectual in blinding him as to my real designs. You have, in bearing this injustice, done your duty as a wife and member of the clan, and your sacrifice will be fully recognized by our honored chief. My dear love, though I shall never see you again in this life, my spirit will be ever present, watching over your welfare and that of our children.

"WHEN THE MEN HEARD THIS THEY WEPT AND BEGGED
HE WOULD RE-CONSIDER HIS DECISION."

"I can now face death without a pang, knowing you will understand what has hereto appeared unnatural in my behavior. Admirable wife and noble mother, your name will be remembered longer than my own, for you have made three offerings at the shrine of loyalty—your husband, your son, and yourself.

"I now bid you a temporary farewell. Oh, wife of my heart! When the duty to our lord is accomplished and I have departed to the land of shadows, think of me as tenderly as you have done during my life, and when the time comes for you to travel the Lonely-road, rest assured I will be waiting to greet you at the termination of your journey.

"I leave the education of our sons entirely to you, and hope my poor example will teach them to live and die loyal men and to be true to their duties.

"Herewith I send you a letter from our brave son, Good-gold.

"To my dear wife, Stone.

"BIG-ROCK."

CHAPTER XXVIII.
THE MISSION OF SIR HAWK'S-GROVE.

"Snow was in the air and on the house-tops, and the geese flying
high overhead could not be seen by the passers-by."

On the morning of the 14th of December the wind suddenly shifted
to the north, thick white clouds piled up upon the horizon, and soon
the air became filled with feathery particles of snow, which continued
to descend until the city of Yedo was covered with a white veil.

Few people ventured into the streets, and the cold gradually
became intense.

Toward noon a *samurai*, dressed in a rain-coat, entered a
buckwheat-vermicelli restaurant at the western end of the Two-
Provinces Bridge, and after saluting the proprietor, said:

"Mr. Long-time, I have come to ask a favor and to say I am about to
bid you farewell. First of all let me have a drink of *saké* and some of
your famous vermicelli. This snow-storm is enough to chill one to the
marrow."

The proprietor ordered a servant to bring the refreshments, then,
squatting by his friend, said:

"Mr. Hawk's-grove, or rather, pardon me, Sir Hawk's-grove, for I
perceive you are no longer a merchant. What do you mean by saying
you are about to bid me farewell? Has your tobacco business proved
an unfortunate speculation?"

"Yes, somewhat," replied the *samurai*. "The fact is I have spent
much to get very little, and the price of rice being high, found it hard
to earn a living. I have been in consultation with some of my former
comrades, who, like myself, are *ronin*. We have had an offer from a
Prince, related to our old master, and have accepted positions in his
service."

"That's good," said the restaurant-keeper. "You remember the old
proverb: 'One cannot make a merchant out of a *samurai*.' Still I am
sorry you are going away, as after knowing you for three years I regret
being obliged to end our acquaintance. When do you start?"

"Not until to-night. During the day the roads are soft; however,
when the moon rises the frost increases, and the traveling will be more
pleasant; besides, as there are over twenty in our party, we shall not
fear the attacks of highwaymen. The favor I have to ask is this. We
intended to assemble in my house and take supper, but my place is too

small to accommodate such a large party. I have come to ask if you will entertain us here."

"Certainly," answered Mr. Long-time. "That is my business. Do you wish me to prepare anything in addition to our usual bill of fare?"

"Yes," said Sir Hawk's-grove, taking a sum of money from his pocket-book. "I will leave this amount in your hands. Please have ready sufficient *saké*, rice, fish and vermicelli to satisfy twenty-five hungry persons."

The proprietor received the coins, saying:

"Although no advance payment is needed from a friend, I will keep this. How late do you desire the repast ready?"

"By the hour of the Fox (10 P.M.)," answered the *samurai*. "By that time all your regular customers will have taken their departure?"

"Yes," sadly replied the other, "between ourselves, my business is not flourishing; so, to make up for the deficiency in my receipts, I have been renting my rooms to *hai-kai* (verse-making) parties, who seldom stay beyond the hour of the Hog (8 P.M.). There is no fear of disturbing my guests; you will have the whole house to yourselves."

When they had chatted for awhile, Sir Hawk's-grove quitted the restaurant, drew his rain-coat tightly about him, and pulled his broad-brimmed hat well over his eyes, so as to shield his face from the blinding snow. He crossed the Two-Provinces Bridge, and entering the street at the rear of Sir Kira's residence, proceeded to a tea-house, where he engaged rooms for a second party, telling the same story he had related to the keeper of the vermicelli restaurant.

Having accomplished this mission he sauntered toward the back gate of the noble's mansion, and taking shelter in a road-side refreshment stall, ordered some tea, at the same time secretly watching all who entered the opposite portal.

"Ah!" laughingly exclaimed the one-eyed patriarch who kept the stall, "this is like old times; I shall be very busy this evening. The great Sir Kira is to entertain a number of his friends, and my kettles will be emptied many times."

The *samurai* pretended not to be interested, and the speaker, who repeatedly slapped his hands to keep himself warm, continued:

"Ah! There will be glorious doings in the mansion. They have made preparations for over a hundred guests. Sir Kira is a very good man. About an hour ago I saw his lacquered *norimono* enter yonder gateway."

The *ronin* handed him some money, then made the best of his way to the house where Sir Big-rock was staying. He informed the Chief-councilor of what he had heard, when the former said:

"Good, the wary eel has entered the trap."

CHAPTER XXIX.
SIR RED-FENCE AND HIS BOTTLE.

"Every one has a hobby, allow me then the ways of Nihon (to make verses).
Provided a man pays for his *saké*, it is no one's business how much he drinks."

Soon after Sir Hawk's-grove made his report to Sir Big-rock, and while the storm was raging furiously, a *samurai*, whose gait betokened he had taken more *saké* than was good for him, staggered along West Street in the district of Small-stone river. His face was red and his eyes had a wild look, still he appeared to know where he was going, and took great care to protect a large earthen bottle that was suspended from his girdle. Every few moments he would pause, raise the skirt of his rain-coat and ascertain if his treasure were safe, then mutter something about the storm and continue his zig-zag career.

This *samurai* was Sir Red-fence, who had a strange history. He was the younger brother of Sir Turf-ground, of the clan of Autumn-moon, and when quite young had been adopted by a family who acknowledged the Lord of Ako as their chief. Unfortunately, Sir Red-fence had a great weakness, an inordinate love for liquor, and was almost constantly under its influence. This failing greatly be-littled him in the eyes of strangers, notwithstanding which he had many times been employed by his lord to conduct negotiations that required great tact and ability. Why was this? Because, even though Sir Red-fence were intoxicated and lying on the floor in a state of stupefaction, he would, at the summons of duty, instantly arise and perform faithfully whatever was entrusted to him, in addition to which he was very eloquent and possessed sound judgment, and in the capacity of ambassador to the princely families, had done his lord good service.

It had generally happened that when he set out upon one of these errands, he was suffering from indulgence in his favorite beverage, and although at first he would endeavor to preserve a dignified appearance, before he had gone a hundred yards he would drop the reins upon the neck of his horse and begin to nod, leaving the animal to go as it pleased and permitting it to crop the grass growing on the road-side. His attendants, shamed by the grins and remarks of the passers-by, would waken their master and respectfully caution him, when, without even opening his eyes, he would mutter:

"Well, well, I know all about it. I am very sleepy."

He would yawn and resume his slumbers until he arrived in front of the residence of the *daimio* to whom he was accredited and heard the loud announcement:

"An ambassador is at the gate!"

From that instant he would become wide awake, and by his dignity of manner command the admiration of the by-standers. He was like the man described in the old saying:

"Although sent in four directions at once, he would still preserve the honor of his master."

Lord Morning-field had great regard for Sir Red-fence, and would often praise him for his ability; while among the clansmen no one was more devoted to their chief than this drunken *samurai*. After Sir Red-fence became a *ronin* he continued to indulge in his potations, and although he often wanted rice, was seldom without liquor.

Having no regular income and being unable to gain his living by any occupation, he depended upon his brother, Sir Turf-ground, a good man, who, recollecting the last injunction of their father, not only furnished the prodigal with money but bought him good clothes.

Unhappily this benevolence was of little benefit to Sir Red-fence, for upon receiving a new suit, he would sell it to the first purchaser of cast off garments he met and invest the proceeds in drink.

His dissolute behavior, while grieving Sir Turf-ground, never lessened the latter's affection, and he continued to do everything in his power for the wayward man, who would haunt his house and amuse the servants with his drunken antics.

Whenever he made his appearance at his brother's establishment, the domestics, although they looked upon him as an unmitigated sot and good-for-nothing, would quit their work in order to listen to his witticisms and watch his comical tricks. This finally became such a nuisance and so seriously interfered with their occupations, that Sir Turf-ground began to wish his brother would visit him less frequently and the lady of the house positively refused to see her relative.

Such was Sir Red-fence, who, bad as he was, had many virtues.

The snow beat into his face and he from time to time was obliged to pause to take breath and ascertain his whereabouts.

"This wintery storm makes one feel as if stone-pins were being driven into one's flesh," he muttered, as he leaned against the side of a house. "I wonder where my brother's residence has gone to, surely it has not been blown away? Thanks to the gods, I have brought my bottle with me. Those at his establishment are usually empty."

His shabby garments, which were partly concealed by a red paper waterproof cloak, and his old straw rain-hat, which he wore athwart his visage, gave him a very disreputable appearance and he in no way resembled "one who remembers his master."

In a few moments he resumed his weary journey, walking unconcernedly through the snow-drifts and puddles, until he reached the side gate of the mansion of Lord Autumn-moon.

After passing the porter, who was crouching over the fire-bowl in the lodge, he halted, and addressing his bottle as though it could understand him, said:

"The cold does not seem to affect you, my old fellow. Of the hundred medical remedies *saké* is the chief."

The porter waited until the visitor was out of hearing, then laughed and remarked to a companion who was sitting near him:

"There goes Sir Red-fence and his bottle, both of them are full of *saké*."

"Would I were like them," replied the other. "A good, warm cup would not be amiss on such a cold afternoon. I have heard Sir Red-fence has never tasted water."

"I wish I could say the same," growled the porter. "I believe the gods supply some people with their drink. Sir Red-fence always has a drop in his bottle."

The object of their remarks, who had assumed a more sober gait, strode across the enclosure and proceeding to the side door of his brother's residence, entered. Upon beholding him, the two maids who were in the kitchen glanced at each other, and the elder quitted the apartment to inform her mistress of his arrival, while the younger, advancing a step or two, knelt, bowed and addressed him, saying:

"Sir Red-fence, you are welcome. You must have felt very cold on your way."

The *samurai* threw aside his rain-coat and tore off his hat without untying the cords, then carefully placing his bottle upon the platform, seated himself near it and smiling at the attendant, replied:

"Girl, I thank you for your kind words, but, as you see, I am warmed with good *saké* and the cold does not trouble me. How is my brother? Is his health affected by this weather? Is he at home?"

"Sir Red-fence, my master is well. At the present moment he is at the mansion, assisting our prince to entertain some guests. I do not think he will return until late to-night."

"Very good. Tell me how my sister is?"

At that moment the other servant re-entered the kitchen and said:

"Honorable sir, my mistress is indisposed. She begs you will excuse her from seeing you."

Sir Red-fence nodded, saying:

"Oh! This severe cold is quite too much for her. I hope she will soon recover."

He spoke indistinctly and the girls imperfectly understood what he said. After awhile he appeared to doze, noticing which the elder of the servants whispered to her companion:

"I will go to my mistress and leave you to wait upon the honorable brother. You are not afraid of him, are you?"

"Not in the least," she replied. "No one fears Sir Red-fence. He never harmed a woman in his life."

When the old servant had departed, the sleeper suddenly jerked himself upright and exclaimed:

"Let me have a cup."

"Of tea?" she inquired.

"Girl! You know I never drink it. I have too much respect for my nerves! Here is some old *saké* which I have brought as a present for my dear brother. Before giving it to you, I will ascertain whether it has been poisoned."

The maid laughed behind her sleeve, and handing him a cup, said:

"Honorable sir, shall I warm the *saké* for you?"

"A thousand thanks," he replied. "I can do that for myself."

He filled the cup and emptied it, repeating the operation several times, while the girl regarded him with an astonished face. The bottle was quite large, and it took him some time to reduce its contents. When only a small quantity remained in the vessel, he shook it and said to the attendant:

"There is too much poison in this *saké*; still the few cups that remain will not do you girls any harm. Accept it from me and finish it before you go to bed."

The damsel received his gift in a hesitating manner and put it aside, after which the visitor rose, and thrusting his toe into the loop of his left clog, which during the conversation had dropped from his foot, said:

"Please be good enough to listen to what I am about to tell you, and faithfully repeat my words to my brother."

"Of course I will, Sir Red-fence."

"Very well, girl. Now listen, and tell him this: Since I became a *ronin* you have been most kind to me, for which I return my heartfelt thanks. My fondness for *saké* has caused you much anxiety and annoyance. I beg you will forgive my offences. At length I have procured employment under a western prince, with whom I am about to start for his province. I came here to say farewell, and am sorry enough to depart without seeing you. Rest assured, even should it happen that I die without again beholding your face, the remembrance of your brotherly kindnesses will ever remain in my heart."

At this point Sir Red-fence dropped a tear, but the girl did not notice it. He then moved toward the door, upon reaching which he turned and said:

"Also tell him: Hereafter and forever I will entreat the gods to make both you and my sister prosperous and happy."

Thus speaking, he placed his hand to his head, and missing his rain-hat returned to recover it, when he found that in pulling it off he had broken the cords. As he was about to envelope his head in a soiled handkerchief, the girl took a hat hanging upon the wall and handing it to him, said:

"Honorable sir, it storms too much for you to go abroad with your head thus unprotected. This is my master's hat; take it and leave your own."

"HONORABLE SIR, SHALL I WARM THE SAKÉ FOR YOU?" "A THOUSAND THANKS," HE REPLIED. "I CAN DO THAT FOR MYSELF."

"I thank you. I must now be off. I hope you girls will have a happy New Year."

He hastily retired, and conquering his sorrowful reflections, hurried through the snow. Within an hour he was perfectly sober, and had joined the conspirators assembled at the grocery-store of the Three-springs.

Soon after Sir Red-fence quitted his brother's house Sir Turf-ground returned, and on receiving the message from his wife, said:

"I regret not to have seen him. He has remained away so long I feared something had befallen the poor fellow. I understand the end of the year is at hand, and he requires my assistance. I am glad to hear he has at last taken service, though it is a strange time for a prince to proceed to his province. I suppose the girl did not comprehend my brother's words, and suspect he is about to depart upon some important errand. This is bitterly cold weather for a journey. I hope he will not meet with any accident. My dear wife, I am really very uneasy about him."

Had Sir Turf-ground known the truth he would have felt proud of his relative, he hoping that Sir Red-fence and the rest of the clansmen of Ako would some day avenge the death of their lord. As it was, he thought only of the profligate, and with difficulty restrained his tears.

His wife noticing his emotion, placed a repast before him, and bade the servant bring some *saké*. The girl produced the bottle left by Sir Red-fence, and minutely described how he had partaken of its contents.

Sir Turf-ground smiled sadly, and when the maid had retired, remarked to his wife:

"Red-fence has only one fault—when there is a bottle near him he forgets everything else. I believe his nurse was a female *Shojo* (a submarine monster of dissipated habits). Even when my brother was a child he cried for *saké*. We see him at a great disadvantage, for I know he possesses many admirable qualities. May be fraternal affection blinds me, still I cannot help loving and admiring him. The other day, when he was sleeping in the kitchen like a dead man, I looked at him, and thought how sad it was he had fallen so low. While I was thus thinking, I noticed his left hand was clenched about the scabbard of his long sword and that he grasped the hilt with his right, showing him to be on his guard. When I advanced he immediately opened his eyes and partly drew his weapon, then recognizing me, rolled over and resumed his slumber. During that moment I observed the blade, unlike its dilapidated scabbard, was as brilliant as an icicle or a fragment of crystal; therefore, believe, spite of his failing, Red-fence is not unmindful of the duties of a *samurai*, and I am certain we shall yet feel proud of him."

CHAPTER XXX.
"SIR BIG-ROCK'S FAREWELL TO LADY PURE-GEM."

"The years have come and gone, and I am still weeping for thee,
my beloved.
My tears fall day and night, like the waters of Nonobiki."

This poem admirably describes the grief of Lady Pure-gem, who, on the third anniversary of her husband's death, had been all the day prostrated before the family altar, where, with Lady Pine-island, she repeated prayers for the repose of the dead chieftain's soul.

Toward the evening, when the storm was abating, she yielded to the earnest solicitations of her faithful attendant, and retiring to her private apartment, partook of some slight refreshment.

"Ah!" she exclaimed, gazing upon a *manrio* plant placed upon the *tokonoma*, "my dear husband wrote his last poem in praise of yonder beautiful object. That flourishes, while my beloved lord is no more; his family name has become extinct, his retainers are scattered like the seeds of a thistle, and oh, terrible thought! His death remains unavenged."

"My honored mistress, do not despair," said Lady Pine-island. "Sir Big-rock will yet be heard from. The fire of loyalty is only slumbering in the hearts of our clansmen."

The widow covered her face with her sleeves, and after sobbing awhile, said:

"I hope your words will prove true. Remembering the nobility of my husband's character, his thoughtfulness for his retainers, his unbounded generosity, and the love they professed to bear for him, I cannot understand why they have permitted the leaves of three autumns to fall upon his tomb without having made an attempt to wipe out the disgrace of his death. Why has Big-rock not sent me some communication? I am living here secluded from the world, and ought to be informed of what the clansmen are doing."

Lady Pine-island did not reply, she having taken great care to prevent her mistress from hearing the strange rumors concerning Sir Big-rock.

About the hour of the Hog (8 P.M.), as Lady Pure-gem was returning to resume her prayers, a servant announced the arrival of Sir Big-rock.

In an instant the mourner's grief appeared to vanish, and she joyfully directed Lady Pine-island to conduct the visitor to her presence.

The attendant made her obeisance and retired, presently returning with the Chief-councilor, who was clad in his ceremonial robes. He advanced with a sorrowful face and grave demeanor, and kneeling, prostrated himself before Lady Pure-gem, remaining with his forehead close to the mat, mute with grief.

Though the lady was likewise deeply moved, through her sadness came a gleam of joy, as she believed Sir Big-rock was there to announce the good news. When she had somewhat recovered from her emotion she requested Lady Pine-island to retire, then filled a cup with *saké* and offered it to her visitor, saying:

"I am told, after you left our castle you went to reside in Yamashina. What has brought you from so great a distance?"

The councilor took the cup, and bowing, drained its contents, after which he replied:

"Most worthy-to-be-honored mistress, in the days of our dead lord's prosperity the responsibilities of my office gave me no time for relaxation, and during my brief visits to this city I had little opportunity for amusement. Although I am only a man of wave-like fortune, I, through the generosity of my honored chief, possess sufficient means for all my needs. You desire to know what has brought me from Yamashina? It is this: having exhausted all the delights of Kioto, I have visited Yedo to enjoy more fashionable pleasures."

The lady listened as though unwilling to credit her senses, seeing which, Sir Big-rock, who was secretly delighted with the success of his words, said:

"I have been to nearly all the celebrated places in this city, and only one more errand remains to be performed — that I shall accomplish to-night. My companions are notified and are waiting to accompany me. I have come to bid you a respectful farewell, as I may not return to Yedo for some years. Meanwhile may happiness and prosperity attend you."

Lady Pure-gem regarded him with amazement, utterly unable to understand the change in his sentiments. Her soul became filled with indignation, and losing her self-control, she exclaimed:

"Ingrate! Are you the loyal retainer of whom my dear lord said: 'Whatever may occur, I desire you will place implicit confidence in my Chief-councilor and regard his words as though they were mine?' Oh, unfaithful and miserable wretch, you have dishonored the name of *samurai!*"

In her agony and despair she grasped a paper-weight shaped like a horse, and hurled it at him.

Sir Big-rock caught the missile, and reverently pressing it to his forehead, replied:

"This parting gift of a horse,[9] I receive with profound thanks. Most worthy-to-be-honored mistress, have you any message for your dead lord in heaven?"

Upon hearing this speech, Lady Pure-gem clasped her hands, and gazing earnestly at him, thought:

"Can it be possible he is still loyal?" then said, in a faltering voice:

"Sir Chief-councilor, I do not understand your meaning."

Sir Big-rock, recollecting how nearly he had betrayed himself, cautiously answered:

"Honored Mistress, I regard your present as though it came from my dead chief. I beg you will now excuse me. Once more I bid you farewell."

He bowed respectfully to the floor, and rising, slowly retired from the apartment, leaving the lady bewildered and shocked at his inexplicable behavior.

The ante-chamber, to which Lady Pine-island had withdrawn, was merely a portion of the main room, shut off with paper screens so as to form a recess. Against the left wall stood an open press furnished with cupboards and drawers for garments; it likewise contained a number of shelves filled with exquisite specimens of porcelain and old lacquer-ware. The chief attendant was reclining behind a paper-screen, her countenance betraying the indignation that possessed her soul. On her left were a pipe, and a lacquered box holding a jar of finely shredded tobacco, and before her a tiny porcelain stove which supported a tea-pot. The other articles furnishing the place were a lacquered tray containing cups, a wooden pillow, a silken-wadded quilt, and a tall, square lantern, the sides of which were filled with semi-transparent paper.

"Madam," said Sir Big-rock, sinking upon his knees and drawing some books from his left sleeve, "here are a few songs and poems I composed on my way from Kioto. In these volumes are described many places of beauty and historic fame. I believe their perusal will greatly interest our honored mistress; therefore, beg you will present them to her and request she will honor me by reading them."

Although Lady Pine-island was intensely indignant with the speaker, she could not refuse the proffered gift, such a proceeding being contrary to etiquette. She took the volumes, opened one of them upside down, and extending it toward him, exclaimed:

"Sir Big-rock, we expected better things than this. It appears, instead of remembering your duty, you have thought no more of it than of a drop of dew, and have been amusing yourself and spending your time in verse-making. Pardon my plain speech. I cannot remain silent."

The other ladies of the household, who one by one had entered the apartment, united in expressing their contempt for his strange behavior; however, Sir Big-rock merely bowed gravely, and taking his short sword from the floor, retired, followed by the young women, who accompanied him to the veranda, and continued their bitter reproaches as long as he remained in sight.

Lady Pine-island slipped the volumes into her sleeve, deeming it would be an insult to present them to her mistress, after which she proceeded to the adjoining room where she found Lady Pure-gem prostrate before the altar, praying and sobbing as though she would die of grief.

"SHE TOOK THE VOLUMES, OPENED ONE OF THEM UPSIDE DOWN, AND EXTENDING IT TOWARD HIM, EXCLAIMED: "SIR BIG-ROCK, WE EXPECTED BETTER THINGS THAN THIS.""

CHAPTER XXXI.
MARSHALING THE CONSPIRATORS.

Sir Big-rock quitted Lady Pure-gem's residence as the temple bells boomed forth the hour of the Fox (10 P.M.). The storm had ceased, and the full moon, shining through the cloud rifts, brilliantly illuminated the grounds surrounding the mansion. On reaching the shrine of the god-Fox, he paused, and gazing upon the snow-laden branches of the bamboos that overhung the structure, said:

"Thus have the loyal hearts of the clansmen been bowed with sorrow. To-morrow's sun will melt your burden and find us freed of a heavy load."

He moved on and passing the guard, who saluted him with profound respect, entered the street. After walking a few paces, he engaged a public *kago* and directed the bearers to convey him to his lodgings. The journey occupied nearly an hour, the distance from the Blue-hill district to the neighborhood of Sir Kira's mansion being over four miles. While proceeding by that noble's residence, they heard sounds of music and revelry, and one of the coolies remarked to the other:

"Sir Kira is giving a great feast; we had better return here. It will be a good place for us to find another patron. We may earn a large sum between this and mid-night."

When Sir Big-rock arrived at his destination, he detained his bearers until he had changed his robes of ceremony for his armor and the uniform provided by the contractor. After doing this he re-entered the *kago* and was conveyed to the buckwheat-vermicelli restaurant, where he was welcomed by his companions and the proprietor, who quickly set before them an excellent repast.

"Gentlemen," said Mr. Long-time, producing a very large and beautiful cup, "I was awarded this as the champion's prize in a game of *hai-kai* (verse-making). Will you empty it with me? On the point of departing upon a journey, drinking from such a cup always brings good luck."

Speaking thus, he placed the vessel before Sir Big-rock.

The conspirators glanced significantly at one another, and were greatly delighted at his words. When all had filled and emptied the cup, the Chief-councilor said:

"Mr. host, we return you many thanks for offering us the use of your treasure. Will you not confer another favor upon us, and recite the verse that won this prize?"

"It was nothing extraordinary," the man replied. "I gained the championship more by good luck than by the elegance of my stanzas. I fear you will deem it a very poor composition."

"Oh no! Oh no!" they cried. "We are sure it is a most excellent poem. Please oblige us by reciting it."

"Well," he answered, "as you insist, I will comply. This is my poor attempt at versification:

> "During the night
> Sings high in the sky
> (What?) a nightingale."

"That is very good," exclaimed Sir Big-rock. "It may also be read thus:

> "In the world
> What will always attain eminence?
> (This) genius.

"Your poem has set me verse-making. Please bring me writing materials. I will borrow your first stanza and add something to it."

He took a brush, and leaning upon his sword, bent forward and wrote:

> During the night
> Harder grows
> (What?) the icicle.

Upon completing this he turned to Sir Big-eagle, and handing him the brush, remarked:

"Now see what you can do. We will have a verse-making match."

The *samurai* thought for a moment, and wrote:

> The cry of the sparrow-eagle pierces the sky.

To this Sir Hatchet added:

> Already the big *saké* cup has been emptied.

The last to write was Sir Big-rock, Jr., who composed the following:

> The red glow fills the hall of the Pine-trees.

These impromptu verses showed the spirit of their writers, and that, even in the presence of death, they were calm and resolute. Among the party were some more proficient in warfare than in verse-making, who looked on respectfully, yet failed to comprehend the hidden meaning of the sentences.

Sir Unconquerable was of this number. After he had disposed of a good meal, he whispered to Sir Big-eagle:

"HE TOOK A BRUSH, AND LEANING UPON HIS SWORD,
BENT FORWARD AND WROTE."

"Why does that poetry so greatly please our comrades? For my part, I cannot see any sense in it."

His companion replied in a low voice:

"Listen. 'During the night harder grows the icicle' may be read thus: 'During the night sharper grows the blade of the sword.' My verse also means: 'The sound of the whistle pierces the air.' Sir Hatchet's stanza signifies: 'Already Sir Kira has fallen,' and the poem of Sir Big-rock, Jr., may be interpreted in this manner: 'The red glow of the combat fills the hall decorated with the representations of Pine-trees,' the apartment in which Sir Kira has entertained his guests."

Sir Unconquerable's grim visage relaxed into a smile, and filling a cup with *saké* he drained it, then said:

"I understand, this is the hour of the poets; later on I will try to distinguish myself. My poetry is written with the point of my sword."

While the conspirators were feasting, Sir Big-rock noticed the absence of Sir Shell, and conjecturing the cause, quietly called Sir Cedar-valley aside and whispered:

"Your friend, Sir Shell, has not yet arrived. I think it will be as well for you to seek him. In parting with wife and child, one forgets how the time flies."

Sir Cedar-valley retired from the assembly and hastened to the house of his friend, whom he found preparing to depart. Mrs. Home was weeping bitterly, and the child was clinging to her and lisping:

"Mamma, mamma, papa shall not go."

Sir Shell glanced at the visitor, as a condemned man does at his executioner, then turned from him, and folding his arms, endeavored to control himself.

"Comrade," said Sir Cedar-valley, crouching near him, "your companions are ready to start. I am certain you will not be the one to delay our journey."

For a moment Sir Shell remained mute and irresolute, after which, remembering his duty, he gazed sorrowfully at his beloved ones, and silently bidding them adieu, quitted his home, leaving his wife prostrate on the floor, like one struck down by lightning. The last sound he heard was the voice of little Also-five-boy, pitifully exclaiming:

"Papa! Papa!"

When he joined his companions at the restaurant, he seated himself with a calm air and in no way betrayed the distraction of his soul.

Sir Big-rock did not appear to notice Sir Shell's entrance, which had been accomplished so quietly that few of the party knew he had not been with them all the evening.

Toward midnight the conspirators quitted the restaurant and proceeded across the Two-provinces Bridge. The cold was intense, and they did not encounter any one on their way.

Upon arriving at their rendezvous, a spot called Rush-island, they were joined by the second division from the tea-house.

Here they remained until the hour of the Ox (2 A.M.), when they were formed into two companies; the first under Sir Big-rock, and the second led by Sir Big-rock, Jr., assisted by Sir Lucky-field. Each man was clad in uniform, and carried in his sleeve a document describing the reason for the attack, to which were affixed his names and a description of his personal appearance.

The following instructions, issued by Sir Big-rock, were copied from the original document, preserved to this day in the Spring-hill Temple:

1. Do not make any mistake in replying to signs and signals. At the sound of the drum, beaten according to the code of Yamashika, nine

times in three turns, both the front and rear companies are simultaneously to advance.

2. Remember the watch-words—they are most important, and have ever, during the night attacks of all ages, been thus regarded.

3. To the challenge of "Mountain," give as a counter-sign, "Spray," "Bubble," or any word referring to water.

4. To the challenge of "River," answer "Rock," "Valley," or "Top," or give a word referring to mountain.

5. Reply as quickly and as clearly as possible, and avoid combating with a friend.

6. As soon as we have gained an entrance to the residence, search for the enemy's weapons, cut the strings of their bows, destroy the arrows, and break the spears.

7. Put out all lights and pour water into the fire-boxes; the darkness will prevent our opponents from ascertaining our numbers, and the steam from the embers will greatly alarm them. After that be ready to light your candles.

8 . Each man shall carry a bottle of alcohol for the purpose of dressing wounds and making flashes to dismay the foe.

9. Each shall also carry two candles and two bamboo pins to be used for sticks.

10. Before starting take some medicine. Do this, no matter whether you be well or sick; sudden excitement often makes a strong man ill.

11. Do not fail to have your distinguishing letter, not only on your uniforms, but also upon your weapons and accoutrements.

12. Each shall carry a *yatate* (pocket writing-case).

13. After securing an entrance, bar all the doors and guard the places of exit.

14. Each shall carry a blue silk wrapping cloth.

15. When Sir Kira is found, his captors must blow three prolonged blasts upon their whistles, to which every one will respond, then all will assemble on the spot where he is discovered.

16. Do not kill women or children, or any of the enemy who are unarmed.

At the moment when the leaguers were advancing upon the residence of Sir Kira, that noble, inflamed with his potations, was reclining upon his bed, thinking of the pleasures he had lately enjoyed, and never for an instant imagining that the hour of retribution was near.

CHAPTER XXXII.
SIR SMALL-GROVE.

"Good deeds are good seeds;
Bad deeds are foul weeds."

In chapter eighth I related the story of the young merchant, Mr. Bright-stone, and his wife, Little-tiger. I will now fulfil my promise, and describe how they were enabled to return the great kindness shown them by Sir Small-grove, Chief-councilor of Sir Kira.

It will be remembered that the young people were adopted by a mirror-maker. This good man died within a few months after he received them into his family, on hearing which Sir Small-grove advised Mr. Bright-stone to remove his place of business to a street adjoining the residence of Sir Kira.

On the night of the attack, Sir Small-grove, who had been all day in attendance upon his chief, was preparing to retire to bed, when he heard the sound of a drum followed by whistling and the crash of falling shutters. Comprehending in a moment the nature of the disturbance, he hastily awoke his little daughter, whom he loved very dearly. After cautioning the child not to make any outcry, he took her in his arms, and quitting his house, hurried across the enclosure to a corner of the grounds where stood the temple of the god of war, the rear eave of which overhung the street. Sir Small-grove procured a fire-ladder, and ascending to the roof, deposited his burden upon the snow-clad slope, then drew up his means of escape and lowered it on the other side of the wall. This accomplished, he took the child upon his arm, rapidly descended to the street, and started at a run toward the house of Mr. Bright-stone, the inmates of which were fast asleep, and who at first were greatly alarmed by his summons. After a brief delay, during which they had ascertained the name of their disturber, Mrs. Little-tiger directed their boy-servant to withdraw the bolts securing the entrance. When that was accomplished, their visitor pushed aside the door, and entering "the mouth of the house" hurriedly handed his daughter to the lady, who anxiously enquired:

"What is the trouble, Sir Small-grove? Is your dwelling on fire?"

The *samurai* paused a moment, then replied:

"It is as I have often predicted. The calamity, so long deferred, has at length overtaken my master. The *yashiki* is invaded, and I have no expectation of surviving the combat. For myself I care not; my only grief is on account of this dear child, who has already lost her mother, and who, after my death, will have no one to care for her. Remembering this I have snatched a few moments of most precious time to bring her to you. My last wish is that you will bestow your kindness upon her."

"SIR SMALL-GROVE, ENTERING "THE MOUTH OF THE HOUSE"
HURRIEDLY HANDED HIS DAUGHTER TO THE LADY."

He then rushed away without waiting to hear their assurance that "not even an ant should harm the little one."

Sir Small-grove remounted the useful ladder, and hastening to the mansion, threw himself into the thick of the fray, being particularly anxious to keep the leaguers from entering the sleeping apartment of Sir Kira before that noble had time to escape.

He guarded the door with indomitable bravery, and although desperately wounded, contrived to keep his assailants at bay, until, overpowered by numbers, he fell like a true *samurai*, and died in the act of defending his chief, his last effort being to hurl his sword at one of his opponents.

The whole mansion was a scene of confusion, and the cries of the women and children rose loud above the sounds of the combat. Barriers were forced, doors broken down, and the banqueting hall with its decorations of pine trees, crimsoned with the blood of both parties.

Outside, the bright stars twinkled in the clear sky, and the pale moon illuminated the snow-covered landscape.

When the conspirators entered Sir Kira's chamber, they discovered an empty bed. Though Sir Big-rock eagerly listened for the three blasts upon the whistle, no sound was heard but the clashing of weapons and the execrations of the combatants.

"THE WHOLE MANSION WAS A SCENE OF CONFUSION."

CHAPTER XXXIII.
SIR BIG-ROCK'S GIFT.

"The long night is at an end.
Brightly shines the sun of loyalty."

While the combat was raging in the mansion of Sir Kira, Lady Pine-island was seated by the fire-box on the floor of her apartment, thinking of Sir Big-rock.

Her companion was still in attendance upon their mistress and her own maid away visiting, so she felt lonely and disinclined to seek her bed. After smoking several pipes she took the books from her sleeve, and as the golden moments melted, sat musing with a heavy heart, her thoughts running thus:

"The much trusted and long looked-for Sir Big-rock has been here, and the result is a bitter disappointment to us all. How different he is to what we have believed him to be; how rude and stupid! Why, he did not appear to understand the cause of our lady's just indignation, and after outraging her feelings, left these volumes for her. How strangely unreliable is the human heart! There is now no longer any hope of avenging the wrongs of our house. Alas! How well I know it!"

The hours passed swiftly, and presently drowsiness overcame her loyal spirit; her fingers relaxed, the books slipped from her grasp and she slumbered. Then the sliding-door upon her right was gently pushed back and some one stealthily entered the apartment.

The noise, slight as it was, aroused the sleeper, who, fearing treachery, pretended to be unconscious, and with partly opened eyelids watched the intruder, a maid servant she had lately engaged, whom every one believed to be half witted.

The lady closely followed the other's movements, and soon discovered her object was to obtain possession of the volumes. As the thief stretched forth her hand, Lady Pine-island picked up a pipe and dealt her a sharp blow upon the knuckles. This did not stop the girl, who seized the books and endeavored to make off with them; whereupon her mistress, who now began to comprehend the creature's treachery, grasped her by the robe and exclaimed:

"We have been fools to imagine you were one. Ah! You are a spy sent by our enemy, Sir Kira. Wretch! I command you not to move another step."

The intruder finding herself and mission discovered, struggled violently to escape; however, her captor held her firmly, crying:

"Help! Help! There's an evil-doer in my chamber. In the name of our lady, I entreat for assistance."

There was a rush of persons from all parts of the house, and the girl was quickly secured and consigned to safe quarters.

When the ladies had retired and Pine-island somewhat recovered from her agitation, she took the books from the floor, and opening the first of them, began to peruse its contents. After reading a few pages, she placed her hands upright, palm to palm, and exclaimed:

"Spirits of my ancestors! What have I done? This very night Sir Kira is to be punished. The death of our dear lord and the dishonors heaped upon his house, have by this time been avenged. I now understand the motives of Sir Big-rock whom—alas!—we treated so contemptuously. He feared that spies might have entered our household, therefore dared not even whisper the truth, believing, if he did so, the news might be conveyed to Sir Kira and thus put him on his guard. The Chief-councilor indeed came to bid us a long farewell. The act of that wretched girl proves the vigilance of our foe and the necessity for Sir Big-rock's caution. I must hasten to my lady and communicate this joyful intelligence."

She then hurriedly arranged her *obi* (girdle), and taking the volumes in her hand quitted the chamber. As she did so the crowing of the roosters announced the dawn of day. Upon entering the corridor she beheld the ladies-in-waiting sitting in groups, and heard them commenting upon the events of the night.

"Be quick and prepare yourselves to attend upon your mistress," she cried. "You will shortly be required to receive important visitors." At these words they scattered to their apartments and were soon busy with combs, powder and paint.

The chief-attendant found Lady Pure-gem asleep, notwithstanding which she awoke her and related the welcome news.

"Pine-island," joyfully exclaimed the widow, "draw aside the window-screens."

When this was done they beheld the sun-goddess slowly arise from her bed among the purple clouds. The rays glinted across the snowy landscape and all nature appeared to rejoice, while the words written by the Chief-councilor, illuminated with happiness the soul of the Lady of Ako.

"The gods be praised!" she fervently ejaculated. "The spirit of my murdered husband will now rest in peace."

CHAPTER XXXIV.
RETRIBUTION.

"In the day of his power his voice was loud and arrogant.
When justice overtook him he crouched mute and terrified."

It was the hour of the Tiger (4 A.M.); the combat between the large body of well-disciplined warriors who defended the residence of Sir Kira and the small company of resolute leaguers was at an end, and the aides of Sir Big-rock were searching the *yashiki* in order to discover the fugitive noble, when Sir Straight-grove and Sir Lull, Jr., entered a charcoal-house in the rear of the mansion and began to probe the packages with their spears. While they were thus engaged, some one secreted behind a pillar hurled a bag of charcoal at Sir Straight-grove, then rushed at him furiously. At the same instant a second assailant confronted Sir Lull, Jr.

The fight was brief, and the conspirators were the victors.

"Come," said Sir Straight-grove, taking his dark lantern from his belt and flashing the light upon the scene, "where you find one snake it is as well to look for others. Those fellows did not attack us without good cause."

They minutely searched the building, which was half filled with bags of charcoal and billets of wood.

"What is that in yonder corner?" said Sir Straight-grove, advancing to the far end of the shed. "Is it a dog?"

He stooped, and to his delight discovered the object was a man, dressed in a white satin sleeping-robe, blackened all over with charcoal.

Upon being addressed the fugitive refused to reply, finding which Sir Lull, Jr., dragged him out of the corner, and his comrade, turning the light upon the prisoner's face, exclaimed:

"It is Sir Kira! There is the scar upon his forehead!"

The overjoyed *ronin* gave the signal agreed upon, and the forty-five came hurrying to the spot.

Sir Big-rock directed the captors to bring their prisoner into the yard, then proceeded to ascertain the truth of the announcement; meanwhile his followers gathered round and silently awaited the result of his investigation. After looking intently at the blackened features of the man, he said:

"Yes, this is Sir Kira."

He knelt before the trembling noble, and addressing him respectfully, said:

"Sir Kira, we are the retainers of Lord Morning-field, who, at your instigation, was condemned to *hara-kiri*. We have come hither to avenge him, and thus perform our duty as faithful, loyal men. We pray you will acknowledge the justice of our purpose, and beseech you to perform upon yourself the honorable ceremony. I will have the honor to act as your second."

Sir Kira glanced furtively at the assembled conspirators but stubbornly refused to reply, whereupon Sir Big-rock, finding it was useless to persuade him to die the death of a noble, produced the dirk of his dead lord, and handing it to Sir Lull, Jr., directed him to make use of it.

When the day broke the victorious leaguers quitted the *yashiki*, and forming into companies, proceeded across the Two-provinces Bridge toward the Spring-hill Temple.

After marching a short distance, Sir Big-rock ordered a halt, and summoning Temple-cliff, bade him communicate the news to Lady Pure-gem.

CHAPTER XXXV.
THE COMMENTS OF THE CROWD.

"I listened to the voices of the people and heard of the noble deed
done in the night."

The morning of the 15th of December dawned clear and bright, and
the household of Sir Turf-ground slumbered peacefully. To the family
of a *samurai* one day is like another, and there is no difference between
the first month and the last; to the merchant, the settling of accounts
causes December to be a busy time.

It was nearly the hour of the Dragon (8 A.M.) when Sir Turf-
ground, who was still in bed, heard the sound of many persons
passing his window, and voices in loud conversation.

"Look! There they go along that street," cried one. "Come quickly."

"Here, Good-fellow, I must leave you and hurry on by myself. You
move more like a tortoise than a man. We shall not get a glimpse of
them."

"Wait a moment. Confound it! You surely will not go without me. I
was the one to tell you the news."

"Look! Look! They are coming this way," cried a woman. "Hurry,
my son, or we shall miss them."

Then came a noise of persons moving over the frozen snow, and a
dull roar, such as is made by a crowd when admiring a procession.

At first Sir Turf-ground did not pay much attention, but when he
heard the people murmuring their applause, he hurriedly arose,
dressed himself, thrust his swords into his belt, and opening the
window, beheld the people running toward the end of the street. He
called to his wife and while he was interrogating her, one of the
spectators shouted to him, saying:

"Have you seen them? By the gods, it is a glorious spectacle!"

"What is?" demanded Sir Turf-ground. "Tell me the news."

"The *ronin* of Ako have attacked the residence of Sir Kira and taken
his head. They are now on their way to deposit it upon the tomb of
their lord."

As the man was speaking, a store-keeper came rushing up the
street, crying:

"They have just entered the *yashiki* of the Lord of Sendai. Be quick
if you wish to see them. It was a sight to behold the brave ones forcing

their way in regular order and guarding themselves according to the rules of war. Ah! They are loyal and faithful men!"

Sir Turf-ground listened attentively, his first thought being of his brother, and he whispered to his wife:

"I am certain Red-fence is one of that party."

He went out into the veranda where he found his old servant, who was on his knees playing with a pair of puppies, and whom he thus addressed:

"First-fellow, do you know the truth about this great excitement?"

"Yes, my master. Upon hearing the noise I and many persons quitted the *yashiki* and entered the street in order to investigate the matter. The *ronin* of Ako have performed their duty and are now returning. I am sure Sir Red-fence is with them."

"FIRST-FELLOW, DO YOU KNOW THE TRUTH ABOUT THIS
GREAT EXCITEMENT?"

"I know not what to think," said Sir Turf-ground. "The other *ronin* being the hereditary retainers of the Lord of Ako, might be willing to avenge their master's wrongs, but my brother was only affiliated to the clan, added to which he is generally under the influence of *saké* and would, I fear, be unable to take part in such a glorious deed. Yet there is a strange coincidence between his message to me last night and the rumor of this morning. I agree with you in believing he is with them. If this is so, it will be not only a great honor to him, but also to me."

"Honorable master, shall I run out and ascertain?"

"Stay one moment, First-fellow. If I send you on such an errand and my brother is not among the noble band, I shall become a laughing-stock. You had better go out as though by accident. Having ascertained the truth, come back quickly."

"Very well, honorable master, I will return as soon as possible and ease your mind."

He ran to the kitchen and procured a basket and account-book, as if he were going to market, then went out by the side-gate and pushed through the dense mass of people.

After the servant was gone, Sir Turf-ground paced the veranda and prayed to the gods that his brother might be found among the loyal men.

First-fellow moved in and out between the spectators congregated upon the avenue leading to the residence of the Lord of Sendai, and kept his ears open for news.

Presently a tall man, in the front rank of the crowd, looked back and said:

"No one will be able to go any further. The watchmen of the Lord of Sendai have formed a line across the street in front of the residence and made a fence with their clubs."

"*Oi*, Silver-boy!" cried a broad-shouldered fellow, "have you seen them?"

"Yes, I caught a glimpse of the party as they entered the gate. They must have fought bravely, for their armor was cut all to pieces, and many of them were desperately wounded."

Then a number of persons spoke at once, saying:

"Are they going to stay inside?"

"I hope they will soon come out."

"What gallant men!"

"This is just what we expected of the *ronin* of Ako."

Every one was enthusiastic over the courage and loyalty of the forty-seven, and adding rumor to rumor in the exaggerated fashion of a crowd, they wore the time away.

"Pine-boy," exclaimed a young clerk, "where have you been? You look as though you had spent the night in emptying a jar."

The man addressed, who was nodding as though half asleep, opened his eyes and replied:

"Ah! Seven-fields, my boy, is that you? You have, as usual, missed a great sight by not going with me."

"I do not miss your headache," retorted Seven-fields.

"You are mistaken," answered the drowsy man. "I drank very little *saké*; the fact is, I spent the night at the residence of my cousin, Plum-garden, who lives near the *yashiki* of Sir Kira. As we were retiring to bed, we heard the sound of the drum and the crash of the attack, whereupon we ascended to the roof of the house, which overlooked the grounds of the noble's mansion. By the gods! It was a tremendous fight. The armies on both sides, with their banners flying, fought in four directions, the war-cry sounding from the earth to the heavens, and for awhile it seemed as if the mighty mountains would be rent asunder. Presently, from the attacking army, issued a warrior on horseback, clad in purple armor, with a coat of red and white—"

"One moment," cried Seven-fields. "What are you romancing about?"

"I am relating what I heard at the lecture in New Street the other night," replied the joker. "Why don't you attend there and illuminate your mind?"

The young men laughed, and one of them remarked:

"Pine-boy, you are always telling stories; why do you not sometimes speak the truth?"

The merry fellow made a grimace, and glancing round him, answered:

"Because fiction is considered more interesting than history. *Oi*, you in the front rank, do you see anything of the second party of the *ronins*?"

The people craned their necks, and Seven-fields eagerly exclaimed:

"Is there a second party? I thought all the leaguers had entered the mansion of the Lord of Sendai."

"Oh! You are quite behind the times," laughingly remarked Pine-boy. "The second company is far more numerous than the first. It is composed of the ghosts of Sir Kira's men."

As he spoke there was a movement among the watchmen who guarded the entrance to the *yashiki*, and soon the cry went up:

"See, they are coming out!"

"Yes, yes, here they are!"

The people crowded forward, and the noise of their tongues was like the roar of advancing waters.

CHAPTER XXXVI.
SIR RED-FENCE WINS GOLDEN OPINIONS.

"The crooked tree often produces fine fruit.
A sword forged by Masamune is sometimes found in a second-
hand store."

The *ronin* had been entertained by the Lord of Sendai, who, on hearing of their approach, had sent a messenger inviting them to enter his mansion and partake of refreshments; his action showing to the world his thorough approval of their deed.

Upon quitting his residence they formed into three companies, and with their arms ready for use, marched boldly forward.

First-fellow elbowed his way into the front rank of the crowd, and eagerly waited for the approach of the companies.

The vanguard, led by Sir Unconquerable, whose armor hung about him like the rags of a beggar, went by, but though First-fellow closely scanned their faces he failed to see the object of his search.

Then came the second division, under Sir Big-rock. This company, the largest, was almost entirely composed of wounded men, many of whom were carried in *kago* (litters). As these passed, the crowd commented upon the fact, that while a great number of the defenders of Sir Kira were killed, not one of the *ronin* had fallen in the attack.

First-fellow, who began to feel very nervous, anxiously watched for the arrival of the third company. As they came in sight his apprehension vanished, for, marching at the head, he beheld Sir Red-fence, who, instead of walking with his usual unsteady gait, advanced with a firm step and a martial bearing that elicited the admiration of the beholders. His head was bare, his helmet being pushed back and suspended from his neck by its cord; his brow was bound with a white ribbon, and in his hand he carried a spear.

He soon perceived his brother's servant, whom he beckoned to him and thus addressed:

"I am glad to see you, First-fellow."

The man went upon his knees in the snow, and bowing his head to the ground, said:

"Sir Red-fence, I offer you my hearty congratulations. You look very weary."

"If I do, I am not sensible of any such feeling," was the reply. "Last night I went to bid my brother farewell, and was unfortunate enough to miss seeing him, and, to add to my regret, my sister was indisposed and unable to receive me. After leaving them, I, with others, paid a visit to Sir Kira whom we found at home."

While the *ronin* was addressing First-fellow, the latter rubbed his hands together and chuckled to himself as though delighted at beholding such a change in his employer's relative, and when the latter ceased speaking, he replied:

"This morning as soon as my honorable master was told of the attack, he ordered me to run with all speed and ascertain whether you were among the noble band. When he learns the good news his heart will leap with joy. I am delighted to be the bearer of such glorious tidings."

Sir Red-fence laughed heartily and said:

"The fact was my brother rather doubted my presence here? Come now, First-fellow, acknowledge the truth."

"Honorable sir, you are indeed mistaken. The moment we heard what had occurred, my master and mistress, myself and all our people, immediately said 'Sir Red-fence is one of the loyal men,' and I rushed off to ascertain whether you were wounded, and to learn from your own lips the particulars of the victory."

The *ronin* smiled significantly and handed his whistle and spear-badge to the man, saying:

"Present these, my last gifts, to my honored brother. Tell him that we have avenged our master's death and, bearing the evidence on our bodies, are proceeding to his tomb at the Spring-hill Temple, where we hope to join our honored lord. I send both my brother and his wife a parting prayer for their happiness." He next removed his purse from his girdle and presenting it to the kneeling man, said in a kindly voice: "This is for you. Now, First-fellow, I must hurry away or I shall be left behind. Take care of yourself and be diligent in the performance of your duties."

Uttering these words he turned and hastened after his comrades who were already at some distance. For a few moments First-fellow was unable to suppress his joy; meanwhile the crowd collected about him and began to ask questions.

"Look at him!" he cried, as though the *samurai* were still present. "Honorable sirs, that is Sir Red-fence, the brother of my honorable master. He was adopted into the family of Red-fence of the clan of Ako and is one of the party of avengers."

"Why, old fellow," remarked a tanner among the spectators, "what are you talking about? The gentleman you are praising is out of sight."

"PRESENT THESE, MY LAST GIFTS, TO MY HONORED BROTHER."

"Ha! Ha! Ha!" laughed the bystanders. "He is crazy with joy."

These remarks brought First-fellow to his senses, and springing to his feet he ran with all his speed toward the residence of his employer, whom he found anxiously awaiting his arrival.

First-fellow fell upon his knees and, panting, exclaimed:

"Honorable master, I could not return a moment sooner."

Sir Turf-ground's heart beat so quickly that he was unable to reply in his usual voice, and could only whisper:

"Have you seen my brother? Not a shadow of him, I suppose?"

"You are wrong, honorable master. Be happy, he was there. I found the avenues crowded with people. *Samurai*, merchants, old and young, men, women and children, were mingled together without any distinction. I pushed my way through them and, as I neared the residence of the Lord of Sendai, beheld the loyal men emerging from the gateway. There were some fifty of them, and though nearly all were wounded, they offered a bold front and advanced in battle array. It was a stirring sight."

"Wounded did you say?" anxiously enquired Sir Turf-ground. "How is it with my brother?"

"He is uninjured," replied the servant; then, sitting up, he slapped his hands on his knees and exclaimed: "Ah! He is a brave man. As he marched at the head of the third company every one applauded him. Instead of the shabby swords to which our eyes have been so long accustomed, he wore beautiful weapons, the scabbards of which were inlaid with gold and silver, and his spear bore ample evidence of having been used. When he called 'First-fellow' I was so overcome that my heart ceased to beat."

"My thanks to the gods," said Sir Turf-ground. "How bright has the world become to me!"

The servant took the whistle and badge from his bosom and as he handed them to his master, said:

"Sir Red-fence sent these to you and bade me repeat this message: 'Brother, I am on the road to death, receive these trifles as my parting gift.' To me he gave this purse of money. Oh! How we have misunderstood him! He is a most loyal, noble man."

First-fellow burst into tears, overcome with the recollection of the scene through which he had just passed.

Sir Turf-ground, no longer able to repress his emotion, wept with joy, feeling happy beyond measure that his brother should have so nobly fulfilled the first duty of a *samurai*, and conferred honor upon the house of his ancestors.

He dismissed his servant with warm words of approval, and hastened in-doors where he received the congratulations of his wife and the maids. The latter fully appreciated the gallant conduct of their master's relative and were loud in their praises of the once despised Red-fence.

The news soon spread through the *yashiki*, and the house of Sir Turf-ground was crowded with the clansmen of Autumn-moon, who complimented him upon the loyalty of his brother, all agreeing that it was not only an honor to the clan of Ako but also to their own. In their enthusiasm each begged for some memento of Sir Red-fence, and hearing of the bottle, asked for a few drops of the *saké*, with which they bathed the crowns of their heads. Having done this they put on the old rain-hat and prayed that the spirit of its owner might inspire them to follow his example.

Sir Turf-ground, who regarded the earthen vessel as a precious relic, wrapped it in a piece of purple silk and placed it in a box among his treasures.

This souvenir is said to be preserved by his descendants, even to the present day, and is the foundation of the well-known story of "Red-fence and his *saké* bottle."

CHAPTER XXXVII.
SUMMONING THE WITNESS.

"Though the sun is shining, and the snow has melted from the face of nature, our sleeves are moistened with tears."

While the *ronin* were being entertained by the Lord of Sendai, the messenger despatched by Sir Big-rock arrived at the residence of Lady Pure-gem and requested permission to see the mistress.

As soon as his arrival was announced, Lady Pine-island entered the reception hall, and saluting him, said:

"I should imagine by your appearance that you are the messenger we have been so anxiously expecting. Surely I remember your face. Are you not the loyal soldier, Temple-cliff?"

He bowed and replied:

"That is my humble name. I come from the Chief-councilor to bring you joyful news."

"Follow me," she said; "my lady must receive the information from your lips."

She conducted him to the presence of her mistress and announced him, saying:

"This is Temple-cliff, who comes from Sir Big-rock."

Lady Pure-gem glanced at his torn garments and battered armor, which explained more eloquently than words the desperate nature of the attack, and felt that even this humble soldier had done his duty to her beloved husband.

Temple-cliff prostrated himself at the entrance of the apartment, and after saluting her, proceeded in a rough, yet graphic fashion to relate the events of the night. His words, though homely, were full of eloquence, and deeply moved the hearts of the listeners.

As he spoke the tears streamed down his cheeks, and at the conclusion of his recital he bowed his head to the mat and remained exhausted with his effort.

Lady Pure-gem, after directing one of her attendants to give Temple-cliff a cup of *saké*, ordered him to be conducted to a room where he received proper attention and nourishment.

At the hour of the Horse (noon), a number of persons applied for entrance at the outer gate, and upon being granted admittance, proved to be Sir Arrow-head and one Temple-west, a servant of Sir Big-rock.

They were accompanied by six footmen and twenty coolies, who bore the following packages:

Three locked trunks covered with oil paper.

A wooden box labeled "Books."

A small box containing a letter.

Nine thousand *rio* wrapped in paper.

Lady Pine-island directed the party to be conducted into the garden opposite the room in which her mistress was seated.

When the messengers saw Lady Pure-gem, they knelt and bowed their faces to the ground, after which the coolies and foot-servants advanced, placed their burdens upon the veranda and retired out of sight, leaving Sir Arrow-head who still remained in a respectful position.

"What is the meaning of this?" demanded Lady Pure-gem. "Arrow-head, come into the house and explain your mission."

The *samurai* rose, stepped upon the veranda, and prostrating himself, said:

"Your Lady-ship, I come from the Chief-councilor who is now with the loyal clansmen at the tomb of our honored lord. Sir Big-rock desires me to say this to your Lady-ship: 'At the surrender of the castle, I, as Chief-councilor, removed a large sum of money which I had the right to take. I have expended a portion of the amount for the support of certain members of the clan and for the armor and weapons required in carrying out our duty. There are nine thousand *rio* remaining which I beg your Lady-ship will accept. I also forward an account of my disbursements.'"

Lady Pure-gem was profoundly moved by this speech, which not only proved the bravery and loyalty of the Chief-councilor, but showed he was anxious to provide for her future comfort.

"My honored and beloved husband spoke most truly," she exclaimed. "Big-rock is a man of a hundred thousand, brave, honorable, fertile in resource, patient under difficulties, and a thorough statesman. Can any one excel him?"

She then whispered to Lady Pine-island and retired greatly agitated.

The chief attendant ordered the servants to see to the messengers, and when this was done they were conducted to the apartment of their mistress, who feasted them with many dainties and rewarded them with expressions of approval.

"YOUR LADY-SHIP, I COME FROM THE CHIEF-COUNCILOR."

During the meal she made minute enquiries concerning each of the *ronin*, and, as she listened to the sad stories, wept over their sufferings and privations.

When the messengers were dismissed, Temple-cliff, who was the bearer of a letter from Sir Big-rock to his wife, set out for his destination, and Sir Arrow-head departed for the Spring-hill Temple. As the *samurai* quitted the residence, he encountered a third messenger, Sir Three-village, who, hastily saluting him, entered the house and asked permission to see their mistress.

Lady Pure-gem immediately agreed to grant him an interview.

On being admitted into her presence, he bowed profoundly, and raising his head, thus addressed her:

"Honorable mistress, I am charged to deliver this message: 'We, the loyal men, having betaken ourselves to the tomb of our late lord and expecting soon to be in the hands of the authorities, beg that some one be at once despatched from the household of your Lady-ship to witness the offering we are about to make to the spirit of our honored chief.'"

The lady reflected for a moment, then said to her chief-attendant:

"Pine-island, will you proceed with all despatch to the Spring-hill Temple and in my name thank each of the loyal retainers for his devotion to my never-to-be-forgotten lord. At the same time you will ask Big-rock to forgive me for ever having mistrusted him."

Lady Pine-island bowed and replied:

"I am conscious of my inability to perform so sacred and important an errand, yet to this and all your commands I joyfully assent."

She then dressed herself in her ceremonial robes and, entering a *norimono* (litter), was borne swiftly from the Western Hill to the region of the Eastern Sea.

Sir Three-village followed her, and when they arrived at the Spring-hill Temple, announced to the Chief-councilor:

"Comrade, the witness deputed by our lady is in the waiting-room."

Sir Big-rock bowed and replied:

"Conduct her hither. We will now proceed with the ceremony."

CHAPTER XXXVIII.
BURNING THE INCENSE.

"I knelt before the tomb of my chief and reverently addressed his
noble spirit."

The afternoon sun, descending to its resting-place behind the hills,
feebly struggled through the leafless branches of the trees that
surrounded the little cemetery of the Spring-hill Temple. In the centre
of the enclosure was the tomb of Lord Morning-field, consisting of
three tiers of stone, surmounted by a massive, upright slab, which bore
the *mon* (crest) of the house of Ako and the posthumous name of the
daimio.

"Reiko in den Mayeno Shosho
Chosantayu Suimo Genri Daikoji."

(Great-peacefully-reclining-*samurai* of the Cold-shining mansion,
who, blowing aside a hair, revealed the hidden spirit of loyalty in his
retainers; and who, during his life, enjoyed the honorable title of
Major-General and The-great-man-having-the-privilege-of-audience-
with-the-Mikado-(Emperor).)

The tomb was enclosed with a stone railing and surrounded by a
platform of the same imperishable material, the slabs before the
entrance being depressed a few inches so as to form a pathway.

Upon the second step rested a *mizuhachi* (stone trough for water),
on each side of which were stone vases containing evergreens, among
the latter being branches of the beautiful *manrio*.

Maku (cloth screens used for the purpose of enclosing a camp) had
been erected around the edge of the platform, and the spot thus shut
off from the gaze of the spectators who swarmed about the approaches
to the cemetery.

As the bell of the temple slowly announced the hour of the Ape (4
P.M.), Lady Pine-island was conducted inside the enclosure and
assigned a place, after which the *ronin*, who were resting in various
attitudes, rose to the respectful position, and Sir Big-rock, addressing
Sir Lull, Jr., said:

"Comrade, present our offering."

The *samurai* removed the cloth which covered an object resting
upon a white-pine *sambo*, and raising the burden, slowly advanced
inside the railings and deposited it upon the third step, then retired
backward. As he did so a priest approached the tomb and set a

lacquered *Dai* (stand) upon the flag-stone. On the stand was a bronze urn containing live charcoal, and a large jar filled with grains of incense.

The *ronin* then took their positions on the platform, Sir Big-rock kneeling nearest to the tomb on the left, and the others forming a semi-circle, his son occupying the second post of honor on the right.

The scene was most solemn and impressive, and Lady Pine-island bowed her head in her sleeves and wept audibly.

Sir Big-rock, whose face was pale with suppressed excitement, rose, and advancing to the incense stand, prostrated himself, remaining several moments with his forehead close to the stone. Outside all was hushed, and no sound could be heard save the sobs of Lady Pine-island.

After a long pause the Chief-councilor took a scroll from his bosom and read as follows:

"December 15, 1701.

We have this day come to do homage at your tomb, all of us being most willing to lay down our lives in your cause. Spirit of our dead Lord, we reverently announce this to you. Three years ago, you, our honored and beloved master, were pleased to attack Sir Kira, for what reason we know not. You, our honored and beloved Lord, were compelled to put an end to your life, but Sir Kira was permitted to live. Although we fear after you have submitted to the decree, you will be displeased at our having resisted it, still we could not refrain from doing our duty. We have eaten your food and partaken of your bounty; we are yours in all things and have ever remembered the command of Confucius. We would not dare to present ourselves before you in paradise without having carried out the vengeance you began. 'Every day we have waited has appeared like three autumns,' yet, notwithstanding our loyal desire, three autumns have come and gone since we received your legacy. Verily 'we have trodden the snow for one day, nay, for two days, and have tasted food but once.' The old, feeble and sick, the young and strong, have come here joyfully to end their lives. Although men laughed at us as at the sickle-insect, which, trusting in the strength of its puny weapon, will attack a team of horses and bring itself to grief, we have never halted in our duty. Your enemy has hidden himself like a bat, and we have had great difficulty in finding him at home. Last night we called at his residence, and this day have escorted him to your tomb."

The Chief-councilor paused in his reading, and producing the dirk from his bosom, rose, advanced to the *sambo* and deposited the weapon by the offering; then returned, knelt behind the incense-stand and resumed:

"This dirk, which you, our honored and beloved Lord, used upon your enemy and employed to sever the thread of your existence, and which, in your last hour, you solemnly committed to our charge, we now return. If your noble spirit be present, we entreat you, as a token, to once more grasp your weapon, and, a second time, strike the head of your foeman and thus forever end your feud.

"This is the prayer of your forty-seven humble retainers."

Sir Big-rock placed the document upon the tomb and all present prostrated themselves.

After a moment that seemed like an age, they felt the massive structure shaken as though by an earthquake, then came the sound of a dull thud, resembling the stroke of a dirk, and the weapon dropped from its place and fell near the right hand of Sir Big-rock, who reverently received the gift, and raising it to his forehead, cried:

"Master, we thank thee! Now, come what may, we fear not, for you have approved of our deed. Oh noble spirit! Wait a little longer and you shall be once more surrounded by your loyal retainers."

The *ronin* listened to this speech with awed faces, then bowed to the ground and wept tears of joy.

When they became somewhat composed, the Chief-councilor took a few grains of incense from the vessel, and throwing them upon the burning embers, exclaimed:

"As this sweet perfume ascends from this vase, so will my soul soon leave its worthless body and join thee, my honored and beloved Lord, in the land of shadows."

He returned to his seat, and taking the roll-call, opened it and said in a firm voice:

"Big-rock, Jr."

His son bowed, and addressing his parent, said:

"Sir Chief-councilor, there are others who should precede me in this solemn act. Sir Straight-grove, Sir Lull, Jr., Sir Common, Sir Hatchet, Sir Unconquerable, Sir Cliff-side, Sir Thousand-cliffs, Sir Island-in-the-front, Sir Red-fence, Sir Shell—nay all should precede me. I, being the junior, ought to be the last to make my respectful offering."

The *ronin* admired the humility of their young comrade, and murmured approvingly; then Sir Big-rock said:

"Your words fill me with happiness; Sir Straight-grove and Sir Lull, Jr., shall precede you."

Sir Straight-grove advanced and performed the solemn rite, then bowing a second time, prayed for the repose of his mother's soul.

Sir Lull, Jr., took a large pinch of incense, the smoke of which was wafted like a dark cloud toward the offering on the *sambo*.

As Sir Big-rock, Jr., returned to his place he beheld, above the canvas screen surrounding the tomb, the peak of Fuji-yama, and remembering his wish, smiled and saluted it.

Sir Lucky-field, an old man who followed him, on resuming his seat, thought:

"The sun of to-day has dispelled the heavy snow of yesterday. The act I have just performed has relieved my soul of a grievous burden."

Next came Sir Lucky-field, Jr., who, like his father, felt at peace with all the world, and made his offering with a heart full of gratitude.

This young man was succeeded by Sir Common. As the latter shook the incense upon the coals, big tears trickled down his cheeks, for he remembered the heroic deed performed by his mother.

Following him came Sir Hatchet who was, as usual, calm and dignified. After he had performed the rite, he seated himself next to Sir Common, and bowing his head, thought:

"The approval of our Lord fills our hearts with happiness, the reflection of which will render joyful those who are dear to us."

While he was thinking, his adopted son, Sir Hatchet, Jr., made his offering.

Then came Sir Moat, Sr., a very old man, who had been desperately wounded in the attack, and who was supported by his son, Sir Moat, Jr. The patriarch spilt some of the incense, noticing which he said:

"That is a good omen; I shall not die of my wounds, but shall end my life like the rest of my comrades."

After father and son had returned to their places, Sir Lull, Sr., feebly rose, and motioning his sons to remain seated, crawled toward the incense stand, dragging his left limb, which bore a frightful wound. Notwithstanding his injuries, he made his offering in a resolute manner and spoke in a voice audible to those outside the enclosure.

This brave man was followed by his second son, who, having performed the loyal rite, returned to his parent, when the latter said:

"My only regret is I have not forty-seven sons to join in this joyful ceremony."

He was succeeded by Sir Shoal, Sir Shoal, Jr., Sir Inner-field and Sir Inner-field, Jr., who burnt incense and addressed the spirit of their dead Lord.

"Sir Shell!" called the Chief-councilor.

The young *ronin*, who had sacrificed so much, advanced with a firm step, and being unable to use his right arm, made his offering with his left. He bowed silently and invoked the spirit of his chief, saying:

"Oh, beloved master! I pray you remember my helpless wife and child!"

As he rose, Sir Cliff-side prepared to take his place. He, too, thought of his family, but remembering the words of his wife and the benevolent act of the god-Fox felt comforted.

This noble *samurai* was followed by Sir Tide-field and Sir Rich-grove, who, being severely wounded, were carried by their comrades, Sir Arrow-head and Sir Swift-water. These assisted the maimed men to make their offerings.

Sir Pure then advanced, and having performed the rite, resumed his seat, thinking:

"I shall soon make my last journey. This time I shall not require *kago*" (alluding to his quick and painful trip from Yedo to Ako).

Sir Red-fence next responded to his name and reverently followed the example of his comrades. As he resumed his seat, he produced a bottle and cup, and addressing the Chief-councilor, said in a low voice:

"Having accomplished the duty required, I will now empty a cup of congratulation."

Sir Big-rock did not reply, knowing full well it would be easier to check a mountain torrent than to prevent *saké* from descending his comrade's throat.

Sir Tree-village, Sir Rush-valley, Sir Near-pine, Sir Thousand-horses, Sir Cedar-field, Sir Cliff-island and Sir Middle-village then answered to the summons, five of them being too badly crippled to burn the incense without help.

"Sir Unconquerable!"

The *ronin* rose slowly, as he did so the remnants of his armor fell upon the pavement, noticing which he kicked them aside and advanced to the stand.

This *samurai* took a handful of incense, and while it was being consumed, grimly watched the object on the *sambo*. He then offered a brief prayer; as he resumed his place he said to Sir Hatchet:

"The falling of the fragments of my armor, and my ragged condition, reminded me of the time when you called my name from the portal of the castle, though then my heart was heavily burdened, while now it is, like my body, free from encumbrances."

After him came Sir Village-pine, Sr., Sir Store-bridge, Sir Village-pine, Jr., Sir Faithful-friend, Sir Rush-field, Sir Arrow-field, Sir Victory-field, Sir Cliff-field, Sir Cross-river and Sir Three-village. These men being among the wounded, though not completely disabled, assisted one another.

When they had retired, Sir Island-in-the-front, Sir Thousand-cliffs and Sir Big-eagle, made their offerings. The Chief-councilor then said in a loud voice:

"Temple-cliff!" adding: "In the absence of our brave comrade, I will perform the rite for him."

Sir Big-rock burnt the incense, having done which he sent for the chief-priest, who, with his assistants, entered the enclosure, and advancing before the tomb, offered prayers, to which the *ronin* listened respectfully.

At the conclusion of the ceremonies, the Chief-councilor bowed to the *Sojo* (superior of the priests) and said:

"Will your reverence be good enough to take charge of our offering and have it disposed of according to the usual custom?"

The *Sojo* gravely returned his salute and replied:

"Sir Big-rock, it is our duty to attend to the dead."

After the priests had retired, Lady Pine-island completed her errand, and, in the name of her mistress, thanked the loyal men for their devotion to their late lord; then addressing the Chief-councilor, commenced the message she was charged to deliver, on hearing which he politely interrupted her, saying:

"Pardon me, I only carried out the last wishes of my honored and beloved chief. My honored mistress thinks too much of the poor services I have been able to render her." He bade the lady a respectful farewell, remarking:

"You were indeed fortunate to be present when the spirit of our honored chief gave its approval to the act we have performed. May you always be happy and enjoy good health."

As he finished speaking, one of the priests approached him and said:

"Sir Big-rock, the officers of the Sho-gun are in the reception hall and desire your attendance."

At the hour of the Hog (8 P.M.) a procession left the grounds of the Spring-hill Temple. First came a number of armed retainers carrying lanterns, decorated with the *mon* (crest) of Lord Narrow-river, Prince of Higo, who guarded a body of the *ronin*, including Sir Big-rock. Next a second detachment, consisting of *samurai* in the service of Lord Pine-plain, escorting twelve of the ronin, Sir Big-rock, Jr., being among the number. Following these marched the retainers of Lord Mori, who were in charge of the third division of prisoners; then came a party of *ronin* who were in the custody of *samurai* belonging to the house of Lord Water-field.

They moved silently and proceeded slowly, in order that the coolies bearing the litters which contained the wounded, might not increase the sufferings of the loyal men.

Upon reaching the heart of the city the procession separated, and the officers in charge conveyed their prisoners to the *yashiki* of their respective lords.

From that time, pending the decision of the authorities, the *ronin*, though treated with the greatest consideration, were neither permitted to receive visits from their friends nor communicate with them. They were, in fact, dead to the world.

CHAPTER XXXIX.
THE RONINS REJOIN THEIR LORD.

"Fully conscious of having performed my duty, I joyfully salute the messenger of death."

The authorities, having imprisoned the *ronin*, were exceedingly perplexed how to act, their sympathy being entirely with the loyal band.

Early on the morning of the 4th of February, 1702, Lord Narrow-river entered the hall in which Sir Big-rock and his companions were confined, and after enquiring concerning their condition, said:

"It appears to me you must feel very weary of this sort of existence; however, be the news good or bad, I imagine you will soon hear from the Council. Although you are not permitted to receive favors from your friends, still there is no law to prevent me from endeavoring to serve you after your sentence is passed. Can I, in any way, show my appreciation of your loyalty?"

Sir Big-rock gravely saluted him, and replied:

"My Lord, in the name of my comrades, I thank you for the many kindnesses we have enjoyed at your hands. Your benevolence has made us forget we were prisoners and emboldens us to ask this favor. We desire that our bodies may find a resting-place near the tomb of our beloved chief. Could we be assured of this, we should die without a shadow of regret."

The *daimio*, who was greatly affected by this speech, thought for a moment and replied:

"Unfortunately I have no authority in such a matter, yet I here pledge my honor to do everything in my power to bring about what you so ardently wish. Rest assured it shall be accomplished. I have now a favor to ask—a souvenir of yourself—which I will bequeath to my descendants as a precious relic."

Sir Big-rock went to the writing-stand, took up a brush and wrote:

"*Ara ureshi, omoiwa harura miwa sutzuru;*
Ukiyono tzuki ni kakaru kumonashi."

(I am indeed happy, for my desire is accomplished, though, in doing it, I have sacrificed my life.

The moon is no longer obscured by clouds.)

He then bowed respectfully and handed the paper to the *daimio* who received it with many expressions of satisfaction.

As the noble ceased speaking, an officer entered and announced the arrival of the commissioners of the Sho-gun, whereupon Lord Narrow-river saluted the *ronin* and quitted the hall. After a brief interval, one of his councilors entered, and behind him came a number of retainers bearing white dresses and *kamishimo* (ceremonial costumes), which they distributed among the prisoners, who were requested to prepare themselves for their sentence.

The *ronin* cast aside their garments and joyfully assumed the snowy robes; having done which they followed their guide to the audience chamber, where they found the commissioners and Lord Narrow-river, before whom they prostrated themselves and remained in the respectful attitude. The elder of the visitors took a paper from the bosom of his garment, and after glancing at Lord Narrow-river, read as follows:

"Big-rock, late Chief-councilor of Lord Morning-field, the *daimio* of Ako, and forty-six others.

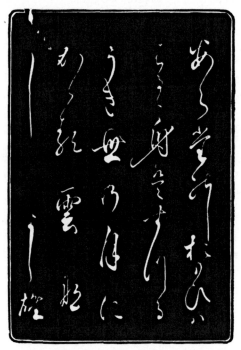

"LAST WRITING OF SIR BIG-ROCK."

"You, men, neither respecting the dignity of the city nor the laws of the country, having conspired against, broken by night into the house of, and slain, Sir Kira, the late master of ceremonies to the august Shogun, Iyetzuna, are, for your audacious conduct, hereby sentenced to perform *hara-kiri*. In addition to this your descendants are banished to the island of Oshima, there to remain during the pleasure of the authorities."

To this the *ronin* replied, as with one voice:

"We acknowledge the justice of our sentence and gratefully return our thanks for being permitted to die such an honorable death."

The commissioners quitted the hall and proceeded to the residences of the *daimio* who had charge of the other *ronin*, to whom they likewise communicated the sentence.

At the hour of the Snake (10 A.M.) Sir Big-rock and his companions were kneeling in two rows upon thick mats placed in the court-yard of the *yashiki* of Lord Narrow-river, behind each *ronin* being two officers who were to act as their *kaishiyaku* (seconds).

In front of the condemned men knelt several *samurai* of the clan of Higo, who were present as witnesses for their lord.

At the same hour and moment a similar scene was enacted in the *yashiki* of Lord Pine-plain, Lord Mori, and Lord Water-field.

Sir Big-rock, whose face and bearing betokened the happiness that possessed his soul, turned to his companions and said in a loud, clear voice:

"Comrades, we will now meet our last enemy!"

Before the sound of the temple bells had ceased to vibrate on the air, forty-six shadowy forms, headed by the spirit of Sir Big-rock, fell into line and began their march down the Lonely-Road.

Together they mounted the Hill of Death, together halted at the place where the three roads meet; here they stripped off their white robes, which they handed to Sanzu-no Baba, and boldly plunging into the dark river, passed over to Gokuraku (Paradise), where they were welcomed by the spirit of their beloved chief.

CHAPTER XL.
THE RETURN OF THE EXILES.

"He who is dutiful to his parents, will be loyal to his chief.
A loyal man cannot fail to be patriotic."

The snows of eight winters had fallen upon the bamboos surrounding the cemetery of the Spring-hill Temple, where forty-seven tombs marked the resting-places of the loyal men of Ako.

On the morning of the 4th of February, 1710, a lady accompanied by two handsome young men, who carried in their hands bouquets of flowers, and followed by a servant, entered the enclosure and proceeded to a tomb which bore the inscription:

"*Zinkuan yoken shinshi.*"

(A true *samurai*, who set an example to all and who used his sword where it was required.)

The visitors were the widow and sons of Sir Cliff-side, and the servant was Original-help, who had on that day returned from their place of exile and come to make offerings at the grave.

After sweeping the tomb, they burnt incense and repeated prayers, then proceeded to the temple where they found assembled many relatives and friends of the dead heroes, who, like themselves, had, by the accession of a new Shogun, been released from banishment.

When all had thanked the *Sojo* for the care he had bestowed upon the graves, they went to an adjoining apartment where they were shown the battered armor and weapons of the forty-seven *ronin*.

Among the party were the wife and two sons of Sir Big-rock, the wife and son of Sir Shell, the family of Sir Common, Miss Quiet, the betrothed of Sir Cliff-field, Lady Pine-island, and the loyal contractor, Noble-plain, whose participation in the conspiracy had caused him to be banished with the families of the *samurai*.

Mrs. Brilliant was not among the number, as on the day of her husband's death, she had joined him in paradise.

The visitors bowed before the souvenirs, which they regarded as good Buddhists do the relics of their saints.

At the hour of the Snake (10 A.M.) the priests led the way to the chapel of the temple. When all had taken their places upon the matted floor, the venerable superior ascended the platform, and placing his hands upright, palm to palm, offered prayers, after which he thus addressed the congregation:

"How can I find words to express the feelings of my heart? My aged tongue can but imperfectly speak the praises due to the loyal men, whose armor and weapons you have just worshiped; who suffered so greatly and died so nobly. Oh, you are the favored ones; the gods have indeed been good to you; you are the descendants, relatives and friends of Immortals! Through all ages and changes, the names and fame of the loyal men, whose bodies rest beneath yonder tombs, will be remembered with respect and admiration. Their glorious deed will shine like a torch at night, and the whole world shall ring with their praise! They were dutiful sons, therefore were loyal men! They were loyal men, therefore were patriots! They have set an example which will be followed forever and ever, and the day will surely come when their worth will be recognized in the highest place (by the Mikado).[10] You, their sons, have an inheritance that will make you envied by all men. It is for you to follow in the footsteps of your fathers. You, widows, how glorious is your dower! You, friends of the departed heroes, how priceless your legacies! I salute you all, favored ones, and welcome you back from exile!"

He then briefly reviewed the lives of the forty-seven, pausing frequently to wipe the tears from his cheeks. His eloquence deeply moved the listeners, who, from time to time, uttered pious ejaculations and bathed their sleeves with the dews of sorrow and joy.

When he had eulogized all the martyrs, he thus concluded his oration:

"The record of their sufferings, their heroism, and their loyalty, is engraved upon a golden tablet, and the friction of time, which obliterates most things, will only add lustre to their honorable names."

THE END.

FROM: A HISTORY OF JAPAN, VOLUME III

BY JAMES MURDOCH

EDITED BY JOSEPH HENRY LONGFORD

CHAPTER VI

THE FORTY-SEVEN RONIN

EVERY historian of the Tokugawa age is emphatic on the subject of the great debasement of the moral currency among the samurai class that began in the Regency of Sakai and culminated under Tsunayoshi in the Genroku and Ho-ei year-periods. Reference to this unpleasant matter has been made in the previous chapter; and although detail was not heaped upon detail, as might very easily have been done, enough was said to indicate that the moral fiber of the two-sworded men had indeed degenerated sadly. And yet it was just when things seemed to be moving downhill with breakneck speed that what the Japanese regard as one of the greatest feats of derring-do that has ever been accomplished within the four seas of the Empire was achieved. There is no tale better known in Japan than the story of the Revenge of Ako, or the Loyal League, while the story of the Forty-Seven Ronin, as it is usually known among Europeans, is the only episode in the Tokugawa annals with which foreigners are almost universally acquainted. The incident has become so famous that it has been deemed advisable to devote a short chapter to its consideration.

In a preceding chapter it was stated that when Iyemitsu reformed the etiquette of the Shogunal palace, he sent the chiefs of the two Koke houses of Kira and Osawa to Kyoto to undergo a special course of training in the ceremonial of the Imperial Court, and that the duty of superintending the reception of the Imperial Envoys at Yedo became an hereditary prerogative of the chiefs of these two families. It became the custom to impose on a Tozama Daimyo the task of defraying the expenses of the Envoy's sojourn in Yedo, and of attending upon and of introducing them at the Shogun's Court. In order to do this properly it was necessary for the host to put himself under a course of instruction from Kira or Osawa, and to discharge his commission under the direction of the Masters of Ceremony, as Kira and Osawa practically were. At this date it was Kira Yoshinaka who usually discharged the duties of the office. Like many of his fellow-officials he was venal, with a most pronounced itch in his palm, and unless the Daimyo, consigned to his tender mercies, took adequate steps to appease his greed, he was apt to make matters very unpleasant for him indeed. To be put to public shame, to be subjected to "loss of face", was a terrible wound to the knightly honor of a feudatory, and Kira, in his position, could easily find the means of exposing his aristocratic pupils to ridicule, if not to contempt. In 1698, he made himself so unendurable to Kamei, Daimyo of Tsuwano in Iwami, that Kamei made up his mind to poniard him. However, that night Kamei apprised his steward of his intention, and the latter at once hurried off stealthily to Kira's mansion, with a load of costly presents. Next day Kira was exceedingly courteous to the Daimyo who, not knowing of the reasons which had brought about this complete change of demeanor, abandoned his anger and renounced his intention of killing him. Thus, by the cleverness of his steward, was Kamei, with all his house, saved from ruin.[11]

In 1701, it was Asano Nagamori, Daimyo of Ako in Harima, that was saddled with the burden, or the honor, of receiving the envoys of the Emperor and the ex-Emperor. On this occasion, Kira must have pushed things too far, for although it was never known what individual incident it was that exhausted Asano's patience, the precise occurrence itself is clear enough from the following testimony of Kajikawa, an attendant of the Shogun's consort:—

"On 21st April I went to the palace. I entered the waiting-room, and there I heard that the Imperial Envoys were to be received earlier than had at first been determined. So I left the waiting-room and went in. In the great corridor I met two priests. I asked one of them to call Kira, but he came back and told me that Kira had gone to the Great Council Chamber. I then got him to summon Asano who was with Daté (Asano's colleague) in the great reception room. Asano came, and I gave him the message from my mistress. Just then I saw Kira coming from the reception chamber, and I went forward to meet him. We met at about twelve or fourteen yards from the corner pillar of the chamber, and I had just asked him whether it was true that the hour of reception had been changed, when behind his back I heard a loud voice: 'Have you forgotten the grudge I have owed you for a day or two?' At the same time, some one fell upon Kira from behind, and cut him on the shoulder. I looked at the speaker, and saw to my great astonishment that it was the Lord Asano. Kira turned round and received another cut on the forehead. He ran a few steps towards me, and then fell to the floor. Asano dashed forward to attack him once more, but I caught hold of his arm. By this time, other nobles had come to the rescue, so that Asano was easily disarmed. He was straightway taken to the Willow Chamber, all the while crying out that he had killed Kira, as he owed him a grudge for his insolence. As to Kira, he was carried, insensible, into the doctor's room."

Of course the penalty for drawing a weapon with lethal intent in the Shogun's palace was death—by *hara-kiri.*

The assault took place at ten in the forenoon. Asano was presently handed over to the custody of Tamura, Daimyo of Ichinoseki, in Mutsu, who sent ten samurai, thirty servants, and fifteen palanquin-bearers to fetch the culprit to his *yashiki.* There he arrived in a palanquin, meshed round with cords, at four in the afternoon. Meanwhile his fate had been settled, and he was presently informed that he had been condemned to disembowel himself. The reason for this unusual haste was that the Shogun wished to be merciful; Kira had not been fatally wounded, and it was well that Asano should not learn that this was so, for he could not then face his doom with resignation. At five o'clock (in the very same day) Shoda, the censor, arrived with the death-sentence. It had been purposed that the *hara-kiri* should take place in the great reception room of Tamura's *yashiki*, but the seneschals bethought them that it would be wanting in respect to let Asano die in the room where the censor sat. So they reared a dais of three mats, covered it with a rug, and hung it about with lighted lanterns. When it was ready Asano, in the ceremonial dress of the samurai (*Kami-shimo*), was escorted into the reception room where Shoda produced the sentence and read it out. Asano calmly returned thanks for being permitted to die as befitted a samurai, and then rising he proceeded to the dais attended by two assistant censors. As he sat down a dirk, wrapped in paper with only two inches of its steel exposed, was placed on a stand before him and one of the censors took his position behind him as his "second" with a naked sword poised ready in his hands. As Asano bent forward to grasp the dirk, the censor's sword fell upon his neck. So Asano did not really disembowel himself.[12]

The reason for this was that Asano's own dirk had been wrested from him in the palace, and, in the haste and confusion, it was a dirk by Bizen Nagamitsu and a precious heirloom in the Tamura family that was placed before him. So, lest it should be soiled, the assistant censor was speedy in his office of second, and struck off Lord Asano's head before he could use the dirk. That evening, Daigaku, Asano's younger brother, sent to receive the corpse, and that very night it was buried at the Temple of Sengaku-ji in Takanawa.

On 26th April, five days after the death of Asano, two of his vassals appeared at the Castle of Ako with intelligence of the calamity. Now, Ako was 420 miles from Yedo by the shortest route, so these men can have lagged but little on the way. That same night, fast upon their heels came Haru and a comrade with a letter signed by Toda, Daimyo of Ogaki in Mino, by Asano's uncle and by his younger brother, Daigaku, announcing that Asano had made away with himself and strictly charging the Ako retainers to surrender the Castle to the Bakufu commissioners without demur. On being questioned as to whether Kira was dead or not, Haru said that although he had repeatedly put the same query to Lord Toda, he had stubbornly refused to answer.

Two neighboring Daimyo were presently instructed by the Bakufu to take charge of the Castle of Ako, and Araki and Sakakibara were the censors dispatched from Yedo to superintend its transfer. When this and the fact that Kira was still alive became known to the retainers, most of them resolved to draw up a petition, hand over the Castle, and then solemnly commit *hara-kiri* at the great entrance to the stronghold; for then, they reasoned, the Bakufu would be sure to punish Kira as he deserved. At the head of this party was Oishi Kuranosuke. But Ono Kurobei headed another section, who argued that such a step would only further offend the Yedo authorities. However, Oishi and sixty others entered into a written compact to carry out their purpose. There were others who did not actually sign the document, but who were nevertheless bent upon following their Lord "upon the dark path". Just then three more retainers came in from Yedo, and they refused to have anything to do with such a compact. But not, like Ono, from fear or prudence. Far from it, for they were clamorous for vengeance on Kira. In Yedo two of their fellows were even then hot upon Kira's tracks, but he was so strongly guarded by the troops of his son Uyesugi,[13] Lord of Yonezawa, that all their efforts to kill him had proved abortive. A band of at least twenty stout and resolute men would be needed for any successful attempt. Asano's stewards in Yedo had been asked to help, but they had cravenly excused themselves, and hence the presence of the three zealots in Ako to find men more of their own mettle.

Meanwhile, Oishi had forwarded a petition to the Board of Censors, setting forth that, as Kira was still alive and in honor, the elders of Ako found it almost beyond them to hold their clansmen in control, and praying that the matter might be settled in a satisfactory manner. The messengers arrived in Yedo only two days after the two censors had left for Ako, and so there was nothing for it now but to give up the Castle. Between the 25th and 30th of May, the two censors inspected and took it over. In the inventory of its appurtenances there was an entry of some half-dozen ailing dogs duly provided for in terms of the law, and for this the clan Karo were highly commended. During these five days, Oishi repeatedly entreated the censors to ensure the succession of Daigaku (Asano's younger brother) to the headship of the clan. They promised to lay the matter before the Great Council, and at first the Great Council thought well of the proposal.

It was the prospect of Daigaku's succession that kept Oishi from making common cause with the zealots from Yedo. They strongly insisted that, as Kira was over sixty, he might die a natural death at any time, and so defraud them of their revenge. In the end Oishi talked them over, dwelling upon the harm they might do to Daigaku's prospects, and proposing that, in the event of Kira's death robbing them of their vengeance, they would commit *hara-kiri* in a body. And so things remained until 1702. In January of that year, Kira became *inkyo*, and was succeeded by his grandson, Sahyoye. In August, Daigaku, who, up to that time had been confined to his own house, was consigned to the ward of Asano, Daimyo of Aki. So Ako did not pass to Daigaku, and the house of Asano of Ako was irretrievably ruined. Then, Oishi Kuranosuke resolved upon taking revenge.

Meanwhile, Oishi had separated from his wife and two younger children, and had taken up his residence in Kyoto. He and his confederates broke up their households and sold their effects, a proceeding which made no small stir in Kyoto and Fushimi at the time. Intelligence of the incident was conveyed to Kira, and he thereupon redoubled his precautions. It was presently rumored that some of the Ako-*ronin* had been seized at the various barriers, and some of those in Kyoto urged Oishi to postpone the journey to Yedo till next spring. When those already in Yedo heard of this they were furious; Yoshida (*aet*[14] 61) and Horibe (*aet* 75) declared that at their age they could not be sure of living till next spring, and vehemently insisted upon prompt and immediate action. Oishi thereupon broke with the more cautious party in Kyoto and proceeded to Yedo, whither indeed the majority of the confederates had already gone. From this time Oishi ceased all communication with Asano Daigaku, so that he might in no way be implicated in the consequences of the project. For two months, after the break-up of his household, Oishi remained in Kyoto, and during this time it is probable that he did play the part of a roisterer to throw Kira off his guard, although the traditional account of his long and inveterate profligacy is certainly incorrect. The Kyoto conspirators left behind anticipated that Oishi's rashness would be his and their undoing, and accordingly they severed all connexion with him. By August, 1702, the confederates, who originally numbered over 120, were reduced to about sixty, and by December, various defections had brought the number down to no more than forty-seven.

Since the summer of 1702, Uyesugi of Yonezawa had been seriously ill, and Kira now frequently visited the sick man in his *yashiki* outside the Sakurada Gate, and often passed the night there, away from his own mansion across the River Sumida, in Honjo. Furthermore, Kira was passionately fond of *cha-no-yu*, and he often visited, and was visited in turn, by other votaries of the cult, so that altogether his movements were very uncertain. Now, it so fell out that in Honjo, there was a *cha-jin*, Yamada Sorin by name, and he was intimate with Kira. One day a certain merchant of Osaka called upon this Yamada, desiring to become his pupil, and he was accepted as such. This man was no Osaka merchant at all, but one of the confederates, who, as luck would have it, had learned *cha-no-yu* in his youth. He soon found out from Yamada that Kira was to have a tea-party in his own house on 23rd November. The date was, however, postponed to 6th December, and then again to 14th December. Now, the 14th was the very day of the month on which Lord Asano died, and the *ronin* thrilled with joy at the omen.

On the afternoon of that day, they set one of their number to watch at Kira's gate, and he presently reported that several visitors, including Yamada himself, had entered. Kira would surely be found at home that night. So late in the evening, the *ronin* assembled in a house near-by Kira's mansion, and made all their preparations.[15] They dressed like officers of fire brigades, only over this dress they wore *haori*, which they threw away at Kira's gate. Inside their sashes they twisted iron chains. They all had white sleeves to distinguish them in the darkness, and a piece of leather with their real and assumed names on the right shoulder. Darkness had fallen when they left their rendezvous and parted into two bands, one to assail the front, the other the back gate of the mansion. The latter section headed by Oishi's son and Yoshida, set ladders against the gate. A few scrambled over, seized and bound the porters, and then admitted their comrades. At the preconcerted signal, the other band, under Oishi himself, lit their torches, poured in through the front gate, battered in the doors of the entrance hall, and burst into the reception room. Four or five samurai opposed them, but these were very summarily disposed of, as were a page and a priest who fought most determinedly. The *ronin* quickly cut all the bowstrings, and snapped the shafts of all the spears in the armory and elsewhere. Oishi had specially cautioned his followers to see to it that there should be no outbreak of fire. Kira's neighbors did at first fancy that the disturbance was caused by a fire, but, as they could see no flames, they sent their retainers up on the roofs of their *yashikis* to find out what was really occurring. Two of the *ronin* at once informed them of their purpose, and charged them not to interfere, as they would take hurt if they did so.

Some of the *ronin* broke in the door of Kira's chamber. Kira was not there, and all hurrying and scurrying to and fro in quest of him was in vain. One of them bethought himself of the charcoal shed, and when they entered it, plates, tea-cups, and lumps of charcoal came whizzing about their ears. When one of the band thrust his spear into the dark interior two men sprang out, and laid about them lustily, but they soon went down. Another man who drew his sword as a *ronin* thrust at him shared their fate. As far as age went, the *ronin* fancied that this corpse might be Kira's, but the face was so besmeared with blood that there was no sign of the scar left upon it by Lord Asano's dirk. But to their joy they detected the marks of an old cut upon the shoulder, and when they fetched one of the porters they had bound, he assured them that it was indeed Kira who lay before them. So, forthwith, they sounded their whistles to summon their comrades, and all assembled at the rear of the mansion. In a loud voice one of them called out to the neighbors on the housetops that now that Kira was dead their object was accomplished, and that they had no other purpose in view. Only six of the forty-seven were wounded, while, of the inmates of the mansion, sixteen men lay dead, and twenty sorely wounded, while twelve had made their escape. Sahyoye, Kira's grandson and successor, was himself wounded in two places.

With Kira's head the *ronin* left the *yashiki*, and proceeded towards the Eko-in. They had intended to commit *hara-kiri* there, but they found the gates closed. So they paused and bethought themselves that it would be well to await the sentence of the Shogun, as the world would then better understand their motives. They had also expected to be assailed; and the space in front of the Eko-in would have afforded them a vantage-ground. But no one interfered with them, so they proceeded across the Sumida, and passed on through the whole extent of the city to the Sengakuji in Takanawa. Here the *ronin* entered the cemetery, and placing Kira's head, duly washed and cleansed, before Lord Asano's tomb, they prostrated themselves in prayer to his spirit. (The head was then put in a box, and on the following day two priests took it to Kira's mansion.) They then went to the temple porch, laid down their weapons, and asked to see the Abbot, who was well acquainted with them all. Oishi handed to the Abbot a list of their names, telling him that two of them had just been dispatched to the Censorate with a written report of the affair. From ten in the morning till four in the afternoon they remained in the temple. Then they were summoned to appear at the censor's office, and they left Sengakuji in an ordered column, marching two abreast, Oishi and his son at their head, while six of the wounded and the aged were borne along in palanquins.[16]

At Sengoku, the censor's mansion, the *ronin* were officially examined, and then informed that they were to be consigned in four parties to the ward of as many Daimyo, which for lordless men was very flattering treatment indeed. After this, the censor ceased to speak as such, and for his own personal satisfaction proceeded to ask them many questions about the happenings of the previous night. It was to Hosokawa of Kumamoto (540,000 *koku*) that Oishi himself, with sixteen of his comrades, was entrusted, the others were distributed among the smaller Daimyo of Matsuyama, Chofu, and Okazaki. Hosokawa sent no fewer than 750 men to fetch the seventeen committed to his charge. It was past ten o'clock when the cavalcade reached his *yashiki* in Shirokane, and yet, late as the hour was, Hosokawa at once proceeded to the officers' room to meet them, and to load them with expressions of admiration and praise. He felt highly honored, he assured them, to be entrusted with the care of such staunch and loyal samurai as they proved themselves to be; he begged them, though many attendants were set about them in obedience to the Shogun's order, to be quite at their ease, and to repose themselves after their laborious exertions. He then ordered supper to be set before them and withdrew. As for the other smaller Daimyo, they did not see the *ronin* that night, but, on learning what had taken place at the great Shirokane *yashiki*, they were not slow to take their cue from the powerful *Kokushu* Daimyo of Higo,[17] and they personally bade the *ronin* welcome on the following day.

Meanwhile Yedo was in a ferment. The castle officials, no less than the clan samurai, were exceedingly anxious that the lives of the *ronin* should be spared. The Hyojosho had the matter submitted to it, and after due deliberation formulated the following propositions : —

1. Kira Sahyoye whose duty it was to have fought to the death, but who escaped with a few slight wounds, should be ordered to disembowel himself.

2. Such of Kira's retainers as had offered no resistance to the *ronin* should be beheaded; those who were wounded in the fight should be made over to their relatives.

3. Those in Kira's mansion who were not *samurai* should be cast adrift.

4. Iyesugi (Kira's son and Lord of Yonezawa) who did not so much as attack the *ronin* as they marched from Kira's mansion to Sengakuji should be punished. At the least, his domains should be confiscated.

5. The fact that the *ronin* staked their lives to avenge the death of their lord showed that they were truly loyal men. Their deeds accorded with the injunctions of the First Shogun which incite men to loyal and filial acts, and though their confederacy and their use of arms had the color of a disturbance of the peace yet, had it been otherwise, they could not have accomplished their purpose.

6. The law forbade confederacies and the taking of oaths, yet that they harbored no malice against the Shogun was apparent from the quiet and peaceable manner in which they had surrendered the Castle of Ako in the previous year, and there was no doubt that nothing but absolute necessity had led to their forming a confederacy (in defiance of the law).

The report ended with a recommendation that the *ronin* should be left permanently under the charge of the Daimyo to whom they had already been respectively consigned. It bore the seal and signature of every member of the Hyojosho (High Court), of the three Temple Magistrates, of the four Chief Censors, of the three City Magistrates, and of the four Finance Magistrates. The Shogun Tsunayoshi himself was really anxious to save the lives of these men, but even he, in such a case as this, could not set aside the claims of the law. If the Princely Abbot of Uyeno had interceded for them, he would have been heard, and Tsunayoshi did go so far as to see His Eminence and indirectly hint that such a course on his part would be appreciated. But the Abbot either did not understand or did not choose to do so, and so the law had to take its course. On the forenoon of 20th March, 1703, each of the four Daimyo above-mentioned received notice from the Great Council, with whom the final decision rested, that censors would be sent to pronounce sentence upon the men of Ako they had in ward.

When these officials arrived the following sentence was solemnly read out:—

"When Asano, Takumi no Kami, who had been ordered to receive the imperial envoys, heedless of the occasion and the place, attacked Kira in the palace, he was commanded to perform *hara-kiri*; while Kira, Kodzuke-no-sake was pronounced innocent. Vowing vengeance for the death of your Lord, you, forty-six retainers of Takumi, leagued yourselves together and assaulted Kira's dwelling with missiles and weapons. The manner of your attack showed contempt for the authorities and now for your heinous crime it is ordered that you commit *hara-kiri*."[18]

At Hosokawa's, Oishi bent forward, and in the name of all thanked the censor for a sentence that enabled them to die as samurai. Araki, who was censor on this occasion, then expressed his concern at having failed to compass Daigaku's succession to the Ako fief, and also his sorrow for their doom, although the accomplishment of the revenge must be a source of keen satisfaction to them. He further informed them—although he was careful to say that he did so privately and not in his official capacity—that that very day Kira Sahyoye's estates had been confiscated, and the house of Kira ruined. Oishi voiced the gratitude of the *ronin* for the punishment meted out to the house of their foe, though indeed, he said, they had no cause for ill-will against Sahyoye himself.

Then one after another, according to their rank, they were summoned to the platform expressly reared for the purpose outside the great reception hall, and there in due order calmly made an end of themselves.

It must not be forgotten that at the time, Oishi and his comrades were lordless men, and so not legally entitled to the privileges of samurai. But, as a matter of fact, the death sentence on them was pronounced and carried out in a fashion that had never before fallen to the lot of mere ordinary retainers. The treatment accorded the whole band was such as was wont to be accorded great Daimyo, and other immediate feudatories of the Shogun.

For an exhaustive examination of all the official and other documents bearing upon this famous episode, we are indebted to Mr. Shigeno, one of the most scientific of modern Japanese historians. One result of his laborious researches is that, while a certain amount of the picturesque gets consigned to the limbo of the storytellers' hall (Yosé), the true story of Oishi Kuranosuke adds considerably to his moral and intellectual stature. The authentic evidence goes to show that his conduct throughout was marked with singular moderation and foresight, and, when it came to the point, determination and audacity. His single-mindedness for the honor and welfare of the house of Asano is apparent at every turn. Nor were his clansmen by any means unworthy of their leader. On the little fief of Ako, with its assessed revenue of 53,000 *koku*, there were in all 322 vassals drawing official stipends. To the feudal Japan of the time, with a dry-rot of moral decadence sapping the fiber of the city samurai so disastrously, it seemed nothing short of marvelous that among this number so many as forty-seven should have been found eager to follow their Lord to the "Yellow Streams". And it must not be overlooked that among the other 275 there were not a few ready to persevere in case Oishi and his band should fail, as they fancied he would do. As for those who refused to co-operate in the enterprise, or who afterwards withdrew from the league, so much is to be said at least, that not one among them turned traitor or played the part of informer at the expense of his fellow-clansmen.

Whenever mention is made of the vendetta in old Japan this episode of the Forty-seven Ronin is at once cited as the typical case. But it is far from being a typical case, indeed it is a highly exceptional one. Before 1703, there were many instances of the vendetta in the Empire, but perhaps the best-known, and most often referred-to, were those of the Soga brothers, and of the Iga *Kataki-uchi*. The former occurred in Yoritomoto's days; five centuries before—the latter so late as Hidetada's time.[19]

Then the year preceding the Ako episode saw the accomplishment of the Ishii-Akahori vendetta.[20] It made a great sensation at the time and, had it not been so completely overshadowed by the episode of the Forty-seven Ronin, would doubtless have become one of the most often-told tales of the country.

In every one of these latter cases it was to punish the murderer, or at least the slayer of a father and not of a lord that the Avenger of Blood imbued his hands. Such a duty was strongly inculcated in the Chinese Classics. In the second book of the Book of Rites the law is thus laid down:—

"With the slayer of a father a man may not live under the same heaven; against the slayer of a brother a man must never have to go home for a weapon; with the slayer of a friend a man may not live in the same state."

Here, be it observed, nothing is said about the slayer of a Lord.[21] Nowhere it would seem did Confucius say anything authoritative as to how the murderer of a Lord was to be dealt with. The classical precedent for this in China dated from the Sengoku, or "Warring Country" period, several centuries after the compilation of the Canonical Books. A certain Yojo was in the employment of three successive Lords, the first two of whom treated him with no special consideration. He then took service with a certain Chikaku, who afterwards compassed the deaths of Yojo's two former masters, and who was in turn killed by one Cho Joshi. Now, Yojo had been held in high esteem by Chikaku, and he made three abortive attempts to avenge him. On the last occasion he was seized by Cho Joshi, who asked him why he was so eager to avenge Chikaku while he had shown himself so lukewarm about the murder of his first two lords. Yojo frankly replied that it was the nature of the treatment he had received in each case that had been the determining circumstance.

"This story," remarks the commentator, "as well as many others bearing on the Chinese and Japanese custom of avenging the death of a master, shows that the execution of the vendetta was not held obligatory in cases where a retainer was not specially attached to his master and where the benefits he received were not sufficient to call for the risk or loss of his own life."

In matters of loyalty and filial piety, Arai Hakuseki was at once a purist, and a great authority. In 1682 he entered the service of Hotta, the Tairo, who was assassinated in 1684.

"His son was very unfortunate," says Arai, "and cut down the allowance of his samurai, and *many left his service*. I was not in confidential relations with him or his father but would not leave at such a time, for if one has enough for oneself and family *such desertions* are not loyal even though the service be unsatisfactory. It is natural that a samurai should be poor, yet he must maintain his station, but finally my funds gave out."

And he left. Now Arai had originally been a vassal of Tsuchiya, Lord of Kururi in Kadzusa. After a short time as a *ronin* he became a vassal of the Hotta family. After another brief space as a lordless man he entered the service of the Daimyo of Kofu, who presently became the Shogun, Iyenobu. Thus, Arai had at least three different lords, and he would readily have taken service under a fourth, if Yoshimune had seen fit to utilize his talents. In Japan, no less than in feudal China, the high-sounding precept that "a faithful vassal should not serve two lords" was formally endorsed and approved. But when it came to the plain prose of practice, Arai's case is by no means the only contemporary one, which seems to indicate that the maxim was taken as a counsel of perfection. It might serve very well as a copy-book head-line, but, in the ordering of his life, the samurai plainly felt that the injunction was better honored in the breach than in the observance. As a simple matter of fact, the despised plebeian now and then made a much better showing in this matter than did the samurai. When Arai became a *ronin* he was followed by two domestics who would not leave him, and who said they could provide for themselves somehow. Some of the famous Forty-seven Ronin were accompanied into beggary by their household servants and, in these cases, the servant not only provided for his own wants but for those of his (economically) helpless master as well. Scores of analogous instances crop up in the course of a perusal of the old documents of the Tokugawa age. It is true that in Japan there have been many cases of murderers of their lords being punished by their fellow-vassals. The instance of Kosai being killed by Miyoshi for compassing the death of their common chieftain, Hosokawa Masamoto, in 1507, and of Akechi paying the full penalty for the assassination of Nobunaga in 1582, will at once occur to the reader.[22] But, in nearly all such cases, it usually jumped very nicely with the personal interest of the righteous vassal to assume the office of the Avenger of Blood. In the Ako vendetta, the case was vastly otherwise. To accomplish their purpose the forty-seven had perforce to outrage the law in one of its most strictly enforced provisions. There could be no hope of worldly material profit in any shape or form to any one sharing in any way in the plot. At the best it was death by *hara-kiri*, and death by decapitation as a common criminal was a by-no-means remote probability, while it was possible that all the members of their several households might be involved in their doom.

It will be observed that the *ronin* were punished not for the actual killing of Kira but for the *manner* in which they accomplished their purpose. The indispensable preliminaries for legalizing the vendetta had not been complied with. The so-called "Legacy of Iyeyasu" is a fabrication, penned a full century or more after the first Tokugawa Shogun was entombed among the forests and mountains of Nikko. But, in many of its articles, it sets forth the established customs and jurisprudence of Tokugawa feudalism correctly enough. One paragraph in it deals with the subject of the vendetta.

"In Japan, there is an old saying that the same heaven cannot cover a man and the slayer of his father, or mother, or *master*, or elder brother. Now, if a man seek to put to death such a slayer, he must first inform the Ketsudansho office at the Hyojosho, and say in how many days or months he can carry out his intention. This is to be entered in the records of the office. If he kills the slayer *without such previous intimation he is to be regarded as a murderer.*"[23]

Now, to have made any such notification would have put Kira so thoroughly upon his guard that he could never have been touched; so much is recognized in the fifth and sixth paragraphs of the Hyojosho report on the episode quoted a few pages back. In the peculiar circumstances, it was generally considered that the *ronin* were punished for a mere technicality. Even Hayashi, the official Chinese scholar, wrote Chinese stanzas lauding them as heroes, and although the Bakufu spoke to him about the matter privately, no public censure was passed upon him. Ogyu Sorai, who had been Kira's lecturer or reader and who was a protégé of Kira's son, Uyesugi, issued a pamphlet in which he assailed the *ronin* for failing to commit suicide at the Sengakuji, without sending any notice to the censor at all. This gave rise to a great commotion among the Chinese scholars of the time, and an embittered controversy over this point went on for years. Modern authors have divided these writers into pro-Bakufu and anti-Bakufu according to the view they supported. This betrays a serious misconception of the actual circumstances of the time—it was only in the nineteenth century that perfervid loyalists began to exploit the episode of the Forty-seven Ronin for their own special purposes. The Shogun was inclined to save the *ronin*, from their doom, and the Great Councilors, though they had to administer the law, had the greatest admiration for, and sympathy with, the "criminals". They, in common with every Daimyo in Japan, readily perceived that the incident could be turned to the greatest possible profit. Dr. Aston has well remarked on the "commanding position of loyalty in the *Table of Moral Precedence*" which, "in the morals and ideas of this period, overshadows and dwarfs all other obligations." Before 1703, the tendency on the whole may have been in this direction, but it was only after the Ako vendetta that it became so pronouncedly dominant. The Japanese is frequently not merely a man of sentiment but a sentimentalist, and, in common with the generality of mankind, is ruled more by the figments of imagination than the calculations of reason. Now this episode was so startling and thrilling that it appealed to the imagination with greater force than any other single incident that could be named in the history of the empire. From Satsuma to Tsugaru it focussed the national attention—for the time men spoke of nothing else, thought of nothing else. Everything else was for the moment forgotten—except perhaps the Dog-Laws, which even Oishi had so faithfully obeyed. Two days after the attack on Kira's mansion, we hear of broadsheet accounts of it being hawked about throughout the whole city of Yedo. The popular writer was soon at work upon a more or less imaginative treatment of the whole incident, and, during the Tokugawa age, about one hundred different versions of the tale were published. In 1703, Chikamatsu Monzaemon (1653-1724), one of Japan's three greatest dramatists, was in the full vigor of his powers, and he at once seized upon the Ako vendetta as a theme. His play held the stage until 1744, when Takeda Idzumo (1691-1756) produced his thrice-famous *Chushingura*, the most popular play ever put upon the boards in Japan.[24]

More than a century and a half later the tale was told to Sir Rutherford Alcock, the first British representative to Japan, then installed in the Tozenji, only a few hundred yards' distant from the tomb of the *ronin*, before which the incense has never ceased to smoke.

"As this story was recited to me I could not help reflecting on what must be the influence of such a popular literature and history upon the character as well as the habits and thoughts of a nation. When children listen to such fragments of their history or popular tales, and, as they grow up, hear their elders praise the valor and heroism of such servitors, and see them go at stated periods to pay honor to their graves centuries after the deed—and such is the fact, it is quite obvious that general talk and unhesitating approval of what with us, perhaps, would be considered great crimes, may have very subtle and curious bearings on the general character and moral training of the people. What its exact influence may be we cannot determine, perhaps, but that it is deep and all-pervading, affecting their general estimate of all deeds of like character, whether it be the slaying of a Regent, or the massacre of a Foreign Legation, is very certain, and presents a state of things well worthy of serious consideration."[25]

In connexion with this episode, one rather important point remains to be adverted to. In view of the resolute daring displayed by Oishi and his comrades, it may well seem that the general moral degeneracy of the samurai of this age has been greatly exaggerated. We have no reason to distrust the accounts of contemporary writers who have touched upon the matter, but we must bear in mind that it was with Yedo and the state of things there prevalent that they dealt. Now, the Yedo of 1700 was to the rest of the empire what London was to England at large in the reign of Charles II. In spite of the scandalous and brazen-faced depravity of the English court and of the fashionable circles in the metropolis at that date, there were tens of thousands of households in the country where a sober, healthy, robust, and "God-fearing" family life was quietly and unobtrusively led. From such accounts as those Arai Hakuseki gives us of his father's life, it is not unreasonable to suppose that a somewhat analogous state of things prevailed in contemporary Japan. In many of the castle-towns, on many of the outlying fiefs, the samurai were still under a tolerably strict and salutary regimen. The strenuous ferocity of Kato Kiyomasa's time had indeed been tamed; in many cases tamed only too effectually. But, in many remote country places, the fierce old spirit was by no means dead, it only slumbered and needed nothing but a suitable stimulus to rouse it to vigorous action. Still, it was gradually passing even in the country districts; it was by the old men (Yoshida *aet* 61; Horibe *aet* 75) of the former generation that Oishi's hand was finally forced. In Yedo, the resident Ako *Rusu-i* made rather a poor showing—at first they absolutely refused to move in the matter, when appealed to. In Yedo, in truth, the case seemed well-nigh hopeless. On Iyenobu's accession an attempt was made to stem the *debâcle*. Tsunayoshi's favorites were cashiered, Yanagisawa found it advisable to shave his head and enter religion. The Shogun's harem was broken up and his forty "boys" restored to their relatives. Gambling was prohibited, actors were deprived of their swords and forbidden to associate with samurai; the wearing of silk crêpe and the visiting of temples in bodies by women were interdicted; and street walkers and private prostitutes were drastically dealt with. But something more than these negative or superficial measures was needed. Iyenobu had good intentions, and his counselor, Arai, had ideas; but neither Iyenobu nor Arai was really capable of diagnosing the malady correctly, and devising and applying a radically effective remedy. That was to remain over as work for a greater man than either of the twain.

AN ACCOUNT OF THE HARA-KIRI
(FROM A RARE JAPANESE MS.)

BY LORD REDESDALE, G.C.V.O., K.C.B. (A. B. MITFORD)

Seppuku *(hara-kiri)* is the mode of suicide adopted amongst samurai when they have no alternative but to die. Some there are who thus commit suicide of their own free will; others there are who, having committed some crime which does not put them outside the pale of the privileges of the samurai class, are ordered by their superiors to put an end to their own lives. It is needless to say that it is absolutely necessary that the principal, the witnesses, and the seconds who take part in the affair should be acquainted with all the ceremonies to be observed. A long time ago, a certain Daimio invited a number of persons, versed in the various ceremonies, to call upon him to explain the different forms to be observed by the official witnesses who inspect and verify the head, &c., and then to instruct him in the ceremonies to be observed in the act of suicide; then he showed all these rites to his son and to all his retainers. Another person has said that, as the ceremonies to be gone through by principal, witnesses, and seconds are all very important matters, men should familiarize themselves with a thing which is so terrible, in order that, should the time come for them to take part in it, they may not be taken by surprise.

The witnesses go to see and certify the suicide. For seconds, men are wanted who have distinguished themselves in the military arts. In old days, men used to bear these things in mind; but now-a-days the fashion is to be ignorant of such ceremonies, and if upon rare occasions a criminal is handed over to a Daimio's charge, that he may perform *hara-kiri,* it often happens, at the time of execution, that there is no one among all the prince's retainers who is competent to act as second, in which case a man has to be engaged in a hurry from some other quarter to cut off the head of the criminal, and for that day he changes his name and becomes a retainer of the prince, either of the middle or lowest class, and the affair is entrusted to him, and so the difficulty is got over: nor is this considered to be a disgrace. It is a great breach of decorum if the second, who is a most important officer, commits any mistake (such as not striking off the head at a blow) in the presence of the witnesses sent by the government. On this account a skilful person must be employed; and, to hide the unmanliness of his own people, a prince must perform the ceremony in this imperfect manner. Every samurai should be able to cut off a man's head; therefore, to have to employ a stranger to act as second is to incur the charge of ignorance of the arts of war, and is a bitter mortification. However, young men, trusting to their youthful ardor, are apt to be careless, and are certain to make a mistake. Some people there are who, not lacking in skill on ordinary occasions, lose their presence of mind in public, and cannot do themselves justice. It is all the more important, therefore, as the act occurs but rarely, that men who are liable to be called upon to be either principals or seconds or witnesses in the *hara-kiri* should constantly be examined in their skill as swordsmen, and should be familiar with all the rites, in order that when the time comes they may not lose their presence of mind.

According to one authority, capital punishment may be divided into two kinds—beheading and strangulation. The ceremony of *hara-kiri* was added afterwards in the case of persons belonging to the military class being condemned to death. This was first instituted in the days of the Ashikaga[26] dynasty. At that time the country was in a state of utter confusion; and there were men who, although fighting, were neither guilty of high treason nor of infidelity to their feudal lords, but who by the chances of war were taken prisoners. To drag out such men as these, bound as criminals, and cut their heads off, was intolerably cruel; accordingly, men hit upon a ceremonious mode of suicide by disemboweling, in order to comfort the departed spirit. Even at present, where it becomes necessary to put to death a man who has been guilty of some act not unworthy of a samurai, at the time of the execution witnesses are sent to the house; and the criminal, having bathed and put on new clothes, in obedience to the commands of his superiors, puts an end to himself, but does not on that account forfeit his rank as a samurai. This is a law for which, in all truth, men should be grateful.

ON THE PREPARATION OF THE PLACE OF EXECUTION

In old days the ceremony of *hara-kiri* used to be performed in a temple. In the third year of the period called Kan-yei (A.D. 1626), a certain person, having been guilty of treason, was ordered to disembowel himself, on the fourteenth day of the first month, in the temple of Kichijôji, at Komagomé, in Yedo. Eighteen years later, the retainer of a certain Daimio, having had a dispute with a sailor belonging to an Osaka coasting-ship, killed the sailor; and, an investigation having been made into the matter by the Governor of Osaka, the retainer was ordered to perform *hara-kiri*, on the twentieth day of the sixth month, in the temple called Sokusanji, in Osaka. During the period Shôhô (middle of seventeenth century), a certain man, having been guilty of heinous misconduct, performed *hara-kiri* in the temple called Shimpukuji, in the Kôji-street of Yedo. On the fourth day of the fifth month of the second year of the period Meiréki (A.D. 1656), a certain man, for having avenged the death of his cousin's husband at a place called Shimidzudani, in the Kôji-street, disemboweled himself in the temple called Honseiji. On the twenty-sixth day of the sixth month of the eighth year of the period Yempô (A.D. 1680), at the funeral ceremonies in honor of the anniversary of the death of Genyuin Sama, a former Shogun, Naitô Idzumi no Kami, having a cause of hatred against Nagai Shinano no Kami, killed him at one blow with a short sword, in the main hall of the temple called Zôjôji (the burial-place of the Shoguns in Yedo). Idzumi no Kami was arrested by the officers present, and on the following day performed *hara-kiri* at Kiridôshi, in the temple called Seiriuji.

In modern times the ceremony has taken place at night, either in the palace or in the garden of a Daimio, to whom the condemned man has been given in charge. Whether it takes place in the palace or in the garden depends upon the rank of the individual. Daimios and Hatamotos, as a matter of course, and the higher retainers of the Shogun, disembowel themselves in the palace: retainers of lower rank should do so in the garden. In the case of vassals of feudatories, according to the rank of their families, those who, being above the grade of captains, carry the bâton,[27] should perform *hara-kiri* in the palace; all others in the garden. If, when the time comes, the persons engaged in the ceremony are in any doubt as to the proper rules to be followed, they should inquire of competent persons, and settle the question. At the beginning of the eighteenth century, during the period Genroku, when Asano Takumi no Kami[28] disemboweled himself in the palace of a Daimio called Tamura, as the whole thing was sudden and unexpected, the garden was covered with matting, and on the top of this thick mats were laid and a carpet, and the affair was concluded so; but there are people who say that it was wrong to treat a Daimio thus, as if he had been an ordinary samurai. But it is said that in old times it was the custom that the ceremony should take place upon a leather carpet spread in the garden; and further, that the proper place is inside a picket fence tied together in the garden: so it is wrong for persons who are only acquainted with one form of the ceremony to accuse Tamura of having acted improperly. If, however, the object was to save the house from the pollution of blood, then the accusation of ill-will may well be brought; for the preparation of the place is of great importance.

Formerly it was the custom that, for personages of importance, the enclosure within the picket fence should be of thirty-six feet square. An entrance was made to the south, and another to the north: the door to the south was called *Shugiyômon* ("the door of the practice of virtue"); that to the north was called *Umbanmon* ("the door of the warm basin"[29]). Two mats, with white binding, were arranged in the shape of a hammer, the one at right angles to the other; six feet of white silk, four feet broad, were stretched on the mat, which was placed lengthwise; at the four corners were erected four posts for curtains. In front of the two mats was erected a portal, eight feet high by six feet broad, in the shape of the portals in front of temples, made of a fine sort of bamboo wrapped in white[30] silk. White curtains, four feet broad, were hung at the four corners, and four flags, six feet long, on which should be inscribed four quotations from the sacred books. These flags, it is said, were immediately after the ceremony carried away to the grave. At night two lights were placed, one upon either side of the two mats. The candles were placed in saucers upon stands of bamboo, four feet high, wrapped in white silk. The person who was to disembowel himself, entering the picket fence by the north entrance, took his place upon the white silk upon the mat facing the north. Some there were, however, who said that he should sit facing the west: in that case the whole place must be prepared accordingly. The seconds enter the enclosure by the south entrance, at the same time as the principal enters by the north, and take their places on the mat that is placed crosswise.

Nowadays, when the *hara-kiri* is performed inside the palace, a temporary place is made on purpose, either in the garden or in some unoccupied spot; but if the criminal is to die on the day on which he is given in charge, or on the next day, the ceremony, having to take place so quickly, is performed in the reception-room. Still, even if there is a lapse of time between the period of giving the prisoner in charge and the execution, it is better that the ceremony should take place in a decent room in the house than in a place made on purpose. If it is heard that, for fear of dirtying his house, a man has made a place expressly, he will be blamed for it. It surely can be no disgrace to the house of a soldier that he was ordered to perform the last offices towards a samurai who died by *hara-kiri*. To slay his enemy against whom he has cause of hatred, and then to kill himself, is the part of a noble samurai; and it is sheer nonsense to look upon the place where he has disemboweled himself as polluted. In the beginning of the eighteenth century, seventeen of the retainers of Asano Takumi no Kami performed *hara-kiri* in the garden of a palace at Shirokané, in Yedo. When it was over, the people of the palace called upon the priests of a sect named Shugenja to come and purify the place; but when the lord of the palace heard this, he ordered the place to be left as it was; for what need was there to purify a place where faithful samurai had died by their own hand? But in other palaces to which the remainder of the retainers of Takumi no Kami were entrusted, it is said that the places of execution were purified. But the people of that day praised Kumamoto Ko (the Prince of Higo), to whom the palace at Shirokané belonged. It is a currish thing to look upon death in battle or by *hara-kiri* as a pollution: this is a thing to bear in mind. In modern times the place of *hara-kiri* is eighteen feet square in all cases; in the centre is a place to sit upon, and the condemned man is made to sit facing the witnesses; at other times he is placed with his side to the witnesses: this is according to the nature of the spot. In some cases the seconds turn their backs to the witnesses. It is open to question, however, whether this is not a breach of etiquette. The witnesses should be consulted upon these arrangements. If the witnesses have no objection, the condemned man should be placed directly opposite to them. The place where the witnesses are seated should be removed more than twelve or eighteen feet from the condemned man. The place from which the sentence is read should also be close by. The writer has been furnished with a plan of the *hara-kiri* as it is performed at present. Although the ceremony is gone through in other ways also, still it is more convenient to follow the manner indicated.

If the execution takes place in a room, a kerchief of five breadths of white cotton cloth or a quilt should be laid down, and it is also said that two mats should be prepared; however, as there are already mats in the room, there is no need for special mats: two red rugs should be spread over all, sewed together, one on the top of the other; for if the white cotton cloth be used alone, the blood will soak through on to the mats; therefore it is right the rugs should be spread. On the twenty-third day of the eighth month of the fourth year of the period Yenkiyô (A.D. 1740), at the *hara-kiri* of a certain person there were laid down a white cloth, eight feet square, and on that a quilt of light green cotton, six feet square, and on that a cloth of white hemp, six feet square, and on that two rugs. On the third day of the ninth month of the ninth year of the period Tempô (A.D. 1838), at the *hara-kiri* of a certain person it is said that there were spread a large double cloth of white cotton, and on that two rugs. But, of these two occasions, the first must be commended for its careful preparation. If the execution be at night, candlesticks of white wood should be placed at each of the four corners, lest the seconds be hindered in their work. In the place where the witnesses are to sit, ordinary candlesticks should be placed, according to etiquette; but an excessive illumination is not decorous. Two screens covered with white paper should be set up, behind the shadow of which are concealed the dirk upon a tray, a bucket to hold the head after it has been cut off, an incense-burner, a pail of water, and a basin. The above rules apply equally to the ceremonies observed when the *hara-kiri* takes place in a garden. In the latter case the place is hung round with a white curtain, which need not be new for the occasion. Two mats, a white cloth, and a rug are spread. If the execution is at night, lanterns of white paper are placed on bamboo poles at the four corners. The sentence having been read inside the house, the persons engaged in the ceremony proceed to the place of execution; but, according to circumstances, the sentence may be read at the place itself. In the case of Asano Takumi no Kami, the sentence was read out in the house, and he afterwards performed *hara-kiri* in the garden. On the third day of the fourth month of the fourth year of the period Tenmei (A.D. 1784), a Hatamoto named Sano, having received his sentence in the supreme court-house, disemboweled himself in the garden in front of the prison. When the ceremony takes place in the garden, matting must be spread all the way to the place, so that sandals need not be worn. The reason for this is that some men in that position suffer from a rush of blood to the head, from nervousness, so their sandals might slip off their feet without their being aware of their loss; and as this would have a very bad appearance, it is better to spread matting. Care must be taken lest, in spreading the matting, a place be left where two mats join, against which the foot might trip. The white screens and other things are prepared as has been directed above. If any curtailment is made, it must be done as well as circumstances will permit. According to the crime of which a man who is handed over to any Daimio's charge is guilty, it is known whether he will have to perform *hara-kiri*; and the preparations should be made accordingly. Asano Takumi no Kami was taken to the palace of Tamura Sama at the hour of the monkey (between three and five in the afternoon), took off his dress of ceremony, partook of a bowl of soup and five dishes, and drank two cups of warm water, and at the hour of the cock (between five and seven in the evening) disemboweled himself. A case of this kind requires much attention; for great care should be taken that the preparations be carried on without the knowledge of the principal. If a temporary room has been built expressly for the occasion, to avoid pollution to the house, it should be kept a secret. It once happened that a criminal was received in charge at the palace of a certain nobleman, and when his people were about to erect a temporary building for the ceremony, they wrote to consult some of the parties concerned; the letter ran as follows—

"The house in which we live is very small and inconvenient in all respects. We have ordered the guard to treat our prisoner with all respect; but our retainers who are placed on guard are much inconvenienced for want of space; besides, in the event of fire breaking out or any extraordinary event taking place, the place is so small that it would be difficult to get out. We are thinking, therefore, of adding an apartment to the original building, so that the guard may be able at all times to go in and out freely, and that if, in case of fire or otherwise, we should have to leave the house, we may do so easily. We beg to consult you upon this point."

When a samurai has to perform *hara-kiri* by the command of his own feudal lord, the ceremony should take place in one of the lesser palaces of the clan. Once upon a time, a certain prince of the Inouyé clan, having a just cause of offence against his steward, who was called Ishikawa Tôzayémon, and wishing to punish him, caused him to be killed in his principal palace at Kandabashi, in Yedo. When this matter was reported to the Shogun, having been convicted of disrespect of the privileges of the city, he was ordered to remove to his lesser palace at Asakusa. Now, although the *hara-kiri* cannot be called properly an execution, still, as it only differs from an ordinary execution in that by it the honor of the samurai is not affected, it is only a question of degree; it is a matter of ceremonial. If the principal palace[31] is a long distance from the Shogun's castle, then the *hara-kiri* may take place there; but there can be no objection whatever to its taking place in a minor palace. Nowadays, when a man is condemned to *hara-kiri* by a Daimio, the ceremony usually takes place in one of the lesser palaces; the place commonly selected is an open space near the horse-exercising ground, and the preparations which I have described above are often shortened according to circumstances.

When a retainer is suddenly ordered to perform *hara-kiri* during a journey, a temple or shrine should be hired for the occasion. On these hurried occasions, coarse mats, faced with finer matting or common mats, may be used. If the criminal is of rank to have an armor-bearer, a carpet of skin should be spread, should one be easily procurable. The straps of the skin (which are at the head) should, according to old custom, be to the front, so that the fur may point backwards. In old days, when the ceremony took place in a garden, a carpet of skin was spread. To hire a temple for the purpose of causing a man to perform *hara-kiri* was of frequent occurrence: it is doubtful whether it may be done at the present time. This sort of question should be referred beforehand to some competent person, that the course to be adopted may be clearly understood.

In the period Kambun (A.D. 1661-1673) a Prince Sakai, travelling through the Bishiu territory, hired a temple or shrine for one of his retainers to disembowel himself in; and so the affair was concluded.

ON THE CEREMONIES OBSERVED AT THE HARA-KIRI OF A PERSON GIVEN IN CHARGE TO A DAIMIO.

When a man has been ordered by the Government to disembowel himself, the public censors, who have been appointed to act as witnesses, write to the prince who has the criminal in charge, to inform them that they will go to his palace on public business. This message is written directly to the chief, and is sent by an assistant censor; and a suitable answer is returned to it. Before the ceremony, the witnesses send an assistant censor to see the place, and look at a plan of the house, and to take a list of the names of the persons who are to be present; he also has an interview with the *kaishaku*, or seconds, and examines them upon the way of performing the ceremonies. When all the preparations have been made, he goes to fetch the censors; and they all proceed together to the place of execution, dressed in their hempen-cloth dress of ceremony. The retainers of the palace are collected to do obeisance in the entrance-yard; and the lord, to whom the criminal has been entrusted, goes as far as the front porch to meet the censors, and conducts them to the front reception-room. The chief censor then announces to the lord of the palace that he has come to read out the sentence of such an one who has been condemned to perform *hara-kiri*, and that the second censor has come to witness the execution of the sentence. The lord of the palace then inquires whether he is expected to attend the execution in person, and, if any of the relations or family of the criminal should beg to receive his remains, whether their request should be complied with; after this he announces that he will order everything to be made ready, and leaves the room. Tea, a fire-box for smoking, and sweetmeats are set before the censors; but they decline to accept any hospitality until their business shall have been concluded. The minor officials follow the same rule. If the censors express a wish to see the place of execution, the retainers of the palace show the way, and their lord accompanies them; in this, however, he may be replaced by one of his *karô* or councilors. They then return, and take their seats in the reception-room. After this, when all the preparations have been made, the master of the house leads the censors to the place where the sentence is to be read; and it is etiquette that they should wear both sword and dirk.[32] The lord of the palace takes his place on one side; the inferior censors sit on either side in a lower place. The councilors and other officers of the palace also take their places. One of the councilors present, addressing the censors without moving from his place, asks whether he shall bring forth the prisoner.

Previously to this, the retainers of the palace, going to the room where the prisoner is confined, inform him that, as the censors have arrived, he should change his dress, and the attendants bring out a change of clothes upon a large tray: it is when he has finished his toilet that the witnesses go forth and take their places in the appointed order, and the principal is then introduced. He is preceded by one man, who should be of the rank of *Mono-gashira* (retainer of the fourth rank), who wears a dirk, but no sword. Six men act as attendants; they should be of the fifth or sixth rank; they walk on either side of the principal. They are followed by one man who should be of the rank of *Yônin* (councilor of the second class). When they reach the place, the leading man draws on one side and sits down, and the six attendants sit down on either side of the principal. The officer who follows him sits down behind him, and the chief censor reads the sentence.

When the reading of the sentence is finished, the principal leaves the room and again changes his clothes, and the chief censor immediately leaves the palace; but the lord of the palace does not conduct him to the door. The second censor returns to the reception-room until the principal has changed his clothes. When the principal has taken his seat at the place of execution, the councilors of the palace announce to the second censor that all is ready; he then proceeds to the place, wearing his sword and dirk. The lord of the palace, also wearing his sword and dirk, takes his seat on one side. The inferior censors and councilors sit in front of the censor: they wear the dirk only. The assistant second brings a dirk upon a tray, and, having placed it in front of the principal, withdraws on one side: when the principal leans his head forward, his chief second strikes off his head, which is immediately shown to the censor, who identifies it, and tells the master of the palace that he is satisfied, and thanks him for all his trouble. The corpse, as it lies, is hidden by a white screen which is set up around it, and incense is brought out. The witnesses leave the place. The lord of the palace accompanies them as far as the porch, and the retainers prostrate themselves in the yard as before. The retainers who should be present at the place of execution are one or two councilors (Karô), two or three second councilors (Yônin), two or three Mono-gashira, one chief of the palace (Rusui), six attendants, one chief second, two assistant seconds, one man to carry incense, who need not be a person of rank—any samurai will do. They attend to the setting up of the white screen.

The duty of burying the corpse and of setting the place in order again devolves upon four men; these are selected from samurai of the middle or lower class; during the performance of their duties, they hitch up their trousers and wear neither sword nor dirk. Their names are previously sent in to the censor, who acts as witness; and to the junior censors, should they desire it. Before the arrival of the chief censor, the requisite utensils for extinguishing a fire are prepared, firemen are engaged,[33] and officers constantly go the rounds to watch against fire. From the time when the chief censor comes into the house until he leaves it, no one is allowed to enter the premises. The servants on guard at the entrance porch should wear their hempen dresses of ceremony. Everything in the palace should be conducted with decorum, and the strictest attention paid in all things.

When any one is condemned to hara-kiri, it would be well that people should go to the palace of the Prince of Higo, and learn what transpired at the execution of the Rônins of Asano Takumi no Kami. A curtain was hung round the garden in front of the reception-room; three mats were laid down, and upon these was placed a white cloth. The condemned men were kept in the reception-room, and summoned, one by one; two men, one on each side, accompanied them; the second, followed behind; and they proceeded together to the place of execution. When the execution was concluded in each case, the corpse was hidden from the sight of the chief witness by a white screen, folded up in white cloth, placed on a mat, and carried off to the rear by two foot-soldiers; it was then placed in a coffin. The blood-stained ground was sprinkled with sand, and swept clean; fresh mats were laid down, and the place prepared anew; after which the next man was summoned to come forth.

ON CERTAIN THINGS TO BE BORNE IN MIND BY THE WITNESSES.

When a clansman is ordered by his feudal lord to perform *hara-kiri*, the sentence must be read out by the censor of the clan, who also acts as witness. He should take his place in front of the criminal, at a distance of twelve feet; according to some books, the distance should be eighteen feet, and he should sit obliquely, not facing the criminal; he should lay his sword down by his side, but, if he pleases, he may wear it in his girdle; he must read out the sentence distinctly. If the sentence be a long document, to begin reading in a very loud voice and afterwards drop into a whisper has an appearance of faint-heartedness; but to read it throughout in a low voice is worse still: it should be delivered clearly from beginning to end. It is the duty of the chief witness to set an example of fortitude to the other persons who are to take part in the execution. When the second has finished his work, he carries the head to the chief witness, who, after inspecting it, must declare that he has identified it; he then should take his sword, and leave his place. It is sufficient, however, that the head should be struck off without being carried to the chief witness; in that case, the second receives his instructions beforehand. On rising, the chief witness should step out with his left foot and turn to the left. If the ceremony takes place out of doors, the chief witness, wearing his sword and dirk, should sit upon a box; he must wear his hempen dress of ceremony; he may hitch his trousers up slightly; according to his rank, he may wear his full dress—that is, wings over his full dress. It is the part of the chief witness to instruct the seconds and others in the duties which they have to perform, and also to preconcert measures in the event of any mishap occurring.

If whilst the various persons to be engaged in the ceremony are rubbing up their military lore, and preparing themselves for the event, any other person should come in, they should immediately turn the conversation. Persons of the rank of samurai should be familiar with all the details of the *hara-kiri*; and to be seen discussing what should be done in case anything went wrong, and so forth, would have an appearance of ignorance. If, however, an intimate friend should go to the place, rather than have any painful concealment, he may be consulted upon the whole affair.

When the sentence has been read, it is probable that the condemned man will have some last words to say to the chief witness. It must depend on the nature of what he has to say whether it will be received or not. If he speaks in a confused or bewildered manner, no attention is paid to it: his second should lead him away, of his own accord or at a sign from the chief witness.

If the condemned man be a person who has been given in charge to a prince by the Government, the prince after the reading of the sentence should send his retainers to the prisoner with a message to say that the decrees of the Government are not to be eluded, but that if he has any last wishes to express, they are ordered by their lord to receive them. If the prisoner is a man of high rank, the lord of the palace should go in person to hear his last wishes.

The condemned man should answer in the following way—

"Sir, I thank you for your careful consideration, but I have nothing that I wish to say. I am greatly indebted to you for the great kindness which I have received since I have been under your charge. I beg you to take my respects to your lord and to the gentlemen of your clan who have treated me so well." Or he may say, "Sirs, I have nothing to say; yet, since you are so kind as to think of me, I should be obliged if you would deliver such and such a message to such an one." This is the proper and becoming sort of speech for the occasion. If the prisoner entrusts them with any message, the retainers should receive it in such a manner as to set his mind at rest. Should he ask for writing materials in order to write a letter, as this is forbidden by the law, they should tell him so, and not grant his request. Still they must feel that it is painful to refuse the request of a dying man, and must do their best to assist him. They must exhaust every available kindness and civility, as was done in the period Genroku, in the case of the Rônins of Asano Takumi no Kami. The Prince of Higo, after the sentence had been read, caused paper and writing materials to be taken to their room. If the prisoner is light-headed from excitement, it is no use furnishing him with writing materials. It must depend upon circumstances; but when a man has murdered another, having made up his mind to abide by the consequences, then that man's execution should be carried through with all honor. When a man kills another on the spot, in a fit of ungovernable passion, and then is bewildered and dazed by his own act, the same pains need not be taken to conduct matters punctiliously. If the prisoner be a careful man, he will take an early opportunity after he has been given in charge to express his wishes. To carry kindness so far as to supply writing materials and the like is not obligatory. If any doubt exists upon the point, the chief witness may be consulted.

After the Rônins of Asano Takumi no Kami had heard their sentence in the palace of Matsudaira Oki no Kami, that Daimio in person went and took leave of them, and calling Oishi Chikara,[34] the son of their chief, to him, said, "I have heard that your mother is at home in your own country; how she will grieve when she hears of your death and that of your father, I can well imagine. If you have any message that you wish to leave for her, tell me, without standing upon ceremony, and I will transmit it without delay." For a while Chikara kept his head bent down towards the ground; at last he drew back a little, and, lifting his head, said, "I humbly thank your lordship for what you have been pleased to say. My father warned me from the first that our crime was so great that, even were we to be pardoned by a gracious judgment upon one count, I must not forget that there would be a hundred million counts against us for which we must commit suicide; and that if I disregarded his words his hatred would pursue me after death. My father impressed this upon me at the temple called Sengakuji, and again when I was separated from him to be taken to the palace of Prince Sengoku. Now my father and myself have been condemned to perform *hara-kiri*, according to the wish of our hearts. Still I cannot forget to think of my mother. When we parted at Kiyôto, she told me that our separation would be for long, and she bade me not to play the coward when I thought of her. As I took a long leave of her then, I have no message to send to her now." When he spoke thus, Oki no Kami and all his retainers, who were drawn up around him, were moved to tears in admiration of his heroism.

Although it is right that the condemned man should bathe and partake of wine and food, these details should be curtailed. Even should he desire these favors, it must depend upon his conduct whether they be granted or refused. He should be caused to die as quickly as possible. Should he wish for some water to drink, it should be given to him. If in his talk he should express himself like a noble samurai, all pains should be exhausted in carrying out his execution. Yet however careful a man he may be, as he nears his death his usual demeanor will undergo a change. If the execution is delayed, in all probability it will cause the prisoner's courage to fail him; therefore, as soon as the sentence shall have been passed, the execution should be brought to a conclusion. This, again, is a point for the chief witness to remember.

CONCERNING SECONDS (KAISHAKU).

When the condemned man is one who has been given in charge for execution, six attendants are employed; when the execution is within the clan, then two or three attendants will suffice; the number, however, must depend upon the rank of the principal. Men of great nerve and strength must be selected for the office; they must wear their hempen dress of ceremony, and tuck up their trousers; they must on no account wear either sword or dirk, but have a small poniard hidden in their bosom: these are the officers who attend upon the condemned man when he changes his dress, and who sit by him on the right hand and on the left hand to guard him whilst the sentence is being read. In the event of any mistake occurring (such as the prisoner attempting to escape), they knock him down; and should he be unable to stand or to walk, they help to support him. The attendants accompanying the principal to the place of execution, if they are six in number, four of them take their seats some way off and mount guard, while the other two should sit close behind the principal. They must understand that should there be any mistake they must throw the condemned man, and, holding him down, cut off his head with their poniard, or stab him to death. If the second bungles in cutting off the head and the principal attempts to rise, it is the duty of the attendants to kill him. They must help him to take off his upper garments and bare his body. In recent times, however, there have been cases where the upper garments have not been removed: this depends upon circumstances. The setting up of the white screen, and the laying the corpse in the coffin, are duties which, although they may be performed by other officers, originally devolved upon the six attendants. When a common man is executed, he is bound with cords, and so made to take his place; but a samurai wears his dress of ceremony, is presented with a dagger, and dies thus. There ought to be no anxiety lest such a man should attempt to escape; still, as there is no knowing what these six attendants may be called upon to do, men should be selected who thoroughly understand their business.

The seconds are three in number—the chief second, the assistant second, and the inferior second. When the execution is carried out with proper solemnity, three men are employed; still a second and assistant second are sufficient. If three men serve as seconds, their several duties are as follows:—The chief second strikes off the head; that is his duty: he is the most important officer in the execution by *hara-kiri*. The assistant second brings forward the tray, on which is placed the dirk; that is his duty: he must perform his part in such a manner that the principal second is not hindered in his work. The assistant second is the officer of second importance in the execution. The third or inferior second carries the head to the chief witness for identification; and in the event of something suddenly occurring to hinder either of the other two seconds, he should bear in mind that he must be ready to act as his substitute: his is an office of great importance, and a proper person must be selected to fill it.

Although there can be no such thing as a *kaishaku* (second) in any case except in one of *hara-kiri*, still in old times guardians and persons who assisted others were also called *kaishaku*: the reason for this is because the *kaishaku*, or second, comes to the assistance of the principal. If the principal were to make any mistake at the fatal moment, it would be a disgrace to his dead body: it is in order to prevent such mistakes that the *kaishaku*, or second, is employed. It is the duty of the *kaishaku* to consider this as his first duty.

When a man is appointed to act as second to another, what shall be said of him if he accepts the office with a smiling face? Yet must he not put on a face of distress. It is as well to attempt to excuse oneself from performing the duty. There is no heroism in cutting a man's head off well, and it is a disgrace to do it in a bungling manner; yet must not a man allege lack of skill as a pretext for evading the office, for it is an unworthy thing that a samurai should want the skill required to behead a man. If there are any that advocate employing young men as seconds, it should rather be said that their hands are inexpert. To play the coward and yield up the office to another man is out of the question. When a man is called upon to perform the office, he should express his readiness to use his sword (the dirk may be employed, but the sword is the proper weapon). As regards the sword, the second should borrow that of the principal: if there is any objection to this, he should receive a sword from his lord; he should not use his own sword. When the assistant seconds have been appointed, the three should take counsel together about the details of the place of execution, when they have been carefully instructed by their superiors in all the ceremonies; and having made careful inquiry, should there be anything wrong, they should appeal to their superiors for instruction. The seconds wear their dresses of ceremony when the criminal is a man given in charge by the Government: when he is one of their own clan, they need only wear the trousers of the samurai. In old days it is said that they were dressed in the same way as the principal; and some authorities assert that at the *hara-kiri* of a nobleman of high rank the seconds should wear white clothes, and that the handle of the sword should be wrapped in white silk. If the execution takes place in the house, they should partially tuck up their trousers; if in the garden, they should tuck them up entirely.

The seconds should address the principal, and say, "Sir, we have been appointed to act as your seconds; we pray you to set your mind at rest," and so forth; but this must depend upon the rank of the criminal. At this time, too, if the principal has any last wish to express, the second should receive it, and should treat him with every consideration in order to relieve his anxiety. If the second has been selected by the principal on account of old friendship between them, or if the latter, during the time that he has been in charge, has begged some special retainer of the palace to act as his second in the event of his being condemned to death, the person so selected should thank the principal for choosing so unworthy a person, and promise to beg his lord to allow him to act as second: so he should answer, and comfort him, and having reported the matter to his lord, should act as second. He should take that opportunity to borrow his principal's sword in some such terms as the following: "As I am to have the honor of being your second, I would fain borrow your sword for the occasion. It may be a consolation to you to perish by your own sword, with which you are familiar." If, however, the principal declines, and prefers to be executed with the second's sword, his wish must be complied with. If the second should make an awkward cut with his own sword, it is a disgrace to him; therefore he should borrow some one else's sword, so that the blame may rest with the sword, and not with the swordsman. Although this is the rule, and although every samurai should wear a sword fit to cut off a man's head, still if the principal has begged to be executed with the second's own sword, it must be done as he desires.

It is probable that the condemned man will inquire of his second about the arrangements which have been made: he must attend therefore to rendering himself capable of answering all such questions. Once upon a time, when the condemned man inquired of his second whether his head would be cut off at the moment when he received the tray with the dirk upon it, "No," replied the second; "at the moment when you stab yourself with the dirk your head will be cut off." At the execution of one Sanô, he told his second that, when he had stabbed himself in the belly, he would utter a cry; and begged him to be cool when he cut off his head. The second replied that he would do as he wished, but begged him in the meantime to take the tray with the dirk, according to proper form. When Sanô reached out his hand to take the tray, the second cut off his head immediately. Now, although this was not exactly right, still as the second acted so in order to save a samurai from the disgrace of performing the *hara-kiri* improperly (by crying out), it can never be wrong for a second to act kindly. If the principal urgently requests to be allowed really to disembowel himself, his wish may, according to circumstances, be granted; but in this case care must be taken that no time be lost in striking off the head. The custom of striking off the head, the prisoner only going through the semblance of disemboweling himself, dates from the period Yempô (about 190 years ago).

When the principal has taken his place, the second strips his right shoulder of the dress of ceremony, which he allows to fall behind his sleeve, and, drawing his sword, lays down the scabbard, taking care that his weapon is not seen by the principal; then he takes his place on the left of the principal and close behind him. The principal should sit facing the west, and the second facing the north, and in that position should he strike the blow. When the second perceives the assistant second bring out the tray on which is laid the dirk, he must brace up his nerves and settle his heart beneath his navel: when the tray is laid down, he must put himself in position to strike the blow. He should step out first with the left foot, and then change so as to bring his right foot forward: this is the position which he should assume to strike; he may, however, reverse the position of his feet. When the principal removes his upper garments, the second must poise his sword: when the principal reaches out his hand to draw the tray towards him, as he leans his head forward a little, is the exact moment for the second to strike. There are all sorts of traditions about this. Some say that the principal should take the tray and raise it respectfully to his head, and set it down; and that this is the moment to strike. There are three rules for the time of cutting off the head: the first is when the dirk is laid on the tray; the second is when the principal looks at the left side of his belly before inserting the dirk; the third is when he inserts the dirk. If these three moments are allowed to pass, it becomes a difficult matter to cut off the head: so says tradition. However, four moments for cutting are also recorded: first, when the assistant second retires after having laid down the stand on which is the dirk; second, when the principal draws the stand towards him; third, when he takes the dirk in his hand; fourth, when he makes the incision into the belly. Although all four ways are approved, still the first is too soon; the last three are right and proper. In short, the blow should be struck without delay. If he has struck off the head at a blow without failure, the second, taking care not to raise his sword, but holding it point downwards, should retire backward a little and wipe his weapon kneeling; he should have plenty of white paper ready in his girdle or in his bosom to wipe away the blood and rub up his sword; having replaced his sword in its scabbard, he should readjust his upper garments and take his seat to the rear. When the head has fallen, the junior second should enter, and, taking up the head, present it to the witness for inspection. When he has identified it, the ceremony is concluded. If there is no assistant or junior second, the second, as soon as he has cut off the head, carrying his sword reversed in his left hand, should take the head in his right hand, holding it by the top-knot of hair, should advance towards the witness, passing on the right side of the corpse, and show the right profile of the head to the witness, resting the chin of the head upon the hilt of his sword, and kneeling on his left knee; then returning again round by the left of the corpse, kneeling on his left knee, and carrying the head in his left hand and resting it on the edge of his sword, he should again show the left profile to the witness. It is also laid down as another rule, that the second, laying down his sword, should take out paper from the bosom of his dress, and placing the head in the palm of his left hand, and taking the top-knot of hair in his right hand, should lay the head upon the paper, and so submit it for inspection. Either way may be said to be right.

NOTE.—To lay down thick paper, and place the head on it, shows a disposition to pay respect to the head; to place it on the edge of the sword is insulting: the course pursued must depend upon the rank of the person. If the ceremony is to be curtailed, it may end with the cutting off of the head: that must be settled beforehand, in consultation with the witness. In the event of the second making a false cut, so as not to strike off the head at a blow, the second must take the head by the top-knot, and, pressing it down, cut it off. Should he take bad aim and cut the shoulder by mistake, and should the principal rise and cry out, before he has time to writhe, he should hold him down and stab him to death, and then cut off his head, or the assistant seconds, who are sitting behind, should come forward and hold him down, while the chief second cuts off his head. It may be necessary for the second, after he has cut off the head, to push down the body, and then take up the head for inspection. If the body does not fall at once, which is said to be sometimes the case, the second should pull the feet to make it fall.

There are some who say that the perfect way for the second to cut off the head is not to cut right through the neck at a blow, but to leave a little uncut, and, as the head hangs by the skin, to seize the top-knot and slice it off, and then submit it for inspection. The reason of this is, lest, the head being struck off at a blow, the ceremony should be confounded with an ordinary execution. According to the old authorities, this is the proper and respectful manner. After the head is cut off, the eyes are apt to blink, and the mouth to move, and to bite the pebbles and sand. This being hateful to see, at what amongst samurai is so important an occasion, and being a shameful thing, it is held to be best not to let the head fall, but to hold back a little in delivering the blow. Perhaps this may be right; yet it is a very difficult matter to cut so as to leave the head hanging by a little flesh, and there is the danger of missing the cut; and as any mistake in the cut is most horrible to see, it is better to strike a fair blow at once. Others say that, even when the head is struck off at a blow, the semblance of slicing it off should be gone through afterwards; yet be it borne in mind that; this is unnecessary.

Three methods of carrying the sword are recognized amongst those skilled in swordsmanship. If the rank of the principal be high, the sword is raised aloft; if the principal and second are of equal rank, the sword is carried at the centre of the body; if the principal be of inferior rank, the sword is allowed to hang downwards. The proper position for the second to strike from is kneeling on one knee, but there is no harm in his standing up: others say that, if the execution takes place inside the house, the second should kneel; if in the garden, he should stand. These are not points upon which to insist obstinately: a man should strike in whatever position is most convenient to him.

The chief duty for the assistant second to bear in mind is the bringing in of the tray with the dirk, which should be produced very quietly when the principal takes his place: it should be placed so that the condemned man may have to stretch his hand well out in order to reach it.[35] The assistant second then returns to his own place; but if the condemned man shows any signs of agitation, the assistant second must lend his assistance, so that the head may be properly cut off. It once happened that the condemned man, having received the tray from the assistant second, held it up for a long time without putting it down, until those near him had over and over again urged him to set it down. It also happens that after the tray has been set down, and the assistant second has retired, the condemned man does not put out his hand to take it; then must the assistant second press him to take it. Also the principal may ask that the tray be placed a little nearer to him, in which case his wish must be granted. The tray may also be placed in such a way that the assistant second, holding it in his left hand, may reach the dirk to the condemned man, who leans forward to take it. Which is the best of all these ways is uncertain. The object to aim at is, that the condemned man should lean forward to receive the blow. Whether the assistant second retires, or not, must depend upon the attitude assumed by the condemned man.

If the prisoner be an unruly, violent man, a fan, instead of a dirk, should be placed upon the tray; and should he object to this, he should be told, in answer, that the substitution of the fan is an ancient custom. This may occur sometimes. It is said that once upon a time, in one of the palaces of the Daimios, a certain brave matron murdered a man, and having been allowed to die with all the honors of the *hara-kiri*, a fan was placed upon the tray, and her head was cut off. This may be considered right and proper. If the condemned man appears inclined to be turbulent, the seconds, without showing any sign of alarm, should hurry to his side, and, urging him to get ready, quickly cause him to make all his preparations with speed, and to sit down in his place; the chief second, then drawing his sword, should get ready to strike, and, ordering him to proceed as fast as possible with the ceremony of receiving the tray, should perform his duty without appearing to be afraid.

A certain Prince Katô, having condemned one of his councilors to death, assisted at the ceremony behind a curtain of slips of bamboo. The councilor, whose name was Katayama, was bound, and during that time glared fiercely at the curtain, and showed no signs of fear. The chief second was a man named Jihei, who had always been used to treat Katayama with great respect. So Jihei, sword in hand, said to Katayama, "Sir, your last moment has arrived: be so good as to turn your cheek so that your head may be straight." When Katayama heard this, he replied, "Fellow, you are insolent;" and as he was looking round, Jihei struck the fatal blow. The lord Katô afterwards inquired of Jihei what was the reason of this; and he replied that, as he saw that the prisoner was meditating treason, he determined to kill him at once, and put a stop to this rebellious spirit. This is a pattern for other seconds to bear in mind.

When the head has been struck off, it becomes the duty of the junior second to take it up by the top-knot, and, placing it upon some thick paper laid over the palm of his hand, to carry it for inspection by the witness. This ceremony has been explained above. If the head be bald, he should pierce the left ear with the stiletto carried in the scabbard of his dirk, and so carry it to be identified. He must carry thick paper in the bosom of his dress. Inside the paper he shall place a bag with rice bran and ashes, in order that he may carry the head without being sullied by the blood. When the identification of the head is concluded, the junior second's duty is to place it in a bucket.

If anything should occur to hinder the chief second, the assistant second must take his place. It happened on one occasion that before the execution took place the chief second lost his nerve, yet he cut off the head without any difficulty; but when it came to taking up the head for inspection, his nervousness so far got the better of him as to be extremely inconvenient. This is a thing against which persons acting as seconds have to guard.

As a corollary to the above elaborate statement of the ceremonies proper to be observed at the *hara-kiri*, I may here describe an instance of such an execution which I was sent officially to witness. The condemned man was Taki Zenzaburô, an officer of the Prince of Bizen, who gave the order to fire upon the foreign settlement at Hiogo in the month of February 1868, — an attack to which I have alluded in the preamble to the story of the Eta Maiden and the Hatamoto. Up to that time no foreigner had witnessed such an execution, which was rather looked upon as a traveler's fable.

The ceremony, which was ordered by the Mikado himself, took place at 10.30 at night in the temple of Seifukuji, the headquarters of the Satsuma troops at Hiogo. A witness was sent from each of the foreign legations. We were seven foreigners in all.

We were conducted to the temple by officers of the Princes of Satsuma and Choshiu. Although the ceremony was to be conducted in the most private manner, the casual remarks which we overheard in the streets, and a crowd lining the principal entrance to the temple, showed that it was a matter of no little interest to the public. The courtyard of the temple presented a most picturesque sight; it was crowded with soldiers standing about in knots round large fires, which threw a dim flickering light over the heavy eaves and quaint gable-ends of the sacred buildings. We were shown into an inner room, where we were to wait until the preparation for the ceremony was completed: in the next room to us were the high Japanese officers. After a long interval, which seemed doubly long from the silence which prevailed, Itô Shunské, the provisional Governor of Hiogo, came and took down our names, and informed us that seven *kenshi*, sheriffs or witnesses, would attend on the part of the Japanese. He and another officer represented the Mikado; two captains of Satsuma's infantry, and two of Choshiu's, with a representative of the Prince of

Bizen, the clan of the condemned man, completed the number, which was probably arranged in order to tally with that of the foreigners. Itô Shunské further inquired whether we wished to put any questions to the prisoner. We replied in the negative.

A further delay then ensued, after which we were invited to follow the Japanese witnesses into the *hondo* or main hall of the temple, where the ceremony was to be performed. It was an imposing scene. A large hall with a high roof supported by dark pillars of wood. From the ceiling hung a profusion of those huge gilt lamps and ornaments peculiar to Buddhist temples. In front of the high altar, where the floor, covered with beautiful white mats, is raised some three or four inches from the ground, was laid a rug of scarlet felt. Tall candles placed at regular intervals gave out a dim mysterious light, just sufficient to let all the proceedings be seen. The seven Japanese took their places on the left of the raised floor, the seven foreigners on the right. No other person was present.

After an interval of a few minutes of anxious suspense, Taki Zenzaburô, a stalwart man, thirty-two years of age, with a noble air, walked into the hall attired in his dress of ceremony, with the peculiar hempen-cloth wings which are worn on great occasions. He was accompanied by a *kaishaku* and three officers, who wore the *jimbaori* or war surcoat with gold-tissue facings. The word *kaishaku*, it should be observed, is one to which our word *executioner* is no equivalent term. The office is that of a gentleman: in many cases it is performed by a kinsman or friend of the condemned, and the relation between them is rather that of principal and second than that of victim and executioner. In this instance the *kaishaku* was a pupil of Taki Zenzaburô, and was selected by the friends of the latter from among their own number for his skill in swordsmanship.

With the *kaishaku* on his left hand, Taki Zenzaburô advanced slowly towards the Japanese witnesses, and the two bowed before them, then drawing near to the foreigners they saluted us in the same way, perhaps even with more deference: in each case the salutation was ceremoniously returned. Slowly, and with great dignity, the condemned man mounted on to the raised floor, prostrated himself before the high altar twice, and seated[36] himself on the felt carpet with his back to the high altar, the *kaishaku* crouching on his left-hand side. One of the three attendant officers then came forward, bearing a stand of the kind used in temples for offerings, on which, wrapped in paper, lay the *wakizashi*, the short sword or dirk of the Japanese, nine inches and a half in length, with a point and an edge as sharp as a razor's.

This he handed, prostrating himself, to the condemned man, who received it reverently, raising it to his head with both hands, and placed it in front of himself.

After another profound obeisance, Taki Zenzaburô, in a voice which betrayed just so much emotion and hesitation as might be expected from a man who is making a painful confession, but with no sign of either in his face or manner, spoke as follows:—

"I, and I alone, unwarrantably gave the order to fire on the foreigners at Kôbé, and again as they tried to escape. For this crime I disembowel myself, and I beg you who are present to do me the honor of witnessing the act."

Bowing once more, the speaker allowed his upper garments to slip down to his girdle, and remained naked to the waist. Carefully, according to custom, he tucked his sleeves under his knees to prevent himself from falling backwards; for a noble Japanese gentleman should die falling forwards. Deliberately, with a steady hand, he took the dirk that lay before him; he looked at it wistfully, almost affectionately; for a moment he seemed to collect his thoughts for the last time, and then stabbing himself deeply below the waist on the left-hand side, he drew the dirk slowly across to the right side, and, turning it in the wound, gave a slight cut upwards. During this sickeningly painful operation he never moved a muscle of his face. When he drew out the dirk, he leaned forward and stretched out his neck; an expression of pain for the first time crossed his face, but he uttered no sound. At that moment the *kaishaku*, who, still crouching by his side, had been keenly watching his every movement, sprang to his feet, poised his sword for a second in the air; there was a flash, a heavy, ugly thud, a crashing fall; with one blow the head had been severed from the body.

A dead silence followed, broken only by the hideous noise of the blood throbbing out of the inert heap before us, which but a moment before had been a brave and chivalrous man. It was horrible.

The *kaishaku* made a low bow, wiped his sword with a piece of paper which he had ready for the purpose, and retired from the raised floor; and the stained dirk was solemnly borne away, a bloody proof of the execution.

The two representatives of the Mikado then left their places, and, crossing over to where the foreign witnesses sat, called us to witness that the sentence of death upon Taki Zenzaburô had been faithfully carried out. The ceremony being at an end, we left the temple.

The ceremony, to which the place and the hour gave an additional solemnity, was characterized throughout by that extreme dignity and punctiliousness which are the distinctive marks of the proceedings of Japanese gentlemen of rank; and it is important to note this fact, because it carries with it the conviction that the dead man was indeed the officer who had committed the crime, and no substitute. While profoundly impressed by the terrible scene it was impossible at the same time not to be filled with admiration of the firm and manly bearing of the sufferer, and of the nerve with which the *kaishaku* performed his last duty to his master. Nothing could more strongly show the force of education. The samurai, or gentleman of the military class, from his earliest years learns to look upon the *hara-kiri* as a ceremony in which some day he may be called upon to play a part as principal or second. In old-fashioned families, which hold to the traditions of ancient chivalry, the child is instructed in the rite and familiarized with the idea as an honorable expiation of crime or blotting out of disgrace. If the hour comes, he is prepared for it, and gravely faces an ordeal which early training has robbed of half its horrors. In what other country in the world does a man learn that the last tribute of affection which he may have to pay to his best friend may be to act as his executioner?

Since I wrote the above, we have heard that, before his entry into the fatal hall, Taki Zenzaburô called round him all those of his own clan who were present, many of whom had carried out his order to fire, and, addressing them in a short speech, acknowledged the heinousness of his crime and the justice of his sentence, and warned them solemnly to avoid any repetition of attacks upon foreigners. They were also addressed by the officers of the Mikado, who urged them to bear no ill-will against us on account of the fate of their fellow-clansman. They declared that they entertained no such feeling.

The opinion has been expressed that it would have been politic for the foreign representatives at the last moment to have interceded for the life of Taki Zenzaburô. The question is believed to have been debated among the representatives themselves. My own belief is that mercy, although it might have produced the desired effect among the more civilized clans, would have been mistaken for weakness and fear by those wilder people who have not yet a personal knowledge of foreigners. The offence—an attack upon the flags and subjects of all the Treaty Powers, which lack of skill, not of will, alone prevented from ending in a universal massacre—was the gravest that has been committed upon foreigners since their residence in Japan. Death was undoubtedly deserved, and the form chosen was in Japanese eyes merciful and yet judicial. The crime might have involved a war and cost hundreds of lives; it was wiped out by one death. I believe that, in the interest of Japan as well as in our own, the course pursued was wise, and it was very satisfactory to me to find that one of the ablest Japanese ministers, with whom I had a discussion upon the subject, was quite of my opinion.

The ceremonies observed at the *hara-kiri* appear to vary slightly in detail in different parts of Japan; but the following memorandum upon the subject of the rite, as it used to be practiced at Yedo during the rule of the Tycoon, clearly establishes its judicial character. I translated it from a paper drawn up for me by a Japanese who was able to speak of what he had seen himself. Three different ceremonies are described: —

1st. *Ceremonies observed at the "hara-kiri" of a Hatamoto (petty noble of the Tycoon's court) in prison.* —This is conducted with great secrecy. Six mats are spread in a large courtyard of the prison; an *ometsuké* (officer whose duties appear to consist in the surveillance of other officers), assisted by two other *ometsukés* of the second and third class, acts as *kenshi* (sheriff or witness), and sits in front of the mats. The condemned man, attired in his dress of ceremony, and wearing his wings of hempen cloth, sits in the centre of the mats. At each of the four corners of the mats sits a prison official. Two officers of the Governor of the city act as *kaishaku* (executioners or seconds), and take their place, one on the right hand and the other on the left hand of the condemned. The *kaishaku* on the left side, announcing his name and surname, says, bowing, "I have the honor to act as *kaishaku* to you; have you any last wishes to confide to me?" The condemned man thanks him and accepts the offer or not, as the case may be. He then bows to the sheriff, and a wooden dirk nine and a half inches long is placed before him at a distance of three feet, wrapped in paper, and lying on a stand such as is used for offerings in temples. As he reaches forward to take the wooden sword, and stretches out his neck, the *kaishaku* on his left-hand side draws his sword and strikes off his head. The *kaishaku* on the right-hand side takes up the head and shows it to the sheriff. The body is given to the relations of the deceased for burial. His property is confiscated.

2nd. *The ceremonies observed at the "hara-kiri" of a Daimio's retainer.* — When the retainer of a Daimio is condemned to perform the *hara-kiri*, four mats are placed in the yard of the *yashiki* or palace. The condemned man, dressed in his robes of ceremony and wearing his wings of hempen cloth, sits in the centre. An officer acts as chief witness, with a second witness under him. Two officers, who act as *kaishaku*, are on the right and left of the condemned man; four officers are placed at the corners of the mats. The *kaishaku*, as in the former case, offers to execute the last wishes of the condemned. A dirk nine and a half inches long is placed before him on a stand. In this case the dirk is a real dirk, which the man takes and stabs himself with on the left side, below the navel, drawing it across to the right side. At this moment, when he leans forward in pain, the *kaishaku* on the left-hand side cuts off the head. The *kaishaku* on the right-hand side takes up the head, and shows it to the sheriff. The body is given to the relations for burial. In most cases the property of the deceased is confiscated.

3rd. *Self-immolation of a Daimio on account of disgrace.*—When a Daimio had been guilty of treason or offended against the Tycoon, inasmuch as the family was disgraced, and an apology could neither be offered nor accepted, the offending Daimio was condemned to *hara-kiri*. Calling his councilors around him, he confided to them his last will and testament for transmission to the Tycoon. Then, clothing himself in his court dress, he disemboweled himself, and cut his own throat. His councilors then reported the matter to the Government, and a coroner was sent to investigate it. To him the retainers handed the last will and testament of their lord, and he took it to the Gorôjiu (first council), who transmitted it to the Tycoon. If the offence was heinous, such as would involve the ruin of the whole family, by the clemency of the Tycoon, half the property might be confiscated, and half returned to the heir; if the offence was trivial, the property was inherited intact by the heir, and the family did not suffer.

In all cases where the criminal disembowels himself of his own accord without condemnation and without investigation, inasmuch as he is no longer able to defend himself, the offence is considered as non-proven, and the property is not confiscated. In the year 1869 a motion was brought forward in the Japanese parliament by one Ono Seigorô, clerk of the house, advocating the abolition of the practice of *hara-kiri*. Two hundred members out of a house of 209 voted against the motion, which was supported by only three speakers, six members not voting on either side. In this debate the *seppuku, or hara-kiri*, was called "the very shrine of the Japanese national spirit, and the embodiment in practice of devotion to principle," "a great ornament to the empire," "a pillar of the constitution," "a valuable institution, tending to the honor of the nobles, and based on a compassionate feeling towards the official caste," "a pillar of religion and a spur to virtue." The whole debate (which is well worth reading, and an able translation of which by Mr. Aston has appeared in a recent Blue Book) shows the affection with which the Japanese cling to the traditions of a chivalrous past. It is worthy of notice that the proposer, Ono Seigorô, who on more than one occasion rendered himself conspicuous by introducing motions based upon an admiration of our Western civilization, was murdered not long after this debate took place.

There are many stories on record of extraordinary heroism being displayed in the *hara-kiri*. The case of a young fellow, only twenty years old, of the Choshiu clan, which was told me the other day by an eye-witness, deserves mention as a marvelous instance of determination. Not content with giving himself the one necessary cut, he slashed himself thrice horizontally and twice vertically. Then he stabbed himself in the throat until the dirk protruded on the other side, with its sharp edge to the front; setting his teeth in one supreme effort, he drove the knife forward with both hands through his throat, and fell dead.

One more story and I have done. During the revolution, when the Tycoon, beaten on every side, fled ignominiously to Yedo, he is said to have determined to fight no more, but to yield everything. A member of his second council went to him and said, "Sir, the only way for you now to retrieve the honor of the family of Tokugawa is to disembowel yourself; and to prove to you that I am sincere and disinterested in what I say, I am here ready to disembowel myself with you." The Tycoon flew into a great rage, saying that he would listen to no such nonsense, and left the room. His faithful retainer, to prove his honesty, retired to another part of the castle, and solemnly performed the *hara-kiri*.

FOOTNOTES

Mitford:

1. According to Japanese tradition, in the fifth year of the Emperor Kôrei (286 B.C.), the earth opened in the province of Omi, near Kiôto, and Lake Biwa, sixty miles long by about eighteen broad, was formed in the shape of a *Biwa*, or four-stringed lute, from which it takes its name. At the same time, to compensate for the depression of the earth, but at a distance of over three hundred miles from the lake, rose Fuji-Yama, the last eruption of which was in the year 1707. The last great earthquake at Yedo took place about fifteen years ago. Twenty thousand souls are said to have perished in it, and the dead were carried away and buried by cartloads; many persons, trying to escape from their falling and burning houses, were caught in great clefts, which yawned suddenly in the earth, and as suddenly closed upon the victims, crushing them to death. For several days heavy shocks continued to be felt, and the people camped out, not daring to return to such houses as had been spared, nor to build up those which lay in ruins.

2. The word *Rônin* means, literally, a "wave-man"; one who is tossed about hither and thither, as a wave of the sea. It is used to designate persons of gentle blood, entitled to bear arms, who, having become separated from their feudal lords by their own act, or by dismissal, or by fate, wander about the country in the capacity of somewhat disreputable knights-errant, without ostensible means of living, in some cases offering themselves for hire to new masters, in others supporting themselves by pillage; or who, falling a grade in the social scale, go into trade, and become simple wardsmen. Sometimes it happens that for political reasons a man will become Rônin, in order that his lord may not be implicated in some deed of blood in which he is about to engage. Sometimes, also, men become Rônins, and leave their native place for a while, until some scrape in which they have become entangled shall have blown over; after which they return to their former allegiance. Nowadays it is not unusual for men to become Rônins for a time, and engage themselves in the service of foreigners at the open ports, even in menial capacities, in the hope that they may pick up something of the language and lore of Western folks. I know instances of men of considerable position who have adopted this course in their zeal for education.

3. The full title of the Tycoon was Sei-i-tai-Shogun, "Barbarian-repressing Commander-in-chief." The style Tai Kun, Great Prince, was borrowed, in order to convey the idea of sovereignty to foreigners, at the time of the conclusion of the Treaties. The envoys sent by the Mikado from Kiôto to communicate to the Shogun the will of his sovereign, were received with Imperial honors, and the duty of entertaining them was confided to nobles of rank. The title Sei-i-tai-Shogun was first borne by Minamoto no Yoritomo, in the seventh month of the year 1192 A.D.

4. Councilor, lit. "elder." The councilors of daimios were of two classes; the *Karô,* or "elder," an hereditary office, held by cadets of the Prince's family, and the *Yônin,* or "man of business," who was selected on account of his merits. These "councilors" play no mean part in Japanese history.

5. *Samurai,* a man belonging to the *Buké* or military class, entitled to bear arms.

6. It is usual for a Japanese, when bent upon some deed of violence, the end of which, in his belief, justifies the means, to carry about with him a document, such as that translated above, in which he sets forth his motives, that his character may be cleared after death.

7. The dirk with which Asano Takumi no Kami disemboweled himself and with which Oishi Kuranosuké cut off Kôtsuké no Suké's head.

8. A purist in Japanese matters may object to the use of the words *hara-kiri* instead of the more elegant expression *Seppuku.* I retain the more vulgar form as being better known, and therefore more convenient.

Tamenaga:

9. The horse is considered a lucky animal. Japanese history records many instances where a general, upon sending a warrior into a desperate combat, presented him with a steed, such a gift being regarded as a good omen.

10. This prophecy has been fulfilled, H. I. M. Mutsuhito having in the year 1869 bestowed upon the tomb of Sir Big-rock the high honor of the Golden-leaf, thus recognizing the devotion of the loyal *ronin.*

Murdoch:

11. Kira's full name and territorial title were, Kira Yoshinaka (according to Brinkley, Yoshihide) Kozuke no Suke. Kozuke is a province to the north-west of Tokyo. The title Suke is peculiar. The

usual title of feudatories of all degrees was "Kami", a word which has many meanings according to the ideographs in which it is written, but generally involving the idea of superiority in rank or office. In this case, it was applied to the provincial Governors of former times and from them transferred to the feudatories under the Tokugawa. Suke was an assistant or helper, and in three fiefs in the Empire it was substituted for Kami in describing the feudatories, not that they were of any lower degree in rank than their fellow feudatories, who were known as "Kami" but because the latter title in these three cases were reserved for princes of the Imperial family. Ako was a fief in the province of Harima with a revenue which had been reduced to 20,000 *koku* at the time of the Restoration, though at this period it was of much greater wealth and power. *Koke*, which has previously in this volume been translated "Chamberlains", here signifies "noble houses".—J. H. L.

12. The following from Titsingh is fairly correct. "All, military men, and persons holding civil offices under the Government are bound, when they have committed any crime, to rip themselves up, but not till they have received an order from the Court to that effect; for if they were to anticipate this order, their heirs would run the risk of being deprived of their places and property. For this reason all the officers of the Government are provided, in addition to their usual dress, and to that which they put on in the case of fire, with a suit; necessary on such an occasion, which they carry with them whenever they travel from home. It consists of a white robe and a habit of ceremony made of hempen cloth and without armorial bearings. The outside of the house is hung with white stuffs; for the palaces of the great and the places at which they stop by the way when doing to, or returning from, Yedo are hung with colored stuffs on which their arms are embroidered—a privilege enjoyed also by the Dutch envoy. As soon as the order of the Court has been communicated to the culprit, he invites his intimate friends for the appointed day and regales them with *saké*. After they have drunk together some time, he takes leave of them; the order of the Court is then read to him once more. Among the great this reading takes place in the presence of their secretary and the inspector; the person who performs the principal part in this tragic scene then addresses a speech of compliment to the company; after which he inclines his head towards the mat, takes up the dirk from the stand before him, and cuts himself with it across the belly, penetrating to the bowels. One of his confidential servants, who takes his place beside him, then strikes off his head. Such as wish to display superior

courage, after the cross cut, inflict a second longitudinally, and then a third in the throat. No disgrace is attached to such a death, and the son (usually) succeeds to his father's place.

"When a person is conscious of having committed some crime, and apprehensive of being thereby disgraced, he puts an end to his own life, to spare his family the ruinous consequences of judicial proceedings. This practice is so common that scarcely any notice is taken of such an event. The sons of all people of quality exercise themselves in their youth for five or six years with a view that they may perform the operation, in case of need, with gracefulness and dexterity, and they take as much pains to acquire this accomplishment as youth among us do to become elegant dancers or skilful horsemen; hence the profound contempt of death they imbibe even in their earliest years. This disregard of death, which they prefer to the slightest disgrace, extends to the very lowest class among the Japanese."

13. In 1664, the last of the Uyesugi of Yonezawa died childless. Kira's son was then adopted as head of the Uyesugi House but the domains of the clan were reduced from 300,000 to 150,000 *koku*.

14. AET - Aetatis (about the age of).

15. The City Companies of Firemen were not instituted until a score of years later. The tradition that makes the *ronin* wear coats-of-mail, with the forty-seven characters of the syllabary for their distinguishing badges, is without any foundation.

16. The document (*saimon*) which the *ronin* in Mitford's story are said to have placed before the tomb is a fiction of later times. That which Mitford saw must have been written afterwards. In 1721, Sengaku-ji was burned down and most of the *ronin* relics then perished in the flames. The official account of their doings styled Sengaku-ji Kakiage, prepared under orders from the Shogun, is not really authentic. The Abbot of Sengaku-ji finding no means of getting any information in his own temple after the fire, borrowed an account penned from hearsay by Shoten, who, in 1703, was Abbot of the neighboring temple of Kogaku-ji.

A Satsuma man caused a stone to be raised to the memory of Hayano Sampei, a page of Asano, who killed himself rather than serve another master, nearly a year before the execution of the vendetta. On this stone appears the name of the man who erected it. Hence the story of the Satsuma man spitting upon Oishi lying drunk in a Kyoto gutter. It has no other foundation, but it is current through all Japan, and not only implicitly credited, but the subject of numerous paintings by artists of high degree.—J. H. L.

17. The province of which Kumamoto is the principal town.

18. It will be noticed that the number of the band is here officially given at 46 and not 47. At the Sengaku-ji when Oishi handed in a list of their names, the Abbot counted them over, and found no more than forty-four, two men having gone to the censors. When the *ronin* assaulted Kira's mansion, they had posted a placard setting forth their reasons for doing so, and had all signed the document. The names then ran to 47; and the last among them was a certain Terazaka. It was this man that had disappeared. Whenever questioned on the matter, the *ronin* answered that Terazaka, being a mere *Ashigaru*, had run away after the attack, probably from love of life. Accordingly he was branded as a coward. But, in 1704, Terazaka appeared before Sengoku, the Censor, and begged to be punished according to law as he had taken part in the night attack in Kira's mansion. The censor reproved him severely for what was tantamount to finding fault with the Shogun's government, at the same time secretly furnishing him with money for travelling expenses. On the night of the attack Terazaka had been dispatched by Oishi to convey the tidings of their success to Lady Asano and to Daigaku who was then in Hiroshima. Terazaka afterwards lived at the Sokeiji in Yedo, dying at the age of eighty-two.

19. The story of the Iga vendetta is given in Mitford's *Tales of Old Japan* under the title of "Kazuma's Revenge". His version is, however, incorrect in some details. The learned translator is, of course, not to be held responsible for that, for his purpose was merely to reproduce the legends that were most famous in the Japan of his time. His volume has become a classic, and it is well worthy of the distinction, for no other single book has succeeded in conveying a sense of the real social and moral atmosphere of Tokugawa Japan so thoroughly and effectually as Mr. Mitford's perennially interesting volume has done.

20. This incident has been previously referred to more than once in this present volume. I have no recollection of ever having heard of it before, and have not only failed to find any reference to it in such authorities as are at my disposal but inquiry among the most qualified Japanese literates in London has only shown that their knowledge of it is on a par with my own.—J. H. L.

21. The Tokugawa jurists asserted that the duty of assuming the vendetta was partly answerable for the severity of the penal code. When a man was sentenced to death for any, and especially for a political, offence it was only prudent to see to it that there should be no

subsequent risk from the Avenger of Blood. Hence, it was common to exterminate the whole household of the condemned man.

22. For Hosokawa *vide* Vol. I, p. 625, and for Akechi, Vol. II, pp. 176-81, both of this work.—J. H. L.

23. According to certain authorities the man-slayer even then could not be assailed with impunity within the precincts of the Imperial palace, or of Yedo, Osaka and Suruga Castles, in Nikko, or in Uyeno, but that is a doubtful point, as would appear from the Ishii-Akahori case. In 1698, the following document was handed to Ishii Genzo and a copy of it entered in the official register: "Know all men that I, Kawaguchi, Settsu-no-Kami, the City Magistrate of Yedo . . . hereby give full permission to Ishii Genzo and Ishii Hanzo to slay their father's murderer, Akahori Gengoemon, wherever they may find him in Yedo, *even though it should be within the sacred precincts of the Castle.*

Besides those mentioned in the text, there are scores of other cases of vendetta (*Kataki-uchi*) which were sufficiently marked by the circumstances that attended them, both in their inception and execution, to earn records in history, and no doubt many more scores in remote districts of the Empire or among samurai of lowlier grade which have been passed over in silence. Sometimes, the revenge was accomplished in a fairly fought duel, sword to sword; sometimes by an ambush, and not infrequently by what seems to us assassination pure and simple. In the latter cases, it is to be remembered that the murder, which provoked the revenge, was probably effected in the same fashion. The last recorded incident was in the years 1867-8, when a samurai of high degree of the Mito clan was murdered in the most wanton manner by another samurai of the Tosa clan, who silently crept up behind his victim and cut him down from the back. The clans, among whom the practice was most prevalent were, it may be mentioned, the very powerful ones of Satsuma, Tosa, Aidzu, and Mito. In this case it will be seen that the parties were of two of these rival clans. The murderer fled but he was seen and described by a beggar, and the two sons of his victim devoted themselves to their sacred duty of revenge with patience and self-sacrificing determination that were worthy of Oishi Kuranosuke himself. They even abandoned their homes and disguised themselves as common coolies. Their story is long to tell here with all its striking incidents, and it must be sufficient to say that they were at last successful, and within a year from the date of the murder, the murderer fell beneath the swords of the two devoted brothers. As they had complied with all the legal formalities, they suffered no penalty. Their deed was lauded in the official gazette, and "all men praised their conduct". This was in the last days of the Shogunate. In 1873 the practice was forbidden by a notification of the Imperial Government which declared that "henceforth no one shall have the right to seek revenge or pass judgment for himself, no matter what the cause and those who follow the ancient custom will be punished according to law". Since then, there has been no case of it. Unlike "*hara-kiri*" and "*junshi*", it is dead.

24. On the anniversary of the attack on Kira's house, the *Chushingura* is still acted in most of the theatres throughout the Empire. In the great warlike fief of Satsuma, the *Sha*—something originally like the old Spartan mess organization—are still maintained in a modified form; and in every one of these the reading of the *Chushingura* begins with the lighting of the lamps and continues through the night of the fourteenth of the twelfth month (old style) as regularly as the year comes round.

A very scholarly and complete translation of the *Chushingura* was made and published by the late Mr. F. V. Dickens under the title of *The Chushingura, or the Loyal League, a Japanese Romance*. The play occupies a greater position on the Japanese stage than even Macbeth or Hamlet on the English and deservedly so, as it is full of thrilling incidents, vividly illustrative of the life of the period. It is always well put on the stage, and well acted.—J. H. L.

25. Sir Rutherford Alcock almost invariably, both in his admirable description of life in Japan in his day in what is still one of the most interesting books that has been written on Japan (*The Capital of the Tycoon*, 2 vols., 1863) and in his official dispatches, took the very worst view of the character and disposition of the samurai. The samurai was, in his eyes, "of that extinct species in Europe, still remembered as 'swash-bucklers', swaggering, blustering bullies, many cowardly enough to strike an enemy in the back or cut down an unarmed or inoffensive man, but also supplying numbers ever ready to fling their own lives away in accomplishing a revenge or in carrying out the behests of their chief . . . no mean adepts in the use of their swords from which they were never parted; one a heavy, two-handed weapon, pointed and sharp as a razor, the other, short like a Roman sword and religiously kept in the same serviceable state—both as dangerous and deadly weapons as man can well possess. Often drunk and always insolent, the samurai is the terror of all the unarmed population and street dogs, and as a general rule, offensive in gesture and speech to foreigners." Sir Rutherford may well be excused for not having taken a more roseate view of the knighthood of Japan. Twice his Legation was

attacked at night by bands of samurai with the object of murdering all its inmates, though he was himself not in Japan on the second occasion, and he never stirred outside the Legation boundaries without justifiably feeling that he was incurring a very present risk of assassination, a risk shared by all his fellow Europeans, which culminated in the death of many by the terrible swords he has described.—J. H. L.

Mitford (Hara-Kiri)
26. Ashikaga, third dynasty of Shoguns, flourished from A.D. 1336 to 1568. The practice of suicide by disemboweling is of great antiquity. This is the time when the ceremonies attending it were invented.

27. A bâton with a tassel of paper strips, used for giving directions in war-time.

28. See the story of the Forty-seven Rônins.

29. No Japanese authority that I have been able to consult gives any explanation of this singular name.

30. White, in China and Japan, is the color of mourning.

31. The principal yashikis (palaces) of the nobles are for the most part immediately round the Shogun's castle, in the enclosure known as the official quarter. Their proximity to the palace forbids their being made the scenes of executions.

32. A Japanese removes his sword on entering a house, retaining only his dirk.

33. In Japan, where fires are of daily occurrence, the fire-buckets and other utensils form part of the gala dress of the house of a person of rank.

34. Oishi Chikara was separated from his father, who was one of the seventeen delivered over to the charge of the Prince of Higo.

35. It should be placed about three feet away from him.

36. Seated himself—that is, in the Japanese fashion, his knees and toes touching the ground, and his body resting on his heels. In this position, which is one of respect, he remained until his death.

GLOSSARY

Chanoyu: Japanese tea ceremony.

Daimio/Daimyo: A feudal lord. Subordinate only to the shogun, the daimyo were the powerful territorial lords who ruled most of the country from their vast, hereditary land holdings. It was usually, though not exclusively, from these warlords that a shogun arose. Daimyo often hired samurai to guard their land and they paid the samurai in land or food.

Dirk: Dagger.

Edo/Yedo/Yeddo: The former name of Tokyo.

Eta: Low caste.

Hatamoto: A samurai in the direct service of the Tokugawa shogunate.

Hara-Kiri/Junshi/Seppuku: Ritual suicide.

Mikado: Old term for the Emperor of Japan.

Ronin: A samurai with no lord or master.

Samurai: The military nobility/warriors of Japan.

Shogun: A hereditary military governor of Japan from 1192 to 1867.

Tokugawa: A clan and powerful family of Japan. The Tokugawa period (also known as the Edo period) ran from 1603 to 1867 when Japan was under the rule of the Tokugawa shogunate and the country's 300 regional daimyo. The Tokugawa shogunate ruled from Edo Castle. The period came to an end with the Meiji Restoration on May 3, 1868, after the fall of Edo.

Tozama daimyo: Nonhereditary feudal lord considered an outsider.

Tycoon: Another title for the shogun, from the Japanese word taikun meaning "great lord".

Purple Rose Publishing

You can find out more about Purple Rose,
view our catalogue, and
find out about our newest releases at:
www.purplerosebooks.com

Our email address is:
purplerosebooks@gmail.com
we would be happy
to hear from you with any feedback,
comments, suggestions or requests!

Also published by Purple Rose:

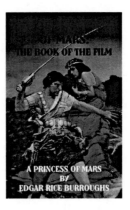

Lightning Source UK Ltd.
Milton Keynes UK
UKOW03f2125291013

220015UK00001B/3/P